WILD BRIGANTIA

Tina Zee

DreamEngine Publishing

Email: publishing@dreamengine.co.uk
Website: DreamEngine.co.uk
Social Media: @DreamEngineuk
Twitter: Tina_Zee_111
Facebook: TinaZeeAuthor
Website: tinazee.com Illustrator: info@louisetodd.com

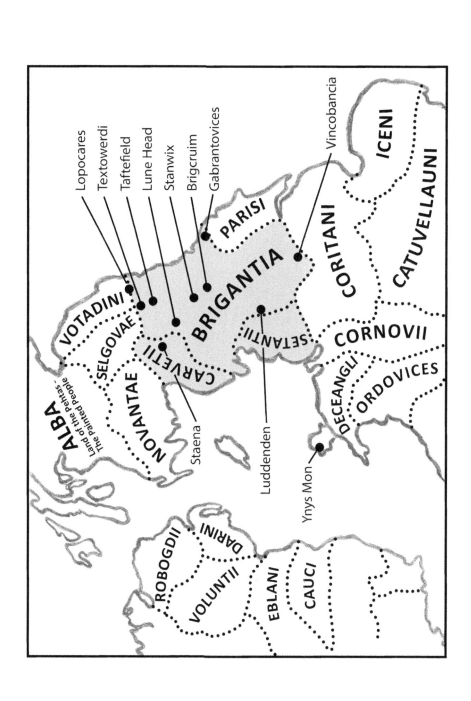

Lopocares
Textowerdi
Taftefield
Lune Head
Stanwix
Brigcruim
Gabrantovices

Vincobancia

ICENI

CATUVELLAUNI

PARISI

BRIGANTIA

CORITANI

VOTADINI

SELGOVAE

CARVETII

SETANTII

CORNOVII

NOVANTAE

DECEANGLI

ORDOVICES

ALBA
Land of the Pehtas -
The painted People

Staena

Luddenden

Ynys Mon

ROBOGDII

DARINI

VOLUNTII

EBLANI

CAUCI

In Memory of Michael

FORWARD

Cartimandua was Queen of Brigantia, a powerful Celtic warrior tribe in Albion [ancient Britain]. From 43AD to 69AD she was crown head and overlord, seeing Brigantia spread over the whole of northern Britain. It covered the land between the River Tyne and the River Humber and spread from the Irish Sea on the west coast to the North Sea in the east. Under Cartimandua's leadership Brigantia became the largest Brythonic Kingdom in ancient Britain.

At that time Britian was occupied by many and varied Celtic tribes. The Brigante people consisted of several tribes and disparate groups who continuously squabbled and fought each other but came together against a common enemy; the invading Romans. They did not want to lose their way of life to a foreign Empire whose main intent was to expand their own wealth by robbing Britain of hers. I have attempted to draw out the desperate fear the Brigante felt, and indeed the other tribes of Britain, when faced with the prospect of losing their lands, beliefs and unique identity. The hierarchical Druid aristocracy were revered and respected. They held the judgements and religion of the people of Britain by using mystical knowledge, interpreting signs and seasons, and executing their wisdom of the earth and her nature as the foundation for everything. The Romans understood that to take the land and hold power, they must destroy the Druids and their religion.

My story, 'Wild Brigantia' is woven round this period in British history when the iron age was coming to a close, and Britian was destined to become part of the Roman Empire. To bring some sense of authenticity, I have used ancient Celtic words which are indicated in italics throughout the story. You will find the glossary of these and other unusual words at the end of the book, followed by a list of Celtic seasons and celebrations and a timeline. I hope this helps to set the mix of factual and fictional characters into a coherent read.

"Four things greater than all things are —
Women and Horses and Power and
War."

— **Rudyard Kipling, 1865-1936,**
English writer, Nobel 1907

"There is no beast like woman so untamed."

— **Aristophanes, 445-386 BC,**
Ancient Greek comic playwright - *Lysistrata*

"O hard, when love and duty clash."

— **Alfred the Great**

PART ONE

CARTIMANDUA SERIES

THE DRUID TALE

In the dark days before the beginning of time, before the Earth woke, the *Eòlas* grew from a single idea, sprouting green shoots and new saplings. These saplings twisted and curled around each other, extending upwards, forming into a mighty oak tree which stood in the centre of thought.

As the tree flourished in presence, the Earth's knowledge became entwined in the growing expansion. Through its roots, it sucked up the nature and goodness from the ground below and drew from the warmth and cycles of the heavens above. From root to cloud, the *Eòlas* gathered strength and perception.

And so, the awakening began.

As the Earth circled, another ring was added to the knowledge of the great oak. Each new eon brought a fresh layer of life, strong and sturdy, pressing it into the thoughts of the people gathered under the shadow of the bowers of the great oak.

The ancient ones who lived under the spreading canopy began to watch for fruit forming on the branches of 'The Knowledge,' savouring the pickings that fell in the autumn sun. Seedlings and fruits spread far and wide. The elite among the ancient folk tasted the fruit. The drupes fused with their spirits until they became one with the very core of the earth. Understanding flowed through the sap veins from the central thought, passing into the psyche of these ancient mortals. Translations of the throbbing beat of the earth turned this rhythm into a language that touched the nucleus of their being.

These elite, these carriers of the understanding, were known as Druids: people who were given The Knowledge of *Eòlas* and became keepers of the sacred groves and kingdoms long since hidden from our world.

CHAPTER ONE

ULTIMA THULE
Extreme Limits

BEFORE THE WILD EARTH had been tamed by man in the furthest of the far places, stood the broch. Hidden at the foot of a voe, this broch was built across water, where fairie strength held it, floating as an island on the edge of the mighty ocean.

It was double walled and round. The long and slim rectangular stones were placed on top of each other in a circular fashion, narrowing the structure with each layer, until it resembled a giant beehive. The roof beam was iron; a huge wheel with eight spokes, made by Taranis himself, 'tis told. It was laid flat on the top of the tower.

The wheel was not covered over, and the spokes were left open, so smoke could escape up from the central fireplace at the base of the structure. The spokes created eight windows, left open as a 'seeing port' for studying the heavens and the stars.

Each stone was placed there by the Fey, creatures not from this world, but from the other side of knowledge.

The broch had one door opening on the south side. The entrance had a magic seal, which only The Knowledge could unlock. The

Knowledge lived in the *broch*, ready for the unfolding, and waiting for the golden fire to come.

Taragh and the woman walked toward the broch. The desperate cries of the hungry child could be heard above the howling winds and roaring thunder which hurtled incessantly over the bleak landscape. The Druid spoke compassionately to the woman. 'You know we must do this. There is no other way. We must leave the child for the fairie to claim. It has been ordered by the gods. Taranis, God of Thunder, will speak again to call our return. Listen. He speaks now.'

At that moment thunder rumbled, warning of the coming rain.

'But the weather is so cruel, Taragh,' she said. 'Surely, we cannot leave him here, alone. What if the gods do not watch over him? What if the boar steals him away?' She clung to the small bundle in her arms; trying to cover the child as best she could with a blanket and the shawl around her shoulders. The woman sobbed as if her heart was broken as she lay the child down in the hollow by the south side of the wall.

'My dear, I have seen his beginning and his end. Was not his birth foretold in the heavens? He will be safely guarded. The gods are watching even now,' he promised, turning his gaze skyward. 'Come. We will be away. We will go before the door is opened, lest we be taken too. Come.' He pulled the woman away from the child, leaving him to the shadows and spirits.

They turned to retrace their steps, choosing not to listen to the child's cries or the thunderous sounds of the satyrs battering the dark crannog.

They had walked a mere twenty steps when there was movement behind them. Keeping their faces forward, and with heightened steps they kept walking. A shaft of light from behind broke into the darkness, illuminating the path around and in front of them. Then, just as suddenly, the light disappeared. They looked back. The child was gone; gone into the depth of the earth. He would remain there until the calling.

Six years later

Mugh Ruith arrived on the isle one spring day. He had come over land and sea to seek "The Knowledge," travelling for many days to reach this far. In the thunder of a stormy night, he saw a vision and heard a voice directing him to the most northern isles of Albion; a place so remote that very few had ventured there. He had journeyed this far without knowing where his destiny might lead, nor whether the golden vision revealed to him some moons ago, was real. 'Just a foolish notion from a mage wanting affirmation from his peers,' he muttered. 'Foolish and silly. Silly and foolish.'

He yawned. His legs stiffened. He stretched his back and breathed the air deeply, reminding himself, 'but the voice was full of promises, of knowledge and sight. I have no choice but to continue.' Though weary and hungry he resumed his stride north easterly toward the rising sun. Sometime later Mugh rested on a large granite stone wondering why he had ever wanted to become a Druid, and why the God of Thunder had spoken to him at all. He beheld the sun reach its zenith; still watching as it fell lower in the western sky.

'There is no warmth in the sun here. No shelter either. No trees grow in this desolate place,' he muttered to himself. He had known when he set out that this would be an arduous journey, and that a Druid's life was meant to be laborious and onerous.

'Give me one good reason why I should continue this life,' he asked himself aloud, as he surveyed the desolate landscape rising from the sandy beach. Tundra moorland rose in tufts, fighting for life among the barren granite stones. Rising also from shore to sky, myriad guillemot tysties cacked their raucous throats as if answering the lone druid. Mugh glanced round to see where the noise emanated. He snuggled his cloak more tightly round his shoulders for protection from the blustering wind. Making a moue with his mouth, he scowled at the clangourous birds. 'Just one good reason. That would do,' he called to them. Then lowered his face, he answered his own question. 'Well, you know why. Because you cannot see properly. If you could just see better, then, my lad, you might have become a scribe. *Ogham*. Yes. You might have learned to write the old language and been of use.'

The birds circled above. He yelled to them. 'The day I lost my eye. Ah! I had been training in *tomus*, and was quite good at it, I thought, when a few of the older trainee Druids decided to play around with the stone weights. One of them threw a heavy stone and I was smacked hard. It gouged my left eye. It was immediate.' The Druid caressed his left eye, rocking back and forth on the stone seat.

'The pain! Oh. It was horrendous and unbearable.' Alas, shaking the memory away, he pulled his *tippet* across the sightless wound, so that the scar was hidden from the indifference of the birds. The fact that his right eye was not so good meant he struggled with seeing at all.

'No good feeling sorry for me,' he said. 'A job is a job, whether it's one I choose, or one the god does choose for me.' With a determination, Mugh rose from the stone seat to continue his way.

Mugh knew he must find a place to shelter before the night fell. 'Oh! Where shall I shelter?' he called to the wind. 'Is there anywhere I can rest?' He knew it was highly unlikely that he would get a response, so he was startled when he saw the broch.

A door opened. He approached cautiously. A voice beckoned him inside.

'Walk this way,' the voice said. There was the sound of shuffling feet and a whimper. The aroma of hot stew washed over him. He followed the scent out of the cold and into the warm embrace of the broch. Round the fire in the centre of the broch hall, three men helped themselves to the pot of stew. 'Come,' said one, inviting Mugh to sit with them.

Another handed him a wooden platter, filling it with the braise. 'Eat' he said.

Mugh moved near the fire and took the meal. The men ate in silence. Mugh was so pleased to see other humans again he could hardly contain himself and prattled on. 'Thank you. I had been wondering where I might shelter and eat. You are so kind. I am grateful to you all. This meal is delicious. What is in it? It tastes like nothing I have ever tasted before. Could you tell me where I am? Have I arrived at the home of 'The Knowledge? Could you confirm the whereabouts of the magnificent Knowing?

He glanced from one to the other, waiting for a response. When none came, he decided that they had not heard him. 'Hello,' he said, almost shouting at them. 'I am Mugh Ruith from Carvetii. That is south from here, by about four moon cycles. I got the call. Taranis called me, speaking through thunder, so I am here to meet with The Knowledge. Please tell me if I have arrived at the right place. I have travelled over land and sea; the farthest distance imaginable, just to parley with him.'

Again, the three did not respond. They continued eating the stew. 'Perhaps they are deaf.' Mugh waved his hands in the air, making signs as he mouthed the words, 'I'm here to see The Knower of the

Oak Tree.' With his finger, he made the shape of a tree, then touched his head. The men began to laugh.

'What's funny?' Mugh asked.

'You,' said the biggest of the men.

Turning from the fire Mugh shrugged his shoulders, offended by the amused attitude of his hosts. 'Well. I cannot see what is funny, when I am trying to be friendly and you do not respond,' he thought. He pursed his lips.

One by one, as if they had read his thoughts, the men spoke. The first was a small, stocky man with a wry grin which was almost hidden under his long beard. Beads of bronze held the beard in long tentacle-like strands. 'I am King Neart. I hold The Knowing of Bronze.'

Mugh was so relieved that the silence had been broken that he sprung in prattling with polite utterances in the direction of the spokesman. 'So pleased to meet you, King. I wonder, could you tell me what kingdom you are from?'

'Silence,' King Neart ordered. Mugh watched in horror as the King placed his hand in the fire. Horror turned to amazement when the hand withdrew unharmed bringing from the flames a large *auroch* horn made of golden bronze. Inside the horn was an iridescent burnished liquid. Neart drank from the vessel, then offered it to the others. Each took a sip and passed it on.

'That was some trick. Maybe when I meet with The Knowledge, he will show me how to do that too.' Mugh took the cup and wondered at the coolness of the *adarc* in his hands. He drank a little. It felt as if the substance took the shape of his body as it flowed through him. He felt a strengthening in his being, a reinforcing of his human frame. He cocked his head while he considered the effects of the solution. 'Incredible…' said Mugh in amazement. 'I'll have another drink of that, please.' But the horn had disappeared back into the fire.

'I am King Misnech,' said the second host, who had spoken earlier. This man was huge and hairy, with rippling muscles bursting through his sleeveless jacket made of skins. His voice was deep and gruff.

'Please to meet you, Misnech.'

'*King* Misnech,' repeated the hefty chief, glaring at Mugh. 'I am *King* Misnech. I form the earth to produce iron,' he explained, and with one punch, his fist beat the ground at his side. A crack appeared, revealing an open well. He reached into the well and brought out a *glaive* from its depths. 'This has been fashioned by the Fairie Kings, and will not be beaten in battle,' he said. He waved the short sword in the air above him. He passed it to the third man, who cut his wrist to show the sharpness, then passed the knife. Each took it, making a similar cut, enough to prove their bravery and prowess. Mugh was offered the glaive.

'If you don't mind, I think I will miss this little amusement.'

King Misnech, ignoring Mugh's comment, held the implement for the visitor, and waited. Mugh waited until the expression on Misnech's face was changing from a calm expression to something more threatening. 'Oh! I see.' Mugh laughed. 'Well, obviously, I do not see. You understand. I am blind. Well, not totally, but enough.' He took the iron and screwed his face up placing the knife on his left wrist. 'He cried out in pain, as he pulled the blade over his skin. 'I'm glad that's over,' he said, with a sigh, passing the knife back to the King.

King Misnech grabbed Mugh's wrist to examine the wound. There was nothing to see, as Mugh had cleverly performed an act of pretence. Misnech took the blade and slashed at Mugh's wrist without hesitation. Mugh cried out. 'You idiot! You have killed me!' he slid from his seated position onto his back, clutching his bloody wrist to stop it from falling off. He writhed in agony, calling for his mother. The three kings gazed on as Mugh cried and sobbed, shouting obscenities at them. The kings remained silent. Mugh stared at his wrist and stopped the moaning abruptly. He twisted it round, checking to see the cut. Nothing. There was no sign of bleeding. He inspected the wrists of the others. Also, nothing: The cuts had instantly healed, leaving only a faint scar. He took his place by the fire again, pouting, and silent.

The third man finally introduced himself. He was a weed of a specimen, wearing an oversized multi-coloured cloak upon which a myriad of silver stars had been embroidered. Mugh had already dismissed this trivial non-person, deciding that anything he said would be worthless.

'Anyone who needs to create a spectacle by wearing an oversized cloak like that is obviously struggling with life disorders,' Mugh thought. 'Though I might like one of those sparkling cloaks myself sometime in the future.'

'I am King Gliocas. My clarity and focus produce silver, the symbol of night and purity.'

Mugh looked at Gliocas, all the time humouring him by nodding his head. 'This should be good,' he thought, wondering if from within the sparkly cloak, this third king might bring something wondrous to behold.

Gliocas picked up a stone from the ground and threw it into the fire. The fire spluttered and crackled. A whorl of smoke rose in the air, spreading insidiously around the group. The smoke rose into the air. Mugh coughed. His eye began to water; his mind clouded over. He felt he was rising into the air, floating upwards to the roof of the tower. The wheel of Taranis was falling from the roof, heading straight for him; swirling and twisting above where he levitated. He was going to crash into it. But just as he braced himself for the collision, he stopped. He was hovering by the spokes of the wheel with his head poking through the gaps, peering through a giant round window. The full, lustrous white moon and shooting stars moved across the sky with speed. Then, in the distance, swirling spectres of green and pink, orange, and purple appeared; dancing and moving in the night sky; throwing out vivid fingers of light, like merry dancers moving in and out of focus. As if in a dream, a picture emerged in front of him. A flash of lightning, brighter than the sun, stretched across his vision, blinding the only eye he could see through. Thunder followed. He blinked hard, trying to clear his vision. Unexpectedly, he saw himself walking familiar paths; roads he knew from home, holding a child's hand and talking to him on the walk.

Then, the dream melted away, and Mugh started to fall; softly, softly, until he was once again by the fire with the three kings.

'Rest now,' said Neart. 'Tomorrow we will talk more.'

The following morning, the sun poked a finger of light through the wheel roof, allowing a little warmth into the darkness of the broch. The fire from the night before had died; the ash particles, fanned by a small breeze moving round the hall, danced in the sunlight. Mugh opened his eye. He did not move. He allowed the day to invade his mind. Carefully, he glimpsed around, checking that his vision was still with him.

There was a stairway near the doorway to the hall, which ran internally around the circular wall of the tower. It climbed to meet with *entresols* above. Mugh thought he could see three or more levels within the tower. His eye became accustomed to the flaky brightness, then movement on the stairway and around the hall. Mugh couldn't make out who or what was climbing the stairway, but they seemed very much like fairie folk. He had seen none before, but he had heard tales of small people living on the far shores of Albion. These miniature men were running up and down the stairs, carrying items in baskets and jabbering in a language that Mugh did not understand. 'Food supplies,' Mugh mused. Women were busy in a particular area of the hall. Mugh thought that they must be preparing the food brought by the dwarfs, as wooden platters were laid out on the table there. He began to salivate as food was being spooned onto the platters, with jugs and drinking pots placed at the side. 'I'm hungry,' he thought. 'I think I will get up now and have something to eat.' He sat up to stir his body awake. 'Oh! My back is a bit sore,' he thought, rubbing the painful area while trying to get up from the stone floor. 'Never mind. It will be better when I get moving. Up you get,' he told himself. As soon as the women saw his movements, they gathered round him to watch.

'Good morning, one and all,' Mugh said, hoisting himself up. Now at his full height, it was obvious that he was considerably taller than these females. 'They are little people,' he commented to himself, wondering if they also might be fairy folk.

'Would you mind if I just went to the table and helped myself to a morsel or two?' he asked. 'I can see a cake and I'm partial to cakes.' The women scattered as he stood. They held their hands to their mouths and faces in fear. Mugh was surprised. He had never had such an effect on anyone. 'Are they afraid of me?' He neared the table and the women made way for him. He reached out for one of the fruits on the table. The women gasped.

'What?' asked Mugh. 'What is wrong?' One of the women waved

her arms about, shaking her head in a warning. In the old language, she shouted for him to stop. Mugh had no idea what he was doing wrong, but replaced the fruit, and decided he would have to wait until someone came to explain. One by one, the women began to bow. 'There is no need for this,' mumbled Mugh, although he quite liked the effect he seemed to have on these women. But then, soft music drifted round the room, and Mugh realised the women were singing a welcome as King Gliocas arrived.

'Good day, Mugh Ruith. Will you break the fast with me?' He pointed to the table, and Mugh realised that he had broken concords by moving to eat before the kings had offered him a place at the table.

'It all looks so delicious, thank you.' Mugh grabbed the fruit he had chosen earlier, then bending low in front of the King, he took a great bite of the huge red apple, ripe, fully sweet with juice which ran down his chin.

'Sit,' beckoned the King. 'Talk to me of your quest.'

Mugh perched on a stone bench by the table and continued to eat whatever was in reach. 'I have come for an audience with The Knowledge. I seek wisdom for a healing,' he said as he reached for one of the small oat cakes and stuffed it into his cloak bags.

Gliocas chewed some meats from the table, then some fruit, as he ruminated over Mugh's seeking. 'And the healing you seek?'

'I would have my sight. I want my eye to be restored, so I can see.'

'There are many ways of seeing, Mugh Ruith, and not all to do with eyes,' said the King. Mugh decided that Gliocas knew very little about anything, if he didn't understand that you need eyes to see.

Gliocas opened his fist to reveal a signet ring. Mugh was taken aback by this response, as well as the item that King Gliocas presented to him. 'Can you see this, my friend?'

Mugh nodded.

'Some things are revealed but are not seen. Some perceive nothing. There are those who look without comprehending what is before them, and few that understand. Which are you, my little friend? You have the capacity to see and understand that which is not revealed, that much is plain to me. But eyes are useless when the mind is blind.'

'Well, that's as may be, King. But I will wait to ask The Knowledge, who might give me what I require,' he said, moving to take the ring from the palm of the King. King Gliocas snatched his hand away and fastened the jewel tight in his fist.

'This is not for you, Ruith, though you may well hold it for a short time. This belongs to another time when the great one who brings warmth and healing will be revealed. One day, if it should ever be granted to one so lowly as you, you would see godly glory stretched out across the vast darkness and would touch the hand of that glory with this ring. All things will be seen, and all things will be understood.'

Mugh gawked at Gliocas, giving himself time for this utterance to sink into his already fuddled mind. He stroked his chin, deep in thought, before he said, 'No,' then shook his head. 'No. I don't understand. You talk in riddles, and I am hungry.' Without another word, Mugh continued to pick at the food from the table.

The other kings arrived then and joined in the meal. The women fussed round the three kingly men, bringing further platters of succulent meats and vegetables until the table overflowed. The fire had been lit whilst they ate, and when Mugh had eaten enough to last for three days, he shuffled from one foot to the other, eager to get on with his intent. Before he had time to bring the conversation round again to his quest, the kings simultaneously rose and moved closer to the fire. They neared it, forming a circle with arms outstretched, touching fingertips. The fire blazed bright. Mugh observed in awe, as the arms of the kings developed new growth; their fingers and nails flourishing as strands of rope. They spread at a rapid pace, coiling and weaving round the three kings, until they intertwined in a cortex of wood-like bark. The king's cloaks merged into this cortex, adding autumnal colours and shivering stars of grey–white ridges and black arboreous furrows; growing until the kings were so tightly bound together that Mugh could not see the beginning or ending of each one. Branch-like tendrils sprouted from the king's shoulders, revealing green buds and blossoming bows. The roots continued down past what had become a living bole, digging deeply into the ground, and anchoring into the earth beneath. Mugh rubbed his eye. 'I am not seeing this. This cannot be real.' Before him, in place of the kings, a white oak tree towered. 'I am losing my mind! Gods, have mercy on me…' Trembling before the great oak, he felt his knees weaken. 'I do not understand this.'

A booming voice emanated from the oak. 'I am Eòlas: strength, courage, and wisdom; fused and united. Together, I hold the knowledge you seek. Sight will be given. You will see far beyond this world, into the otherworld, where the spirits of all others live. You will use this sight to call into being the Sacred Flame, created before the Earth was formed, which now shelters in the depth of the sacred place.'

For the first time in a long time, Mugh was silent. His breathing was rapid and his eye, weepy.

The Eòlas continued. 'You have been chosen, above all other Druids, to complete this task. But there is a cost to pay. You must listen and obey the voice of "The Wheel" and for the sake of your land, you must be ready to serve. You will tend the growth of the seed of Brigantia; until such times that the harvest is ready.'

'Please, Eòlas, speak plainly,' begged Mugh, bowing to the ground in awe. He scraped the earth with his hands, holding his head low. His voice trembled as he spoke. 'I don't understand what you are saying. Please. I only want to "see" again. I want nothing more. I am only a poor Druid, still learning the art.'

A great rush of wind roared into the broch, whipping round the Oak tree, and blowing the branches till Mugh thought they would break, and he would lose his life under the fall. He ran to the trunk and clung to it for safety. 'The gods are angry with me,' he thought, his teeth chattering. 'I am sorry. I am sorry,' he prattled. 'I will do whatever you ask. Just let me be free of this nightmare.'

The wind subsided, disappearing into the atmosphere as quickly as it had arrived. The Eòlas spoke again, gently. 'You *will* understand, Mugh Ruith. And you *will* follow the path set before you. Sight will be given, as you journey onwards. Sight will come. Strength too, as you move in the right direction.'

'I will.' Mugh squeezed his eye tightly shut and prayed for the day to end. He did not open his eye again until he felt a warm breeze caressing his face. Looking round gradually, there before him, the three kings stood.

From under his cloak, King Gliocas brought a small leather pouch tied with a silk string of blue. He took Mugh's right hand and placed the pouch in his palm, then folded the Druid's shaking fingers tightly round it.

'Bring the child,' King Gliocas ordered, before settling his gaze back on the face of Mugh. With a gentleness that surprised Mugh, Gliocas spoke calmly and quietly. 'Mugh Ruith. One day you will learn that size does not make the man, nor does sight.'

A small child was ushered into the middle of the room by two women who held his hand: a beautiful boy with golden hair. He smiled as he entered the group. Mugh recognised him. His mouth dropped open. 'Oh, this is the boy in the vision from the night before.' As he spoke out, lightning flashed above them. Thunder could be heard rumbling across the skies, enouncing in Drueidan. Although Mugh did not understand much of the old language, the voice was clear enough.

'This child, you must nurture and protect, for he is the future of Albion. He rises from the goddess, and in time, to Brigga, he must return. Take him to your home and rear him to know the druid ways. Teach him to battle as a druid warrior. Do this until the gods call to you, then you will receive your request. Sight will be given.'

Mugh fidgeted as the weight of this edict dawned on him. He opened his mouth to protest, only to close it again. He stood there, good eye closed, hoping this was all but a dream. A dream from which he would awaken, standing in front of The Knowledge and receiving his sight. He stood there in the darkness, screwing up his face and ignoring all the sounds and delicious smells of roast boar and sweet fruits. Finally, he felt a small hand pushing its way into his fist, squeezing his fingers. The Earth began to spin. Dizzy with the turning, Mugh felt sick. When the spinning stopped, he opened his eye to discover that he was outside the broch, with the small golden-haired boy holding his left hand and a bag in his right.

CHAPTER TWO

LONG LUM
Tall Chimneys

UGH AND THE CHILD walked in silence heading for the coastline in search of a ship which could transport them back to the mainland of Albion. A small group of shelters stood by the seaport, one of which offered sanctuary from the cold while they could find a vessel willing to take THE pair for little cost. The druid had influence, simply because of his training and appointment. Although druids were revered and respected across Albion and the outlying islands, not everyone welcomed the priests into their home. Whilst some were so in awe of them to the point of fear, others hated them and their privileged life, which seemed to be given so easily to them. Others still, consumed by jealously craved The Knowledge and position of these high-powered men and women.

The couple who took in Mugh Ruith and the boy were simple people who had great respect for the cloaked order. They quietly welcomed them to stay as long as necessary. Whispering to his wife, the man said, 'These are travellers come from the Broch. Such auspicious guests would surely bring good fortune into our home.'

The woman nodded.

That evening, while settled round the fire in the small shelter, they enjoyed a hearty meal served in wooden bowls. Tender herb-rich mutton enhanced with barley had been stewing for some days. The pot was continuously refilled with any vegetables the hosts could find, which seemed to be beans that day. This thick and filling meal was all the pair needed before quietening down ready for the night. Little was said during the evening, apart from general words of gratitude. Soon the woman of the house prepared mats and a wool-filled bag as a pillow, so Mugh and the boy settled down for the night.

They lay on the mat by the fire; the Druid's back turned away from the boy. Sweat glistened on his brow and his chest. His stomach churned as his mind raced. 'There are so many questions I want answers to, but where do I start? What if he does not answer? What if he does not know the answer? What if he does not like me? I need wisdom in how to deal with a young boy like this.'

Without moving from his position, Mugh cleared his throat, hesitating a few moments before finding the courage to question the boy. 'What is your name, Boy? How long have you been in the broch with the kings? How old are you?' he rattled off. The boy ignored him mostly as he drifted off to sleep.

'I am known as Eachann *map* Belinus,' he said, yawning, 'though the fairie folk called me son of Beli Mawr.' That was as much as Mugh found out that night.

The following morning brought good news: their host informed him that a small ship was ready to leave the harbour. Mugh almost dragged the boy down to the water's edge before ordering him aboard the craft. Thoughts of the sickness he had endured on his way to meet with The Knowledge, rose like waves on the ocean before him. He hugged his stomach as he recalled the surge of the affliction on his first journey. The vessel—a willow framed ovoid, covered in greased skins stretched over the skeleton of woven branches—bounced easily in the harbour; crude, but robust and seaworthy. Mugh positioned himself at the side of the bulwark, so as to be able to deposit any vomit into the brine, rather than down his cloak. Mugh pulled the boy to his side and resigned himself to the hell of the sea.

Four days later, they landed safely on the northern coast of mainland Albion, avoiding the *Seal isles*. From there, they travelled southwest in the direction of home. The journey was hard and treacherous, with little time for rest; but the boy showed remarkable determination to keep up with Mugh.

They made a resting place and built a fire near a cave in the highlands, Mugh began to engage with the lad again.

'Eachann, tell me about your parents, if you can remember.'

'I don't remember them. I have been told very little, and most of it was in stories woven by the Little People. I know nothing of my father except he was mighty. And of my mother, I know nothing. Her name was whispered on one occasion, but I did not hear clearly. I think it was "Eanna," but I cannot be sure. The Eòlas told me of my destiny, but my past, I do not know.'

Mugh mused at the lad's ability to speak as an equal, and not as a child. 'Can you tell me the stories, Eachann? What do you remember?'

The boy lifted his eyebrows and pouted his lips. Then, with a shrug, he opened his mouth to sing a tale; one he had learned at the hand of the Little People.

"Beli, great rider of the sky, in chariot pulled by horses.
Son of Thunder and of light, releases and discharges
healing and power in his right hand. Then linked like iron to
another,
warrior spirit with warrior spirit holding sacred Brigga.
One day **Eòlas** *will require the iron and bronze and stone.*
With strength and courage to overcome, the fire will bring the word.
When Bel melts into the earth and Brigga rides again,
the soul of Albion once more will burn as fire through the domain.'

Mugh waited a moment, thinking through the story. 'And what do you think that means, Eachann?'

'Well, obviously I am going to be a great warrior,' he simply said as he turned away from the fire and settled down as if to sleep.

Mugh had a million questions for this lad to answer, but for once in his life, he could not find the words. The fire flickered warmly, as both he and Eachann inspected their thoughts. Eventually, Mugh remembered the bag that he had been given by the Eòlas when he was expelled from the broch. He had meant to look earlier, but the thought of having to are for the boy had taken his mind away from the situation and into a state of worry and anxiety.

'What am I to do about this responsibility?' he wondered. 'I've never had such a responsibility. Who would want to give *me* this load to bear? I can't even look after myself.' His mind had been in turmoil since finding the small hand grasping his when they walked away from the magic door to made for the coast. 'I could really do with the thunder, or some other god to bring help, or at least some understanding. I simply wanted my eye fixed,' he thought. Sweat ran down his brow and panic set into his heart. He searched for a distraction.

He searched inside his cloak for the bag. He pulled out a cake – stale and green. He discarded it. 'I forgot about that. That's a shame. I would have enjoyed eating that.' He fumbled again in his cloak and drew out his finding. Untying the string, which was wrapped around the gathered cloth, he unfolded the small sack to reveal the contents. The items exposed allowed a shimmering silver cumulus of light to escape into the air, and there in front of Mugh was a ring, a stone, a short dagger, and a phial. Mugh gasped, immediately recognising the items.

'These are the things the kings showed me.'

The boy, noticing the brilliant ray escape into the night sky, jumped up to look at the items displayed on the cloth. He moved to take the dagger, but Mugh grabbed the boy's wrist to stop him. 'Wait, Eachann. We do not know why we have been given these items, nor yet their purposes.' Smiling kindly at Eachann, Mugh releasing his grip on the lad, then patted his hand. He wrapped the cloth round the four mysteries and folded the bag once more into his cloak. 'The meaning will be revealed, in time. I have no doubt. But let us be patient for a while. When we get home, I will enquire of the Druid priests and all will be well.'

'Where is "home," Mugh?' Eachann asked.

'Home is Carvetii, on the west coast of Albion. My home sept is called Long Lum. It is a place like no other. The sept is large, and the families are good people. Resourceful, too. Their building experts are renowned, though some of them have heads bigger than the broch from where you came. The homes are built of stone in rounds with roofs of straw. You will know it when you see it, for a few of the people have built tall smokestacks from stones for fumes from the house fires to escape. There is no place quite like it,' he said, staring wistfully into the darkness beyond the flames of the fire. 'Long Lum will be your home until you are grown. And as you grow, we will see what the gods have in store for you, Beli Mawr. But until then, we must keep your birthplace a secret. I fear you are a star in the sky of Albion, and significant purposes are at work in your life,' prophesied Mugh. He felt quite good about the prophecy, too. Never had he been able to say anything with such authority! A surge of confidence ran through his veins reminding him of when he drank the bronze liquid in the broch.

'The journey will take us several weeks, through the territory of our enemies, the Painted People. They are known as the *Pehtas* and the *Goidi I*,' Mugh explained to his young companion. 'These tribal warriors paint their bodies with blue and purple tattoos till no skin is left to show. They often live in Souterrains; underground passageways and tunnels.' Mugh spread his hand over the scene displayed before them, intuitively pointing out the hidden underground mines where the Pehtas might be concealed. 'They are savage in life as they are in battle. They can cut off any part of a man's anatomy to take whatever they want, - fingers for rings, hands for amulets. You name it, they will have it,' he warned. 'I need you to have a keen eye, looking out for any sign of them. Do you hear me, boy? Their arrows are sharp, and they wield axes with fervour.'

The pair travelled through this dangerous land where the only safety cover Mugh and Eachann had was the Druid cloak; and the hope that anyone they came across would have respect for the old traditions. Eachann obeyed Mugh, continuously eyeing the horizon for movements or omens.

Mugh was undeterred. He had already travelled this route once when following the 'voice of thunder' in his quest for The Knowledge. Mugh knew (or rather, hoped) that Taranis would continue to watch over their return and bring resolution to his godly intent.

Each day Mugh found a fresh place to rest and fresh places to lay traps for rabbits and hares.

Each evening, they found a suitable place by a stream or river to camp and eat. The fish were plentiful, as were the foraged berries and fruit from the shelterbelts along the bleak paths. Mugh showed the young boy the art of fire raising; a simple magic which the Druids had long ago shared with the people. An iron splinter and some twigs were all that was needed to start a roaring campfire. They both slept fitfully, warm and well hidden under the Druid cloak.

The journey took them through rocky ground, up mountains and down into glens. The landscape was stunning, though often they were soaked by torrential rain. Mugh made time to stop and rest, taking in the air and scenery. Without conscious effort, Mugh instinctively recalled and traced the paths home in his mind.

'My eyesight might not be so good, but my memory is excellent.'

Eachann found two tall sticks, and each took a support for the arduous walking. That evening, Mugh took out his own small hunting knife and allowed Eachann to use it to whittle the staffs into smoother holds. He enjoyed teaching Eachann about hunting and fishing; about surviving out in the wilds and defending himself, if need be. He explained about the moon cycles and the shifting sky; of his people's dreaded fear that one day the sky might fall from its place and heaven would be lost in the great ocean. He taught him some of the Druid ways with old traditions, and explained about the two pillars which hold up the sky.

'Though, Eachann, you need not worry yourself about such things at this point in your life. But take care to always honour the gods, and they will take care of you.'

'I know. I learned some things from Eòlas, but there were many things they said I needed to find for myself. "Truth can be passed from father to son," they said, "but it is in the experience that the son really stands the truth." I can understand how to make fire, but I will not know its' truth; its' power until I hold my hand in the flames.'

Mugh blinked, repeatedly. Then coughed. 'You amaze me, young Eachann,' he smiled, nodding his head. 'You amaze me, indeed.'

'But please continue, Lord Ruith.' The child bowed his head.

Mugh passed on the understanding of Taranis, the god of thunder, whose wheel of time and lightning flashes could be seen blazing across the sky. He explained that Taranis reveals himself in the storms on Earth.

'It is this God to whom I have vowed to revere; Him and Beli, the God of lightning and of bright fire.' Observing the boy intently, Mugh told the tales of Beli the Great, once High King of Albion and the warrior who fought against enemy invaders led by Julius Caesar. He spoke of the great Casswallen, son of Beli, and other warrior kings from across the land. Mugh wondered if the lad would understand the connection he might hold with those kings.

Closing in on the northern outskirts of Carvetii, a fire ignited in Mugh's breast, his excitement soaring to the highest heights. He chattered away to himself in the way he had always done, but with a gabbling speed.

'We are almost there. Another few days' walk, and we will be home. One foot in front of the other. Hold fast. Good. Now what do I tell the people in my grove? I could tell them this, or I could tell them that. I could tell them I found the boy on the way home from my mission… But you haven't got your sight back, Mugh. No, No. This is a problem,' he ranted, knocking his forehead with his fist. 'I need to think of something… think. Get your thoughts in order. Put one foot in front of the other… This is the way to do it.' All this was spoken out loud, and in well within Eachann's earshot.

'Why don't you just tell them the truth?' asked Eachann calmly.

'I could tell them the truth,' repeated Mugh, tossing his head from side to side, flipping the thought over. 'I could tell them the truth, yes. What truth? The truth about the Little People and the Kings of the Knowledge... I don't think they will believe me. No. They will laugh and say I have lost my head.' Then he added, with a determination in his voice. 'They will, though. They will believe me. I am a Druid. And Druids know these things.' He tried to convince himself, but somehow the thought of being ridiculed grew in his mind until his earlier excitement turned to fear, choking at his throat. He coughed, spluttering mouth juice over the head of the young lad. 'I won't worry about it yet. No, I won't worry. Oh! dear gods. Yes. I need the gods to help me. The gods will give me understanding.' He left the thought dangling somewhere suppressed, deep in his brain as saliva dribbled to his chin.

They travelled southward, following the river *Easg*, stopping at Longtown to rest. But to avoid the boggy peatland at Mosse Bawne and the marshes where the sept at Rock Cliff rose, they had to venture more to the east, then continue along the banks of the river Lyne.

Turning south again, they arrived at Harker camping for a few days, before moving on the road leading to the river Ituna. They made their final camp of the journey between the tall elder and willow trees lining the lush margins of the river.

With each stretch of the journey behind them, Mugh's excitement increased tenfold. Eachann was weary, but Mugh amused the boy with stories and magic. Sleight of hand and a skill in performing conjuring tricks, creating the illusion of invisibility. Eachann was quick to unpick the trick, and before too long, he had mastered the cunning craft. Then, wanting to divert the conversations they were having, Mugh asked, 'Eachann, we have exhausted all the tricks I have. Why don't you tell me a story for a change?'

'What can I speak of, Mugh? I have no knowledge to share.'

'Everyone has knowledge of sorts, young lad. Tell me about your life with Eòlas. What was it like to be with them?' Mugh regarded every movement of the boy while asking the question. Eachann fidgeted while he thought.

'It was as it has always been,' he said. 'The thoughts take root and grow. I did not understand, but I did not need to understand. Understanding flowed from their love.' He tossed a twig into the fire as he spoke. The gesture and the statement from the lad seem so natural and just as obvious as the flames burning in front of them. 'I am learning that the world of Eòlas is but the foundation of our world and is in itself incomplete. There needs to be continuous increase and progress developed in the thought, for it to manifest for the good of the earth.'

Mugh moved his glance away from the boy; his one eye opened to its full extent. He gawked into the darkness of the surrounding shadows. 'Well, well. What have we here?' he thought.

'Do you not agree, Mugh?'

He stuttered. 'Indeed. Indeed.' In silence they sat, watching the flicker from the blaze; lost in their own thoughts for a while. Then Mugh continued. 'Could you make that statement into something that ordinary folk would understand, Eachann? We have to consider the people we will meet who do not have your experience with The Knowledge.'

'Of course, Mugh. What I learned from the Eòlas is that there should be no eagerness to fight when you have limited knowledge of your enemy. Gather insights before battle.'

Mugh sighed with relief. This he understood. 'Now you are thinking like a Druid!'

'Druid sight is everything,' said the boy, smiling at his protector. Mugh adjusted his tippet over his blindness, wondering if the lad was making fun of him.

'What I would give for that clear Druid sight,' he thought.

A small boat crossing the Ituna brought them to the confluence of both the rapid water and the *Peitriana* River. Following the smaller river, they travelled southward, past the large settlement of *Staena*. There was much activity and fresh building work being carried out there.

Mugh had been away for so long now that he couldn't tell who was doing the work or why. The pair stayed just outside the busy trading post, only to rest for a short time before continuing on.

When they finally arrived at Long Lum, the rectangular elder-weave gate parted, granting them entry. There was movement toward the gateway as people came to witness the return of Mugh and his young companion. They passed onto the main pathway through the village; and through the eager townspeople, shouting questions, greetings and even the odd bit of teasing and abuse. 'Hi! Mugh. You made it then.' called one young man carrying a bucket toward the pigpen. 'And you have grown a beard!' he added, laughing at the tufts of hair on the Druid's chin.

Another shouted, 'Yes, he's back, and look… He has indeed, grown a beard! And there are two of them now: Little Mugh and Tiny Mugh!'

'Did you follow the thunder instructions like you should have, Mugh?'

'Who's your companion, Druid?'

'Can you see well enough now?'

Ignoring the taunting and jeers, Mugh dragged the boy round the side of the sept; where the homes were made up of simple one-roomed stone, mud and twig roundhouses, topped with pointed thatched roofs. Though the houses were meagre in size, they allowed a space for storing food, for beds made of straw covered with animal skins, and for an open central fire. These dark, smoke-filled places without chimneys housed potters, ironsmiths, fieldworkers, and their families. Others were farmers. The lands outside the sept had been furrowed and worked on to produce wheat, flax, and barley. Geese ran freely round the sept, whilst goats were fettered to the side of homes; pigs grunted and snuffled in muddy pens and provided a constant supply of meat.

But to one side, three houses had been built in a new way. They had a central hearth and chimney made from wicker daubed with clay. Having helped in the planning somewhat, Mugh was proud of the Druid invention which took the smoke from the fire directly through the roofs, instead of leaking between thatch or shingles. These larger homes had been erected round a sacred oak tree and belonged to the Druids of Long Lum

The insults and bullying carried on until Mugh arrived at the entrance of the grove; where sacred elder, yew, and hawthorn trees formed a barrier of protection around the Druid quarters. There was only one way in: a gate of woven willow held together by an iron frame and hinged with iron pins. Mugh opened the gate and turned into the roundhouse of the High-Druid of Carvetii, Audigus Raigon. Raigon was visiting the sept, on behalf of Venutius, King of Carvetii, who had instructed him to take stock of Carvetii lands. Using this knowledge, Venutius was able to find the population of his land, who and where tribal power was held, and the measure of fighting men who could be called on swiftly should the need arise.

He had commenced regulating an army, deploying them in areas where Carvetii borders were weak. His intent: to increase Carvetii by pushing north, taking the tribal lands beyond his borders once they were secure. Venutius had only recently moved to take the regal seat of Carvetii; passed on to him after his father's death. He was yet new to his position.

Mugh was glad that the Druid was still at Long Lum. He hurried to the open door of the sacred cloak.

'Audigus Raigon.' Mug bowed low in the doorway; his frame blocked the light. 'Chief Raigon. It is I, Mugh Ruith. I have returned from the far north shores of Albion with tales to tell and adventures to share.' He hesitated in the doorway, wary of the response he might receive from one who was known for his acid tongue and sarcastic comments.

'Move away from the door, Ruith, so I can see you better,' called a gentle voice, belying the reputation of the priestly Druid.

Mugh stepped inside the hall, pulling the boy behind him and hiding him underneath his cloak.

'Ah! Mugh Ruith. You are returned to us in good health, I hope?' Raigon was sitting by the hearth and chimney. He wore his black Druid cloak; the white cloak edgings and hood making him stand out from the rest of the Druid family of Carvetii. It spoke of his high status. His long white hair was tied back in a tail. His bejewelled rings glistening as he turned a venison steak on a skewer, twisting it over the flames. The meat cooking on the spit smelled wonderful to Mugh, who couldn't help the saliva running down his chin.

'Come. Join me,' invited Raigon. 'Talk to me.'

Mugh neared the bench by the side of the door, perching clumsily, almost squashing the boy underneath his cloak. He positioned himself awkwardly and, to little avail, tried to keep the boy hidden;

his golden hair covered.

'Have you grown extra legs while you have been travelling Mugh?' asked the Druid. 'Or have you brought something extra for the spit?'

Mugh pulled the boy out from under his cloak and pushed him in front of the King's priest. 'I found him on the road, Lord,' Mugh lied, wondering at his own reticence to tell the chief Druid the boy's origin. 'I thought he would make a good apprentice.'

Mugh noted the old sage run a gimlet eye over the boy, then sniff. 'Indeed, Mugh. Please continue.'

So Mugh regaled him with tales of his adventures. 'I travelled to the far corner of the land, even as far as the farthest isles. I came upon this boy while I travelled. He was helpful to me as we returned home.' But when it came to the part about the little folk; the fairie kings and the boy, he remained silent. He talked about the sea journey and his sickness due to the length of time in the water before land appeared again. Of the desolation of the furthest of the far places; the lack of trees and growth he recounted. He chronicled the night he saw the coloured sky and the chariot of gold streaking across the dark night. Mugh embellished his ordinary days with talk of spirits in the night and scenes of horses galloping across the terrain on the pathway of the silvery moon goddess. He talked of the thunder of Taranis, who had led him there, and the purpose and knowledge he had gained in his understanding. His voice wavered when he talked about his deep belief that sight was to be granted to him as he undertook to serve Taranis, the god of the wheel. But of the boy and the bag of secrets, he did not speak.

Raigon seemed interested, asking some questions of Mugh while the tale unfolded.

'On your journey to the far places, Mugh Ruith, did you come across the deep secrets of the Other World? Did the gods speak prognostications? I have heard tell of great truths being revealed, showing how to gain great power and riches. Did you hear of any of that?'

Mugh avoided the penetrating gaze from Raigon. His face lowered to the floor, with brows furrowed. He remembered the words of Eòlas proclaiming to him:

> *'You will see godly glory stretched out across the vast darkness,*
> *and you will touch the hand of that glory with this ring.*
> *All things will be seen, and all things will be understood.'*

Mugh looked up, meeting Raigon's gaze. 'No.'

For some moments, Raigon scrutinised Mugh's face, searching for some veracity to his answer, perhaps. Then, looking away, Raigon continued to probe.

'I have heard tell of a Druid king to be born when Taranis rides in the sky. The ancient Druids spoke of such a king. Are you sure you heard nothing?'

'I am sure.'

'Well, you have some wonderful tales to tell, Ruith. When the light prepares to sleep, I hope you will be able to sing your stories to the people of Long Lum; perhaps even to the people living in the centre of Carvetii, at the Dykes, should you be called. Venutius, our new king, is in training there, though he has plans to make Staena his headquarters. He has already started a building project to extend the sept there for that purpose. He is a tough lad, growing fast. His warrior prowess increases daily, and his wisdom is beyond his years. He will make a favourable king. And I am sure he will delight in hearing such tales as you have to sing.'

Raigon pulled the meat from the skewer using his teeth. He

chewed as he spoke. 'You may know that Venutius is showing signs of becoming an exceptional warrior and leader of men. He is an ordinary-looking boy, but his muscles are taut, and he stands well. His aspiring leadership has encouraged many followers to his side. I personally am one such follower, so when the Druid priesthood declare me as High-Druid over Carvetii, I was pleased to become the senior advisor to Venutius.' He picked at a piece of fat caught in his teeth and flung it aggressively into the fire. Drawing his face close to Mugh's, he threatened, 'One day I will become Arch Druid of Albion.' he vowed. 'And woe betide any who stand in my way.'

That night, and for many nights after, Mugh mixed among the people of Long Lum and sang tales of travel and sunrises from the far shores; places that most of the Carvetii could only dream about. He expanded the stories to encompass many magical myths. He spoke of the voice of Taranis uttering a prophecy about the boy with golden hair, then had the boy appear from nowhere to sit by his side.

Mugh explained that the boy—the apprentice—was a gift from the God for Mugh's obedience. He wrapped the essence of fantasy with truth within the yarns, so much so that he started to believe his own tales.

He gave the boy the name of Beli Mawr; 'The Shining One,' and this fable attached itself to Eachann as he grew. His golden hair shone like the sun, so it seemed natural for the people to think of him as a radiant gift from the gods. Although blue eyes were not unusual, the colouring of the boy was so different from the dark skins and dark curly hair of most people in Albion. Thus, it was easy for the legend to manifest. As the stories were shared among the people, so the legend grew. Mugh became known far and wide as the keeper of the Golden One; a title he cherished.

Mugh guarded the boy, leading him and encouraging him on the path to priesthood. Eachann was a quick learner, and by the time the boy was ten years old, he had already mastered the art of reading the moon and the sky patterns. He understood the flow of rivers, the tides of the oceans and how they were powered by the *Gealach;* the god of the silver boat, who carries the brightness of the night. Mugh taught him how to speak in Drueidan, the ancient language; as well as many wisdoms, such as festivals and blessings for the land. Each year as Eachann grew, they attended the gatherings to celebrate the changing seasons. Mugh explained the way the festivals pinpointed the movement of the moon, and how the Earth held the time within that season.

He explained about crops and herb medicines, linking them to the sun and moon phases and to the gods. He taught which gods to respect and follow and which to avoid. But most of all, he taught about his glorious God, Taranis.

'His voice can be heard as thunder and his chariot wheels spit sparks from the sun as he speeds across the heavens. He holds a thunderbolt in one hand and the sun-wheel in the other.' Mugh explained. 'This is the God who chose me into his service. This is the God that you, Eachann, must take to your own heart,' Mugh urged.

One bright spring morning Mugh woke up with a heavy head. 'I drank too much ale last night,' he said to himself, cradling his brow. 'That was quite a celebration, when Eachann picked a fight with three older boys in the sept and won. He flattened them one by one, pinning them against the wall of one of the houses, then dragged them to a tree with their own belts,' laughed Mugh, muttering to himself. 'Then he tied them to the trunk so they could not come back and bother him. I slapped him on the back. He had my approval, alright. And I noted his growing height, which has already exceeded my own. The boy is ready to take the next step into manhood,'

Holding his head, Mugh rocked gently backwards and forwards. 'I could do with a rest from all this chatter. I probably shouldn't have allowed my charge to drink in celebration. I shouldn't have handed him a horn of mead.' Lifting an imaginary cup to the sky, Mugh repeated his words from the night before, 'A salute to your youth, and passing childhood. Drink, Eachann Beli Mawr. Drink your childhood away.'

Eachann had tasted the mead, in obedience, but soon returned to his cup of water. Mugh continued to drink that night as though it might be his last, but regretted it now, in the morning light.

Cradling his thumping brow, Mugh mumbled under his breath, 'I need to go to the river and wash it away.' He took himself to the side of the stream that ran into the river *Peitriana* making its way to join the bigger waters. He bathed in the natural pool, cooling his banging head and thinking of the breakfast to be had when he returned to his house. The stream was gentle and bubbling.

A shrine to the Goddess Peitra had been built at the side of the stream. A small hollow in front of an upright stone, positioned under a young oak tree was ready to receive votive offerings to the Goddess. In the hollow, acorns soaked in the water had been placed; therefore, ready to prepare as food for the weary traveller. A small horn hung by the shrine also. Mugh remained before the shrine and for a few moments, held his breath. The sound of the stream by his side relaxed him. Mugh raised the horn, and reached down into the stream, filling it with water. Lifting the horn high, he blessed Taranis, then poured an offering to Peitra, the Goddess of the river, before drinking the remainder of the water himself. The liquid ran through his body. 'I feel a little better, now.'

Startled by a flash behind him he spun round and almost toppled with dizziness. He could not detect the source of the light. Whilst looking round for what had caused him the surprise, a roar of thunder crossed his sound path, a rumbling, warning of things to come. Mugh put his hands to his ears to stop the pain from thunder-triggered hyperacusis. He cried out as agony seared through him, doubling over while he tried to hide his ears from the intolerable sound. Suddenly a voice in the thunder; faint, but undeniable, vibrated. If the voice was in his head, or behind him, or above him, he could not say; but the voice became more distinct the more he tried to block out the deafening, resounding rumble.

The thunder roared a thick, deep explosion of sound. The Earth reverberated in response. From the midst of the rumbling, a kaleidoscope of colours emerged, circling, then surrounding his vision, pulling him through a tunnel of lights. In front of him, a young warrior on horseback, holding high a thunderbolt in his right hand. His scarlet cloak thrashed in the sunlight. He seemed to mouth a single word on the thunder…

'Donannu.'

As swiftly as the pain had started, it left, and Mugh was back in his right mind. 'Oh, that hurt. What on earth is Donannu? Am I going out of my mind?' he asked himself. But just in case Taranis was still watching, he promptly wrapped his cloak round his small frame and returned to Long Lum. 'I better start an adventure,' he decided. 'I will ready myself and the boy.'

CHAPTER THREE

TREANADH
Training

Four years later

THE CARVETII MESSENGER RODE hotfoot in the direction of Staena as fast as his steed was able. The news of any uprising at the borders of Carvetii carried grave concerns for the people living near the fringes of the land, so they called for help from their king. The Pehtas troubled continuously, occasionally overwhelming the small farming settlements and villages across the edges of Carvetii. This irritation, like an itch that could not be scratched, caused Venutius great consternation. 'I need to rid my lands of this vexation. They try and take what belongs to me. I vow I will take what belongs to them. And in the process, I will expand my power northward over their lands.'

Venutius sent messengers in every direction. 'Call your mighty men, your warriors and fighters. We have work to do to.' Soon, he was ready to present a tactical plan to the priest Druids, who were to judge the probability of victory in this endeavour.

'Where is Raigon, my High-Druid?' The King, reclining on a cushioned bench, did not rise as the Druids entered his new throne hall. He stroked his wispy moustache which grew dark against his pale skin. The tattooed markings of weapons on his shoulders and well-defined pectus made him look menacing and formidable. Despite that, his fair character warmed the hearts of those who knew him, while the *bhaírds* sang of his victories and battle wins.

The four Druids convened at the King's request, shrugged their shoulders. 'We expect he is on his way,' answered one of the gathered.

'No matter,' Venutius responded, waving his hand away. 'He will have to catch up with my plans when he deigns to appear. Now, this is what I want from you.' He unfolded his thoughts on the scheme, while the seers listened. 'We need to travel north to strengthen any areas where the boundaries of Carvetii have been breached.' He talked about the confrontation he anticipated. He presented his plans as a truth already accomplished. 'I have called together the mightiest men from across Carvetii. We will march as one army to the weakest point of our borders. I have been told of a vantage point facing the northern lands where we can camp. We will head there, and from that position, with a wide view of the landscape before us, we will be ready to relentlessly annihilate the blue vermin that dare to defy.' Fist in hand, Venutius pounded his knuckles as he paced the room. 'We will take them one by one if need be. But take them we will. Now, leave me and seek the gods' blessing for Carvetii and its King. Come back when they have spoken, and you have the victory outcome for my plan.'

The Druids assembled round a fire in the grove. Three wore blue cloaks depicting their high status in the grove. One other wore a green cloak; a trainer in *Ogham*, and one who would lead the 'asking.'

The rain fell in rhythm to the chants from the Druid priests seeking mystical insight into the outcome of Venutius' plans. A bucket, already half full of water, collected the rain, though it was but a mizzle.

The Blue Cloaks lifted cupped palms to receive the water from the *heafan*. The Green Cloak produced a small mug holding sacred oil and proceeded to pour a few drops into each of the open hands. Feeling the liquid, they rubbed the water and oil together, then sniffed each hand. Trance-like now, the Druids commenced the chant.

We call on you.
Oh! Gods of our lands,
To protect and to guard
Venutius' plans.
Give insight we ask.
In advance of this task,
That victory marches with us.'

They circled the fire, repeating the last few words many times, 'Victory marches with us. Victory marches with us.' The rain stopped falling. The fire sparked. The green cloaked Druid held aloft two venerable oak sticks, engraved with Ogham signs. One wand bore the sign for victory. The other; defeat.

Turning his back to the fire, the green Druid threw both tally sticks over his shoulders, into the blaze. All five stretched their hands out allowing the clenched drops of water-oil to fall into the flames. Sparks flew. Lifting the bucket, green cloak threw the contents into the sparks, enough to douse the heat for a few moments. Grabbing the nearest ogham stick, he pulled it from the flames. 'Our gods have heard our supplications.' Lifting the divination tool high above his head, he announced, 'We have victory!' then headed to inform Venutius. 'The gods have spoken. Your plan will succeed.'

Venutius immediately called for the best of his warriors from tribes scattered around Carvetii: sixty brawny fighting barbarians, afraid of nothing. They desired only two outcomes: to show their prowess in battle, to death if necessary; or return home victorious, displaying their spoils of war and trophies.

Within two weeks, the army was assembled, ready to leave.

'Move ahead!' shouted Venutius. With their young king leading the way, horsed men, charioteers, footmen and camp makers headed up to the border territories, which butted onto Carvetii.

By the end of the second day, they had made camp on the west side of Staena by *Ituna,* where it meets the larger tidal bore flowing into the western channel: a dangerous area of tidal flats and shifting waterways. A swathe of fertile land was by the bogs and marshes at Carreg Bainn; more than suitable for the Carvetii to rest and feed the horses. It was a vantage point, making it easier to strike any marauders, hunters; or battle warriors from Selgovae or Novantae, should they try their hand at entering Carvetii.

Once settled into his royal marque, he instructed six men, armed with bows, spears, and swords to venture across the Ituna, into enemy territory. 'Go into Selgovae, to discover where the raiders are pitched. Travel silently. Search out the truth of their numbers and any other information you can glean.'

Over the next few days, Venutius called a council of champions, laying before them his plan to bring slaughter onto the tribes who had irritated him for so long. 'I have learned at the hand of my father; simple action is the one most likely to win battles.' He noted the men in this gathering, watching eye movements and reactions.

'We must be ready, not only to defend ourselves against any attacks that might come from the painted tribes, but ready to overcome. We have the advantage here. We will see them long before they can attack us. Our brute strength and determination are more than matched by the amount of weaponry we can utilise. Divide and separate any groups of these varmints. Single them out. Pursue them to death.'

The men nodded and cheered in agreement. A chorus of 'Whatever moves on our borders, we will slaughter.' 'Aye! We are ready.' 'Man, or beast!'

'Do not wait for my signal if you are confronted. Be fearless and ready to kill or be killed. Make it your resolve to stop any advancement.'

Within three weeks, the trackers arrived back at the camp with rope-tied captives walking behind the horse train. They were taken to the King's tent and paraded in front of him.

'We found these men on our exploration of the northern lands. They were camped near our borders, and all had spears and shields. They signed that they are hunters, but their attire, or rather lack of it, tells a different story,' The warrior who led the expedition explained.

The prisoners were naked, except for blue paintings covering their entire bodies; even their faces showed embellishments of spears and swords, flowers, patterns, and gods.

The King remained silent for a while before he asked, 'Do they speak?'

'Not our language, Lord. There are similarities, but they spoke very little we could understand. We did catch some of their meaning as we captured them. We suspect that there are hordes of them gathering just north of where we found these men.'

'Is there anyone here who can understand these verminous *Pehtas*?' asked the King. He scanned round. No one came forth.

'Then take them and try cutting their fingers off. Then, if this does not work, and we get nothing from them, you may have their heads as trophies.'

The men bowed down before dragging the captives out.

Evening fell and Venutius became unsettled. He paced the covered room, then, taking a torch, ventured outside. He patrolled round the camp, listening to the chatter from his men, and inspecting the horses. Suddenly, he froze. A sound made him stop. He waited, listening, holding his breath. A whisper on the wind caught his attention. Without another thought, he called out to his men.

'Enemy approaching! Sound the alarm!'

The men grabbed their weapons just as a score or more of horses stampeded across the centre of camp. Wolf dogs followed in their wake. The ear-splitting barking and hoof noise was fused with the shouts of their riders. The Carvetii warriors, although taken by surprise, responded instinctively. Arrows showered onto the coloured bodies of the attackers. The King's men charged at the horses, grabbing the riders and pulling them from their mounts. They swiped at the horses and riders, cutting at the legs of the raiders with short glaives. The raiders slashed back. Dogs ran in circles, looking for escape. The Carvetii were merciless, stabbing their swords into the chests and hearts of the fallen men. One warrior chopped at the necks with his iron axe, while others used long spears to wound and impale. Only two escaped their demise, running into the river to save themselves. Eighteen *praedetari* died that night. The fire burned bright with their bodies.

Venutius grinned while glancing at the results of the night. Trophies were collected from the dead: a sword and a shield or two, beads and amulets, rings, and ear brooches. All was placed in the coffers of the King, until the time came to make a share among the sixty men.

Only two of the King's men were wounded, though not fatally.

Ten more horses were rounded up the following day and added to the sum of Carvetii battle mounts. When morning arrived, Venutius woke with a smile on his face. He smiled when he thought about the raiders and how rapidly his men had responded to the attackers. 'But I want more from them. I wanted them to be continuously alert. If it had not been for my unsettling apprehension and walk of the perimeter last evening, the raiders would have arrived without warning,' he thought. 'This is not as I planned.'

He called for his trackers. 'Have you any news from the men you caught?' Venutius asked.

'Yes, Lord King. It is as we expected. There are hordes gathering just beyond Birrens, intending to take Carvetii. We suspect these are Selgovae and Novantae people, but we cannot be certain yet.'

'Well done. Now get rid of them. Serve them up to Belatucadrus, the god of war, as, in his benevolent shadow, we are victorious.'

Venutius then called for more support from the whole of Carvetii, asking that fighters would come and help with the subjugation of the northern realms. 'Send messengers throughout Carvetii. Tell them of the spoils to be won in exchange for their support in the battle against these boundary breakers.'

Mugh and Eachann, doubly purposed, set out to join with the battling, and to search for the god's revelation, 'Donannu.' Snippets of talk overheard among the people in Long Lum suggesting that the High-Druid of Carvetii, on his way to meet with the King, travelled the same path.

Heeding the call from Venutius, they rode a pony each, though

Eachann's was so laden with baggage there was little room for him to sit comfortably now that he had grown.

'We will follow the north route, which meets with the river Peitriana, and then continue conforming to the river until we reach the rushing water of Ituna, east of Staena. This route I have travelled previously, and I know the outlay.' Mugh explained with confidence.

They camped that first night at the side of the river at Cumquinton, eating the bread they had packed in the bags attached to the sides of Eachann's pony. Eachann had been learning to ride for some time, and Mugh was pleased with his horsemanship. 'You are a natural handler.' Mugh encouraged as he marked the boy caring for the beast with an unusual kindness.

'I have given him a name, Mugh. Is that a good thing?'

Mugh found this soft side of Eachann beguiling but wanted to encourage his stronger inner soul. For that, he would require a warrior trainer. Recalling the voice in the thunder, Mugh chatted away to himself instinctively. 'I must follow the instructions given to me. The timing is right for Eachann. I hope that Raigon may be able to help.' Addressing Eachann, Mugh mumbled louder 'It would be good if we met with Raigon. It has been a good few years since we last spoke, and I hope I may be able to ask about Donannu then. I can ask and he might know. I can ask. I will ask. He should know.'

Eachann squatted by the fireside, clicking his teeth, and breaking twigs into even smaller fragments with a definitive snap.

'For god's sake, Mugh. Do you have to talk all the time?'

'I thought you would be well accustomed to it by now.' Mugh chuckled.

'Even so, it's enough to send a man mad.'

'Well, there's an obstacle, as you haven't arrived at manhood quite yet, though clearly you are on your way.' Mugh retorted.

'Yes, Mugh. But that day will soon arrive. Even this adventure might bring the opportunity for me to prove I am already there. I am almost a man. By the turning of the seasons, I will be sixteen soon.'

'Pride, my friend, does not become you. Be aware. A Druid should be humble. There is no room for boasting or hubris.'

'I apologise, Mugh, for my arrogant comment. But I do hope the time for me to prove myself will not be far away.'

'I am already arranging for your training in battle, Eachann. Do not rush life.'

The two chatted easily with one another, talking of expectations for the future days. Eachann's pony became unsettled, snorting and hopping from foot to foot. Eachann was beside him in seconds.

'Easy, Cahir, easy,' Eachann cooed, exploring the black shadows beyond the tether; checking the perimeters of their camp for marauders or intruders and sure enough, a group of four hooded men on horseback, holding swords and axes appeared to circle round the fire and encase Mugh in the midst. Eachann ducked behind the pony, pulled his hood over his head, and spied.

Mugh poked the fire. Not lifting his head, he spoke quietly to the visitors.

'Good eve, my brothers. Please, warm yourselves by the fire,' he said, offering a hand to the men. 'It is late for you to be without camp. Is all well?'

The men grunted, dismounting their steeds. Three lifted their hoods, but one stayed back, edging into the shadows. He led the horses to the tree where the other ponies were tethered, crouching within a spit of where Eachann concealed himself.

While the fourth hooded visitor stayed in the shadows, the others entered the warmth of the fire circle and sat. Each helped themselves to the bread and the mead which Mugh offered, relaxing in the Druid's company. Eachann relaxed too but stayed by the pony.

'We are trackers, on an errand for our master who rides toward Staena. We have orders to clear his way, so we must ask why you are here and what is your intention?' said the heaviest of the land spies.

Mugh breathed in before answering. 'I am travelling to Staena myself and hope to meet up with other Druids. Especially Audigus Raigon, the High-Druid of Carvetii.'

'Then all is well. We are Raigon's men. He will be travelling this way in a short time. Do you travel alone, Druid?'

'Alone, but for my apprentice, who tends the horses.' Mugh beckoned to Eachann to come and join him by the fire. With hesitation, Eachann closed in on the men, eyeing them cautiously.

The men conversed together about the raiders from the northern lands, and their intention to join Venutius in the subduing of these hostile usurpers. They included Mugh in the discussion. 'You are a Druid. Have you insight into the situation in the north?'

In response, Mugh said, 'I know little of the strategies or schemes of kings. I have no wider knowledge, though I have noted the call for support from King Venutius. But I will seek wisdom from the gods to furnish further discernment.'

The night developed. The mead accomplished its purpose, as the talk round the fire became loose and careless. 'When Raigon is settled, I am going to join with the warriors. I am ready for the fight,' said the middle tracker, a tall man with a scar over his left hand.

'You could not fight a sparrow,' his fellow pathfinder said with a smirk.

'Indeed, I can! And I will prove it,' he said, rising and making his way to the hooded shadow by the horses. 'I can fight this runt,' he said, grabbing the hood of the cloaked figure. 'Then I will enjoy the fruits of my winnings.' Pulling the hood away from the stranger's face, the drunken traveller revealed the long, black hair and sweet face of a woman of eighteen or nineteen years.

Eachann sprang up, but Mugh held his wrist to stop him.

'Stay here,' whispered Mugh. 'Good men, I wasn't aware that there was a woman in your group. Please, bring her to join us.' The assailant stopped, considering the Druid's words. He dropped the hood and dragged the girl nearer the fire and sat beside her, clutching her hair to stop her from running.

'Why are you travelling with her? Who is she?' asked Mugh.

'She is a token for Raigon. He called for her. She travels to him. She speaks with some local knowledge regarding the lay of the land. She offered to show us a shorter route to Staena, in exchange for food and safe passage with us.'

'Then we must make sure that you keep your side of the bargain.'

Mugh nodded to Eachann to fetch fuel for the fire. 'I have an impression that this night may be a long one.' he whispered. 'But pour some more mead for our friends, Eachann before you load the fire,' urged Mugh. Talking quietly to himself Mugh repeated the conversations with the three trackers over and over until it almost became a refrain; lilting, singing notes. A faint drone of sound escaped his mouth until the three trackers fell into a sleep trance, one by one, mesmerised by the Mugh's humming voice and the flickering flames from the blaze.

Once the three were sleeping, Mugh addressed the woman. 'Please, may we introduce ourselves to you, fair traveller?' Mugh asked. 'I am Mugh Ruith, the blind Druid who has travelled to the farthest of the Far-Lands to meet with the Eòlas and returned safely from those dangerous coasts. You may have heard of me.'

The woman stared at Mugh and then back at Eachann. 'Then you are the fabled one who safeguards The Shining One?'

'I am he,' confirmed Mugh. 'And you are Donannu *Scáthach*?'

The woman leaped in surprised. 'How did you know?'

'When the god speaks, he also ratifies. I have been expecting you. I knew that you would also be searching for us. My function is to bring you and this young man together. Tomorrow we will start work.' The woman nodded. Eachann did not interrupt, but his face wore a puzzled look. 'Sleep now. Tomorrow we will be on our way.'

Before the dawn broke, Mugh directed Eachann to prepare the horses. 'We will break fast some distance away from our fellows here,' he whispered. Donannu was already saddled on her horse. With her hood up, she silently left the camp, followed by the Druid and apprentice.

Once they were far enough away so as not to waken the three left behind, they progressed to a gallop; making headway on the road to the flowing river, which would eventually lead them to Staena and to the field beyond, where Venutius and his men were assembling.

Coming to a wooded area by high noon, they dismounted to give the horses rest. They laid camp by the side of a rock formation which gave security from the open riverbanks, deciding to stay until dawn the following morning.

Mugh unpacked his travelling items, disbursing the bag to reveal the Eòlas mysteries. Taking the glaive from the mix, he held it for Eachann to see.

'Eachann. Now the time is right, I feel, and your size speaks of sixteen years. I give you this glaive for your own. The Eòlas have determined its victorious power. This day I pass to the competencies of this weapon. Donannu is to be your teacher in all things warlike. Take note from her, so it goes well for you,' he said. 'In the thunder I heard her name, and I saw a bright warrior. I know in my Knowing that this woman is gifted by the gods. She will teach you how to be the man you are intended to become. I cannot teach these ways, for my sight hinders me. But you can become my eyes in the coming times, and I will become your understanding.' The little Druid touched Eachann's forearm, handing him the glaive. He smiled from ear to ear, then tucked the long golden tresses out of the young man's face lovingly.

Mugh watched for a reaction from Eachann, who, searching the face and stance of Donannu, disputed the necessity of a woman pedagogue. 'But she is so slight. I am already taller than she. Where will her stamina lie?' he questioned. But Mugh raised his palm, and the young lad became silent.

Donannu laughed. 'This is good, Eachann. I like the fact that you do not argue with your mentor. Do not argue with me, either. Then our paths will speed toward success,' she explained. At this, she took out a glaive from her cloak, and flashing it around, showed Eachann how to handle it.

They practiced the art of cutting, piercing, and slicing all afternoon and well into the evening. She showed him how to stab at an object for instant death, or simple wounding. By the evening, Eachann had already grasped the rudiments of battle. Whilst they travelled north, Donannu imparted her warrior knowledge to Eachann; promising to continue training him until he was initiated into full manhood. This knowledge, it seemed, dictated that he collects trophies from his enemies, after rendering them to the gods.

'I am sorry I was callous at our first meeting, Donannu. I can see now that you are versed in battle-knowledge more than anyone could be aware. Where did you learn such arts?' enquired Eachann, sharing the warmth from a small fire, over which a pot of herbs and rabbit cooked.

'My training was granted by *Braint* from Brigantia. I was sired by a king, or so I was told, but my mother hid me away, protecting me from the dangers of being a king's bastard. I have a brother; Erix, who cared enough to give me a chance at life. It was he who arranged for my training. The gods were good to me. And although granted nothing from my father, I want for nothing.' She shuffled a little, taking a stick and poking the fire. Ash and flames licked the cauldron. 'I entered the order of Druids and spent some time at *Ynys Mon*, achieving completion of my re-doing in just two years.'

'Then you are already an accomplished Druid,' stated Eachann, raising his eyebrows.

'But, we all have so much still to learn from each other, Eachann,' she answered modestly. 'Audigus Raigon has purchased my services from my brother, who gave his pledge to give me a livelihood. But the gods uttered other thoughts into my ear. So, I fled. Instead, making my way toward Venutius in the hope that he would release me from the pledge that had been made between Raigon and my brother.'

'Thank you for your honesty, Donannu. If the gods have been kind to you, then I will respect your blessing.' He smiled at the young woman before him, but a troubled expression crossed his face. 'What sort of king would disown his own blood? But I ask the same question of myself. Who is my father that he should disown me and leave me in the hands of Mugh the Sightless?' he thought. Eachann glanced at Donannu. 'She looks insignificant and frail. Not at all as a warrior should be.' But Eachann challenged his own thoughts, pronouncing, 'You are a Princess, then.' He bowed before her.

'No. Do not pay homage. It is I who should bow before you.'

Eachann, puzzled by this response, 'But why?'

'Now then, Donannu,' Mugh interjected. He pointed to the pot over the fire. 'Let us get on with the matter in hand,' he said, pouring the hot broth into horn cups and handing them to the two.

The following morning, the three men they had met a few days previously arrived on the same stretch of road approaching the outer borders of Staena. They flanked the sides of a chariot in which Raigon was perched, his black and white cloak hung loose round his shoulders. Coming closer, they hailed Mugh Ruith. 'Druid, we meet again. We wondered why you had departed our company so swiftly and taken our fellow traveller with you.'

Raigon stopped his chariot. 'Why, Mugh Ruith, is it really you? What has happened to cause this exchange?' he asked.

From his position on the horse, Mugh bowed before the High-Druid and rode to the side of the chariot. 'Lord High-Druid, we left hurriedly before dawn so as to catch the god, Taranis and receive his instructions concerning the journey and our preparation in support of Venutius,' he explained.

'But you took the woman with you,' called one of the three by Raigon's side. 'She was mine.'

The high priest faced the man and scoffed. 'Phhff. Your orders were to bring her to me. Fetch her now and all will be well.'

Mugh neared. 'Your highness, she is of no use to you. Could we not keep her until you are settled at Staena? We could train her to serve you and add to her usefulness. Then we can bring her to you, or any other more suitable token we might find? It may give the wrong impression should your highness arrive on a battlefield with a woman *tarraing.*'

The High-Druid stopped for a moment, kissing the ring on his little finger, and lifting his eyes. He nodded. 'I see your point. But I do not care what others think, so she will come with me. I have paid a price for her service, and therefore she belongs to me. Get her,' he called to his companions. The three moved closer to Donannu.

She edged away as they closed in on her pony.

'Do not reveal your capabilities,' Mugh mouthed silently. 'You are more than capable of dealing with all three of these opportunists, but it may be unwise to reveal your hand so soon.' In a blink he manoeuvred his horse between Donannu and her opponents, taking the middle ground. From the side-line, Eachann took out his dagger; readying himself should Mugh give a signal. The heftiest of the three men shifted round Mugh to grab her, but her cloak slid from her shoulders, and his grasp slipped with it. She swung round to hit him with her open hand. The sound echoed round the trees by the route, sounding an echo of thunder. It startled Cahir, Eachann's pony; causing him to rear up in front of the trackers' horses. Alarmed, the horses stampeded; running like bolts from lightning in the direction of Staena, while the two riders frantically holding on, tried to control their runaways and break their speed.

The third man, blind with anger and humiliation, drew his sword. The glint of polished iron dazzled and Eachann drew his glaive. The High-Druid's agent rushed forward, lifting his sword, Eachann came under him with a charge that sent his short sword into the open armpit of the assailant, causing him to fall from his horse.

Immediately, Donannu and Eachann pulled back their steeds and galloped in the direction of the forest to escape.

Instantly Mugh followed Donannu and Eachann, whilst Raigon waved his fist in the air.

'I will have you! I will have you, Ruith. And that acolyte of yours!'

Mugh's cloak flapped like a giant bird in flight whilst he galloped away. 'You will have to catch us first.'

CHAPTER FOUR

BREITH BANRIGH
Birth of a Queen

T HE ROTUND ARSE OF Bellnorix was spread on his chair. It had been that way for almost two weeks, as he waited for this day, - the day that he hoped his daughter would produce for him a grandson; heir to the tribe of Brigantia, and one worthy of taking his place on the throne.

Bellnorix allowed his mind to wander into a warm remembering of all the roads his life had roamed up to this point. 'I remember the land here in the north and building this tribal hall here; east of Tafte Field.' In his mind's eye, he recalled himself surveying a wooded upland where once the people had built homes in trees. With arms held high and hands open, he pointed at the imagined scene. 'I was born here and plan to be buried here… Whenever that day should arrive. This is the centre of my kingdom and, will soon become the epicentre for the whole of Brigantia.' His thoughts continued. 'Here I met my beloved wife, Riganta.' He smiled thinking of the beautiful woman with the biggest breasts he had ever seen. Their marriage had cemented the unity between Brigantia and the smaller tribe of Textowerdi.

His mind travelled to her sister, Anna. 'She should have never left Brigantia,' he mulled, shifting his gaze to the floor 'No good can come of it.'

Then lifting his eyes again to look at the landscape before him. 'Here we raised our daughter, Ferelith. Saw her married to that… insignificant… overweight, snippersnapper.' The thought of Brennus, his daughter's spouse, caused Bellnorix to screw his face so tight that it hurt.

'Bahh!' he shouted, his face burning red with frustration. 'He couldn't even live long enough to see his child born. Idiot,' he yelled. 'He should have been more like me.'

Fearless in battle and more powerful than three men, Bellnorix had led his warriors across the northern lands of Albion, teaching them the art of horsemanship, stealth, and then the art of victory in battle. They fought opposing tribes and added daily to their captors and allies until Brigantia was swelling under his power. He was a formidable leader and a formidable king. It had always been his hope that Ferelith would marry a dynamic king or warrior, who would be an asset to the leadership of Brigantia in its enlarging. But even though Brennus, Raven Prince, was *Breehin* of Roecliffe, and held lands and sept, these he had simply inherited; not acquired through his own ambition or prowess in battle.

'His abilities lay in his power to dodge the enemy, rather than face them,' thought Bellnorix. 'Until the day he had no choice. The enemy came too close and took his head, as well as his horse.' Bellnorix shook his head, his cheeks sagging. 'For all that. For all that, I loved him. The blubber Knob!'

Just then, the messenger ran to the hall of the King, shouting as he ran, 'My King, my King! I have the news!'

Turning his full attention on the messenger, he bellowed, 'What news? What news? Is the child born? What is it?'

'It's a girl, Lord! Full lusty and screaming already,' he replied.

Bellnorix rose from his seat slowly, taking in the news. He drew breath. Rage took over his pumping blood and rushed to his throat and face. Words would not spit from his mouth. He walked to the door of his hall, and outside, the fury spilled over into a shaking frenzy. 'A GIRL! A blasted feeble, fumbling wet piece of useless cow dung fanny! NO!'

He took deep huffing breaths; his anger subsiding little by little, till his breathing steadied. He walked from his hall to the birthing room across the muddy path. His huge shoulders, covered in furs, trembled. He stopped outside the covered doorway and listened. The child within cried loudly; the wailing, miserable squall of a caterwaul pitched pain to his ears. Bellnorix turned away.

That evening, his daughter Ferelith died. The birth had taken too much blood, and the midwoman could not stop the flow. Even the Druids could not help. They had gathered by the birthing room, chanting healing and incantations throughout the delivery, but to no avail. The child was given to a wet nurse and stayed with her for the period of weaning.

Bellnorix did not visit the child again.

The young princess grew fit and sturdy. The wet-nurse and other women from Taftefield helped in her raising. But although Bellnorix would not see the child, he remained aware that she was his only heir. At some point in the future, he would need to redress his anger concerning her lack of masculine ability. So, as it was, when the princess was ten years old, he called for her.

The women who had been caring for her came first. They bowed before Bellnorix and shuffled for a position out of his reach, but near enough for him to see and hear them.

The king gawped at the maidens before him. 'Hmm. Does it take all of you to bring one child to see me?' Bellnorix asked. More shuffling went on before one woman dared to step forward and speak.

'Lord King. The child is quite a handful. She is wilful and headstrong. We have tried to bring her to order, but she is like a feral pony, untamed,' said the woman, bowing and bobbing her knee before the King.

The King thought about this, and a grin spread across his face. 'Wilful, eh? And wild, you say? Bring her to me,' he demanded. 'The child might have some spirit yet.'

They yanked the girl into the hall in front of Bellnorix. He eyed the child, wondering if they had brought the right girl to him. She was dressed in a skirt, which she had hitched up between her legs to make *braccae*. Her hair chestnut red, fell over her face, unkempt, and wild. Her face was unwashed, as were her tunic and feet.

'Bow before your grandfather, the king,' said the woman angrily, directing her authority at the child. The child stood stiffly and defiantly silent.

'Well child, what is your name?' asked the King.

'Child.'

'Just "Child"? Do you not have another name?' Bellnorix asked.

'If I have any other names, I do not know them,' she answered.

'This will not do. Was she not named by her mother? A name you must have. I will give you a one, and you will use it,' determined the Brigante King. 'It will be a name suitable for a wild child, and heir to the Kingdom of Brigantia.' Choosing the youngest of the women carers, a woman of about seventeen years; aglow with health and with a kind face, he asked. 'What is your name, woman?'

'I am Raegan, Lord. I serve you in the home of my father, Lord Erebus. He is one of your warrior champions and fought long side you in the battle against the Votadini some time ago.'

'Good. Then you will do. Raegan. I want you to take the child, wash her and get her dressed suitable for her position. Find rooms in my halls for the both of you and bring her to me when she is clean. Meanwhile, I will decide on her name.'

Raegan pulled the child kicking and screaming in defiance, dragging her from the hall to act on the King's orders.

Disobediently, the child screamed 'I do not want to move into the halls of my smelly grandfather. I like playing with the other children in the sept, and I do not want to be separate from them.' She spat at Raegan several times until Raegan sat with her and gently explained that she needed to take her royal position and use her spirit and anger against the enemies who would come against her and her people.

'Great wealth and victory will bow at your knee, child. But you must obey your grandfather, the King, and learn to become a formidable queen.'

'I do not want to become a queen,' she argued. 'It's bad enough having to wash until I'm scrubbed raw.'

Raegan combed the girl's wild hair while talking delicately to her. 'Your life is planned out, child. You have choices to make as you get older which will decide your future. Choose to become a victorious ruler rather than a weak slave,' Raegan coaxed, tying the girl's thick mane into a braid, then helping to dress her in finer linen than the rough cloth kirtle she had been wearing. 'Do not turn your skirts up into braccae,' the woman said. 'Wear them as a young woman should. Wear the tunic loose. There, you look acceptable. Now, we must go to the King.'

On the way across the grassed cortile in front of the Great Hall of Bellnorix, Raegan and the child stopped at a ring of ponies being brought into obedience by the trainer. These wild ponies, [a sturdy breed of high intelligence] roamed the Peneinz; the Brigantium mountainous backbone. They were traded among the merchants and vendors from as far overseas as Belgica and Celtica from the uplands at Epicus and surrounding areas. Their hardy disposition and swiftness in battle made them suitable, once trained, as war *Còmhdhail;* battle horses that pulled the light chariots of the Brigante warriors.

For a while, the two heeded the ponies trotting round the wooden ring.

One of the ponies was startled by the unexpected chatter and laughter from a group of men passing on their way into the village forge. The pony reared up in a sudden frenzy and lifting his foot, stampeded, crashing into the wooden fencing which formed the ring.

Raegan called to the girl to get away out of danger, but the girl stood her ground. She called to the animal. 'Ssshhhsh, little pony. Shuuush.' Carefully she stretched out her hand, touching the mane of the frightened mare, bringing calmness to the situation.

'You have a gift, young one,' the trainer said, taking the horse back into the fold.

'I can ride them too,' the child said.

'Really?' questioned the trainer, lifting his eyebrows and smiling.

Really!'

'Then come into the ring and show me,' he said, helping her climb over the fencing. She slowly approached the skittish pony, and taking the rope fastened round its neck, she circled in front, encouraging the animal to follow. Pulling the horse's head low, and almost dancing, the girl swayed from side to side in front of him; then, sensing calmness in the beast, she made for the sheepskin pad on the horse's back and swung effortlessly on top. Gently at first, she rode round the ring, gathering speed within a few moments. She patted the long neck and all the while, leaning into the ear of the horse, talked quietly to him.

'Where did you learn how to do that?' asked the trainer.

'There was little to do during the day, so last summer I regarded their ways, and practiced when the warriors rode out.' She furrowed her eyebrows, the corners of her mouth turned down, then she tossed her head. 'Why? Was I wrong to do that?'

The trainer grinned, so she dismounted the pony and climbed back over the fence to Raegan.

'Adjust your skirts, child,' directed Raegan grabbing the child's hand and marching her briskly to meet Bellnorix, who had been by his hall door, looking for the child's arrival. He had observed the taming of the pony.

'I am so sorry Lord, King,' Raegan said, bobbing her knee in front of Bellnorix. 'I had the child washed and clean, but the pony was startled, and she darted over the fence before I could stop her.'

The King waved his hand and ignored Raegan. He beckoned the child to follow him into the hall, where he took his place on the huge wooden chair which was intricately carved with animals, aurochs, horses and flying snakes. He gazed intently at the child.

'I saw you with the pony, child. Do you like ponies?'

'Yes,' answered the child, rolling her eyes and sneering at the King.

'Then you shall have one of your own,' the King granted. 'You may choose any one you like, and you may give it a name you like.'

The child shrugged her shoulders, bewildered at the King's offer.

'I don't need one of my own. I ride whenever I like, on the wild ponies outside the wall.'

The King rubbed his eyebrow, holding his head back in disbelief at the child uttering this frank statement. He scanned the room to see who had noticed this flout in protocol.

'You do not argue with the King in this room, child,' bellowed the King's High-Druid, standing beside his lord and master. The girl glared rebelliously into the face of the chief Druid. She shuddered, averting her eyes, then returned to stare at the King in defiance.

He rubbed his long moustache and thought for a moment. 'Then what can I give you that you would like?' he asked.

'I would like a sword and a shield. I would like to ride with the warriors, and I would like to show you that I might be a girl, but I have a boy's heart!' The King gave a snort, then laughed so loud that the child covered her ears. 'I think your laugh might blow the roof off the hall,' she giggled. Showing no fear, she continued, 'Oh! And I want to wear braccae. Not these silly skirts!'

'I like your spirit, child. It is like one of the wild ponies; strong and courageous; defiant. I will name you *Mandua* – yes! You are a little pony, and just as wild. You will be known as "Mandua," for you are indeed a wild pony!' The King grinned at his choice, 'I feel it suits the wild child standing in front of me. What do you think of that, Mandua?'

She pouted her lips, and cocking her head to one side, she weighed up the sound of the name. 'Yes.' She nodded. 'I like that very much.'

'I like her,' the King chortled. 'And that is all that matters at the moment.' He rose from his throne and took the hand of the little girl. 'You will ride with the warriors as you ask. And be treated as any boy in this land would. You will become a glorious ruler and leader over the lands you will inherit, my *Boann* Mandua.' The King bowed in front of his granddaughter, laughing heartily, then gripping her hand so she could not escape, he strolled round the hall to introduce her to his champions, bodyguards, servants and ladies.

All the excitement had created quite a stir in the town. The King ordered a feast, giving a reason to introduce his new successor more widely among the people of Taftefield. He declared loudly, 'If the gods had given me a girl for an heir, then I will make sure that the girl has the Brigante spirit burning in her breast, until the day she becomes a great queen and warrior. Even greater warrior than I, if that was at all possible.' He quipped, laughing raucously.

So Mandua enjoyed all the privilege that was bestowed on her, and promised herself that she would become a worthy warrior princess, if it meant she could prod the boys in the village and smack them whenever she liked.

CHAPTER FIVE

POLLENS NOBILATATE
Royal Lineage

ANDUA WAS GROWING IN might and wisdom. Her skill in riding was astounding. She favoured a grey, almost white fell pony; sleek and fast, which she named Tormaig. She spent much time training and riding until she and her equine seemed to merge as one. Much of her training was allocated to one of Bellnorix' own champions, Camulo. He was a big man in stature, good natured and with a penchant for filling his belly with whatever food was on offer. He could always be found in the kitchens helping the cooks and helping himself to any morsel. His moustache was long and continuously greasy. But his liking for tasting did not affect his ability with weapons and warfare. He was a fighter of experience and a champion in his own right. He had been reared in the household of Bellnorix and understood the nuance of ministrations to the high throne. Mandua was well served.

Bellnorix had a smaller seat made especially for Mandua. He had it covered in red cloth and a cushion atop. She installed herself at his side, watching and learning as he ruled over the Brigante people, and was included in the confabs with Druids and warriors when discussions took place concerning enemy tactics and battle news. Her opinion was requested on various topics, helping her learn the art of discernment.

But above all else, her reputation of passion, power, and prowess in the slaughter grew to such heights that Mandua became synonymous with the goddess, Brigantia herself. Her people took the "wild, white pony;" the *boann* with the spirit of sacred horses, as their talisman.

Each skirmish or incursion that Bellnorix planned and executed, Mandua joined. She rode out with the warriors until she knew instinctively her position and ability. She was quick and agile on the horse and fearless in the battle. Her trophy collection became vast, competing with her grandfather for space in the sept.

'Make friends whenever you can, Mandua. Do not make enemies, unless that is the only possibility,' Bellnorix advised his agrestal young princess. 'Always look for the light. You will be safe in the light.'

People saw the likeness of her ancestry in the bone structure of her cheeks, akin to those of Bellnorix. Her colouring was his colouring, her strong limbs, his stance. Her laugh and grin reminded the Brigante people of her father before her. For though he never achieved victory on the battlefield, he had been well liked for his quick wit and great-hearted generosity. The people saw in Mandua the obdurate spirit of her grandfather; the beauty and softness of her mother; and a tactical munificent brain, which they believed must have been gifted from her father. That she was to become heir to Brigante lands, sat well with her people.

Many disparate tribes surrendered to Bellnorix, joining the lands of their fathers with the lands already under the Brigante banner. So it was that Brigantia swelled both in size and in legend, from the great Northern Sea to the west coast of Albion; from the borders of the *Pehtas* in the north to the borders of the Coritani and Setanti tribes in the south. Except for the Parisii on the east coast, Setanti on the west, and Carvetii, Bellnorix ruled over almost one third of the land mass of Albion. This made Brigantia the largest tribal area in the land. Bellnorix planned to take Parisii, then Setanti, into the Brigante confederation, with or without their consent.

As Mandua grew in stature, so did her victories in battle.

Mandua stood at Bellnorix' side when each tribal king bent the knee to her grandfather, offering their loyalty and allegiance. She enjoyed the admiration. 'I will be the greatest queen in Albion,' she promised herself.

On the day they set off heading to Parisii, Mandua astride her horse Tormaig, looked in every part the queen she was to become. No longer a girl, but a woman of fierce stature; beautiful and formidable. Her long, chestnut hair (still untameable, much like her nature) was tied back from her face by a band of red cloth, adorned with iron droplets. The unruly mane glowed as a halo of fire in the morning sun. Atop her white tunic, she donned a white cloak of thickly woven flax, fastened by two gold brooches: one at the neck and one at the shoulder. Far thicker than wool, the flax cloak provided some protection against the sword or axe. Hemming the edges of the cloak was a pattern of linked chains and roses stitched in fine gold thread. She had wrapped round her waist a long length of softer wool cloth, pinning it, and then bringing it up and through her legs to form braccae trousers. On her back was a scabbard holding her iron sword; one forged especially for her size. In one hand was a short glaive, and in the other a round polished shield bearing the symbol of a pony depicted in white.

The Brigante fighters rode with Parisii in their sights. Mandua accepted her fate. Invoking the help of the gods, she breathed deeply. 'In the name of Taranis and Epona,' she inhaled, allowing her lungs to swell with the passion which stirred in her young breast. The spirit of Brigantia flowed from the air, filling her body, imbibing the energy of her people. Mandua rode at the head of the cavalcade of heavily armed warriors. Valas, the High-Druid of Brigantia, followed behind, along with the Druid warriors aligned to the High King.

Holding her head and her hand high, Mandua called out, 'Onwards! May the gods be with us.' In his chariot, Bellnorix travelled at her side for the first twelve miles before dropping back to ride with the other charioteers. Thus, he allowed Mandua to take authority in the outcome of the operation.

The first day saw them arrive at *Gabrantovici*, on the east coast. Approaching the sept in his chariot, Bellnorix took the sea air into his lungs. At the cliff edge, indicating with his hand toward the Northern Sea, he said, 'Look at this. This is the edge of our land. How beautiful is this?' The sun shone over the water, and each tidal lap produced thousands of sparkling fairie chariots ebbing and flowing in rhythm with the earth.

Mandua dismounted her horse to stand by her grandfather. 'It is a sight touching the soul,' she said. 'It is worth any fight to keep.'

'But remember, my little wild one: make friends first. Do not make enemies when you don't need to.' He patted Mandua's arm. 'The way of peace is the path to greatness.'

Only a short distance from the shoreline, atop a hill overlooking a fine cove like bay, was the sept. The prime position protected the area from pirates and marauders who might sail the choppy waters to invade Brigantia from the seas.

The chief welcomed them, having made a pact with Bellnorix some time ago. Peace had followed a turbulent past, when Ninniau

Beornraed ceded to Bellnorix, allowing him overall command of his lands and people. A positive relationship had flowed between the two; one which Bellnorix hoped would continue.

The *Beornraed,* aided by his daughter the Lady Cynifrida, opened the gates, offering food and sleeping arrangements for all the company. Ninniau, with open arms, welcomed the King.

'Bellnorix. Come. Let me present my daughter, Cynifrida. It is some years since you last saw her. She is grown, is she not?' Cynifrida, a small woman with jet-black hair and a serious countenance, curtsied before the King. He took the hand of the young mistress, his eyes never leaving her face as he kissed the signet ring on her little finger. Mandua also eyed Ninniau's daughter as her kissed hand dropped to her side.

Beside Cynifrida, a comely warrior stood; even featured and bearing a bushy bristle of a moustache. Edwin Bloodeworthe furtively touched the kissed hand of the lady. She did not retract her hand from his touch but held it there for a few moments.

Bellnorix beckoned to Mandua, 'This is my granddaughter.' He drew Mandua close to him and held her by his side.

Ninniau bent his head, touching his left shoulder with his right hand, the sign of respect. Mandua acknowledged with a nod. Holding her head high, Cynifrida positioned herself between Mandua and her father, ushering him to the hall. Then, bowing before the visiting king, she left the hall, ordering the servants to bring food and wine on her departure.

The gathering settled at the tables in the Great Hall. With assent from Bellnorix, Mandua called a conclave of the highest and esteemed men and Druidae travelling in the venture. She asked Ninniau to include his favoured men, also. Ninniau called Edwin Bloodeworthe, the escort of Cynifrida, to join the discussion, along with two Druids and three warriors. One by one they proclaimed name and bearing. Valas, the High-Druid of Brigantia, took his position at the head of the table as judge and law lord. He wore the white priestly cloak conveying his Druid authority and carried an oak fey in his right hand. It was expected that the voice of the High-Druid would be acknowledged, and his advice acted upon. He had served Bellnorix well and had stated his intention to continue serving the heir presumptive, after the esteemed king's death.

Clearing his throat, he showed his readiness to speak. Mandua snorted and shuffled down the bench and away from Valas. Valas glared at the princess, showing bared teeth. Ignoring him, Mandua called to the meet her personal bodyguard and champion, Camulo, who had safeguarded her when she first entered the halls of Bellnorix. He had been at her call ever since. 'Come, Camulo.' Mandua patted the bench by her side.

With jabbing finger, Valas, specified to Mandua that she should occupy the seat by him. 'Here, Princess,' he said, pointing to the empty space, his tone, heavy with threat. He waited. Mandua, feeling the hairs on the back of her neck bristle, and the smell of rotting fish invaded her nostrils, hitched a little nearer to him, but as far away from his odour as possible. Snarling, Valas grabbed her arm, forcing her to closeness. She snatched her arm away, then slid away again, showing only contempt for the High-Druid. She snorted again.

The men and their young mistress discussed the best way forward. Mandua was grateful for the insights Edwin Bloodeworthe gave concerning the landscape on the approach to Parisii; and his suggestion that they should send scouts to meet with the lords of that tribe if they were willing.

'I believe there are four kings over the land called Parisii,' he explained. 'And each one should be approached individually. They hold equal power. If you can encourage them to join with Brigantia against the threat from the south, then it may be possible they will give support without lives being lost.'

'You talk of the threat from the south, Lord. Can you give us news of their movements?' asked Mandua.

'We have heard that Gaius Caligula, their emperor, is planning campaigns against us, and is readying his troops to move into the southern channel. We have winter in our favour, and maybe a few more winters, but small numbers of the enemy are already infiltrating. They have control already, to some degree, using trade and bargains to seduce our people. There has been talk of the prince of Cantiaci having bargained with Rome against Albion. Though some tales arriving home tell of the Latins collecting war trophies to take home to Roma. They collect shells from the beach.'

Mandua leaned backwards in disbelief. 'Maybe they want to make pretty neck bands for their women as gifts to take back to their lands when we defeat them,' Mandua jibed. An uproar of laugher filled the room. 'We may have nothing to fear, but it may be a ruse to allay our concerns before attacking.'

'The invader's intent would most likely be, first, to take most of the lands south of your own, Lady, before moving northward.' Edwin divulged. 'Though they will struggle to take Iceni. Lord Prasutagus and his wife, Boudicca, are a vicious and formidable terror. They are, however, considering opportunities which may be offered, should they cede to the invading adversaries.'

Ninniau interjected, 'Prasutagus is a grey beard; a man with age on his back, like me. He worries about his two daughters and his queen, Boudicca. The world is changing. The Romans are cunning. These intruders threaten our very existence. So many of our young people have been taken as slaves in the past; our women are used, raped, and killed as if it does not matter. They have no regard for our people, our ways, or our lands. Over the many years, we have had to accept their infiltration.'

We are now at a stage when, should the need arise, we can be ready to fight against these murderers and slave takers.' Edwin spat into the ground. 'They disgust me!' He spat again.

Acknowledging the polymath of the chief of Gabrantovices, Mandua asked, 'Lord Ninniau, what advice do you give?'

'Call to yourself as many tribes and honest men as you can. Build a defence against these enemy legions along the borders of our lands. Fight with every portion of Brigante spirit you can muster. These opponents will not take my land, nor my people,' he vowed.

Bellnorix nodding in assent banged his fist on the table.

'Aye!' the gathered war lords agreed.

'I will send three trackers and an emissary to find and lay before the lords of Parisii our request for fraternity,' decided Mandua. 'This would be the optimum outcome. Should they not agree, then the ramifications will weigh on their heads. We will discuss the outcome on their return.' Bellnorix again assented his approval.

A banquet was brought to the Great Hall: platters of fruit and meats; pig and stag, sliced and hot from the spit, were placed on tables round the room. Cynifrida entered the hall, followed by her brother, a boy of about seventeen cycles. He helped Cynifrida orchestrate the meal, filling the main table with stew, breads, and cheeses, along with nuts and apples. Around this table, the lord of Gabrantovices and Lady Cynifrida faced the King and Mandua. A fire had been sparked and candles lit as the two companies gathered in friendship. The boy located himself near the fire, but close to his sister.

'Tell me of your life here,' Bellnorix queried the elderly Ninniau, each sharing wine. 'Are you safe from the tyrants? What is your armoury like? Have you enough stocks?'

'Since the passing of my dear wife Arnemetia, life has taken on a different shade. When she was taken by marauders, I vowed to bring better protection for our people. I vowed never to let Gabrantovices suffer in the same way again. I have made it my work to build our homes and this sept into a fortress on this hilltop. We have a goodly stock of weapons. Our forge is at work constantly,' responded Ninniau. He leaned back, beaming a confident smile. 'We have excellent warriors. My young son is growing into a well-trained warrior, too. He learns quickly and is a clear thinker.' Then, leaning into Bellnorix' ear, Ninniau divulged, 'I have another comfort, Bellnorix. Latis warms my bed at night. She is both comforting and affectionate. I never expected to have such a full life again.'

'We have fertile land, and the great Northern Sea holds ample fish. Our supply is plentiful,' added Edwin, who had positioned himself at the other side of Lady Cynifrida.

Facing the young Bloodeworthe, the King asked, 'And what of your brother, Edwin? Is he still at Ynys Môn learning the dark arts and Druid ways?'

Edwin's brow furrowed at the question.

Bellnorix chuckled and continued. 'You look bemused, Edwin. Did you not think that your family situation is known to me? I have long held the friendship of your father, Ogma. Before he died, I spoke with him of his desires for the future of his sons.'

'My Lord,' responded Edwin. 'My brother Donn is indeed learning the ways of our religion. He is already gaining a reputation as an exceptional Druid, and I suspect he will be ready very soon to take up a high position. His knowledge of warfare and magic is reported with wonder.' Edwin's expression showed no emotion, but his face flushed red, and his breathing became heavier.

Mandua's eyes, alert to the slightest movement, noticed Cynifrida touched her escort's hand, patting it gently, and then continued to answer the King's questions.

She held her gaze downward, away from the eyes of Bellnorix. 'My Lord, I do not think that Donn Donnlugh will return to Gabrantovices any time in the future. He has a bigger plan for his life, I think.' Concluding, she picked a plate of sweetmeats to offer the King. 'Please, take some of our delicacies.'

The King took some small cakes from the platter and continued. 'Then I must see if there is a place for him at my seat, when he has completed his training.' He glanced at Mandua, and for the first time, introduced her formally. 'Lord Ninniau and Cynifrida, I want you to meet Princess Mandua, my granddaughter and the future Queen of Brigantia.'

Edwin sprang to his feet and bowing, followed by the ensemble. Greetings and well wishes directed toward the future queen could be heard resounding around the hall. Clapping and celebrating began in earnest; *bhaírds* played music and dancing began.

The princess glanced round the room, taking in the admiring smiles of her people. She noticed that the heads of Valas and Edwin were very close while they whispered together. She also noticed the furtive look from Valas, checked to see who might be in earshot before continuing his conversation. Mandua's heckles raised. Seizing an opportunity to speak with Edwin herself, later that evening, she asked, 'Lord. Can I call on your support in our ventures to keep Brigantia in unity with Gabrantovices?'

'My Lady. Indeed. You show sagacity in your judgements, which are beyond your years. But you need not question my loyalty. I am quite offended that you should. May I ask with what reasoning you imply any other?'

'I see ambition in your eyes, and they reflect Cynifrida. Do I need to concern myself?'

'My Lady. I am Brigante first, and therefore loyal to the people of Brigantia and her leader. If that be Bellnorix or his heir, I will serve until death. This I vow.' Mandua tilted her head.

Hesitating, Edwin continued. 'Lady, should you have any concerns, do not look to me. Rather, have a care of my brother; lost to the family through mistrust and anger. He is ambitious like no other. It is he you should be aware of.'

Mandua stared at Edwin, puzzled by his response. 'I know nothing of your brother, or indeed your family, but I sense green eyes, Edwin. Envy can be a very destructive emotion.'

The three trackers and the emissary set forth the following morning to approach the four kings of Parisii. 'Be swift. Return safely,' mandated the princess, on their leave.

Within a day, they had entered the northern border of Parisii and touched Bredla, the first settlement holding. They arrived at the gates of the sept, where a few warriors rode out to meet them.

'Who are you, and what is your purpose here?' one asked, brandishing his sword.

The emissary spoke calmly. 'We are here on behalf of Bellnorix, High King of Brigantia. We come in peace and seek an audience with your king. Where can we find him?'

'In Parisii, there are four kings. Which one do you look for?' he asked.

'We seek all four. There is reward in it for you, should you help us find them.'

The emissary was quick to enquire. 'What reward? Show me?'

'First, tell us which direction. Then we will show you the spoils.' Each of the trackers drew their swords and lined up on horseback. The Bredla warriors match the actions of the Brigante.

'Your skills in battle are known, Brigante. We do not want to fight. Give me some show of trade and I will tell you what you want to know.'

The emissary pulled from his sack, four or five gold rounds and showed them to the Bredla. The Bredla mouthpiece nodded. 'There are four kings. I will give you the name of one, and the others, with more trophies.'

The emissary tossed one piece of gold at the warrior opposite him, holding back the others for each name the Bredla revealed. 'Rig Drust lies within these gates.'

'I will test your honesty, before giving more,' said the emissary, putting his handful of coins back into his sack. He made to ride on, and the warriors opened a path giving access to the gate. '*Rig* Drust,' shouted the emissary. '*Rig* Drust. Show yourself.'

A whistle shot round the village. Men and women showed their faces at the doorways of their houses. From the central house walked a man: impressive in size, wearing a cloak with fur shoulder pads, which extended the width of him considerably.

'Who calls me? Who dares to disturb my repose?' he bellowed from the doorway. His hands rested on his hips, and the sound of his booming voice caused his belly to tremble.

The emissary, without hesitation, yelled, 'I ask after you Rig Drust. I have a message from High King Bellnorix of Brigantia. He asks you to consider joining with him in the fight against the threatened Roman invasion. Will you consider?'

The King laughed a hefty belly laugh. 'I will consider this, if my brother kings will also consider.' He turned his back on the emissary, dismissing him.

Over the next four days, the emissary and the three trackers, having paid for information about the other three kings of Parisii, set off to enquire from them. Vercinge, Aongus, and Karnos refused the request. 'We have already been approached by the Romans, and find they offer us a better deal for our support. Take that news to Bellnorix. We have assessed peace and good fortune through the Romans,' said Rig Vercinge. The company returned to report to Bellnorix.

'I will chop off their heads for their treason,' vowed Bellnorix, seething on hearing this report.

'Where might he find the body power to fulfil that vow?' Mandua wondered.

Bellnorix discussing with Lord Ninniau, deciding on ways to keep Brigante safe from Parisii and Romans on the Gabrantovices borders of Brigantia. The high king promised warriors, should the need arise, which would bolster Ninniau's own troop.

'I can offer men and weapons,' he said. 'Place a guard on your borders for some weeks and watch. It may be that the Parisii will do nothing if you remain inside our lands. Watch and be ready.'

'King, should we not attack?' asked Mandua.

'I think we should ride on to *Setanti* and gather their support first. I know that they are against the Romans, so they are more likely to join us. Let us prepare to leave Gabrantovices, knowing that Bloodeworthe will hold our borders here.'

Mandua agreed, though her face told another story. She clicked her lips in frustration.

As the cock crowed the following morning, Bellnorix was helped onto his chariot, and lifting his hand in the air, he signalled to Mandua to lead the warriors, charioteers, and cavalcade in parade out of Gabrantovices, toward Setanti.

The terrain from Gabrantovices to Setanti gave no easy access, allowing only three rough rest camps on the way. They skirted the boundary of Parisii southward heading for the growing settlement of *Vincobancio* which housed the tribe of Corinota. The place was buzzing with traders from the south and east, whose tents and camps had spilled out onto the surrounding fields. A market held the main focus of activity in the centre of the large sept. Hawkers and traders vied for deals from the wooden carts which displayed all manner of goods and food. King Bellnorix, parading in his chariot, rode through the open gate into the centre of the market. He had instructed Mandua to take a more cautious entrance.

'Cover your war cloak with a black one and your face with your cloak hood, my princess. I am not sure who holds this place. When we have assurances of our safety, then I will introduce you.'

High-Druid Valas rode by the side of the King's chariot, taking the lead at this point. On entering, the King's men circled the inner walls of the enclosure, surrounding the people.

'Halt,' called Valas. 'Bow before your King Bellnorix, High Over-Lord of Brigantium.'

The people stopped. A moment later, bowing, they showed their fealty for the King. A few ran to the centre of the sept to let the leaders know of the arrival of Bellnorix.

Two warriors, huge hulks in leather braccae appeared in the open. Each carried a staff taller than their height. They displayed ostentatious moustaches, grown so long that they touched their bare chests. Each had rings on every finger, and several pins in their ears. The similarities between the two ended there; for one had fair hair, shaved at the sides with the rest long and tied back into a braid. The other had black hair, falling like rope spirals around his face and shoulders. Some he piled high on his head and fastened with a stick of willow, till it appeared as if the tree itself grew out of the bush. A wolf hound moved out of the shadows to sit at his feet. Both stood tall, saying nothing, but grinned at the King.

'Welcome, Lord King,' they said in unison, while making an exaggerated bow in front of the entourage.

'To what do we owe this good fortune?' asked the fair-haired warrior.

'Never before have we been honoured in this way,' said the dark-haired warrior.

Valas made his way forward on his horse, till he was between the King and the two men.

'We are here on our way across Brigantia, bringing good tiding and news. To whom do we speak?'

The fair-haired man bowed. 'I am Beombran Byrde. One of the *Braint* originally from this tribe of Corinota. I am Lord of this sept, and the outlying lands.'

'And I am his cousin, Belinos, also of the Braint. I am visiting my cousin here, though originally from *Brigcruim*. I am head of *Coria Toutas* in that area. I am not originally from there; but I have made it my home. Over a hundred men stand at my order. We are at your service, Lord King.'

The two powerful men bowed before Bellnorix, then stepping to the side, stood wide of each other, allowing a path between them. They offered their hands to direct the King and his company between them and into their home. The windowless hall, built from stone and fully round, was warm and filled with candlelight. Two tables at each side of the room were already being rammed with fruit and nuts, water, and wine: a meal for the travellers.

'Come. Come,' encouraged Belinos. 'Rest and restore yourselves.'

His hand gesticulated to the tables. 'Sit wherever you feel comfortable.'

The room was decorated with trophies from battles; heads hung from the single end rafter, like baubles dancing on a tree. The King made his way to the far side of the room where a larger seat signified the place for the tribal chief. Valas took a seat at the opposing end. Mandua made her way to her grandfather, but Valas grabbed her arm in passing. With one stern look of warning, he pulled her to his side and pursed his lips, a sign for her to be silent.

'Who does he think he is dealing with?' she thought. Although flushed with temper, Mandua acquiesced and obeyed the High-Druid. He continued to hold her wrist, pulling her closer to his chest. Struggling to break free from the hold, Mandua tugged, but Valas held onto her with a lock so tight that the blood flow in her arm restricted. She sat with her back to the room so her presence could not be known.

Camulo took a seat near Valas and Mandua. His hand was on the hilt of his sword in readiness, should he be needed. The other warrior and Druid company placed their bodies where the seating allowed. The two Braint positioned either side of the King. They faced into the room, all the while watching the King's men.

'We are honoured by your presence, King. Our allegiance is yours,' said Belinos. 'But I have to ask why you are travelling over our lands?' He grunted and flicked one of his braids behind his ear.

The King responded. 'Do not concern yourself, my friend. I merely bring news, and hope that I can count on your support against the enemy, who would take your lands away from you. I am here only to seek your further assistance, should the boundary of Brigantium be breached in the coming months.'

'Aye! We have heard of their southern movements, and tales

abound of the way they have edged closer to our shores,' uttered Beombran. 'But we will not allow the foreign armies to take what is rightfully ours.'

The King leaned forward as if delivering a secret. His voice dropped low. 'How are your dealings with the kings of the Parisii?'

'We have no dealings. They keep inside their borders. Apart from the occasional scramble, we see nothing of them. We have heard that an approach has been made by Rome, offering them riches and peace.'

The King proceeded to tell them of the reports he had received and to warn the Corinota chiefs of the lack of support from the Parisii kings.

He spat on the ground. 'They are not true Albions. I need to be sure of your resolve should they attack. My intention is to deal with them in the coming months. But first, we must see where our strengths lie.'

Both warriors placed their right fists against their left shoulders in a sign of fealty. 'You have our support, if we can count on yours.'

Talks continued for some time. The two warrior lords spoke of their needs for the people they protected. 'New arms and more metal for trade would help in our preparation against any future battle defences,' they suggested. The King listened and agreed to send further supplies to the men in exchange for their continued loyalty.

'We are Braint. Our word is tied to Brigantia,' Belinos vowed, though his top lip curled with the words.

The King nodded. 'Also, we hear stories about your granddaughter. She is hardy and beautiful, they say,' continued Belinos. 'Does she ride with you, Bellnorix? Will we meet her? Will she also join our agreements?' Turning to slap his lord on the back, he added, 'My cousin is in need of a wife.'

Beombran Byrde pulled the hand from his body; his face reddening a little. 'I can find my own wife, cousin, thank you,' he growled.

The King put his head down and glanced to one side. Thoughtfully, he answered, 'She will join us later.' But the two men were insistent.

'We hear talk, Bellnorix. If she is to become our queen, then we need to know her qualities, her battle capabilities. We will not be led by a weak woman who is only good for opening her legs and producing brats.' Mandua nostrils flared. She lurched forward, grabbing her dagger.

Camulo held his hand up. 'No!' he whispered.

'Your concerns are well spoken,' continued Bellnorix. When the time comes, your queen will fearlessly lead an army into battle. Her nature is feral and stubborn; swift and sleek, like a wild horse. She will not be caught, and she will not be weak. Have no fear.' An assurance in the King's commanding tone quietened the chief and his cousin. 'She is the daughter of Brennan, The Prince of Ravens who married my daughter Ferelith. She is my granddaughter—her lineage is without contestation.' The King rose from his seat, and with a firm voice, spoke loud enough for the whole assembly to hear. He banged his fist on the table. 'When she marries, no doubt she will produce strong heirs; sons who will inherit my own capabilities. Be under no illusion. She will be queen, and when she is, you will all bend the knee.'

Beombran Byrde stood, meeting the King in stature. He held his hand out, palm uppermost, offering it to Bellnorix. 'We are your men, King,' he said, bowing low before Bellnorix.

The wide grin on Mandua's face spread. She couldn't help

fidgeting in her seat. Valas tightened his grip.

That night, a celebration was called. The Cortinotai became alive with singing and dancing, eating, and drinking. Cups were raised in honour of the gods; Epona the horse spirit, Maponus the god who offers youthfulness, and Ludd, the god with invincible strength in battle. Shrines were covered in amulets of iron and rings of gold, gifts to these gods, and others.

Drums beat a steady rhythm. Maidens danced round the shrines and the sept centre. The braint lords of Cortinotai linked arms with the King of Brigantia, hailing the friendship and unity of the land.

Almost hidden in the shadows of the hall, Mandua sat quietly observing the festivities. She heard a rumble. 'I believe I hear the gods speak,' she thought. From outside the hall, the horses shuffled and snorted. 'And I do not like what I hear.'

CHAPTER SIX

CAILLEACH
The Winter Queen

MANDUA CREPT OUT OF the hall, away from the noises and merriment. Curiosity called to her senses. 'What is unsettling the horses?' The moonlight was bright enough to reveal a path, beckoning her to the outer edges of the sept. Hood wrapped tightly around her face and shoulders; on tiptoe she crept along the beam of light. Her shadowy figure merged with the darkness of the tree-lined path; silhouetted in the silver light of the moon. The cold of the night showed in her breath. A gust of winter wind whistled behind her, pushing her forward. From the woods beyond, the faintest flicker of firelight caught her eye.

Carried on the wind, the neighing sounds of wild ponies could be heard in the distance, followed by an overpowering stench of herbs and onions. Like a moth drawn to the light, so Mandua was compelled to discover these sights and sounds hiding in the night. Silently she crept on the pathway, cautiously stepping forward, until only a fairie tree of hawthorn stood between her and a solitary figure dressed in a long grey woollen tunic. A dun-coloured shawl covered the shoulders of the wizened old woman. She bent over the fire; her back to Mandua, stoking the flames with a long wooden staff. It warming the pot hung atop. 'Welcome child,' she said, almost coughing the sounds through a thick, gravelly voice. 'Come and sit with me.' Using the staff, the *Cailleach* continued to poke the flames, then stir the herby liquid in the cauldron. The pungency of stewed fish made Mandua feel sick, but she stepped forward, hand on her dagger in readiness. 'You have nothing to fear from me, child. Come.' The woman kept her back to her visitor, beckoning her to the fire with a flick of her left hand. 'It's cold, child. Come nearer for warmth.' Mandua took one more step, but the woman continued to stir without so much as a glance.

Silence fell unnaturally from the sky like a perverse shroud over the earth. A covering of white frost veiled the ground. The night stopped breathing. Mandua also held her breath. She felt faint as the surrounding air became bitterly cold. Frozen in that moment, the princess was unable to move at all.

When the woman spun round to face her, fear gripped Mandua's heart. The woman's stone-coloured skin oscillated from grey to blue, then back to grey. Every pore was filled with slimy pus-like worms jostling for position. Her oversized mouth oozed slobber, which ran down her chin, wetting the neck of her cloak and hood. A veil of gossamer web fell over her eyes, hiding them from the unbelieving stare of her visitor. Then suddenly she disappeared.

Mandua stared hard into the distant darkness, trying to catch a trace of the old woman, but she was gone. All was dark, except for the fire and the cauldron. Then a flash of grey, then blue, then black; and the old hag returned. On her head was a crown of white gnarled brushwood tangled in her long white hair. It glistened with thousands of diamond sparkles of frost.

'Come, Mandua, Wild Pony of Brigantia.' The woman's breath turned ice blue as her words caught the night air. 'I have been waiting to give you a gift.'

Mandua, in a trance, allowed the Cailleach to guide her to the fire. The frozen air disappeared as warmth took its place. The woman pulled the fine mesh covering her forehead over the whole of her face to veil herself. Mandua breathed again.

Seated by the fire, the crone spoke in the old language of the Druids. Almost spitting out the words, she hissed:

'O shiorruidheachd fhada nan dia, Tha 'n teine gairm a mach
Spiorad an Ti ard,'

Facing Mandua she translated, 'from the long eternity of the gods, the fire calls forth the spirit of The High One, bringing victory, strength, and determination for her people. From the winter into the spring, the fire, and the chariot travel.'

Looking heavenward, emphasizing the route of such a sight, the wizened arm of the Cailleach directed her finger, tracing it in an arc across the sky. As if by magic a shooting star appeared in the darkness, following the line of the invisible arch. She continued. 'Chariot of fire carries the sacred seed. It is an omen. The time is approaching. But I see many shadows around a flame. Do not let the dark invade your heart. Let the sun be your light.' Using her staff to steady herself, the Cailleach banged the ground with the stick. Instantly, the ground froze. Pacing her next words, she scowled. 'But for now, *I* hold winter.'

Mandua saw the star trace its path across the night sky. Though the old woman, the possessor of winter, was still speaking, Mandua's mind was pulled to another place.

'I hear the gods calling,' she thought. Without uttering a word out loud, she spoke into the silence. 'I hear you, my gods. If the battle is coming, I will hold the seasons…all of them!' She grabbed the staff supporting the old hag. She slipped but held onto the staff in spite of the ice around them cracking. The frozen earth started to melt away. Mandua and the hag grappled for possession of the staff. Mandua held the two outer ends, grasping it in front of her, like a war weapon. The hag held the middle, gripping with two hands, while chanting an old spell, cursing the youth of her opponent. They tugged to free from one another, not wanting to release the staff. Age and strength battled against experience and magic. Fire and ice battled for victory.

Suddenly, a rustling sound came from the hawthorn bush behind Mandua. It took them by surprise, and momentarily, they relaxed their grip. The staff fell onto the hardened ground, splitting in two.

The old hag grabbed the wooden pieces and fixed them in her hands. She called:

'Bheir Dhithan siorruidh a' gheamhraidh. Thoir dhomh ord a' chatha.

The words appeared inside Mandua's head. 'I will have the battle hammer, Crone,' she responded, without thinking as to how she knew what the old woman had said.

'Will you make a bargain for it?' asked the hag.

'Why? Why should I not just take the staff?'

'Because of this,' said the woman holding the two pieces of the blackthorn staff high above her head. Fire burst forth, fusing the two sticks. At one end, the head of a hammer formed. Just as quickly, the fire disappeared, and in her old, gnarled stone-like hand, was a golden battle hammer. Mandua backed off from the blaze, but beholding the hammer, now perfectly forged, she wanted it.

'This is the bargain, Mandua. This hammer is the power hammer of the Cailleach, the Queen of Winter. I have seen the omen in the sky. I know the gods speak of a great battle over the land. This battle may bring the sky down upon us.' Admiring the hammer in her hand, she continued. 'This hammer brings victory in battle. It holds power over the land, the seasons, and the days of Albion. This is my bargain. Once you are queen, you may hold this hammer, and you may own it for a time. But after that time, and as Sanheim approaches, you must bring it back. When the prophecy is fulfilled, before Imbolc, I must hold the hammer again.'

'So, I must wait until I am queen before you will give it to me?' Mandua spat on the ground.

'You will be queen sooner than you think. At Imbolc, I will bring the weapon to you, and victory will follow you to every battle. Even so, there will come a day when you must return it to me.'

'Why should I not take it now, old woman? You are feeble and frail. The worms will have eaten your body before we have the chance to meet again. I could snatch it from you and leave here before you have noticed.' Mandua, scowling into the ugly face of her opponent, controlled the fear trembling in her breast. She drew herself to her full stature and thrust her chin out in defiance.

'Because Mandua, I am not as frail as you think. I am the eternal goddess of winter. You need me as the Earth needs the heat of the sun, the cold winter sleep, and the waters of the rivers and oceans. I hold the Earth in the cycle of seasons. Do not think about betraying me. That would be one battle you cannot win.'

A flash produced by sparks from the fire created a puther of smoke, and the old hag was gone.

Mandua, rubbing the smoke from her eyes, wondered if it had all been a dream. She breathed deeply, then checked to make sure that the old woman had truly disappeared. She cautiously made her way back to the festivities.

Valas and Camulo were searching for her. Camulo eyed her first and ran to her side.

'Where have you been, princess? We were concerned for your safety. Valas is distraught, and I… I was almost ready to accuse the braint of your disappearance. Are you well? Has anything befallen which would cause me to ask for the ear of the King?'

Mandua waved her hands. 'Do not be alarmed, Camulo, my trusted friend. All is well,' she whispered strutting in front of her champion, beckoned him to follow her. With sword drawn, he marched behind as guard. Valas picked up the path at her side.

Bending to her ear, Valas whispered, 'My lady. Is there anything the High-Druid of Brigantia should know about your solitary walk tonight?'

Looking Valas squarely in the eye, Mandua spat. 'My dear High-Druid. I would be surprised if there was anything you did not already know. I think you are a *sgondrell*,' mocked Mandua, defiance edging her voice. She leaned closer to Valas. Whispering into his ear she sniped, 'but there is nothing for you to be concerned about. My conversation with my grandfather is mine to be had. Do not concern yourself. I am well and have not been harmed. I do not need your constant attention, nor will I accept it when I am queen.' Between her finger and thumb, Mandua pointedly picked a twig of hawthorn which had embedded into the Druid's cloak. She twisted it under his nose, then flicked it away.

When they arrived back at the hall, the music and merriment was in full flow. The disappearance of the princess had not been noticed, except by the two guards at her side.

Mandua waited for an opportunity to speak with the King. When the music was particularly loud, she sidled up to his chair and caught his eye. The King, at this point, was exceedingly drunk. He tried to stand, but his corpulent body overbalanced, and he fell. His armed men ran to help him up. He rolled around, laughing and slipping with each flat footstep that failed to grip the floor. Once again, he rolled, unable to get his balance; until no less than five men managed to pull him upright and plonk him back into his chair.

'He is drunk indeed,' called Belinos. 'How can he lead us? He is an old man who cannot hold his wine.' A roar of laughter ascended the room. Mandua was incensed. With a ready hand, she felt her sword, but Camulo stopped her, drawing his sword and taking a champion stance.

'Who would dare to stand against the High King of Brigantia?' he bellowed. The room fell silent. Each heeded the others around the room. Whispers ran swiftly to every corner, as questions were asked.

'What does this mean?' rippled among the crowd of revellers.

'Who is this?'

'Is he the King's champion?'

Belinos raised himself in front of Camulo and eyed him. Both knew that a fight was inevitable. One had made a statement against the High King, and one had called the challenge. The position of Bellnorix stood in parity. The throng of jovial imbibers and dancers changed stance; dividing on either side of the room, making way for the challenge which could decide the future of Brigantia. Beombran Byrde spoke, addressing the King. 'Forgive my cousin, Belinos. He is a fool who opens his mouth and his sense rides away. The King has our loyalty. We vowed this to him only today. Do not let a hot head with fire in his belly bring our friendship to an end. Say what you would have us do, my king. But not this. Not a fight to the death.'

The King, though still wobbly, rose cautiously. Though his head was fuddled with wine, he was experienced enough to know how to bring a situation round when his life depended on it. He addressed the room.

'Belinos. Camulo my champion, has rightfully challenged your treachery. But as this is a day of unity among brothers, a fight there will be. But there will be no death. You two will fight for the position of champion of my army. The winner will be declared High Champion.' The people cheered at this, and the contest time was agreed. 'Tomorrow, before the noon sun, you will fight.'

The sun was slow to rise the following morning. Frost was in the air, and a cold dew covered the ground. Yule waited to descend upon the land in all its winter glory. The King lay snoring on a mattress made of straw, while all around him rabblement woke to greet the day. Servants were busy drawing the fire in the centre of the room and the kitchen was buzzing with the sound of people preparing food. Outside, a stream ran around the outskirts of the settlement, and already some had moved to wash in the raw winter dawn, allowing the icy water to clear their heads from the night before.

Mandua ventured outside, still hidden in her cloak. She soaked up the air and let her lungs expand with the freshness. Thoughts of the night before hung heavily on her mind.

'Could it all have been a dream?' she asked herself. 'But I heard the gods speak. I am sure I did.' Observing the people washing and chatting quietly between themselves, she noticed how her own people and the people of Cortinota mixed in friendship, and her heart felt glad. 'I do not know what the gods have in store for me, but here I see a unity that cannot be wrong. Our enemies should not come from within our homes.' Gathering her thoughts, she rose from the ground with a smile on her face and a determination in her heart. Swearing quietly to the god of thunder, she vowed, 'Taranis, have this: with all my strength, Brigantia *will* be united. They call me "wild." I will show them what wild is!'

Camulo had moved behind the young woman while she prophesied to her god. As she spoke, he remained motionless, then rested his right hand lightly on her shoulder. 'Princess. My Queen.'

With her left hand, Mandua covered the hand on her shoulder. 'My champion, and friend. Today, you must win this challenge. Today your strength must triumph, so that Brigantia is not broken, but forged together as never before.' The two walked back to the hall to find that the arena was already being prepared. Around the circle, benches had been placed. A line of Druids appeared from the Druid grove, making their way in formation to the benches to find their place. The sight was a colourful one, as each Druid wore the cloak of his office. A long line of priestly white cloaks and warrior red cloaks were followed by the blue of the *bhairds*; singers of the histories and stories of Albion. The lesser ovates, the Druids in training and workers in brown followed. Valas wore the golden cloak of the High-Druid and carried the weighty oak staff of Brigantia. It was topped by an iron sphere, painted in red and gold. This staff showed his authority and power to speak on behalf of the King, the Druids and the people.

Two large throne-like chairs covered in red and blue linen had been positioned at a strategic viewing point between the Druid benches. It wasn't long before Beombran Byrde and King Bellnorix walked together nearing those seats.

Activity within the sept started in earnest. The crowd was already seeking vantage points around the site, in which to sit and enjoy the promised spectacle. They jostled against one another, laughing and chattering in family groups. Others pushed and shoved one another, vying for the best seats as near to the King as possible. Children carried mugs and drinking vessels; first to Bellnorix and Byrde, then through the crowd. As directed by their elders, they poured wine and mead, till it overflowed from the cups. When the King held his hand high, all fell silent. Then like a mallet, he slammed his fist down on the wooden arm of the chair. The crowd responded. A roar went up to the sky.

The first into the ring was Belinos, swaggering with arrogance, he moved to centre place. His braided strands of hair had been piled even higher on top of his head and slotted through rams' horns. The horns made him look larger and fiercer than any other warrior in the sept. From a distance, Mandua regarded this champion, weighing the differences between him and Camulo. She noted the way he held his sword and his square wooden shield. It was painted black with a symbol of a wolfhound depicted in white. His long moustache ends had both been tied then fastened back round his head like a scarf. He was naked, apart from the daubing of blue dye which covered his upper body and arms, and the leather thong shoes on his feet; though every finger flashed and glinted from ring adornments. He walked round the arena, lifting his sword and shield in hubris. Mandua laughed to herself, as she felt a rising of heat from her body. Growling fiercely at the crowds, he presented himself to them, waving his manhood for all to admire. The crowd growled back, even louder. He continued to pace the ring, showing his arse to the crowd, who roared with laughter.

'Linos! Linos!' They chanted. 'Champion! Champion!'

Camulo walked out of the hall, also dressed in a horned helmet, and quietly joined the throng. He carried a staff with the head of a slaughtered enemy staked to the top. He had donned leather braccae and leather shoes. His shield and his torso, both painted in white, bore the wild pony insignia of Mandua. On his back, he carried his sword and sword belt. He walked into the ring appearing just as fierce as Belinos, when he slammed the staff and severed head into the ground. It swayed menacingly back and forth. Taking his sword from his back, he leered at the crowd. Lifting his voice, he shouted. 'For Bellnorix and Brigantia!'

Mandua sighed when she saw her champion. 'Yes. We will win,' she said with conviction. 'We must win!' she begged the gods.

A roar went up from the supporters of the high king. The sept became alive when the two giants faced one another and, with feet apart, swung their swords. Belinos was the first to swipe at his opponent. He shouted as the sword fell heavily downwards, but Camulo ducked out of the way of the attack.

'You will have to do better than that, lord warrior,' Camulo, sneered. Belinos surged forward, dropping his shield to grab Camulo's neck, but Camulo easily dodged; side swerving to conceal himself behind Belinos in his blind spot.

Belinos glanced round, puzzled. 'Hello, little wart. Here I am,' Camulo chuckled into his opponent's ear, then jabbed him with his sword.

Belinos growled, spinning round to face Camulo. He swiped at him, but Camulo was too fast. Camulo lunged at the naked warrior's back, striking him hard in the back of the knee with the flat of his sword. Belinos' knees flexed. He winced. He stalled to the floor, winded.

Bellows from the crowds ascended into the air. 'Brigga. Brigga. Brigantia!' Clapping and waving banners encouraged the fallen warrior to rise.

Belinos yelled to Camulo in a rage. 'I will have *your* legs, you fannybaws!" With mad fury he blindly swung at Camulo. Camulo ducked then skilfully leapt out of his range. He parried the attack, the clash of iron sending sparks into the crowd as each man hit hard the opposing weapon.

Once, twice, three times, their weapons collided. Camulo was the faster of the two.

Camulo switched sword hands, slicing from the left and into the stomach of the unprotected Cortinotan. Blood rushed from the wound of Belinos' exposed body. His weapon fell. He grabbed his belly to stem the red river. His legs buckled and he tumbled.

Camulo also dropped his weapon. 'Get the Druids. Help him,' he shouted into the crowd. The onlookers were stunned by the swift action which had rendered the warrior hero to the ground. They fell silent, then hurriedly ran for medicines and bandages. The Druids ran into the ring to help.

Bellnorix stood. Beombran Byrde ran to his cousin. 'Clear the ring. Get him inside. Druids follow.'

Throughout the night, Belinos suffered. People built a shine to Bormo, seeking healing for Belinos. They left gifts and tokens of food before the shrine, praying that the god would stretch out his hand and tie the wound.

By morning light, the wound was dry; and Belinos was out of death's shadow. The King and the Lord of Cotinota visited the afflicted champion.

'You fought well, Lord. But not well enough,' said Byrde. 'The King has spared your life, and now you must once again offer your loyalty and fealty.'

Belinos, who was propped up on a mattress of straw and sheepskins, bowed his head acknowledging the King, wincing with every movement. 'Your champion is fast, Lord King.' He stammered. 'I would gladly stand with him in battle and stand in the name of Bellnorix of Brigantia.'

The King moved closer to the wounded man. He leaned forward and whispered, though with a hint of menace in his voice. 'I accept your vow. But tomorrow, I would have you solemnly covenant your loyalty for my heir to the high throne.' Turning to Byrde, he ordered, 'Call a public meeting, and in front of your people, I would have you all bend the knee to her.'

CHAPTER SEVEN

BRIGCRUIM -AN T-AONADH
The Uniting

A S THE DAWN BROKE, Mandua rose, full of the excitement for the new day. Looking out of the doorway of the hall, she sniffed the air as a pony might sniff. She dressed quickly and covering her head with the hood of the dark cloak, ventured forth into the open settlement of Cortinota. 'Autumn is over,' she said aloud, looking out to the distant hills. 'The reign of the Winter Queen is ahead.' Wrapping her cloak closely to her body, she walked to the shrine of Taranis, wanting to pay homage to the warrior god. Kneeling before the shrine, she offered her prayers and a token of apples from the hall kitchens, which she had gathered into her tunic. Freeing the apples from their containment, she poured them around the foot of the shrine. All the while, she silently mouthed the words of her heart.

'As Sanheim approaches, and the winter takes root, I will run with the disciplines before me to become the queen I am required to be.' Turning her face upward, she whispered to the air, 'Through the winter of desolation, I will bring my people. I will battle for them seeking a unity that has been unheard of in past years. With or without the golden hammer, I will hammer into my people, the need to link together in order to become a force to be reckoned with. Changing the past, we will stand - as Brigante against our enemies; no longer battling against our brothers. We will slaughter our enemies and become the great peoples we are destined to be!'

In response, a streak of lightning flashed from east to west across the sky, chased by a thunderclap. Mandua nodded, her jaw set like flint.

She retraced her steps back to the centre of the Cortinota seat, as the rain began to fall. She quickened her pace to avoid the downpour.

Valas was waiting for her. 'My lady. The King calls,' he said, beckoning Mandua to follow quickly.

'What is it, Valas?'

'He is ill, my lady. He asks for you.'

Mandua rushed into the room which had been given over for the King's use. She entered through the gap, pushing away the curtain and stepped into the room. Her grandfather was stretched out on his bed, propped up by furs and cushions.

'Grandfather. What has happened?' she asked, running to the sick man, wafting away the stench of Valas.

'Listen Mandua.' The King, though weak, was still lusty of voice. 'We have work to do, and quickly. I feel my time is almost gone and the gods call for this body. But before that happens, we must make sure that all things are in place. I want you to be presented today to these people. We will start the process of announcement in Cortinota, today.'

'Oh, King. This can wait until you are well.'

'No. It must happen today, Mandua, and then we ride back to Taftefield. You will be pronounced Queen of Brigantia then.'

Mandua put up both hands to object, but the King shouted her down. 'Do not argue with me, Mandua. I will have your head cut off!' His face, red with frustration, showed his anger. He sat up to force his point and in so doing, let free a belch that shook the room. 'By the gods, my little one. That feels better!'

'Grandfather. You caused me so much concern!' she laughed, fanned away the stench from the old man's mouth. 'You drank too much last night, I think,' she laughed.

'Nevertheless, my orders still stand. Get me ready,' he commanded, rising from his mattress. Mandua called for Valas to help her pull at her grandfather's fulsome body. She attempting to lift him upright. 'Leave me, Mandua. Valas will assist. You must go,' he said, waving his arms around to push her away. 'Go. Get ready. Dress as a queen!' he ordered. The High-Druid called for two men to help the King dress so that Mandua could leave.

She was grateful that her grandfather was only troubled by wind in his gut. 'I will miss him when he goes,' she thought. 'I didn't realise how much I have come to love him. But my concern is real. He is aged, and not as strong as he was. I must be alert to enemies who would take the power of Brigantia from him.' A niggling thought entered her heard. 'And Valas,' she thought. 'He whispers in the wind. He says it is in the name of Brigantia. And he has tried to hold me once too often, the dung weevil. He will not do it again.'

The rain stopped just as the people gathered once again in the grassed centre of the sept. Belinos, on a stretched skin bed, was carried into the middle of the arena, and at his side, Beombran Byrde walked. Bellnorix had requested his royal chariot be pulled into the centre. He had plans to speak to the people of Cortinota from that vantage point. The Druids arrived from the sept sacred grove, walking in line behind the High-Druid of Cortinota. A single drumbeat timed the rhythm of the walkers. Byrde took his position, elevated on a table, so all could see him. When all was ready, he signalled for the King to take his place. Valas walked at the side of Bellnorix, ready to support him if he floundered, but Bellnorix was steady.

The King had on his head a crown of copper, which had been polished till it appeared to be gold. It was a plain band, etched with the symbols of Brigantia; the sun, the moon, and stars, linked together by intricate rope patterns. His cloak was also adorned with golden symbols. Under this, he wore a tunic of red with brown linen braccae. On his wide shoulders, a cape of feathers and fur moved in the wind, making the King look as if he were twice as wide, and more fierce and regal than any other. He climbed into his chariot.

Beombran Byrde spoke. 'Lord High King of Brigantia. Today I and my people standing before you, offer loyalty and fealty to you and your kingdom. Not through any weakness of ours, but because we join with your intention to fight the invaders; the ones we know as Romans. We promise to be ready and willing to rush wherever you send us to alleviate ourselves of this dark, overbearing prospect. We stand with you.'

Valas took up the central position, saying, 'People of Cortinota. Bow low before your high king.' And so, the people bowed low, swearing allegiance to Bellnorix. The King held his hand high, accepting adoration from the people bowing before him. Taking a deep breath, he said, 'My people. I welcome you into the fellowship of Brigantia. You will remain under the leadership of Beombran Byrde, in whom I hold much trust. He is a mighty warrior and a man with power and understanding. But today is not about fealty to me. No! rather I look for your loyalty to the next Queen of Brigantia; my granddaughter, Mandua.' He pointed to the gateway of the sept. All eyes focussed on the entrance, and as if by magic, Mandua appeared suddenly, riding toward the centre on the back of the white Tormaig. The wind caught her wild hair, released from her braids. It hung loose round her shoulders, blowing up with every movement, until it appeared as if her head was crowned by fire. She wore the white tunic and white cloak of status. The linked pattern of roses and chains decorating the cloak glistened in the morning light. A golden torc embraced her neck. High in her left hand, she held her polished bronze shield, flashing the pony insignia for all to see. In her right hand she whipped her sword marking time with her horse's steps. The sun caught the metal, sending flashes of brilliance into the sky, dancing as they sparked all around Mandua. She moved to the side of her grandfather's chariot and rested. Awe struck the hearts of the watchers. Riding behind her, Camulo; battle ready.

The people clapped and cheered at the sight. Word went round the crowd 'This is our goddess. It is Brigantia in person!'

'We have been waiting for such a queen; such a goddess.'

'She looks to have the gods in her. She will do for me!'

'We have heard of her battle prowess, but she is so young. She must be marked of the gods.'

Bellnorix beckoned to her to take his hand. Handing her weapon and shield to Camulo, who rode behind her, she took the King's hand, and continued to hold it. Raising his voice above the crowds of cheering, he spoke. 'This day, I give you the future Queen of Brigantia. She will be crowned on our return to my home, and from there she will take her position as leader of the armies of our peoples. Bow before her.'

The first to bend his knee was the lord of Cortinota; Beombran Byrde, followed by the line of Druids and warriors of the sept. The men, women, and children in the gathering, all moved toward

Tormaig, stretching out a hand to touch either Mandua or the pony. Two of the Druids helped Belinos to the chariot, and in front of Mandua, he bowed.

'I give you my life, my lady, if you require it,' he promised. Mandua nodded. Belinos took a step nearer to Mandua. She looked on him intently. Leaning on one of the men in his company for support, Belinos met the stare of the princess.

'I give not only my promise to you, my queen, but also, I offer my allegiance to Brigantia. I offer my army in *Brigcruim,* promising that they will stand with Brigantia for her freedoms and liberties, her faith and beliefs.'

Presenting her hand to Belinos, Mandua responded. 'In return for your loyalty and battle alliance, I vow that you will be given all the help available, so you will be ready to fight when the time comes.'

Taking her hand, Belinos kissed it. 'Therefore, my lady, when you leave Cortinota, I would seek your permission to travel with you.'

Mandua felt a flush of heat passing through her body. She nodded quickly in assent, averting her eyes.

The sun rose high in the sky, and though the day was wet, the sun cheered the hearts of the people who were beginning to do what they enjoyed the most, feasting, drinking, and dancing in earnest celebration of the festival of Samhain. Hunters rode out to fetch even more wild boar and stag to the table. The women prepared the fires and spits. Bards, using willow whistles, bagpipes, drums and rattles, took up their positions to sing the events of the day:

> *'Cortinota is blessed in the winter sun.*
> *As the leaves fall from branches around.*
> *And promises of battles won.*
> *With future queen, our songs resound.*

So Bellnorix speaks of brothers together.
And so, it will be done.
The future queen rides the white pony.
Brigantia rides as one.'

The music continued while hunters returned with their spoils. The butchers first placed the carcasses in a row, ready for Druids to inspect them. One was chosen for sacrificial offering and was dragged to the main table set out as an altar to Taranis. Valas, the High-Druid, along with the lord priest of Cortinota, stood behind the table and in front of the people. The chosen pig was drawn, and the blood allowed to run freely. The High-Druid, using sacred knives and axe, opened up the animal in order to read the entrails escaping from the body.

The word from Valas was inviolable. When he spoke, silence reigned. Anticipation hung in the air. 'There is blessing today as Bellnorix is honoured. Our future queen will bring wealth and comfort to her people. Today, we will celebrate the word of our goddess, Brigga. She speaks a good word. Rejoice! Rejoice!'

Mandua sat at her grandfather's side while the feasting and music continued into the night. Bellnorix whispered in her ear. 'My princess. We must be heading home before Sanheim is concluded. Tomorrow we will begin the journey.'

Mandua questioned the King's decision. 'Why, Grandfather? Are we not venturing outward to Setanti to gather further support against the intended invasion of our lands? Surely, we should go and speak with them. We are so near.' With fisted hands, Mandua thumped the air in temper. 'This is stupidity. We cannot leave the situation here. We have added but a small allegiance with Cortinota. Many more warriors are needed for our preparation.' Frustrated,

Mandua bellowed out her concerns. The passive expression on Bellnorix' face angered her. She stamped her foot, then turned and marched off, shouting obscenities; her wild hair flying behind her. Bellnorix laughed.

Heavy rain led the way from Cortinota, followed by chariots and horse riders bidding farewell to Lord Byrde and the people who had ventured into the deluge to wave a god-blessing on the Brigante entourage. In his chariot, and with several other charioteers, Belinos travelled behind the King. The mud paths leading northwards made chariot wheels stick.

'It is not the best time to be riding,' Mandua thought. 'I do believe that my grandfather may be losing his mind. The horses will tire far too soon in this mud bath of a road.' But obediently they continued to head north.

Belinos called to the King, 'Lord Bellnorix, would it be prudent to make headway through to Brigcruim, where we can rest the horses and have proper shelter from this damned rain?' The King did not answer. He called again, 'Lord King. We will all but pass Brigcruim and my people would be grateful to have an eye on you and our future queen. Please consider this an invitation to rest, eat and revel in our good fortune.'

'Very well,' answered the King. 'Turn toward Brigcruim,' he shouted, pointing in the direction of the hills and moors in front of him. The rain continued to pour. It was with relief that they saw the four *menhirs* near *Kringlekarr,* and the river known as Tutt, where a shrine to the god Toutatis had been built. It was here, just as the rain began to ease, that they camped to rest overnight. They erected shelters using animal hides, animal bones and tree branches, which had been conveyed on chariots for the purpose. Soon the King and his *comraich a-staigh* of Druids and warriors were enjoying the heat from the fires outside the circle of *teanta*, drying out under the protection of the hides. Mandua sat a little apart from her grandfather. She did not drink. Her eyes scrutinised Belinos in the circle, talking to his few men. Mandua moved nearer to Bellnorix. Belinos, catching sight of her, smiled. Mandua reddened, lowering her eyes and glancing away.

Belinos approaching the King again, neared Mandua. She could almost feel the heat of his body. Her breath became rapid. She began to nod to herself. 'Yes. I have decided on an action and the gods will know about the outcome.' She rose to kiss her grandfather. 'Good night, my lord,' she said, then entered the tent of the King where she was to sleep that night. There she lay. 'Tomorrow I will act,' she thought.

The journey to Brigcruim the following morning found the travellers in autumn sunshine, a welcome change after the wet torrent of the recent days. All were in good spirits on entering the gates of Brigcruim later that day. The people gathered outside, making way for Belinos and the King's retinue to enter. Within the hour, Belinos called to his cognoscenti who lined up, and one by one, were introduced to their High King.

'This is chief Druid Lochru of Brigcruim.'

The Druid bowed low. 'I am at your service, King. May the moon and stars follow your path; guiding and protecting you and our great lands,' he said. A trail of six Druids, including two female priestesses, also bowed in passing, then followed ten warriors.

'These are some of the leaders of my army, King. They are overseers of ten others. I discovered this is the Roman way of training. It seemed wise to me, so I have begun to use this strategy with my own. These men and women fighters are famed for their ability on chariots, are hardy and strong and at your call, whenever you need them,' promised Belinos. 'But enough for now. Bring the bhaírds and bring the mead,' he called. It was but a short time before wine and mead flowed, and the singing began.

Valas and the King's Druids sat with Lochru and the other Brigcruim Druids. They discussed in earnest, considering the blight of the south, the threatened invasion, and strategies to defend and attack any infiltration into Brigantia.

'The King is old, Valas. Is it true that his granddaughter is strong enough to take his place?' asked Lochru.

Valas leaned into the ear of the High-Druid of Brigcruim. 'If she fails, I will be waiting. Have no fear, Lochru. Brigantia will be strong with or without that little piece of rebellious marplot. I am too long in the tooth to worry about her.' Lochru stared into the eyes of Valas, but Valas stared back showing no emotion. 'I have friends, Lochru. I have friends in many places who will make sure that I am always the High-Druid of Brigantia. Give me your loyalty, and all will be well.'

Lochru questioned, 'But Lord Valas, where are your supporters? Are they near and eager to see a change in the leadership of Brigantia? If so, then this is something I would be interested to know.'

'I have plans already in place, Lochru. If the princess is strong, then all is well. But…' He allowed his voice to tail off, his attention attracted to the exuberance in the place.

The warriors arm-wrestled and drank; their good humour holding through the day and evening. Music played, and songs flowed in the night air; songs of battles won and lovers lost in tribal feuds. Bhaírds sang into the night, composing new tales of honour and battle and wrapping them round the outstanding High King, and his heiress.

Brigcruim celebrated the visit of Bellnorix and Mandua, and the return of their Lord Braint Belinos. The jovial night was full of laughter and good will. The Shrine to Belenos, the healing god of Brigcruim, and from whence Belinos had taken his name, had been laden with offerings. These included a bloody bowl of entrails from the sacrificial pig, scraped from the 'table of seeing.' The Druids had pooled over the gory omens, interpreting the signs and expounding them as prophecies for the good of the people. The night brought together the two tribes, in joint ambition – to stop the land being overrun with the infernal Latins.

Belinos sat with Bellnorix for most of the night. They drank and saluted each other like brothers in blood. 'Tell me of your childhood, Belinos. You speak with authority among your men,' prodded Bellnorix.

'I am, in fact, from the south. I travelled over the land in my quest for understanding of the tribes and how we might prepare against the enemy.'

'Who is your father, Belinos? Is he of royal lineage?'

Belinos glanced away. His reticence to answer did not evade the King. 'My father is a great warrior, and one who has disowned his sons. I no longer desire to know him.'

Bellnorix nodded, understanding the undertone of Belinos' answer. He did not pursue.

Mandua, waited for her time. As befitting her status, Belinos had arranged a private place for her to sleep; a screened teanta within one quiet area of his hall. It was covered in woven red and blue wool sheets. A small bowl of animal fat and a wick burned in the tent, throwing enough light and shadows to make the place feel warm and safe. A mattress of straw and feathers had been placed on the floor, adorned with animal skins and cushions in various colours. Earlier, Mandua had placed her goatskin bag holding her regal cloak, torc and tunic in the tent, before joining the festivities. She walked round the hall, admiring the deep red curtains and ornately carved chairs. 'Iron work at its best,' she mused. Her fingers smoothed over the tables, feeling the levelled plane of each. She traced the filigree ironwork of the torch sconces in admiration. A smile covered her face. 'Yes,' she thought. 'This seems right to me.'

Bellnorix drank and ate and squeezed the bottoms of various women who passed within reaching. He laughed at the dancers more, with each new cup of wine he drank. Belinos whispered in his ear, 'Do any lasses take your fancy, King? I can arrange.'

'Then arrange away, Lord. It would be fitting for the King to take his pleasure while here. Your hospitality is applauded.'

'Then, when you are ready, King, she will be waiting in your teanta.'

The eyes of the Brigcruim warrior hooked onto the young princess. Mandua became aware that he was watching her circling the hall. She wanted to know what he was thinking. 'I hope he likes how I am moving my body,' she thought, instinctively swaying her hips from side to side.

He leaned over to comment to one of his men. 'There is something feral about the young princess; a wildness about her. I am captivated by her, but I would like to captivate her,' he laughed.

'She is ready and ripe,' the companion jibbed. 'Have you a mind to take her?

'I have a wife. Hold your tongue.'

Once more circling the walls of the hall, Mandua approached, leaning forward into him. Loosening her tunic belt slightly, she pulled the side of the top to reveal her breast.

'Come to me,' she said.

Belinos waited until the evening was drawing to a close, and warriors, heads on arms, had fallen asleep at the tables. His wife had left the proceedings earlier, when the first signs of feasting was approaching an end. She, like most of the married women, knew not to bother their husbands on such auspicious occasions. His drinking and battle strategic exchanges, at times like these, were private affairs. The Druids had left the hall to sleep in the sacred grove, and the King had been helped onto his feet and almost carried to his sleeping place. The girl was waiting for him. Bellnorix fell on the bed, blacked out and crocked.

Belinos crept onto Mandua's bed. 'Come,' whispered Mandua. 'Do not make a sound. I will tell you why you are here.' She patted the bed, indicating for Belinos to lay at her side. Her voice was level and firm. 'I am a young girl, and I will soon be queen. Then the gods will dictate my future. But here and now, I want to know what it feels like to be a woman. I have chosen you to show me.' Mandua faced Belinos and met his gaze. She did not turn away, but stared, until he could not stare back. His silence irritated Mandua. 'Get on with it. I am not so naïve as you might think. I know I have to open my legs.' At this point, she lifted her skirts and showed him the full opening. Drooling, Belinos complied.

He laid back on the bed, gathering his breath and his thoughts. 'Will you have my head, my lady?' A smirk spread across his lips.

'I will have your obedience, and your sept,' she responded, but turning away, her lips opened, and a snigger escaped. 'I am to be queen, and I can do what I like. Now go. Your usefulness has been depleted.' She bent her leg to give her foot one forceful push in the chest of Belinos. He left, smiling with satisfaction. Mandua laid silently, savouring the time she had just spent.

'So, that's it?' she mouthed to herself. 'Not really a lot to be bothered about.' She turned over and slept heavily.

The King's company stayed at Brigcruim for several more days.

Belinos visited Mandua at every opportunity. She played with his need, accepting or rejecting on a whim, and enjoying the power she felt she had over Belinos.

On the seventh day, a message came from beyond the sept. A tribe not far from Brigcruim, sent warrior raiders in an attempt to find and kill Bellnorix. They had laid siege to the road north, intent on interrupting the King from travelling home and capturing him, or worse. One of the insolents had been captured in the attempt, his trophy head hung from the hall doorway, but not before Belinos had him tortured for information.

'We are from the northeast of Brigantia, from Lopocares, though we have been sojourning near Stanwix for some time. Our orders and intent were to take Bellnorix, and therefore Brigantium. Our own tribal leader of Lopocares, Vello, would then take the position of overlord.'

Belinos called his men to organise a raid of retaliation. They gathered in the hall.

'Stop this,' shouted Bellnorix 'Stop. I will give the orders.'

'Lord King. Forgive me,' declared Belinos, bowing his head. 'We will follow your lead.'

'And what about me?' asked Mandua, glaring at Belinos. 'Is there any consideration for me?'

The King did not hesitate. 'I will ride out, followed by the chariots. The warriors on horseback will be led by Mandua. She knows how to fight. You may order your men to follow as you will, Belinos. But this fight will be mine first.'

As the gates of the sept opened, and the company rode out, the stench of battle-ready warriors and horses filled the air. Swords rose high over the heads of the warriors. Shields clashed against their iron weapons in a battle rhythm. Voices called like thunder over the clamour of chariot noise and hooves. Bellnorix bellowed, 'Beware Lopocares! We'll have your bloody balls!'

Mandua lifted her voice and shouted over the fray, 'For Bellnorix, Brigcruim and for Brigantia!'

Inside, Mandua was shaking. 'This will be the last battle that Bellnorix will lead,' she thought. 'He is becoming frail as his age grows. I am moving closer to full leadership of Brigantia and as the queen I will have a responsibility so charged that I dare not fail this day.

CHAPTER EIGHT

AIR SON NA GLOIRE
For the glory

E ACHANN STIRRED THE CAULDRON of mutton and vegetables, as Donannu ordered the bowls and water jug for the meal. Mugh sat by the fire, seeing into the flames.

'There is fire in your soul,' Mugh maffled. The flames spat onto him, burning little holes into his tunic. He flicked the hot sparks away, standing in order to do it. 'Fire! Fire,' he continued. 'Eachann, there is fire ahead.'

'What are you saying, Mugh?' Eachann scratched his head.

'I saw in the flames. It was you, Eachann. You were covered, head to toe in golden flames. Flames of glory.' Putting down the stick he was using to stir the meal, Eachann gave Mugh his full attention. Mugh continued, as if seeing the vision afresh. 'You were riding Cahir. He seemed splendid, as did you. Trophies and accolades were being presented to you, and Venutius…Venutius was there too. He was cheering you. We must prepare, Eachann. Donannu, we must prepare.'

'For what?' asked Donannu.

Ignoring the question, Mugh ordered, 'tomorrow, we ride to the camp of Venutius. Tomorrow we will see the future unfold.'

Mugh continued to mutter, but the syllables coming from his mouth were undecipherable. Eachann and Donannu shrugged their shoulders at one another; their eyes wide with questions. Mugh bounced up and paced the floor, muttering all the time to himself. 'Tomorrow…. must prepare…. must prepare. if I put a foot forward like this...Venutius …. timing is right…then that will happen?' Mugh busied himself around the Druid hovel which had become home to the three. Eachann continued to prepare the meal. 'Donannu,' he asked, 'have you any idea?'

Donannu shook her head. 'Why we must go to the royal camp, I do not know. We have just spent the best part of the last five years avoiding it - and Raigon. If he catches up with us, we may have a fight on our hands again. Though I will be glad to leave this place of hiding, I don't want to rush into a head-on clash with death just yet. We haven't completed your training yet.'

'I am as trained as I can be, woman!' Eachann laughed and slapped the back of Donannu in good fun, though his hand lingered a little longer, turning more into a caress than a slap.

Donannu did not move, allowing his fingers to move slowly down to the middle of her back. Then Eachann stepped back, pouring the stew into the bowls. Both sat silently by the fire. Mugh came to join them, picking up his food and hastily eating the fill of it.

'Are you two not eating?' Both looked at each other, reddening a little, before looking down at the bowls. They began to eat.

'Mugh, may I ask?' Donannu queried tentatively. 'Is it wise to go so near the camp when Raigon is there? Do you not recall why we have been avoiding him?'

'You know as well as I that we cannot, nor should we, stay in hiding for the rest of our lives. We have used this time well. You have trained Eachann to this day, and now it is time. The god calls for him to show himself again.'

'But Mugh,' protested Eachann, 'How can you be so sure that the timing is right? I am ready to fight. I am well trained, I know.' He glanced over to Donannu and smiled. 'But is there a purpose in us heading there tomorrow?'

Mugh adjusted his tippet, and showing his blind eye, he said, 'I do not see clearly, Eachann, as you know. But when the Gods speak in visions, I see very clearly. The acuity of mind gives me sight. Now, be sure that this is the right time. Tonight is the last evening we will spend in this god given hovel. Enough!' he said, raising his hand showing his open palm, even as Donannu also started to protest.

That night, laying by the fire's embers, Donannu called to Eachann. 'Will you come closer and hold me for a while? I worry so much that this life you are destined to lead will bring you upon hard times. I worry for your safety, Eachann.'

Eachann wrapped his strong arms round the young warrior and held her close. The tautness of his muscles, and the strength in his young body was now fully developed.

'Donannu, you have taught me well. Everything you know, you have passed on to me. If the gods dictate the end of my life, or yours, then together we will seek one another in the afterlife. This will not be the end. This is the beginning.'

'This is my fear, Eachann, that this - your beginning - will be my end.'

Eachann drew her face closer to his, wanting to comfort her, but found his lips touching hers.

'This is our beginning,' he said quietly. Donannu took his hand and placed it on the inside of her thigh. He found his hardness pressing close to her. She took him in her hand, and revealing where to go, she received him. 'This is your rite to manhood,' she whispered. 'I am honoured to be part of that.'

They rose early that morning, ate a hurried breakfast, and packed their needs. Leaving the hermitage that had given them shelter for so long, Donannu faced her men. 'I will not travel with you, Mugh. My job so far is completed. I will leave to return to my brother.' Focussing directly into Eachann's eyes, she said, 'Do not try to dissuade me. I will leave now. But remember this – I will hear your call, should you need me. I will be there. But I need to lead my own life, and so it is time for me to go.' She swung her legs up onto her horse, and without looking back, she left.

Momentarily stunned, Eachann paused his actions, at once going as if to follow, then hesitating. He searched Mugh's face for direction. Mugh, reading his expression, raised his palm and waved down. 'No. Eachann. She is right. Let her go. This next adventure is for you, and you alone.' And without another word, Mugh rode northeast heading for the new camp of Venutius at Staena. Eachann wiped his eyes and followed.

Keeping alert for other travellers on the journey, they turned their backs on the sacred hovel which had given them a safe place to hide from Raigon through three long winters and the following summer. It had been a sanctuary where Donannu encouraged Eachann in the finesse of battle art, and in that secret place, she showed him deeper secrets of Brigante warfare. He had turned twenty during this time. Mugh was aware of his eagerness to see the field where trophies and acclaim could be won.

They left the small hamlet of Bullgill and ventured with speed, following the river Eilidh as far as they could, settling camp at Beorgrow, on the side of the mound which had been deserted long ago. The only evidence of life ever touching the place was an altar to Bitucadros, where a cleaned horned skull of a goat had been placed and fastened there.

'That skull is a good omen for us, Eachann,' commented Mugh. 'Warriors must have passed this way before. We will rest here till the morrow.'

'I will be wary, Mugh. The horns of the ram do not always show favour. Is this not the altar of the wild god? It could be a warning.'

'Indeed. Indeed. But we should have no fear. The gods are calling you to act. We are protected.' Mugh was sure that he had seen in the fiery vision enough to know that Eachann should be by the side of Venutius, and no man could stop what is written in the fire.

Eachann, unsettled through the night, tossed and turned. Mugh slept fitfully, though at every moment, the bleak night brought new sounds to be deciphered. The scape was wild and agrestal. A wind blew from west to east across the open land and whistled round the hill mound.

'There is little possibility of anyone sneaking up on us,' Eachann voiced to himself. 'But still my gut tells me all is not well.' With one hand on his sword and the other on his shield, he huddled down. The sky was clear of clouds, and the stars shone brightly. A frost crept toward the camp, covering the moon in a white haze. Eachann got up to load the fire from the small supply on the back of Mugh's horse. It burst into fresh flames as the sticks and twigs fell on the needy embers. He sat for a moment, chin in hand. Under his breath he whispered, 'Donannu.' His hand found an uncontrollable rush in his loins, which, now awakened, struggled to leave him. Vibrations throbbed from the ground to his groin. The trembling became more rhythmic, like the hooves of horses galloping, thundering, making the earth beneath him tremble and convulse. Eachann jumped up. A thick fog suddenly rose up-slope cloaking the hill.

'Mugh,' he shouted. 'Mugh. Wake. Horses…' He went to shake Mugh from his deep sleep, but it was too late to hide. 'This was too open an area,' he said. 'The only hope of hiding is in the folds of this murc.' Mugh stirred. Both stared into the darkness, unable to see further than an arm's length. The pounding of the hooves heightened. Eachann instantly killed the fire.

'Mugh,' Eachann whispered. 'Can you spread a spell?'

Mugh at once acknowledged the danger and with hands swaying, wove a shroud of concealment into the foggy fibre before them. They sat a little way from the smoking embers of the snuffed-out flames, waiting for the arrival of the riders. Four ghostly figures dressed in black tunics and cloaks stopped short of the fire and dismounted. Their faces and moustaches wore the blue dye of woad, though it was a greyer shadow; the signs that it had been on their faces for some time. The grey gave an eerie quality to their appearance, and in the shadows of the night they looked fierce, intimidating. They searched the area, looking straight at Eachann, then back round again. Mugh continued to hold the spell, mumbling inside his head, so the words could not escape into the air. No sound left him. Only the words formed on his lips.

'Ceo draoidh achte
Hide us from the world around.
Cover us in mist.
Protect us from the evil shadows.
Till evil does desist.
ceo draoidh achte'

It seemed that the spell held, for the four men peered straight through Eachann and Mugh.

'Here. They have been here,' said one of the shadows. 'The fire is still hot.' He kicked the fire with his booted foot. The ashes scattered into the mist.

'They must have gone further that we predicted. How could they have disappeared?'

'We have been watching them for so long, and now they have just melted away. Impossible. We must find them.'

'I don't like our chances of a future when we go back to report that we lost the trail. It took us long enough to discover where they were hiding out.'

'What will it matter?' asked another.

'Don't be stupid, man. Of course, it matters. Our orders are to bring the golden boy to him. And that we must do.'

'I don't understand the importance. Do you?' the third asked, questioning the other riders. 'He's only a squirt of a boy.'

'Yes, but now he realises who the boy might be.'

'But how does he know?'

'Because his birth was prophesied. It has been foretold…. "From the beginning of time, Taranis holds the power." You know the fairie telling?'

> *"Son of Thunder and of light, releases and discharges*
> *healing and power in his right hand.*
> *Then linked like iron to another;*
> *warrior spirit and warrior spirit holding sacred Epona.*
> *One day* **Eòlas** *will require the iron and bronze and sword…."*

and so, it goes on. When our leader heard this prophecy, he knew that the power of Brigantia would never be his while the boy lives.

So, he must act to hold the boy. The boy must not join forces with any other.'

'It seems to me, it's a bit of fanciful thinking. How can a boy hold the power over a whole land?'

The one who had been trying to explain put his hand to his head in exasperation. 'Because, my idiotic friend, this boy could snatch the future of Brigantia from the one who aspires to the seat. See?'

They debated among themselves and continued to argue while mounting their ponies and setting off along the river into the mist; their voices and shapes disappearing in the darkness.

The magic fog began to dissipate. Eachann sat, stunned. 'What was all that about?' he asked, though more to himself than Mugh, as his memory recalled a time long ago, and a song he learned at the knee of a king.

Mugh rose and, shaking the dirt and damp moss from his cloak, proceeded to his horse. 'Eachann. We cannot let those four men get to Staena before we have had a chance to speak to Venutius. Come. We must follow them and make sure of their end.'

They followed the riders, keeping well back, so the men were not aware that they were no longer the pursuers, but now they were being pursued. They travelled the riverbank, lined with trees, which thickened into a wood. The river was joined by a beck, and at this point, the four dismounted. They made camp, and although it was almost dawn, they led their ponies to the shallower part of the water, allowing them to drink and rest. Silently approaching, Eachann and Mugh dismounted also. Tying their steeds to a branch, they readied their weapons. With sword in one hand and a glaive in the other, they crept around the thick growth, which afforded them cover from the now growing light of dawn.

Mugh pointed to the boots of the four. 'Notice the quality of the footwear?' All four wore similar boots of leather and polished to a high shine.

'These are no ordinary men folk,' Eachann murmured, stealthily moving behind them. Mugh nodded, to show he understood Eachann's plan. Weapons ready, through the bushes they thrust in and out each sword point, into the exposed backs of the four men. Immediately, Eachann pounced over the cluster of shrubs, followed by Mugh. They pulled their weapons, and with synchronised actions, sliced into the throats of the unsuspecting party. All four black cloaks lay before them. The two Druid warriors sat, gathering their thoughts and their breath.

'Not a chance,' laughed Mugh.

'I'll have the boots, Mugh,' chortled Eachann pulling the best pair of leathers off one of the dead men. He tried them on.

Mugh went to another pair and, choosing the nearest to his size, put them on. They were large and slobby, but Mugh liked them, so decided to keep them. Then he took the others, tied them together, and hitched them over the back of his horse.

'These will make good bargains, should we need them,' he muttered. They stripped the cloaks and belts, the swords and weapons, a battle axe, and an iron chain. They took rings and beard studs before disassembling the heads of the four. The bodies, they kicked into the river; but the heads, they tied by the hair onto the sides of the saddles on their horses. Two each. These trophies would show their prowess to all. 'It will be known that Eachann and Little Mugh Ruith are not men with whom you can trifle.'

They travelled into the dawn, watching the sun as it rose on their right. On arriving at Watch Hill, they decided to rest. It was here, scanning the land from the high point, that they saw a band of travellers heading from the west. Women and children were part of the group, so it was with a trouble-free calm that the two met the band, to ask them where they were headed.

One of the travellers, a heavily set man of about forty, seemed to take the lead. 'It is almost Sanheim, so we are venturing on to Staena for the celebrations and challenges. We are carrying salt from our village to sell at the markets during the festival of Cocidius. It is to be celebrated there, and Venutius is calling for champions to play the fields.'

'May we travel with you, good lord?' asked Mugh.

The leader eyed the two; noticed their Druid cloaks and the heads and boots dangling from their horses.

'We do not want any trouble, Druid. We are peaceful people,' he said. 'Our families, wives and children travel with us.' He pointed behind, where children were huddled in a chariot together, and women walked at the side of the cart.

'You have nothing to fear from us,' assured Mugh. 'We will be able to help in protecting you on the way.' He bowed his head to the leader. Taking a pair of the boots from his horse, Mugh offered them to the leader. 'Please, take these as a token of our peaceful friendship. Let me introduce you to my acolyte. This is Beli Mawr, known as "The Shining One." You may have heard of him. He is a champion of the gods.' Mugh signalled for Eachann to remove his hood and reveal his golden hair. It had grown long over the years, but it still blazed like gold. Mugh continued, 'We also are going to the festival of Cocidius and will celebrate Samhain in Carvetii. It is our intention that Beli Mawr will show his power and take his rightful place as the new champion of Venutius.' The sound of chatter flew round the group of people regarding the two new faces. The old stories that Mugh Ruith had shared, so many moons ago, had travelled on the wind to each corner of Carvetii. These people from Saltlaithe on the west coastline of Carvetii, had heard of the keeper of The Shining One, and were delighted to make acquaintance.

That night, they set camp near the foot of Watch Hill, and soon, the questions began. Fires were lit, food was shared, and stories were spun. Mugh and Eachann sat in the circle, enjoying the admiration afforded to them as they tried to answer the plethora of quizzing.

'Tell us of your journeys to the far, far places, Lord Druid,' they asked, offering a small bag of salt as payment for the evening's entertainment.

'What was it like going through the place of the painted people?'

'Were you afraid?'

'Did you see any of the tribes there?'

Mugh Ruith was pleased to repeat and embellish the tales from his peregrinations; of meeting Eachann on the road home and of the gods' guidance as he grew from a small boy into the fighting man before them. The trophy skulls they displayed weighted the warrior stories that Mugh augmented each night. They shared good company for the next five days, continuing their journey toward Staena. On the sixth day, they came to the large oppidum of Venutius. Mugh mused. 'This is the ideal opening for you, Eachann. This is your chance to show off your battle mastery. This will be the beginning of your shining!'

'Have I any say in this, my mentor?' he laughed.

'No.'

'Then I will obey.' He slapped Mugh on the back, and Mugh realised that this young man was no longer the small boy.

Spluttering from the strength of the slap landing on his back, Mugh announced, 'You have grown brawn overnight. And look at the hardiness of your arms.' He leaned forward to squeeze the engorged bulges of the young man's biceps, nodding with approval.

As an afterthought, Mugh continued. 'But, until we have found our stand in this place, I think it wise if you keep your head covered and your voice low. I want to assess the situation so that the maximum effect can be displayed when you are revealed.' Eachann smiled and nodded.

The approach to the new oppidum of Venutius was imposing and grand. The large access to the sept was bustling with traders and merchants from the surrounding hamlets and dwellings scattered across the area. Others had travelled greater distances to bring their wares, and to compete in the games. Tables displaying many sorts of ironware, jewellery, foodstuffs, and mead had been set up on the approach to Staena. Traders shouted to passing travellers in the hope of catching their attention for a sale.

The formidable gates protecting the sept were made of iron and larger than any the trekkers had seen before. Makeshift tents on the inside of the sept lined the road toward the main hall. It was a long, straight road, cut in the middle by a large circular arena. A sacred oak tree dominated the nucleus. The tree was awash with mistletoe berries hanging in large clusters from the branches of the oak. Around the tree, but outside the circuit circumference, penned market animals were displayed for sale, and for barter. The whole place was a teeming, vibrant mass of movement and noise. Spits holding enormous pigs had been placed around the main market arena. Newly lit fires underneath the spit roasts were fuelled until dripping pig fat made the flames erupt and crackle. Women took turns to rotate the swine. Torches covered in strips of animal fats and skins tied round old bones were being lit to give light as the sun lessened her autumn glow. The Saltlaithe tribe set off to look for lodgings, excited about their arrival, but the two Druids moved into the shadows, disappearing through the throng into the penumbra shroud. With hoods hiding their faces, they tethered their horses at the back of some small roundhouses, and away from the main thrust. A shelter or two had been erected there for the use of visitors at the festival. At the side of these shelters, a few small sleeping teanta perched dismally against one another. An old woman sat by the shelters, with bag open, ready to receive any payment.

'How much for a night or two?' he asked the hag.

'What have you got?' she enquired.

Eachann pulled the bag of salt from his cloak. 'We have seasoning beyond your taste, woman,' he said as he offered the bag.

The woman snatched it. 'Two nights only,' she said. 'And no women in there. That's extra,' she grunted.

A Carnyx sounded, calling the crowd to the opening ceremony of the festival to Cocidius. People stopped what they were doing to gather near the central sacred tree. Whipping his garment of black and white round his shoulders, Audigus Raigon, High-Druid of Carvetii, opened his mouth to speak to the gathered crowd.

'Good people of Carvetii, hear this and tremble,' he called. 'Today our king, the esteemed, and noble Breehin-Venutius, warrior and braint of Carvetii, has called on Cocidius, the god of the forests and sacred mistletoe. It is this god; our red god, who grants to his people good hunting throughout the year, and success in battle. It is Cocidius to whom we offer our own red blood tonight, as an offering of our worship.'

Two men bound with ropes around their necks, legs, and hands, were dragged into the arena by four brown cloaked Druids. They kicked the bound men till they fell at the feet of Raigon. Raigon, looking away, continued to call to the assembled crowd as if the men before him were invisible. 'These animals at my feet have been caught stealing our grain,' he announced. 'What say we do with them for this transgression?'

The crowd shouted out for the death of the two offenders. Loudly and with a rising voice, they called for blood. Raigon raised his hand to silence the noise before he proceeded. Taking a large pebble from his belt, he shouted, 'Should this judging lithos hit the sacred tree and fall, then the men will live. But should the stone be taken by the tree, then sacrifices to Cocidius are required.' Lifting the stone high above his head, Raigon lobbed it at the sacred oak tree. It bounced on the trunk before becoming lost in the cradle of mistletoe.

'Tonight, their ends have been determined. Cocidius demands a sacrifice.'

With one voice, the people called for the demise of the guilty men. 'Death. Death. Death.' they called.

The brown Druids dragged the captives, heaving them onto the altar table. Raigon neared the bodies. Lifting the ceremonial knife high, he stabbed each one. 'In the name of Cocidius,' he called. 'In the name of Cocidius.'

One by one the Druids lined the table, and, passing the dagger, they took turns decimating the bodies. 'In the name of Cocidius,' they called.

The crowd cheered. 'In the name of Cocidius and of Venutius!' 'Venutius!' they called as bleeding guts spilled to the floor, then the remains of the dying men were taken to the tree and hanged from the highest branches.

As the bodies swung, Raigon inspected the viscera spilled on the altar. 'We are rid of the canker that would take our food and leave us to starve. Our god is satisfied,' he promulgated. 'Let us rejoice!'

Deep in the shadows of the crowds, Mugh noted the sacrifice but kept his focus on Raigon. Eachann watched the curtained doorway of the main hall beyond the tree. Venutius stood, observing the action from just within the curtained opening. His face was expressionless. He moved into the shadows, as if waiting for his moment. Then, as the music from willow pipes and the drums started to play again, he stood tall, took a breath, and walked to the centre of the gathering. 'Venutius, Venutius,' the people cried on his arrival.

With hands raised he waved to his people. 'Tonight, we begin the celebrations. I want champions- champions who are fearless in battle and accomplished in war; champions who will be willing to pay any price to protect Carvetii. Champions who will die for the glory! Are there champions here?' Venutius shouted. He swung round a full circle to take in the response from his people.

'Aye! Aye,' the strong echo reverberated round the sept.

Raigon shouted across the heads of the crowd. 'Make a line, you likely champions, and we will proceed with hand-to-hand combat.' Those wanting to prove their worth and receive the accolade as distinct warriors of Venutius lined up in front of Audigus Raigon. There were about fifty in all. Pairing them up, he directed them to areas where they fought to the death. Cheers went up from the crowds as one or the other met his end. The crowd mocked the weak. They celebrated the victors; they drank and sang until only twenty-five men stood. The music began again. The bhaírds sang glory battle songs, while the families of the remining men attended to their cuts and bruises. The bodies of the dead were taken to a mound outside the sept hedge walls and wooden fencing.

CHAPTER NINE

TÁIRNEANACH
Taranis

THE SUN BEGAN TO stretch her lucent fingers across the morning sky. The light touched Mugh's sleeping body, prompting him to wake though darkness still reigned in that place. Rubbing his eye, he straightened out in the teanta. Mugh allowed moments for his head to remember the night before, and what had brought them to this place. The merriment had continued into the night. Bonfires had been lit over the land to honour the arrival of the dark season and the end of the summer. This was the time when access to the world of the departed was granted, and the veil between the living and the dead was thin enough to pass through. Throughout the festivities, there had been many stories of the underworld, told and retold. Druids spoke of dark souls wandering in the mists of time, and others who had battled through exacting challenges in the dark places to return victorious. Mugh had been one of the storytellers that night, though his stories always centred around the rising of Beli Mawr, the Shining One. 'He came out of the night holding a thunderbolt in his hand, and the shield of time in his other. Taranis the glorious,' Mugh apprised.

The Little Druid tossed about in the skins covering him, not wanting to greet the day. With both eyes still closed, he reached to feel if anyone else was in the bed with him. An unexpected gleam of light broke through the dark of his eyelids. It seemed to come from beyond the covered structure where his bed lay, but Mugh ignored it. 'It's only my blind eye flashing in my mind.'

He mumbled, his voice chitter-chatting with random thoughts. 'To do. To do. What is there to do? Beli Mawr must be ready. For the glory…there.' He fell quiet, listening.

'Just the lad. I hear him snoring… sounds like thunder.' Just then, the rain started. Mugh leapt up. 'That's not snoring,' he said. 'It *is* thunder.' A loud explosive bang rattled across the heofones. Mugh sat up on his bedding and listened again. 'Yes,' he nodded, covering his ears to soften the voice in the thunder.

Mugh rolled back into the comfort of his bed, staying there till sleep overtook him again. By the time that Eachann stirred, the rain had stopped, and the thunder had gone. Eachann did not disturb the little Druid.

The old hag crouched by the shelters, eating an apple. She chewed, spitting the skin out from her mouth and onto the ground. A rat ran by her feet, stealing the skin. Eachann bowed in kindness as he passed.

'Good morning,' he said, heading onward to the river which flowed through the sept on the east side. 'A wash is what I need,' he thought. He kept his hair tied under a tippet. Mugh had suggested he wear it until it was time for him to be revealed, but the rest of his clothing he discarded by the bank. He immersed himself in the running water. His muscles rippled when the cold flow hit his nerves. His stomach tightened, showing the full extent of his now fully adult body. Angled, he dived high into the air, then hovering weightlessly he plummeted into the gushing river. He felt exhilarated.

A few strides away, a warrior, but a few years older than Eachann, was also preparing to bathe in the water. He had dismounted his horse and tethered it with his weaponry and outer garments, some paces away. A Druid was with him, ready to help him into the flow. This Druid wore the brown cloak showing his servant status; a Druid in training. Eachann heard the two men talking, so had become aware of his fellow natator, but remained back from view. He made his way to the bank, with the intention of dressing and leaving, when the Druid flung back his cloak to reveal a sword. Drawing it, he made to strike the other from behind. Without a thought, Eachann ran to stop the action. Grabbing the sword arm of the cloaked man, he swung him round and battled him to the ground. The sword dropped from his hand. Eachann straddled over him, stopping the Druid from gaining an advantage. Restraining the attacker, he yelled to the bather, 'Danger. Get out of here.' The warrior spun round to see a man wearing nothing but a head scarf, sitting on top of his Druid. He ran to get his weapon from his horse and wrapped his cloak round his body before nearing the two still struggling on the muddy grass bank.

'Who are you?' he called to Eachann.

'I am a friend who saw this man attempting to attack you.'

'Is this true?' he asked of the Druid. 'Is this true?'

The Druid spat at the two men, as he wriggled to escape. 'May the gods have your soul for this,' he bellowed in anger, squirming under the weight of his captor. The clothed warrior raised his sword, and with one swift movement, thrust the tip of the weapon through the gullet of the traitorous Druid, drawing his lifeblood. The Druid slumped. Eachann moved away from the body.

'Who are you? asked the warrior as Eachann rose from the ground, making toward Cahir for his tunic and clothes.

'I am your humble servant, Lord Venutius,' he replied. He bowed low in front of the King he had just saved, grabbing his cloak as a covering.

'I am grateful to you, young man. Are you here for the festival? You will sit at my table this evening. Give me a name.'

'I am Eachann,'

Venutius slapped Eachann on the back. 'I am pleased to make your acquaintance, Eachann,' he said. Mounting his horse he fled, leaving the traitor's corpse and his horse for Eachann to dispose of. He stripped the body of its belt, pins, and iron rings then shoved the body into the river, kicking it into a roll. The water received the cadaver willingly. Eachann kneeled in thanksgiving to Coventina, the goddess of rivers and springs. 'Receive this sword as an offering, Goddess,' he said, throwing the Druid's sword high, and lobbing it over the water. Then he returned to the humble teanta where Mugh was just rousing.

'Mugh, I have something to tell you. While you slept, I have been to the river to bathe. My horde of trophies grows,' he smiled, showing Mugh the belt and pins he had taken as his own. Unfolding the story, Eachann explained why he had been invited to sit at the table of the King.

'Then we must be prepared,' nodded Mugh furiously, acknowledging the importance of the matter. 'Today, Eachann, I heard the voice of Taranis in the thunder. Your pathway is clear. Tonight, I will open the bag from **Eòlas**, and you must decide which trinket you need.' Mugh mumbled, words which Eachann could not decipher. But the little Druid lifted his arms up high and tossed his head back. 'Oh! Delight. It is happening. Cakes! Good. Food at the table of Venutius. Delight! It is so long since we shared a feast. I cannot wait.' Eachann left the mumble of words to attend the horses, including the horse of the Druid traitor.

Throughout the day competitions, vying and drinking continued in the central cirque and around its perimeters, overseen by Audigus Raigon and his Druid company. Awards for bravery were presented to young men who ran through blazing torch hoops, and for those who could last the longest hanging from ropes within wheels which were turned upside down. Wild dogs and boar were released into pens where warriors dared to grapple with the bloodthirsty beasts. Swimming competitions were added into the mix. The river became alive with divers and water fighting. As the day ran, so did the number of warriors fighting in the tournaments and games, lessen. By nightfall, the competitors for a position as one of the champions of Carvetii had fallen to five. These men (the very best of Carvetii warriors) were ready to fight, even unto death, to claim the glory bestowed on the champion of champions.

As dusk began to grasp the light and hide it, Mugh called Eachann to the teanta. 'Get ready for tonight. Wear your Druid cloak of white tonight. When you are ready, come sit with me a while, Eachann. I have a strategy.'

This was the first time that Mugh had allowed Eachann to wear the cloak. He pinned it over his shoulders, looking solemnly at Eachann. 'This is a serious occasion.'

'I know you would not let me use this cloak, unless you think that I am ready to bear the office of Druid warrior and priest.' Eachann was edgy with enthusiasm. His limbs tense and shivery, caused him to shuffle; his fingers moved restlessly, opening and closing his grip.

Mugh took the bag from his larger travelling sack and placed it on the bed. He opened it carefully. Over the years he had not let curiosity tempt him into uncovering the sacred Eòlas items, 'cepting for the glaive, which Eachann had used since learning the warrior art from Donannu.

'This morning, the voice in the thunder – my god Taranis, made it known to me of this pivotal moment. It holds the balance for you; for us; for our lands.' He untied the rope and the leather pouch fell open. A flash of gold light escaped into the night. Thunder rumbled in the distance. 'Tonight, you must choose one item to use alongside your power glaive. Only those two must be used.'

'But how will I know which to choose, or when to use them?'

'You will know. Now, which?' Mugh separated the ring, phial, and stone, so that Eachann could identify them individually. The young warrior lifted the ring and examined it. Placing it back, he lifted the stone. He turned it over and felt the smoothness of it. Then placed it back. The phial, he put to his nose, and sniffed. He laid it back with the other objects, and rested his hand on his chin, feeling the young beard hair. He sniffed again.

'I wish I knew more, Mugh. I haven't any idea which to choose. If I knew what was going to happen tonight, then I may be able to make a better decision.'

'Flamin' fumin' indecision.' Mugh mumbled. 'You must be sharper than that, son. If this were a life-or-death moment, you would be on the ground with a dagger through your heart already!' With short patience, he almost shouted, 'Oh! Just choose one!'

'Well. Then. I choose the flask,' he said and opening the little potion, he drank it. For a few moments, the two men stared at each other; Mugh, waiting for Eachann to show signs of magic power, and Eachann waiting for something, anything, to happen. 'Nothing,' he said, flatly.

Mugh covered his one eye with his hand and sighed. The thunder roared above them.

The carnyx sounded. Venutius was ready and seated in the master chair; Raigon, by his side with a table placed in front of them. The table was filled with skewered mutton and pork slices, beside dishes of offal cooked in herbs. A whole boar head took pride of place amid fruit and nuts, and platters of roasted turnips and parsnips. Bread and small barley cakes, apples and berries graced the tables. Flagons of beer and wine were served by lasses in hitched skirts and bare bosoms. They smiled at Venutius, offering more than just the wine. Venutius ate heartily.

When Eachann approached, Venutius recognised him immediately. He called out, 'Come, lad. Come.' With a hand gesture, he indicated to Raigon to move from his seat to make way for Eachann. Raigon did as Venutius had asked. Stiffening his lips, he curled the top one, though obeying the King. Eachann, ignoring Raigon, took the seat, then called to Mugh to take the place next to him. Raigon moved one space further away from Venutius, his face reddening with anger, sucking in his cheeks as the one-eyed Druid wearing leather boots pushed in front of him. Mugh hustled onto the bench, taking the position offered, and flopped onto the edge of Raigon's cloak. Raigon did not speak but yanked the cloak from under Mugh. He spat at the little Druid.

'Oh, Thank you High-Druid in the black and white cloak. Where I come from, your spittle is revered. It's a blessing,' Mugh said with biting wit. Raigon shut his eyes, displaying his disgust, turning his face in the other direction.

'You will sit with me during the games, my lad,' Venutius ordered. 'I did not realise that I was in the presence of a priest.' He flicked the white priestly garment between his fingers. 'Hmmm,' he observed and nodded. Pointing at Mugh, Venutius asked, 'and who is this?'

'I am Mugh, the keeper of the "Shining One," Beli Mawr,' babbled Mugh. 'You might have heard of me. I am the Druid who has travelled to the far lands. I met with Taranis, who speaks to me often. I…' Before he could continue, Venutius returned his attention to Eachann, dismissing the ramblings falling from the mouth of Mugh.

'Then, who are you, Eachann?'

Eachann took from his head the tippet covering his hair. It fell over his shoulders, a shimmering cascade of gold. 'I am Beli Mawr, known as "The Shining One," and the one to whom Mugh gives reference.' he said, bowing his head to his king. Raigon flinched.

'I have heard of you,' declared Venutius. Turning to Mugh he added, 'and you, also. Your tales have travelled far, little Druid. I am delighted to meet you, and tonight you will entertain us with your stories. But first, we will watch the battles. Call the five champions we have still. These men have already proved their ability and will become my highest warrior ranks if they survive till the end of today. But we will continue. There will only be one winner this evening. He will be the new Champion of Carvetii, and of your king Venutius,' he proclaimed. 'Call them. Are they ready to show us their chariot skills? One by one- there will be a fight for points against the scum pictish prisoners we captured on our last eruption at the northern borders of our land. Bring them into the ring.'

Two hardy looking men dragged a prisoner into the circle and handed him a sword and a stake. 'Fight for your life, filth,' shouted the watchers.

The first chariot appeared, chasing round the open space. The charioteer, whipping the horse, sped to encircle the wretched opponent. Each time the prisoner lifted his sword, the warrior drove the horse straight at him, thrashing him with his leather whip, then returned easily to retrace his movement. Again, and again the chariot charged, making for the pitiful foe, until the sword dropped from his hand, and the staff fell also. The sword of the victor was swift and thorough. Venutius rose. Holding up his hands, he showed four fingers. 'Next,' he called.

The crowd cheered and hissed at the next four charioteers showing their agility on the platformed wheels. To each one, Venutius gave finger indications of their competence, until each had received suitable honours. The warrior with the highest citation was called to sit with Venutius and enjoy the moment of merit.

'You have done well throughout these games, warrior. What is your name?' The King asked.

'I am Vellocatus, Lord.'

'You desire to be one of my champions? And what is your occupation on a day?' the King asked.

'I serve Carvetii as a chariot maker, ensuring that our chariots are in good condition and ready for battle at all times, but to serve you as a warrior, is my heart's desire.'

'Then, Vellocatus, because of that desire, I have one more test for you before I bestow the honour of being my champion. I have one more fight for you.' With his open hand, he presented Eachann. 'This is Beli Mawr, favoured warrior and god. You will fight him, and whoever wins, it is he who will become the highest Champion of Carvetii.'

Mugh balked. The food he had just placed in his mouth spat out across the table. He choked on the morsel and held his breath in fear. Eachann opened his eyes wide and shook. His whole-body erupting into a shaking that he could not control.

'What is it?' whispered Mugh, showing great concern.

'I feel like I have been filled with a hot substance – my body feels as if it has been stuffed with metal – bronze. I feel unbreakable; indestructible.'

Mugh hoped that the phial of power had commenced to release energy into the body of the young warrior. 'The Eòlas mighty bronze force linking with the power of the glaive will bring victory,' he speculated, breathing again.

Eachann advanced into the ring toward his opponent, raising the gifted glaive in his right hand. Before he had time to utter a word, lightning flashed across the firmament, touching the tip of the glaive. From the tip rained aureate shards and splinters of fire, falling all around the ripped silhouette of Beli Mawr. The sky lit up again as another flare turned the darkening night into a red glow, creating a halo of radiance around the golden locks of this Earth-God. Blood red *welkin*-fire had enveloped both the *heafan* and the earth where the young warrior Druid stood, till there was no seam between them. Thunder was hot on the heels of this blazing brilliance. Booming roars streaked across the night sky, furious and sizzling. The warrior was ablaze with glory.

He had no need to fight, that night. The crowd beheld the extraordinary spectacle and bowed in awe. 'Taranis is among us,' they said, falling to their feet, convinced that the man in the arena was the god himself. Fear and awe overtook the crowd. 'Beli Mawr, The Shining One is with us,' they called. Children hid, and women ran to their families, searching for safety. The King set himself on tiptoe to behold his new champion. Mugh ran to join Eachann in the ring.

News journeyed with speed to all the septs within a short galloping distance of Staena, that night. Before long, hordes were vying for attention from Beli Mawr and from the King. When the rain started, it was with relief that Venutius called Eachann and Mugh to follow him into the shelter of his hall, and away from the awestruck mobs.

Joining a few of the King's men on benches at the back of the room, Raigon had a clear view of all that was happening in the hall that night. He had seen the King giving his attention to the newly appointed Champion of Carvetii. Leaning close to one of the King's men, he blurted out, 'look at the stature of the man, his golden hair and his stance. Pah!' Sucking his teeth, mumbling under his breath, he continued. '…white cloak and… his boots. There is something about this man…' He placed his head in his hand, as Mugh, incessantly chattering, told stories of Beli Mawr the golden, to the crowd who had engulfed the hall. Then lifting his head '… Of course. No longer a boy,' he spat.

'Eachann,' called Venutius, over the noise from the excited crowds. 'I am pleased to call you, my champion. I saw tonight that the gods have blessed you, and I am blessed, also.' Eager to bring Eachann into the midst of his chosen elite, he continued to enquire, 'When will you have completed your Druid tutelage?'

'In fact, my lord, I have only to unlock the art of shapeshifting, and my education will be complete, though my mentor, Mugh Ruith will still stay with me, until the accepted twenty years' training is absolute.'

'Then both you and he will be given lodgings in Staena. From here we will work together on the strategies needed to, not only protect Carvetii from the northern tribes of Novantae and Selgovae, but from the Pehtas covering the north. My plan and hope, starting with Novantae and surrounding areas, is that it will become mine, and my authority will enlarge. But we must not forget the biggest challenge is to be prepared and ready to move against the threatening Roman invasion. Will you give me your fealty, Eachann Beli Mawr?'

Eachann stood, and kneeling before the King, he bent his head. 'Yes, Lord Venutius. I will. This is my promise.'

The days proceeded, and the two arrogated to themselves a shelter in Staena, near the King's Hall. Outside, they hung the heads of the four assassins as a sign that they were famed and accomplished warriors. Following the night of revealing, and for some seasons, Mugh continued to teach Eachann Drueidan ways; enriching his understanding of the local flora, herb collection and potion making, as well as teaching him the two languages of *drueidan* and *daelic*, and how to write in *ogham*. He showed him the way of the sight, using *couchen*, the sacred drink only permitted to the priestly orders, and other abilities including shapeshifting. Although Mugh was unable to shift his mind in this way, he knew the path that pointed to the otherworldly doorway. Eachann took the path easily, touching the portal jambs, ready to enter over the threshold should the gods allow. So, each day, Eachann grew in Drueidan knowledge and understanding, happy to be with Mugh, to fight for Venutius and to take the adoring girls in Staena whenever his body needed. The Earth circled. Imbolc came. Eachann grew in notoriety; his warrior competency growing in equal measure.

Venutius, itching for new challenges, called for his battle lords and Druids. Advice, he was not looking for, but the High-Druid needed to be seen to endorse his decisions.

'In three days, we venture north. The enemy hordes continue to leak across the borders into our lands. We will go and subdue them. Indeed, we take with us my champion, Eachann Beli Mawr, the embodiment of Taranis, the golden god of thunder. As a sign of our allegiance to this god, I order our ironsmiths to make tokens for each of us. They will be as wheel pendants, to wear as a sign that Taranis dwells with us, and of his blessing as we venture forth into the wilds of the northern lands.'

'Do you know anything about this champion of yours?' questioned Raigon. 'Where did he come from? Where did he get those boots? They look very much like the ones my own men wear…and I sent some of them on a mission. They have not returned. If he has harmed them in any way, then he would be a traitor to Carvetii, not the champion,' he spouted, anger gushing from his mouth. 'I do not like him. You are giving him too much power when I, High-Druid of Carvetii, would advise caution.'

'Ptah,' responded Venutius. 'Your men, indeed? Be cautious, Raigon. You take liberties with my power.' Tapping his finger on the table, Venutius continued. 'I trust him, Raigon. When the gods speak, I will not go against their word.'

'But the lightning strike was nothing but a show for you, King. You have yet to see his battle power and Druid magic. What of the mossed areas, Lord?' continued Raigon. 'Are you to take your champion through the marshes to the watery doorway of the underworld? Will you ask him to go where his leather boots may be tarnished? Will he bring a message back from the dead who occupy that land?' A smirk spread over Raigon's face challenging the King.

Venutius glared at Raigon, meeting his sarcastic challenge, he responded. 'Yes. Lord Raigon, indeed, I will.' Then turning his back on the High-Druid, he called for his champion. To Eachann and Mugh, he lifted his voice high enough for Raigon to hear. 'If Taranis wills it, you will fly as the fabled Druid eagle, over the dark marshes, and visit the further reaches of the Pehtas. Return with strategies from the otherworld to bring us victory.' Slamming his fist on the table in defiance, he glared at Raigon, who withered backwards into the shadows. 'Will that suit you, lord?' he asked. Raigon did not meet the King's eye, but faced the ground as he left the room.

Raigon beckoned to one of the guards by the door. 'Where are the four trackers I commissioned some time ago? It has been too long since I heard from them. Send someone to find them. They should be back by now,' he growled in anger.

The procedure for Selgovae took but a few days' preparation. The route had been traversed on many previous occasions, as Venutius and his men had continued to defend the boundaries between Carvetii and the northern primitives. This time, Venutius headed the cavalcade in his battle chariot, taking Vellocatus with him. Eachann and the other Druid warriors, priests and priestesses followed behind the retinue of charioteers and warlords. Raigon held back, slowing his pace.

They made good time, passing Aballava and arrived at the wetlands at the *firth* of the *Sulewad*, also known as *Tràchd Rombra* before the night arrived. The round shaped headland of Mais beckoned. The mud flats and tidal flats in the area made this a most dangerous place to camp. It was not difficult to fall into the salt ponds and swamps which surrounded some of the tidal bars in the area, and stories of lost travellers taken under the quicksand, were many. Venutius had knowledgeable guides who knew the tidal paths of the great river and were willing to show the way from Mais to Annan for a good fee. The guides advised, 'Lord King, the tides are high, and the passage is unsafe. Wait until the spring arrives, and our passage will be secure.' Taking the advice, the host made camp at the side of the salt flats to bide their time.

But Venutius was impatient. Calling for Eachann, he spoke calmly but with authority. 'Eachann, tonight I want you to shift over the waters. Find us a way through, looking at Novantae firstly. I do not want to wait till spring.'

Eachann bowed in acknowledgement. 'What am I to do, Mugh?' he asked when the two shared the warmth from the small fire that evening.

Mugh peered hard into the flames, searching for a sign from the gods. He stared until his good eye filled with water, and he could not perceive a thumbnail in front of him.

'Eachann, I have taught you all I know. I cannot see further than here. You must seek sight from the gods for yourself.' Remembering the Eòlas, Mugh brought out the pouch containing the items gifted to Eachann. He held the two items left in the pouch: the ring and a stone. Offering the stone to his young disciple, he said, 'This stone will help you understand the way to go. But once you have used it, then your future stands only on your holding the knowledge you gain. Take it, feel it, and know that Taranis will guide you.' He placed the stone into the palm of Eachann's hand.

'But what if I cannot see – if nothing comes and my sight is marred?'

'Do not concern yourself, Eachann. You have reached more than twenty-four Earth turnings. Your time is now. Has not Taranis spoken? When Venutius called the champions together, did not the lightning strike you and yet you lived? Use the stone, and all will be well.'

Biting the skin on his thumb, Eachann responded. 'I am reviewing the advice you have given me over the last eighteen years.' He took the stone in his palm, rolling the smooth weighted object over and over. 'What to do?' he asked. 'What to do?' Closing his eyes, he repeated the question to himself, as he continued to turn the stone.

Mugh called, 'Careful Eachann. There is smoke from your fist.'

Eachann opened his eyes to witness a column of mist

smouldering through his fingers. Spreading his fist, he revealed the stone. It resembled an egg broken in two. It sparked like flint against a rock. From the shell, a tiny Druid's bird appeared, instantly growing large until a fully grown eagle perched on the arm of Beli Mawr. A leather jess strap held the leg of the bird, linked to an anklet which had fastened itself round the *Iolaire's* leg, and Eachann's arm. With no time to assess the way of this, the great bird took flight, carrying Eachann with him. 'I rise, as if I have wings,' Eachann declared, his eyes wide in amazement. Following the moon's path slipping below the Earth's edge, he flew. Soaring high, then diving low, he glided over the salt marshes below. With ease, he took to the west, pursuing the flow of the great river, till he reached the end of it, and the vast ocean beyond. Abruptly, he retraced his path. With eagle eye, he peered down discerning the lights from fires on the coastal side, where Mugh monitored the night sky.

'I wonder if Mugh can see me.'

Heading north, the eagle glided over the tidal flats again, but this time bound for the opposite coast of Annan and beyond to Novantae. His eagle eye picked out a shadow, darker than the other areas around, and swirling as if the place was alive with *beithir* and *Boobrie* in a hidden camp. No fires could be seen; just the shifting eidetic figures of the fairie folk. He was so taken with the coiling mass directly below that he did not see the arrow hurtling toward him.

Mugh remained by the fire, observing the still corpse-like form of his protégé. He held the stone in his open palm, but no longer turned it. All around, sound became muted until the silence was deafening. Without warning, Eachann began to rise from his place by the fire, as if the wind had caught him under his arms. He spread them out like a bird taking flight, then disappeared into the night sky.

'The shifting has begun,' said Mugh to himself. Focussed on the flames in the fire in front of him, he urged the gods to allow him to follow. The flames rose higher. Mugh rubbed his good eye, trying hard to peer into the realm of the gods through the smoke which bellowed from the flames. 'I should be able to follow,' he muttered. 'Drivel. That's me. I should be able to conjure up a vision or two. What sort of Druid am I?' He stared hard into the fire before him, feeling despondent by his lack of perception, just as the smoke cleared a little. 'I can see the pathway!' he shouted. 'I can see the pathway!' Through the haze, and between the flickering flames, Mugh perceived Eachann rising high into the sky like a golden eagle. He saw his path across the great river, and the ocean beyond, and him flying back toward the northern coast. Then he saw the arrow.

Mugh shot to his feet. 'Eachann!' The vision disappeared as the flames died. He could do nothing but wait for Eachann to return.

CHAPTER TEN

TORR CHATHAIR
High Throne

The meagre army of Bellnorix leaving Brigcruim that day, found and captured the company of assassins who had dared to make an attempt on the life of the King. Stanwix, a small settlement on the route to Brigcruim, had been their hiding place, from which they ventured to threaten Bellnorix, and the leadership of Brigantia.

The King led the onslaught in retaliation. Surprised warriors appeared from within their shelters with no time to come by arms. Women and children ran for their lives. The other men of the sept fought but could not hold back the retribution of the Brigante attack. Mandua kept Bellnorix in her sight even when charging at the traitors. Waving her sword, and with all her force, she faced her enemy, slicing and chopping whatever came into her margin, all the while, seeking to protect her grandfather. The fight was bloody; limbs and throats were cut and severed, and heads removed from bodies, as Bellnorix and his warriors brought the incursion to Stanwix. Revenge was sudden and final. Any women and children who had avoided the brutal retaliation were captured and tied. Heads were collected, and items of value; rings, weapons, and utilities, were taken. Nothing was left of the people there except the few that were allowed to run to tell the tale of Bellnorix and Mandua, the true leaders of Brigantia. 'Lopocares beware!' he called after them. 'Tell Vello to beware. I am coming next for his head, and the heads of all who dare to defy me!' Shaking his fist in the wind, he raged until the air in his lungs gave out and he swooned.

That day, the company of Belinos and the King's men camped in the ruins of Stanwix. Mandua stayed with Bellnorix, who had collapsed in pain. Grabbing his chest, he stumbled to the bed that Mandua had made for him. She covered him in skins to keep him warm from the damp cold night, making sure that the fire to warm him was kept blazing.

'Mandua,' he called.

'I am here, Grandfather,' she answered, moving closer to him.

'Mandua, you must take the crown before it is taken from me. Tomorrow is Yule. This is the perfect time for me to hand over to you the *Torr cathair* of Brigantium. You will be queen before the winter ends and Imbolc arrives. It is better you take the crown before I leave this world. Go - prepare. Take the support of Valas and of Belinos.'

'But Lord, it is only wind. Sit up, and I am sure a good belch will make you feel better.'

'Not this time, Mandua. I feel the darkening of the season and know it carries with it the darkening of my soul. Now go,'

'I will not have it!' Mandua tossed her hair back and jutted her chin in defiance. 'No. No.'

'Do not argue with me. You are not queen yet.'

Tutting, she left the room. Mandua swore. '*Bescumber* on this!'

Bellnorix shouted after her. 'Send Valas to me, Mandua. I have things to tell him. Mandua did not respond except for raising her hand as she marched away.

Valas entered the King's room, his cloak sweeping the floor and his pungent odour sweeping behind him. Bowing low, he gave acknowledgement to the King. Bellnorix turned from the fire to face Valas. 'My faithful friend,' he said, smiling in pleasure at the sight of Valas. 'I am ready to depart this world.' Valas moved a step forward, raising his hand to stem the words from the King. Bellnorix held his hand up too.

'No! do not protest. This is happening. I feel it in my chest – the pain. I have not long for this world. I want to be prepared for the next. These are my instructions. I want to be buried according to my rank. I want my chariot and horse…my faithful horse…to be with me. Dig the chamber deep and give me my treasures to take into the afterlife. Make the day one that the people will embrace and remember, so that my name and that of Brigantia will forever be engraved in the history of my country. First, take my body home to Taftefield, then after that, celebrate not only my departure, but the arrival of the new queen.'

'Lord, all will be as you desire. I am your servant.'

'Before all this, tomorrow we will travel back to Brigcruim for the festival of Yule. I would have Mandua given the power and throne of Brigantia at that festival when she will take up her royal heritage. Go. Prepare for a banquet tonight. Tomorrow, as the season travels through its darkest days of winter, so Brigantia will travel through the changes. Speak to Belinos. After the ceremony, we will then travel on to Taftefield, for the final honouring rituals needed to hand over the full power of Brigantia to Mandua. I hope I will not be called by the gods before then.'

'And Lord, if I hold any part of your heart, will you ensure my position as High-Druid of Brigantia when Mandua is queen?' Valas asked.

'I will do what I can, Valas. Though I cannot dictate from the grave.'

Valas was swift to direct the fulfilment of the King's wishes. Belinos, happy for this to happen in his oppidum, rode home, calling Lochru and his druids together preparing for the celebration to take place. The people had gathered fuel and supplies, readying their homes for the long winter nights and colder weather. The fires of cleansing had been prepared around Brigcruim, and the ritual tables had been laid with sacred herbs and oils, ready for the sacrificed animals to be offered to the gods. Lochru, Valas and other priests were primed to discern the future of the Brigante people from the inner organs of the carved-up pieces. All lay in readiness.

The night arrived, the bonfires lit. A crowd gathered in anticipation of the revelry and celebration of the darkest day, as it meets the corner to gaze at Spring. Bellnorix was propped on a chariot. The wheels had been removed and poles inserted into the frame so that he could be lifted with ease and moved around the festival sphere. The seat was lifted high by four Druids: two of the King's and two from Brigcruim. All wore brown cloaks of service. Other Druids wearing priestly white cloaks flanked his sides. Drummers beat out a steady rhythm, giving the parade an unrelenting rigidity and formality. With solemnity they made their way through the line of on-lookers, then, circling around, they came to the open green in the centre of Brigcruim. On the north point, they rested the chariot. Lochru stood at the side of Valas, who held in his hands the sacred *fey*; his oak staff carved with magical symbols and tokens of leaves and circles. He lifted it high as Druids do when invoking the witness of the gods. Directing his attention to the crowd, he uttered, 'Good people of Brigantia, for so you are. Belinos, your leader here, giving fealty to Bellnorix our high king, has so joined in unity. Therefore, we are all brothers together. As High-Druid and Priest of Brigantia, I hold authority in spiritual matters, and speak to you with that authority. It is today, on the eve of Yule, that we understand the death of the old and the birth of the new. We move from the darkness into a hope of new light. Today, we embrace our faith in that reality; the circle of life – birth, death, and birth again. And so, we come to offer gifts to our gods, and thanks for the year leaving and the new year meeting us in the morning.

Our high Breehin, Bellnorix, desires to speak. Listen to all he has to say, and consider what wisdom falls from his lips tonight, for with his words, come the blessing of our gods.' Using his staff to redirect their attention, Valas pointed to the King.

Bellnorix lifted his hands. Silence spread across the assembly. Raising his voice Bellnorix thundered, 'Brigantia. Brigantia. This is the land of the great goddess Brigga, whose name we bear. This is the place where Taranis rides, and Esus blesses. This is the land you are honoured to be part of.' He combed the scene before him, surveying his people, then added, 'this day, we make history. Tonight, you witness the passing of the known; the old, and the raising of the new. Behold, the chosen one - our queen of Brigantia.'

Mandua walked smoothly and deliberately from the Great Hall of Belinos. Her cloak edges sparkled in the firelight. Her hair, plaited and long, had been laced with ivy, and crowned with a wreath of holly and mistletoe. Round her neck she wore a golden *torc*, the sign of her highness. In her hands she held a small motto of white willow twigs bound by a long red ribbon. Bards initiated songs, resonating with the drumbeat, to bring harmonious tongues and melodies to the march. The crowds kneeled and bowed as Mandua passed. She approached Bellnorix, who gave her his hand and she stepped onto his rostrum to stand at his side.

Bellnorix bellowed once again, into the crowded camp. 'This day, my granddaughter will take the throne of Brigantia. She will take her position as rightful ruler of these lands; a position she has been destined to hold since the day she was born. She is wild and unafraid, and like wild horses, she will lead you into victory, both in battle and in life. This day, with the blessing of our priestly Druids, I rename her "Queen *Carti-Mandua.*" For she is the wild queen and goddess of Brigantia. Sleek like a pony - she will pursue and cut down the enemy. Victory will be her accolade. Honour will be her legacy. Therefore, honour your queen, oh! People of this land. Honour her and be blessed.'

A cheer rose from the core of Brigcruim, acknowledging the sacred edict.

'Carti-Mandua,' they shouted. 'Carti-Mandua.'

'See how she holds the sacred willow of Brigga. It is a sign of the changing times,' they said.

'Our queen and commander. Our wild goddess.'

The confessions continued for some time while the new queen was raised high on the shoulders of the priests. They carried her round Brigcruim, raising her higher each time the people raised their voices, until the thunderous uproar turned into singing, and words flowed from the celebrating jubilance.

'Brigantia is blessed in the winter sun.
Sacred Mistle covers the branches around.
Promises of great battles won.
With goddess and queen our songs resound.
So Bellnorix speaks of brothers together.
And so, it will be done.
Queen Cartimandua rides the white pony.

Brigantia rides as one.'

When the merrymaking and drinking took hold in earnest, Bellnorix called for the new queen to join him at his table. 'My precious child,' he called her, while resting close to her shoulder. 'When I am gone, and you stand alone, remember this: trust but a few. Power is commanding control of yourself. Power is leading by example; showing resolve in your convictions, and strength in your resolve. These things will give you the right to rule.'

'I have learned so much from you, my king, and I will determine to use the power I have in a way that strengthens our people; one that unites rather than divides, and one that brings peace wherever peace may be found. I have learned this from you, Bellnorix. I will not forget.'

'Then remember this also, Mandua. There are three things that are important to the spirit of Brigantia: liberty, loyalty, and love. Look for all three wherever they may be found. You have a friend in Camulo, and in Anna; the sister of my beloved Riganta, your grandmother. If she can be found, Anna will be your ally when you need her.'

'Anna?' questioned Cartimandua. 'You have never spoken of Anna. Where do I find her? I would like her to be near me now.' Cartimandua grew quiet for a moment. 'I wish I could have met my mother.' Bellnorix, spread his arm around the shoulders of his granddaughter, and squeezed her.

'I wish that too.' Silence fell between them. They could hear revelry from outside, but for a moment, they were transported away from the music and noise of the crowds. Bellnorix sighed, then continued to seek the attention of the young woman at his side.

'Anna will not be far away when she hears of my passing. Of this, I am sure.' His softened voice offering comfort to the heart of the young queen. 'One thing, Mandua,' he enquired. 'Is there one thing you would like today as a tribute of distinction? Is there a way we can mark this moment in glory?'

'Yes, Lord,' and without hesitation, Cartimandua continued. 'I would like Brigcruim as a gift, and Stanwix to become my oppidum. I would like Belinos to build a new centre from which I will reign. The two places together will be a sign of our unity – our purpose to link brother to brother across this land. But I have a vision for one place of power.'

'Whatever you wish, Queen. It is yours.'

'Then let me tell Belinos. I would like to disclose this information myself.'

That night, when the revellers had fallen into drunken sleep, and the dancers had worn themselves out, Cartimandua called for Belinos. Smiling coyly at him, she opened her cloak to reveal her naked breasts. Her hand gently cupped round the orbs and stroking her nipple, she tempted Belinos to follow her.

'Queen,' said Belinos, pulling Cartimandua into his arms. She grabbed his crotch and stroked urgently, feeling his excitement. Then, abruptly taking her hand away, she turned her gazed into the fire which still blazed in the hearth of his hall.

'Belinos. I have a question for you,' she said, touching her lips and playing with her mouth. She beckoned him to her side, patting the cushioned bench. Reaching for his hand, she placed it on her knee. 'Now that I am queen, I need a place in which I can situate my throne, and from which I can easily access my lands; more central to the whole of Brigantia than where my king Bellnorix has sited his seat.' She searched intently the face of her lover, all the while, moving his hand to touch inside her thigh. 'I have asked Bellnorix for Brigcruim and the demolished land, which was Stanwix. I want to combine the use of the two and create a mighty oppidum…a place where I might hold the power seat of Brigantia.' She waited, giving time for her words to find their place.

'Ah! The first night we were together, you warned me that there would be a cost. Now I understand,' said Belinos, removing his hand from her leg.

'I am not asking, Belinos. I will do this, with or without your acceptance. But it would be much better if you comply. I have plans for you; plans which will not embarrass you, but rather elevate you in the eyes of the Braint and all others in Brigantia.'

'And what, might I ask, is this plan?' Belinos breathed deeply, his nostrils flaring. His body flipped from heightened passion, to one of growing vexation. He tapped his knee with his fingers in agitation. 'You have me, Queen. You blow hot and cold, while I boil and freeze. What is this plan of yours?'

Cartimandua untied the cloak from around her shoulder, allowing it to drop to the floor. 'Belinos, you may call me Mandua, for we have a special relationship. Do we not?' Her naked body glistened in the firelight. 'Belinos, give me what I want, and I promise, one day you will be by my side as my king.'

Belinos, hot with passion, grabbed Cartimandua. She pushed away his advances. 'No. My Lord. You will not have me until you agree to my plan.'

'You are rapacious in your desire, Mandua. But how can a mere man, such as I, deny you, or myself?' He spun Cartimandua around, laying hold of her from behind. He took his pleasure while speaking into her ear. 'Yes. Yes, you can have my lands. You can have it all.'

Cartimandua thought, 'How simple it is to acquire lands and power.' She smiled, covering herself once again in her cloak. Belinos lay spent on the floor in front of the dying embers. Silently,

Cartimandua walked away.

That night, while Cartimandua bargained with Belinos, Bellnorix quietly and without acknowledgement passed into the otherworld. Valas found him in the morning light, the death stiffness already upon him. Immediately Cartimandua was called, and the rites of passing from this world to the next were set in place. The face of Bellnorix was concealed in white linen as the Druids, walking in line, circled the bed where he lay. They chanted a *Caim,* while Valas ordered fresh holly and mistletoe to be found and placed it over the body of the King. He lit candles and chanted the old chants in *ogham,* thus preparing the enduring soul of the King for his departure from this world and his access into the next. As Valas chanted the *Caim,* the people joined in:

'Life has beginnings and endings,
The road betwixt leads us on
To the doorway between both the moments
Where each one of us must run.
The circle of life in completion.
Beginnings and ends tied as one,
The journey in this life, departed,
Enters the other world just begun.'

They laid the cold body on a long cart, extended from his chariot. It had been layered in soft branches and decorated with holly, mistletoe, and ivy. They wrapped Bellnorix in a cloak of white and blue, as befitting his high status. Guards shielded either side of the funeral cart, coeval with people lining up to present offerings to him and to their gods. Charms, amulets, and chains; some of iron, some of silver and gold, were placed carefully around the body. Each person with bowed heads, silently circled the monarch, offered their tributes.

Carrying the sword of Bellnorix, Cartimandua marched between Valas and Lochru. The warriors and Druids followed behind. When she reached the cart, she stopped. Her grief overwhelmed her. She sobbed with deep moans. Camulo rushed to her side, and without speaking, put his arm round her, giving her support. He led her to the enfolded head of Bellnorix. She caressed his face before placing the King's sword by his side. Camulo, supporting the Queen, stepped with her leaving the funeral cart and the mourners.

'Camulo, my friend. I am so glad to see you. Where have you been?'

'My Queen, I have been by your side each step of the way. Although I have positioned myself in the background, I have never allowed you to move out of my sight.'

Cartimandua stared straight into the eyes of Camulo, searching his face. Her cheeks reddened.

'Lady,' said Camulo, realising her discomfort. 'I have seen nothing, except what a protector should see in order to keep you safe.' He smiled. Cartimandua regained her composure. 'Besides, I am too often in the kitchens with the cooks to see everything,' he added.

The journey northward to Taftefield took several moons. The way was difficult, and Cartimandua had no desire to rush. In due course, the entourage arrived at the King's sept. On their arrival, the body of Bellnorix was laid to rest in the Great Hall, allowing the people of Taftefield to mourn the passing of their great king. Others came from afar to show their respect for the great warrior and lord. They stepped silently, waiting in turn to approach the funerary cart. A quiet woman in the line of mourners, waited to kiss the ring on the finger of the cadaver. She was with a Druid, who supported her. Tears ran down her saddened face. She laid a torc and bronze drinking cup by his side, then curtsied in front of the great man.

'Anna, come away,' whispered the Druid. 'Your sister, and now her husband, both have gone to a better place.'

The sister of Riganta; Bellnorix's wife made another curtsey, then moved on. A great commotion sounded in the hall as Cartimandua entered. 'One moment,' said Anna, brushing away the tears and peering to see what the din was about. All eyes were mesmerised by the young queen moving to the centre of the hall. Anna pushed for a better view.

A throng of people pressed forward, greeting Cartimandua as their queen. 'Welcome to our new High Queen of Brigantia.' Applause resounded round the hall, mixed with joyful shouting, as Cartimandua approached them. Then the room fell silent once more.

The burial ground and token offerings prepared to receive the body of Bellnorix were chosen by Valas. The following day, several strapping men from the sept commenced the dig. Deep into the hillside they worked, making a chamber large enough to accept the chariot, horse and body of the great warlord, god and king; Bellnorix. Before the body was positioned in the tomb, Mandua bade her final farewell to the man she had come to love and respect. She raised her eyes to the *heafan* for a few moments, breathing in the clear air of Brigantia, until it filled her lungs afresh. Then, without a backward glance, she returned to the hall of her grandfather.

The smell of fish warned Cartimandua that Valas had entered. 'Ah! Valas. I believe that the flower of henbane has a smell like sticky fish, yet it is among the sleep remedies used by the Druid. Is that correct?'

Bowing low, he acknowledged the Queen, who was posing in a sedentary position on the throne of Bellnorix. She was seated on the iron chair, once precious to her grandfather, feeling the comfort of the many soft cushions padding the seat. Her arm lay limp over the side of the chair. Dwarfed by the tall iron sides which climbed upward, then curled outward, almost tapping the roof of the hall, the Queen seemed fragile and delicate. She wore a golden torc; a sign of her position, and one that had belonged her mother. She took from the jewels that had been merited to her, a signet ring, which had belonged to her grandfather. She placed it on the first finger of her right hand, casually twisting it round with her thumb.

'Do you have difficulty sleeping, Valas?'

'Queen,' he called, ignoring the question. 'A word, if I may.' Cartimandua, deep in thought, did not seem to hear him. She spun the ring around on her finger but remained contemplative. 'Queen,' he repeated. Cartimandua nodded, and Valas proceeded to the throne.

Stirring from her torpid state, she spoke. 'Come, Valas. Tell me what is on your mind.'

'Queen, because of my high position, I was wondering if you had any objection to my taking an assistant; an acolyte, to help me with the enlarged undertaking of Brigante Druid leadership. I have one in mind.'

Sighing, she responded. 'Yes. Valas. I have no objections. Who have you in mind?' she asked, though showing little interest.

'I hear that Donn Donnlugh has finished his training and returns from Ynys Mon. He has no desire to return to his home sept, so it seemed right to think on him.'

'Do as you wish, Valas,' uttered Cartimandua carelessly. 'I will return to Brigcruim. I have plans to extend that place and Stanwix.'

She made to leave, then pondering, her eyes flitting from one side to the other, as though she had just woken from a trance, she decided. 'Bring him to me at Stanwix. I will see him there. But first…' A wind blew through the hall. Irritated by the gush, her cloak swung out, taking hold of her. Cartimandua dashed from the room, shouting, 'Call the men. Call the warriors. We will have Vello and Lopocares tomorrow!'

Vello had little warning of the attack by the Brigante force. Swooping into the sept, they took anyone who fought against them. Cartimandua was her most wild; anger filled her body.

'Get Vello,' she called. 'Get Vello. He is mine!' Arrows of fire hit the thatched roofs of the Lopocares round houses, while women and children ran from the blazing firestorms. Charioteers swarmed into the centre ground, grabbing at the women, and carrying them off to be tied to trees outside the gates of Lopocares. Warriors lunged, slashing at warriors until only a few of the rebels remained alive. Lopocares was decimated; all but burned to the ground. Vello, caught in the affray, was brought before Cartimandua. Sitting astride Tormaig, her sword in hand, she looked down her nose on the captured Vello. 'How dare you go against the High King?' she spat. 'How dare you? Are you so foolish that you thought you might stand in his place? You send a few men to trap him and think that he would be so easily captured. You underestimated him and me!' Her presence towered over the weakened traitor. Vello did not respond. 'Where are your Druids?' she asked, passing an eye round the ruined sept.

A few priests cautiously revealed themselves from the smouldering mess which had been Lopocares. Addressing them, Cartimandua continued, 'Here is your leader, found to be an enemy of Brigantium. What say you? What is his fate?'

One Druid spoke out, 'Queen. Welcome to our sept, though it has seen better times. Vello has taken the leadership of our village without our approval. We have lived under his traitorous shadow for so long now, it is hard to remember better times. The people of this place ask for your mercy. Not for him, but for the farmers, women, and children; for our iron workers and traders. We are but a few now. Can you see it in your heart to give us freedom?'

'Who are you, Druid, that I should listen to you?'

'I am Brochfael.' Brochfael bent his neck, keeping his head bowed for some time. Cartimandua, silent for some moments, considered the request. Beckoning to Valas, she whispered in his ear. He nodded in agreement, turning to leave. Cartimandua continued in silence for some time, until the return of Valas a good while later. He whispered in her ear, then left.

Cartimandua spoke to the Druids. 'This is my decision.'

With one sweep, she lifted her flange hilted rapier and smote Vello, leaving him to bleed to death on the ground when he fell.

Lowering her eyes to the Druids, and in a loud voice, she called, 'You are rid of Vello. I grant you mercy.' Addressing Brochfael directly she ordered, 'you are to take up your rightful place in authority over Lopocares. Should there be any sign of treachery, from anyone, anyone at all, I want to know. Do you understand?' Anyone! I hold you personally responsible.'

Taking a breath, she scanned the faces of the Lopocarians and continued, 'When I return, I expect to see Lopocares restored, and your people loyal to me and to Brigantia. Or so help me God, I will finish you all off.' Once more she signalled to Valas, 'I want you to stay here for a while - a moon turning or so. Release the women and children. Stay with the Druid. See if he is to be trusted, then return to Stanwix with any good warriors you can find here. Do not bring all. Some will need to stay, to protect Lopocares now it is part of Brigantia. We will discuss this and the plans I have on your return.'

Speaking again, directly to her people, Cartimandua shouted. 'This day, in the name of Bellnorix, Lopocares is united with Brigantia. Retribution has been met. The last wish of my grandfather has been satisfied. Welcome, people of Lopocares, welcome into our fellowship. Feast tonight in unity.' Satisfied with the outcome, Cartimandua waved her sword in the air. In response a cheer from the people ascended to the sky.

CHAPTER ELEVEN

LAOIDH IAIN
Iron Hand

The rebuilding of Stanwix started in earnest immediately Cartimandua arrived back from Lopocares. She had a plan to exceed the majesty of anything built before, and then to link the build to Brigcruim via a road large enough to take the wheels of her chariots without damage. Her intention was to make Stanwix her seat of power, reigning over Brigantium and enlarging her territory even more. She had chosen well, for the area covering the route north was in prime position to also dominate the routes east and west. It would also grant her control of movements over the Peneinz, the mountain range dividing Brigantia centrally. Using over ten thousand strides to measure the circumference of the settlement, the area which would become Stanwix the regal oppidum, was marked out.

The winter months had been kind, and the promise of Imbolc was palpable. Valas returned from Lopocares. His good reports of the situation there left Cartimandua smiling, though the return of the pungent body odour did not.

'We will enjoy the festival of Imbolc, then we will see the raising of my oppidum to completion,' the Queen told her Druid council.

'A grove for my Druids will be among the first places to be constructed. I need my advisers and the blessing of my gods.'

'But I will stay in the hall of my Queen,' proposed Valas. Cartimandua turned her nose up, thinking of the aroma attached to such a situation.

'You will not.' she ordered. 'You will move into the grove with the other Druids when it is ready. Do not contend with me.' The Queen held her hand up to stop any further suggestions and dismissed the old Druid. Valas reddened. The blood rushed to his throat, pumping tension and anger around his body and into his tightening fist.

All capable workers from Brigcruim, and Cartimandua's own men from Taftefield were called to dig a circumference ditch, cutting into the bedrock of the land. Ramparts were reinforced with retaining walls, which stretched fifteen feet high. An iron gate set in the south side of the oppidum on the approach to the new fortified sept, rose proudly from the ground, exhibiting the high status of the place.

'I don't care if it takes a year before I have a hall suitably large and impressive. But I will have this,' she vowed. Calling on the ironworkers, she ordered the making of a new and impressive throne to be in a centralized position, raised high from the ground. Until the completion of her new abode, she resided with Belinos at Brigcruim, though her spirit could not settle. All the while, the new and elevated status of Stanwix emerged, so the Queen became more determined to incorporate the tribes and land of the Setantii and then Parisii, into the powerful and growing Brigantia.

'Send word to the Lord of Setantii,' Cartimandua ordered Belinos. 'Tell him of my great power. Ask him to come under our protection and unity and to ready his armies against the romans who threaten our shores. If he agrees, then invite him to join us for the celebration at Imbolc.'

'And what if he doesn't agree, Lady?' asked Belinos.

'Then he will find the same fate as Vello.' Cartimandua pulled at the curls in her hair, agitated with the unruly locks.

'Have you enquired of the gods, Mandua? What does Valas say on the matter?'

''Oh. That smelly old fish? I wish I trusted him, Belinos. But I cannot. At the moment, he is busy inculcating his new mentee; Don Donnlugh. He is so taken with him I almost think he has fallen in love with him.' The Queen giggled. 'But I do not care. You *will* follow my instructions, Belinos.'

Belinos set off the following morning with four other warriors of outstanding ability. Their journey would take them across Brigantia heading westward, from where they hoped to engage with Breehin of Setantii, the noble Broccos Maglos.

Meantime, the Queen made plans for the festival. She anticipated the honouring of Imbolc with excitement, and more than any other celebration, for Imbolc signified the return of the spring after the long, dark months of winter. This year, she eagerly awaited the fulfilment of the promise from the Cailleach, and thus the golden hammer of war coming into her hands. There in the morning sun which filtered weakly through the open doorway of her hall, she thought, 'This promise speaks of victory and the expansion of lands under the banner of Brigantia.' She breathed the cold spring air and felt the vigour of expectation in her spirit ripple through the hairs on her arms and neck.

'I want this festival to be the start of a new and greater practice,' ordered Cartimandua. 'I want to create a spectacle with a feast like no other. Grouse, swan, and other birds are to be hung in readiness.' Sweeping her arm across the expanse of the hall, she continued with the unfolding of the grand plan that she imagined in her mind. 'Stag and pig on splendid platters; late fruits and vegetables - fetch them from the stores. Make bread, cakes… and beers until all the barrels are full and ready. I want fresh ideas for games and sports, and they must all be prepared and waiting for the seasonal change. As the season unfolds, so we will show the unfolding of the power of Brigantia, like a flower unfolding its petals in the fullness of the sun.'

Her mind raced with the words she uttered. To herself, she thought, '…and I want the hammer of war bringing victory over our enemies, as never before.'

Taking a few steps, she decided, 'we will have flowers.' She spoke out loud to the servants gathered in the hall. 'Bring whatever flowers you can find. Bring branches and blossom wherever it might grow. I want this place to be filled with the scent of the land as if it is Litha – full summer.' Planting her feet firmly astride, and smiling to herself, she lifted her hands together, picturing them holding a weight - a magical hammer. She swung her skirt round wildly, spinning the imaginary *mallachd*, enjoying the feel of the spin. Once, twice, she spun. Her uncontrollable hair tumbled around her shoulders, a waterfall cascading into a whirlpool. The bháirds watching made songs from her momentary show of delight.

'Oh, she dances to the sound of the Earth,
Her feet light and lovely, each step.
She dances from winter to spring,
Weaving her magical web.
She holds the power of our world.
To bring her enemies down.
The sun, moon and stars are her cloak.
The favour of gods is her crown.'

Cartimandua was delighted with the songs, and insisted that they be sung at the feast, where she promised herself, she would dance as it was shared.

On the first day of Imbolc, Cartimandua rose early. 'As soon as Belinos returns, you must come and tell me,' Valas had been hovering by the Queen's sleeping area, ready to catch her attention as soon as possible. He showed his obedience, lowering his eyes to a slit '...And fetch Camulo, my champion. I need to talk with him.'

'I am here, my lady.' Camulo moved from the shadows where he had been on guard throughout the night.

'Camulo, I want you to be here with me today. Take some rest now but return shortly. I need you to be with me if, ...*when* Maglos arrives.' Camulo bowed his head, then left the Queen's presence.

Valas spoke in a hush. 'All is ready, Queen. Should Breehin Maglos join us, we have honours ready to bestow, and gifts to offer for his support in our quest. We have organised games and competitions for the fun of the sport, along with dancing and music, of course. The fun and festivities will run for eight days at least. There will be enough to cause admiration, and to satisfy your desire, my lady.'

Cartimandua smiled. 'Good. Then our festival of light will be something for him to behold.'

'Queen, may I bring to your attention the new Druid priest, Donn Donnlugh?' Valas pointed to the curtained doorway where Donnlugh was hovering. Donnlugh glided into the room, his black cloak ballooning behind him, like Druid raven wings.

Eyeing the young Druid up and down, Cartimandua dismissed this wisp of a man. 'Yes. Yes. Very good. Is there any news yet? Has Belinos returned yet?'

'No, my Queen, though messengers have reported that they will soon return. The news travels before them. Belinos has been successful. He travels with Maglos. It would seem that your offer to him is, indeed, worthy.'

The festivities commenced instantly her guests arrived. Music played and dancers danced from the gates of the oppidum leading them up to the hall where the Queen waited. Maglos had brought with him three of his men, and a warrior Druid. Belinos led the five men straight into his hall as the Queen turned to meet them. Maglos, tall and erect on approach, bent his knee. He was a husky fellow whose blue war paint had worked into his skin, making him look ill, but his muscular shoulders and arms told another tale. His brown, almost black hair had been shaved round the sides, and left to grow long on the top. He had bungled the length up onto his crown, tying it with a leather thong. When he spoke, his voice was coarse and rough, though his manners were more refined.

'Queen. I have heard of your presence, and I am glad of your offer of unity between us.'

Cartimandua offered her right hand to welcome the King of Setantii. He took the hand, kissing the ring on her forefinger. Acknowledging the ring, Maglos remarked, 'I see you wear the signet of our great king of Brigantia. I am sorry to hear of his demise.' He nodded his head in respect.

Cartimandua confessed, 'We will miss him greatly, but for the sake of our lands we must unite against this awful threat from the latins.'

Maglos agreed, then asked, 'But how will Setantii benefit from our union?'

'I plan to establish a council of kings where we will have a place to speak, to add to the strategies and wisdoms from our Druids and our gods. These insights will be needed to bring victory from the threat.' Cartimandua observed intently the face of her visitor. Shaking his head, he opened his mouth to speak, but she raised her hand to hold him. 'Also, in the matter of war against the enemy, the armies of Brigantia will be at your disposal. They will support and fight with you whenever they are needed. You will agree to do the same with your warriors. It is only by acting together that we may have a chance of victory.'

Maglos thought for a few minutes, then added, 'I will not give up my throne. The Setantii are my people, and I have vowed to protect them. I will not hand over my power to a woman.' The renowned warlord placed his hand on the belt of his tunic, where a short sword hung.

Camulo stepped forward, readying his sword. Belinos also advanced one step. Both stood at the side of the Queen, hand on sword hilt. On their advance, the Queen's guardians hidden in the shadows, also stepped into the firelight, to show themselves.

A moment passed between the party. The air was filled with tension and mistrust.

Cartimandua tightened her fist, then spoke. 'Maglos. I am not asking for your kingdom. I am asking that Brigantia and Setantii link together in one purpose: that of peace. Seeking peace for our people, no matter the cost. You *should* remain king of Setantii. I will remain Queen of Brigantia, and unless you desire to become part of Brigantia, then you will remain in full charge of your lands and power.' Cartimandua reached for the hand of her guest still gripping the sword hilt, and with one finger, she stroked it.

Maglos relaxed. 'This I like,' he agreed. 'In front of these witnesses, I agree to your terms of unity. Setantii will give support where and when needed.'

'Then you will agree to stay for the Imbolc festival? Enjoy your stay and accept these tokens of our friendship.' A table had been set with fruits and gifts, tokens, and riches for Maglos to enjoy. Cartimandua led him to the table. Offering him a cup of wine, the Queen tiled her head coyly, fluttering her eyelashes at him.

The warriors, now pleased with the outcome of the meeting, slapped each other on the back.

'Is there more wine?' they asked. 'Yes, and lasses?'

Belinos, discreetly went to kiss her cheek. 'I couldn't have done that better,' he praised. 'You have a soft way with that iron hand of yours. The art of war belongs to you, my Queen.'

That evening, Cartimandua attended her people, expressing her joy at the new unity between Brigantia and Setantii. Publicly, she welcomed High Breehin Broccos Maglos, begging him to enjoy the sports and games planned over the days of Imbolc. The people, excited with the merrymaking and entertainment, drew Maglos and his men into the midst of Brigcruim. Young girls danced for them, and soon the place was full of cavorting Brigante and visitants, kissing, and coupling whenever they felt the urge.

When Cartimandua retired, Belinos was by her side. Together they rested by the fire and talked over the happenings of the last few days. They drank wine, then Belinos addressed Cartimandua. 'I need to tell you something,' he said. 'I have been called home. A messenger found me on the way back to Brigcruim. He brought news from Caluvellauni. The romans have taken command of our southern shores. War is inevitable. Our challenge to keep the savage romans out of Albion and obviously, Brigantia, is real. The King of *Caluvellauni* has asked for my help in staying the enemy attack, stopping it from proceeding further.'

'Why would he ask you, Belinos? What has it got to do with you? If you stay here, you can help to defend our borders. I will not allow you to go.'

'There is something I haven't told you, Mandua. My father is the high chief there. He is Cunobelinos, known as the King of Albion, and descendant of the mighty Casswallen. My father has called his son home to help in the fight. I cannot refuse him.'

'Cunobelinos is your father? That king who calls himself Rex, and fashions himself after the emperor of Rome?' Cartimandua, dazed and perplexed, pulled at her ear. 'What are you telling me?'

'He has got fat on trade with these people. That is no lie. And his territory has spread over Albion until he holds almost as much of it as Brigantia. In fact, his roots are here in Brigcruim where he was born.'

Cartimandua started pacing the room. 'But this is a puzzle, because I have never heard of a son of Cunobelinos called Belinos.' She glared into his eyes, daring him to explain.

'No.' Belinos hung his head. 'I lied. I have been hiding these years. My name is Togodomus Belinos. I am one of four sons. My father is a violent man. He breathes, and men fall. I have been avoiding his temper, and the fighting in the south. But I cannot avoid it any longer.'

'But what of your brothers? Why are you the one to obey your father after all this time?'

'My eldest brother is Adminius – King of Cantii. He was given the kingdom as his own, to rule in my father's name, but Adminius revolted against my father; a move for which he must pay. Father deposed him and intends to take Cantii back under his power. When I found out that Adminius had been conspiring with the madman Emperor Caligula, I tried to dissuade him from leaving to join those enemies of Albion. My father supposed I was aligning myself with my treacherous brother. He is wrong. But I could not persuade him of the error. I ran, I am ashamed to say.'

'And do you suppose your father has forgiven you, and now knows the truth of the matter?'

'I think he will test me when I return home but return I must.'

'And what of your other brothers?' Cartimandua interrogated.

'Caratācos. He is already home. He was acting as spy and organising counter attacks against our enemies. He is a ferocious warrior and will die rather than cede to the enemy. In him we have a leader who is not afraid to die for what he believes to be right. I must call men from my own territory to join my father and brother. We need to turn attention to the real war in front of us rather than each other. Should anything happen to Caligula, his younger brother Consul Claudius is already presenting himself the bigger threat. He could amass his thousands, ready to take all. We must be prepared against either of these emperors, to defend our lands and our lives.'

Cartimandua stopped her pacing, and staring at the face of Belinos, she weighed up the information he was giving, wondering how this would affect her and her people. 'And another brother?'

'One other brother,' continued Belinos. '…I am told… I do not know what has befallen him. He is but a whisper and a source of gossip against my father. It is probable that he is dead, though it is also probable that he never lived. In all this, my father has called me home to support him in the fierce battle against the Cantii. This battle among brothers must be settled before the real foes of Albion rises. Enemy armies have set sail and look to gather off the southern coastline of Albion. You know they have done this before under orders from Caligula, but then they returned across the channel. But the threat is real. We must be ready to save our country from invasion.'

'Then what do you suggest I do?'

'You have done well today in uniting allies. Now go and do the same with the King of Carvetii. Bring the people together in one purpose. We have a chance of victory if that iron hand of yours can hold Brigantia together.'

Belinos rose to leave.

Cartimandua grabbed his arm. 'Brigantia is mine, and I will not give it to alien forces. I would rather die!' she vowed. Then, softening her voice, she promised, 'I will look after Brigcruim. It will be safe till your return.' A solitary tear escaped her eye. Holding her head high, the Queen flung her hair back and turned toward the doorway. Without a glance backwards at Belinos, she called, 'and what of your wife, oh man of many secrets? What of your wife? Will she travel with you?'

Before he could answer, Cartimandua walked away.

The night was full of shadows and dreams. Cartimandua tossed; her mind did not allow her to rest. Dreams robbed her of slumber. Pain seared through her chest. Tears flooded her eyes. She sobbed with anger and frustration. Wrapping her cloak round her frame, she soundlessly and swiftly headed in the direction of the barn. The horned moon winked above the cold northern wind.

Before Cartimandua reached the shelter, she heard the whinny of Tormaig pacing and pawing, ready for the night. She mounted the powerfully built pony and headed north in a gallop. The wild wind gusts took her cloak from underneath her, whipping it high in the sky, trailing behind her like wings flying full speed. She was away. Without stopping, she exacted the horse, imposing her will into the speed of the horse's limbs, becoming one with the creature. The horse flew as Epona herself; the great mare goddess, embodying the journey physically, mentally, and emotionally. There was no care in the heart of the Queen, only an odd feeling that she was being followed.

When Cartimandua arrived at Stanwix, dismounting, she ran to her new hall. Though the roof was not finished, and the walls had not been plastered with mud linings, still Cartimandua flopped onto the only bench in the room. She sobbed until her voice became husky and hoarse. Then, exhausted and worn, she sank down on the floor, allowing the tears to fall around her.

'Oh! Bellnorix,' she called out into the wind. 'Bellnorix, my grandfather. Who have I left in this world?' She allowed the feeling of desperation to invade her spirit. She fell, groping on the ground like an animal. Deep guttural sounds came from within her soul; painful moaning; deep callings. 'I am alone. To whom can I turn?'

She did not see Camulo follow her into the hall. He hovered in the shadows of the unfinished room, observing her pain; at a loss as to how to help his Queen.

An owl screed from above. The temperature dropped abruptly. An unearthly wind blew across the ground. In its wake, icy fingers of death spread like glass crystals scattering light in all directions. Cartimandua realised she was in the centre of a coating of frost, as if she were sitting in a pool of frozen water. She began to shiver. She tried to lift herself from the freezing ground, but her bones became stiff and frigid. Her mind stopped too, immobilised in that moment. The hall fell under the otiose spell. Camulo, affected by the enchantment, was solidified in the shadows. The whole sept was covered in a ghostly cloak of frost; the workers silenced in their beds. Rain began to fall.

'It is raining,' thought Cartimandua, feeling drops of liquid falling onto her shoulders and splashing onto her face. Struggling to bring sense into her head, she opened her hand, and held her palm out to catch the soft drops. Plop. The drops were thick. 'Not like rain,' she thought. Then glancing upward, she became aware that peering through the hole in the roof, was the worm ridden face and grinning lips of the Cailleach. Saliva dripped down from the open mouth, showering the queen with the putrid liquid. Cartimandua tried to duck out of the way, wiping the wet mucus infused slop from her face and body. The stench lingered like old slops in a cauldron.

The Cailleach laughed. 'Is this not the festival of Imbolc?' Feigning admiration, the Winter Queen continued, 'My Queen Cartimandua. What are you doing here?' she asked.

Cartimandua spoke slowly, for the cold had stopped her muscles from working. She spluttered out, 'Winter! I am indeed your Queen,' she said, with as much bark as she could muster. Cartimandua pushed herself up from the bitterly cold ground. 'I have come to think and pray,' she answered.

'I have the hammer, Mandua. I have the golden hammer of victory.' The Cailleach goaded.

'Then give it to me. You promised. Let me see.'

'It is by my side on the top of the roof bearings. Come and get it.' She moved away from the hole but continued calling to the Queen. 'And remember. It is mine. When Samhain returns, and I come calling. Then you must restore it to me.' Her voice trailed, and the Queen knew that she was gone.

Outside the weather continued to blow across the land, clearing the clouds away to reveal the glistening bright lights of the stars above. A gale whiplashed the building. Hitching her braccae tighter round her waist, Cartimandua carefully climbed the outer walls. Anchoring her fingers into any pockets she could find, she hoisted herself up until she reached the beginnings of the roof structure. The thatching had already been started. Cartimandua gripped the thatch, pulling herself up as high as she dared. The hammer was perched on a willow beam between the open roof struts and the pinnacle of the round building. The thatch hold was flimsy, and the gusting winds made her situation precarious. One fall could be seriously damaging, if not fatal. She reached for the hammer balancing on the beam. Its golden surface shone in the moonlight, deliberating critically.

'One more finger length,' she thought, reaching with all her ability. 'It will be mine! That bloody hag,' she cursed, scrambling up the straw and reed covering. Unexpectantly, an owl flew from the rafters, hitting Cartimandua in the face. She slipped. Her grip on the truss weakened, and she found herself slithering further down the thatch. Grappling with her predicament, she steadied herself, then clinging, she scaled the roof again. This time she made her upward climb more deliberately, judging the strength of the ties round the beams and trusses, until her hand wrapped round the hammer. 'Got you!' she shouted. The owl returned, flying for the back of Cartimandua's head. She could see the piercing eyes and the sharp neb of the *stryx* as its body grew in front of her; its eyes like beacons, flashed from black to green, then black. With its talons, the stryx gorged into the hand of the Queen; wings flapping violently. Cartimandua hung onto the roof with her bleeding left hand, and with her iron fist, aiming for the demon now entangled in her hair, she swung the hammer. The hammer touched the *comachag*. A bloodcurdling shriek escaped its lungs as it flew northward. The shriek could be heard above the wind, like a woman screeching a warning of revenge to her attacker.

Camulo, roused from his stupor by the scream, dashed outside the hall to find Cartimandua hanging from the roof.

'Let go, My Queen. I will catch you,' he called. The wind blasted.

The scuds took his breath. Branches of trees caught the gusts, flying broken to the ground. Benches blown over, rolled and broke up. Tables lay on their sides, while drinking vessels and platters rattled around the sept, crashing into the half-erected houses. With urgency, he called again. Cartimandua released her grip. With a way cleared for her to approach safely, the Queen slid into the open arms of the champion. He carried her back inside the cold, draughty hall. He built a fire, and calling for help from the now aroused workers, he fetched skins and straw, settling the Queen into a cocoon of warmth. Someone brought broth, and bread for the two of them, and mead to drink. Before many moments had passed, the cheeks of the Queen filled with colour again; her breathing fell to a normal rhythm.

'What were you doing up there, my Queen?' Camulo asked after they had finished their meal.

'I don't know. I think I must have been dreaming, and walked in a daze,' she said, then remembering the hammer. 'What has happened to it?' she wondered silently. She inspected her hands. Her right hand felt unusually heavy. She turned both hands over and over, gazing closely. There was nothing to see. 'But it feels different,' she thought.

'What made you ride so far in the darkness of night?' Camulo asked, gently.

'I felt so alone, Camulo. The people I thought would be with me; loyal to me, supportive, they are gone. Even Valas is so full of his own importance that he does not heed my situation.'

'But I am here, my lady. I will be with you until your need has gone. And what of your new ally? What of Maglos and the Setantii? They have given their support to your leadership. Even now he waits for you to join in the observance of Imbolc. A new spring is on the horizon, my Queen. Your people call for you. You must return to Brigcruim and be there as soon as you can. Maglos will expect you to show him hospitality and to formalise your bond. When you are rested, we should go back.'

'Give me one hour, Camulo, and I will be ready. Forgive me for what seems like a weakness, but I suspect other forces called me here tonight. Just one hour, and we can be on our way.' Cartimandua's mind returned to the conversation she had with Bellnorix just before he left this world. 'Camulo,' she said, 'my grandmother had a sister.'

'Yes. Anna.'

'You know of her? Where is she? What do you know?'

'She left Taftefield urgently, with a Druid some years ago. I do not think she has returned there, nor do I know why she left, except that there was tension between her and Bellnorix. Shall I look for her?' he asked.

'Not yet, my friend. But I will require this of you very soon.'

Camulo happed to leave his Queen as Valas broke into the room. 'Queen, you are safe?' he sighed with relief.

'How did you know where I was, Valas?'

'I saw in the wind,' he answered.

For one moment, Cartimandua hesitated to speak. Opening her mouth, she closed it again. She stood to greet Valas and flicked a feather from his cloak. Twisting the feather between her fingers, she mused, 'This looks like a feather from an owl. You must have flown here on the wind, Valas, to be on our tail so soon.' She did not smile but searched his eyes.

Valas, avoiding her gaze, turned in the direction of Camulo. 'I am glad you have kept our Queen safe, Camulo.' He nodded an acknowledgment for the champion, who did not respond.

Cartimandua, speaking directly to Valas, ordered, 'Now go. Leave me for a while. Get some food, Valas, for we return to Brigcruim in the hour.'

Warming herself by the blaze, Cartimandua allowed her mind to recall the events of the night. 'What does it all mean?' she asked herself. 'Camulo, I can depend on, I am sure. But Valas? I know he is not to be trusted. There is something in his manner that unnerves me more tonight.' The flames flickered. The Queen reflected. Remembering the advice from Belinos, the seeds of a plan started to formalise in her mind. When the fire was spent, Cartimandua spoke again to Camulo.

'Prepare the horses. Fetch Valas. I desire to speak with him before we leave.'

Valas returned, bowing low, his cloak scraping the ground on entering the hall. The Queen sat, fully composed.

'I want you to ride to Carvetii, Valas. I want you to approach the King there and offer him the same terms that were offered to Maglos; that of uniting in our readiness against the Romans. Take some men with you, some tough workers from here. I want you to ride with speed. Return also with speed. Tell him that the Romans have already entered the south, and king Cunobelinos of Caluvellauni is already gathering men together to make a stand against their invasion.'

'Queen. How do you know these things?' he asked. 'Is this true?'

'You doubt my sources, Valas?' The blood pumped in the breast of the Queen. 'You give voice to these doubts? Is this treason, Valas?'

'No. No. My Lady. Forgive me. I just wanted to ensure your information.'

'I tell you; I will not reveal my sources. I will just say - I saw in the wind.'

Valas bowed, ceding to the woman before him.

'Now go. Do as I bid. And if you are able, send a "wind message" to that young acolyte of yours. Tell him I will speak with him on my return.' Cartimandua showed her back to Valas conveying the end of this hearing. He turned to leave the presence, but the Queen called, 'Oh! And one more thing, my high and mighty Druid. I plan to return to Stanwix as soon as the festival of Imbolc is passed. I want this hall and as many other houses, ready for my occupation. Tell the workers that they must move more quickly if they want to see their families again.'

The horses left Stanwix at speed. The royal retinue travelled south, intending to endorse the treaty between Brigantia and Setantii and join the celebrations at Brigcruim again. The High-Druid and five others travelling northwest seeking Carvetii.

CHAPTER TWELVE

CARVETII
Stag Warriors

ACHANN COULD NOT AVOID the arrow as it hurtled toward him. It hit hard under the wing of the spectre, causing him to spiral. A gust of wind lifted him momentarily, placing him onto a flight path back to the southern coastline. He fell from his shapeshifting flight into the sandbanks, and lay there, shocked, wet, cold and bleeding, just as dawn broke. After several hours of searching, Mugh found the wounded Eachann. Using his refreshed Druid 'sight' and calling for help from the gods and anyone else within the area, he waded into the soft, dangerous sands. Voices sounded afar. 'I cannot tell where they are.' Mugh muttered, all the time swearing for lack of help. He began to call again. 'Help me. Anyone.'

His soliloquy continued. 'Shaping frequently causes a great mental impact on the shifter. Beli Mawr will be exhausted and feeling incomplete.' The little Druid babbled away to himself, 'but I know that the damage inflicted by the arrow, this is the more difficult to deal with.' Paddling into the water's edge, he called again. 'The gods are not listening, and I am too far away from the camp for anyone else to hear. I will have to do this on my own. I wish I had the strength. But. -He. -Is.-As.-Heavy as a block of iron.' Lifting and dragging Eachann to a safe bank, Mugh began to assess the damage to the body of the young shapeshifter. He rolled Eachann over into a more comfortable position, trying to remove the wet clothing, then called again for help. 'It is no use,' his voice still droned. Puffing from lack of breath, he removed his own cloak, to wrap around the body of the fallen man. 'I am all bone and no muscle. If I put my arm under him here, and then pull …When I have sorted this, and Eachann is back to fitness, I promise I also will work at building my strength. I see it now. If the gods do not bring their help, then the only one I can rely on is me.' His active mind continued to ramble. 'Mind you, I would have to stop eating those cakes and sweetmeats. I am not sure I am ready for all this.'

Mugh checked Eachann for signs of damage when a haughty voice from behind him spoke into the early morning mist. 'Ah! Mugh. You have found him. Is he injured?' Mugh glanced round to see the black and white figure of Audigus Raigon standing on a low bank and looking down on the two of them from a short distance away.

'He is alive, but injured, Lord Raigon. Have you come to help?'

'Of course, Mugh. I will go back and send others to you.' There was no urgency in his manner.

'Thank you,' called Mugh. As Raigon turned to leave, Mugh shouted again. 'Raigon.'

Raigon turned to front the glare coming from Mugh's eye.

'Yes?'

'Oh! Nothing. I just wondered why you are so far away from camp. The gods must have sent you here.' Mugh also added under his breath, 'and have you been hunting?' but followed his outspoken thoughts, added, 'Have you got any cakes in that quiver on your back? No. No. Of course not. I'll wait until we get back to the camp.'

When Eachann was settled back in the camp, Mugh attended to the arrow wound. The damage was not deep, though the blood had spread over the cloak and tunic, covering it in the congealing red. 'A few days rest should be all that is needed to get the warrior back on his feet and fighting fit again.'

But Eachann was unsettled. 'Call the King, Mugh. I have news.'

'Lay still, Beli Mawr. You have been injured. You need rest.'

'No. Call the King. This is important,' he insisted.

Venutius came the following day. Eachann told him what he had seen on the banks of Annan, across the great river. 'There are hordes of them. They were hidden in the night. No fires drew attention, but I could see them moving. Small glinting outbursts of light were exposed in the moonlight. I knew that these flashes showed their weaponry. My insight tells me that there is an army hidden from us, getting ready to attack. I cannot say how many, but certainly there are enough to warrant concern. We have not long to bring our warriors into position to cause their defeat.'

'What happened Eachann, while you were there?'

'I was so intent on gathering an understanding of the hordes, that I lost concentration. An arrow was fired directly at me. I did not know it had hit me until I started to fall. If it were not for Mugh searching and finding me in the quicksands, I would be entering the other world by now.'

'Anyone attempting to interfere with my champion, will find no favour with me. Do you know who might have attempted such a thing?' asked Venutius.

Mugh coughed.

'No King. But this I do know. Who dare menace with me, they

will find their own ending. They are not the threat. We have little time to bring the real peril to heel.'

'Have you a plan?'

'I think so. These foes will want to cross the great Sulewad, and because they are camped at Annan, my guess is that they are already preparing to cross there. The tides are the only thing holding them back. They will swarm when the tide is low enough for a safe crossing. There is a way we can encourage them to take the route we set rather than their own, and this is how we might do it.' Eachann continued to explain his plan to the King. Mugh listened too, offering his own Druid insights to the discussed proposition. Venutius left Eachann to rest but went straight to his advisors and warriors to trundle the scheme.

Wearing their traditional battle headdresses of stag horns, the warriors gathered all the hands they could find. 'Fetch wood and fetch animals; heads, fats, oils,' they were ordered. By the early evening, they had moved twenty carts to the coastline, at a place where quicksand was known to be. Around the length of this place, they emptied the carts, using the wood to build several fire heaps. They placed torches made of stakes tipped with rags and dipped in the animal fats and oils. They were ready to catch as soon as the fires blazed. The animal heads, they filled with more fat and oil and placed them on stakes fastened into the ground in between each fire. As the day light closed, the staked animal heads were lit. The burning heads fulgurated over the great river, lighting up the 'camp' from the shores of Carvetii. The army of Venutius waited.

As the tide began to turn, the army lay silently waiting. A few other men lit the bonfires and began to sing and cavort as though they were celebrating and drinking.

The enemy pehtas paddled silently on small rafts, drawn by the fires and what appeared to them as a small encampment. The fires lit the path all around the marshes. Venutius held his ranks. Eachann raised his Druid staff at the south of the line. Mugh mimicked the action at the centre of the fire line. As the rafts arrived at the marshes and quicksands, Venutius gave the word. 'Fires,' he shouted. Eachann repeated the order. Mugh also called the order. Stags appeared from out of the night, riding on horses and shouting and wailing. The prepared torches were lit from the blazing flames and hurdled onto the rafts. Burning arrows followed, lighting up the sky and landing on the wooden floats of the pehtas. The herd of stag warriors rode in a frenzy up and down the fiery line, throwing more burning shafts into the sands between the enemy and the Carvetii fires. They looked, and were, terrifying and dangerous, galloping along the extent of the coastline. The raiders, in a blind panic, surged for safety from the red-hot rafts, shouting and yelling as they sank in the sands beneath them.

Any that managed to cling to the drier sands, soon found their path to the otherworld, as Venutius and his men drove oiled stakes through their bodies, lighting the palings to finish the undertaking. The aroma of smoking and burning bodies rose upwards and across the land. The air was filled with the smell of Carvetii triumph.

The following day, victorious, Venutius led the march home to Staena. 'Carvetii is now in a position to take the land beyond the great river,' he pronounced, as the people celebrated their success. Venutius praised Eachann. 'Your strategy was excellent. Your protection of our lands is essential.'

Raigon joined in praise of Eachann. 'Well done, Beli Mawr. How did we manage before you found your way to Staena?' he smirked.

Progressively, Eachann continued to protect and uphold the causes of Venutius, even as he grew in grit, wisdom and glory.

Venutius and his army battled into the territory of the Pehtas, taking some of the tribal areas of Novantae and Selgovae. In each new place he took, he had altars and shrines built in honour of Brigga, the goddess who offers new life. He built altars to Belatucadrus, the horned god, and to Taranis, the god favoured by his champion. The Carvetii brought their offerings, establishing the new tribal lands as their own. Mugh Ruith used every opportunity to spread the legend of Beli Mawr, 'The Shining One,' and Beli Mawr was praised.

'Where is my champion? Where is Eachann Beli Mawr? Bring him to me, and yes –bring Little Mugh too,' Venutius called, enjoying the many victories over the Pehtas in the last *bliadhna*. 'Beli Mawr. I have much to thank you for. Your Druid ability has put the next phase for the expansion of Carvetii into my hands. I have decided that I will make you my High-Druid, from this day!'

Eachann objected. 'But what of Raigon, Lord King? I do not want to make an enemy of him.'

'I will choose whom I will. Why? Have you another idea?'

'Let me stand by his side; work with him, be on his council occasionally, along with Mugh Ruith. But allow Raigon to keep his position. When and if the time comes, I will be ready to take his place. But for now, King, if you agree, I would rather be in the fight, than in the council.'

'As you please, Champion. As you please. I trust your wisdom.'

Returning to the Druid grove later that day, Eachann told Mugh of the King's desire. He immediately started to mumble. 'I can't believe this. This can't happen. We have been waiting for something to happen – something great from the gods; but this?' He started to drum his fingers on the table, then he sprang up and began to hop from one foot to the other, as if he were walking on a carpet of fire. 'Not good. I feel it's not good.' He turned to the table where a platter of sweet cakes sat. Almost subconsciously it seemed, Mugh began to stuff the cakes into this mouth, but still continuing to mumble. The cake crumbs splattered from his mouth over the table. 'I should have given an offering to Taranis. I am neglecting my position. You should have waited to ask Taranis for wisdom, Eachann. Now look at us. I don't trust Raigon. You must watch him like a hawk.'

'But Mugh, I must make some decisions. And I would rather keep Raigon close. In any case, I feel that my time is coming, and I need to be in a place where I can be free to move. If I took the position of High-Druid, I would be tied to Venutius and Carvetii. He has my loyalty, of course, but I must be free to fly where the wind takes me. I do not yet know who I am, Mugh.'

Mugh continued to mutter under his breath. 'I just wanted an uncomplicated life. Now this. I will always have to watch his back.' He stuffed another cake into his mouth.

Later that day, Venutius called Raigon to tell him of his decision. Raigon narrowed his eyes and puffed out his chest. 'King, have I no say in this matter?' argued the High-Druid. 'I must allow Eachann to stand by my side as second High-Druid of Carvetii?' His knuckles were tight and red. His body shook with agitation. Controlling his anger, he spluttered, 'I don't trust him. We know so little about him, Venutius. I have little in common with him. And I think he has killed some of my men.'

'Your men? Your men? *You* have no men but mine, Raigon. And I believe that if Eachann did indeed rid the country of any, then it would have been with the blessing of Taranis. Your men, indeed!'

Regaining some composure, Raigon pursued the conversation. 'And he - he knows nothing…nothing that is worth your attention. If it were not for that little peewee by his side, he would be useless.'

'Then you must teach him what he does not know, Raigon, for if you do not accept this position, then I vow that Eachann will be High-Druid, first among my Druids, and not second!' Venutius slammed his fist on the arm of his throne, rising to meet the defiance of his advisor. He touched the hilt of his sword which rested by the chair, tapping it with threat.

Raigon did not bow. Turning to the door, the High-Druid swiftly marched out. A darkness descended in the room when he left. Venutius sat again and pondered. 'It is the first time that I have spoken orders to Raigon in such a way. Am I damned?' he questioned. 'Just because the Druids have such power and authority, does that give them more power than the King?' He answered his own question. 'You know it does. The gods give authority and wisdom and power through Eòlas. Who are you to go against your own faith and teachings?' Venutius sat quietly, his fingers tapping his lips. 'What to do? There is nothing I can do now but to observe my resolve.'

Raigon swept through the sept and to the Druid grove. His anger still seethed from his mouth. 'I will have him. I will have that runt of a god. See if I don't,' he swore.

That night, he drank wine which had been offered to Sucellos, the hound-God of boundaries. He walked to the shrine in the grove. Sitting down on the grass, he closed his eyes, calling for a revelation from Sucellos. The moon was full when the wolf appeared. 'Am I seeing things or is this a vision from the gods? Is this the one I pray to? He is walking on his two back legs as a man. He carries a barrel of wine,' Raigon whispered, rubbing his eyes hard. As the wolf rose before Raigon, the vision became clearer. Standing before the Druid stood a ghostly apparition of Sucellos. Half man, half wolf, changing and re-shaping, until settling again as an old man covered in wolf's fur. He wore the skull of the wolf like a headdress. He offered wine to Raigon, who took it and drank. 'Sucellos, I need help, and your insights.'

Sucellos took his fur skin from round his shoulders and placed it onto the back of Raigon. The warmth of the skin put Raigon in a trance. Before him appeared a wooden gate. It opened easily, but there was no light beyond the gate. Behind him walked the wolf, snarling to block any return. Through the gate into darkness, Raigon ventured. The shaft was undetectable. Raigon felt himself trip, falling into the unobservable space between the earth and the under-world – a place where only Druids dare, and often do not come back. Down, down he fell, only stopping when the hard rock ledge broke his fall. Dazed and shocked, Raigon fumbled round in the darkness, broken momentarily by unpredictable sparks of *ignis fatuus*. All around him stood a field of tall nightwalkers. They moved trancelike and hypnotically circling Raigon, swaying side by side in the night air. Belittling Raigon, they trapped him in a maze of reeds. There was no way through the thick growth, though Raigon pushed against the sinister army with all his might.

In front of him stood the old man again. 'Welcome Audigus Raigon, it has been a while since your last visit. What can I do for you?'

In front of Raigon hovered the master of the black arts of drueidan; someone who could weave the storms and create lightning; he could shift his shape and call on animals to unite in his body. One minute he was a Druid, the next he was the wolf who wore the shape of Sucellos; such was his ability to transform. Raigon bowed. 'Lord Sucellos.' Raigon trembled.

You seek my help, Audigus Raigon?'

Raigon cowered. 'Please, give me your insight. It is that Druid god, Beli Mawr. He bothers me. What can I use against him to stop him usurping my position?' he begged.

Sucellos drew a circle in the air, forming pictures with his claw-like finger. In front of Raigon appearing in the vision, a mighty king who grew and grew, until he towered over his people like a mighty oak. His throne was large. Below his throne, four lords kneeled: smaller than the mighty king, but just as powerful. One lord was taken away on the back of an owl. Another was stripped of his cloak, then he also was sent away. The other two lords reigned, alongside the mighty king until his death. Raigon took in this vision as it unfolded, then turned to Sucellos. 'What does this tell me, Sucellos? What does it mean?'

Sucellos continued to draw in the night sky. Another owl landed on the high roof of a hall in an oppidum. Raigon could hear voices speaking from below. 'My love. You must go home to Brigantia and protect the child. I give you my ring. It will be proof of his heritage.' The woman sobbed, laying the child down in a shallow hollow, covering him only in a shawl. The vision began to fade, but Raigon, eyes wide open, took in the sight. At that moment, the trance left him, and he found himself back in the grove, shivering from the cold, damp night air.

There was quite a stir in Carvetii and in Staena when Valas and his travelling party of five rode into the oppidum. The white priestly cloak of another High-Druid was enough to cause consternation in the sept, and especially in the Druid grove if there had been no warning of the arrival. Druids moved into the centre of the sept, carrying fey and staffs of office. Druid warriors stood with sword in hand, and other warriors wearing black, donned their stag helmets and mounted their horses in a show of intimidation. They surrounded the visitors. Valas was aware that his life was at risk, even before Raigon appeared, or Venutius deemed to show. His age showed in the way he climbed down from his mount. His shoulders were more hunched, and he found it difficult to straighten them after the long journey. His knee joints cracked when he stood. His beard had grown grey in the last few years, and although great age in a Druid can be a factor in presenting his wisdom, it can also leave him more vulnerable to attack from outsiders who do not fear the authority of the cloak. Valas quivered.

Raigon moved forward, swinging his priestly cloak wide. 'My Lord. Welcome,' he said, feigning pleasure at seeing the visitors. 'Have you come far? What is your purpose here in Staena, the centre of the great Carvetii kingdom and our great king Venutius?'

Valas, standing erect in false confidence, responded to Raigon. 'I come in the name of Cartimandua; Queen of Brigantia, who rules the lands far and wide. I desire an audience with your king, Venutius, to express the message I have carried from my Queen.'

'Speak your message, and your name,' said Raigon, moving closer to the six men.

'Lord. I do not mean to offend, but I have instructions to deliver my message to Venutius, and to Venutius only.'

Nodding an indication to the Carvetii Druids, Raigon showed that they were to stand guard over the other five travellers, but to Valas he beckoned. 'Come with me.' He led the way into the Great Hall of Venutius.

Venutius burst into laughter, as Valas unrolled the offer from Cartimandua.

'What? Who is this Queen of Brigantia? I have heard rumours that she lives off the reputation of her grandfather. Who does she think she is, to seek me out and offer so little for my support? Go back to her and laugh in her face. Unity comes with a price, and she has offered me nothing yet.'

Bent over the ear of the King, Raigon murmured, 'Lord. There might be some play in this situation. It would do Carvetii well, if Brigante warriors were at your disposal in the fight to take the more northern lands, extending Carvetii even more.'

'Tell me more, Raigon.'

'What if you should agree to some of the Brigante offer? To agree in principle to joining in preparation against the dreaded Romans; yes. But with many more stipulations on the treaty. What if you should ask for equal rule over Brigantia, for instance, and the land to go with it?'

Venutius stopped to think about the words of Raigon. 'Ah! I see where you are going with this thought.' Smiling, Venutius began to work through the premise. 'Then I shall wait for a response from this queen. Bargaining from her need could make for rich pickings.'

Raigon smirked. 'Tell your Queen, whoever she is, that Venutius likes the offer of unity against the threat from Rome but will need an enlarged offer of lands in order to comply.'

Jumping in quickly Valas blurted out, 'And if there is any way I can be of service to you personally, Lord Venutius, then I will be at your side. I know ways of helping you to a solid position, my lord. I am old, but not without influence.'

Raigon whispered in the ear of the King. 'This priest may be useful to your cause, Venutius.'

Venutius nodded and waved Valas from his hall. Valas bowed low and backed humbly out from the presence of the King of Carvetii. The King and Raigon laughed heartily at his grovelling. The old Druid and his men travelled back to Cartimandua without delay.

CHAPTER THIRTEEN

Drochaid Dia
God's Bridge

THE TREK BACK TO Brigcruim and to Cartimandua, took Valas and his retinue eight sun turnings. He stopped in Stanwix to organise the shaping of the new oppidum. He called builders and stone masons to erect new workplaces, forge, grain stores, animal pens. From the centre of the area, he ordered the shaping of homes, where people could come, build and occupy their own round houses. The protection of such was the fifteen feet high wall built around the circumference of the Oppidum. Iron gates, erected to keep enemies at bay and peace within, were positioned at the four quarters of the site. Another twenty days he gave to the work, and then ventured south to Brigcruim, to see the Queen.

Cartimandua, putting her impatience for news from Carvetii to one side, entertained Maglos until he was ready to return to his home tribe. She ordered carts to carry his gifts and incentives back to Setanti, so when his departure was imminent, she called him into her hall.

'I have a special gift for you Maglos. You are a special ally and one who deserves something from the Queen personally.' Without a blush, she lifted her skirts, flaunting her fanny in front of him.

He moved nearer. 'Oh Queen,' he whispered, reaching out to touch.

Immediately Cartimandua dropped her skirt, and stared at Maglos, smiling with a wide smile. 'This will be your prize when we are victorious over the Romans. I look forward to the day when you take me as your prize.'

'I will hold that thought in my mind, Queen. Until that day, I will anticipate the prospect with eagerness.' Maglos returned to Setanti.

Cartimandua mused, 'will a dream keep Setanti loyal? One look at a fanny, and he is mine?' Her wild heart did not contemplate the promises she so easily gifted.

When Valas returned to Brigcruim, Cartimandua was in the hall, standing by the fire. She watched the flickering flames and did not turn when she smelt the aroma of stale piscine waft into the room.

'Give me the news, Valas. Where have you been and what did Venutius say? Is he in agreement?' Valas bowed low, and grovelling, drew nearer to the waiting ruler of Brigantia. He coughed to clear his nervous throat. 'Well?' quizzed the Queen.

'Queen. Good news from Stanwix. The shape of our grand oppidum is already standing tall.'

'Good. Yes, yes. But what of Venutius?'

'I saw Venutius, who was very pleased with the idea, but wondered if there might be more for him before he gives his authority to you.'

'He wants more, when our country is under threat? He wants more? What sort of a man is he, and more to the point, what sort of a leader?' Cartimandua turned to face the grovelling Druid bent to the ground. Looking at his position, she spit on the ground at the side of him. 'Get up, Valas. What are you doing?' Contempt flowed from her voice.

'I have failed, Queen.'

Cartimandua's face turned blood red. 'Then get back to this…. this… Venutius and make him change his mind. Belinos brought Maglos and Setanti. You can get Venutius and Carvetii. Get him here. I will do the rest, you useless imbecile. And before you go, fetch Donnlugh to me. He can take over as High-Druid in your stead, while you are away.'

Valas did not argue with the Queen, but instead, slithered toward the doorway. Looking back over his shoulder, he sneered. 'I'll be damned if anyone takes the high place which is rightfully mine.'

Donn Donnlugh advanced nearer the Queen who had resumed her position of staring into the fire. Three women hovered round her, ready to bring drinks or food; whatever she desired. A servant Druid in a brown cloak mended the fire, until it flamed high, warming the chilly spring air.

'Queen,' acknowledged the young Druid. He was dressed completely in black. A cloak made of fine linen hung from his shoulders, attached round his neck with an iron *fibula* of a raven, intricately wrought. Under his cloak, he wore black leather boots and a tunic. Round his waist, a leather belt held an iron dagger. A talisman showing the sacred oak tree, hung from a fine gold chain round his neck. He was small, but his presence loomed large in the hall.

The Queen acknowledged the young man. 'Donnlugh. Welcome.' I have heard some things about you, and I know that Valas is inspired by you. I have sent Valas on a special mission, and I want you to stand in his place as high priest until his return.'

'Lady,' bowed Donnlugh. 'It is my honour to serve you.'

'I expect you to advise me when asked, and to shift the *heafan*, if necessary, to see and do what is imperative for the safety and growth of Brigantia. I expect your total loyalty, and should you fail me, your head will be staked. Do you offer this loyalty? Do you understand?"

'Queen, indeed, I do.' Donnlugh did not shift in expression or stance.

'Then you must make your living space in my hall to be near, should I require you for whatever purpose. For now, I would like your advice. I would like you to tell me what you "see" as the outcome of my message to Venutius.' Then, just before Donnlugh left, she added, 'And do not use henbane in your magic rituals, Donnlugh. I cannot stand the smell of rotting fish.'

Donn Donnlugh took his leave, preparing to move into the Great Hall as the Queen had ordered. He set up a shrine to Brigga, and had it positioned to one side of the door to the hall. It was a table upon which he placed a polished bronze bowl, ready for offerings to be left. An iron statue of Brigga was attached to the bowl. She stood in fighting position with spear and hammer in her hands. A chair was placed at the side of the shrine, from which Donnlugh was able to sit and contemplate Brigga as she revealed her visions to him. It was here, hidden under the hood of his black cloak, that he petitioned the great goddess. Sipping *couchen*, in the early hours of the morning, Donn fell into a trance. His eyes remained open, but his body was inactive and corpselike. When the morning broke, he crept toward Cartimandua's bed chamber. She was still sleeping, so he stood by her bed and waited. Suddenly aware of his presence, the Queen jumped with alarm. 'Oh! Argh!' she shouted, startled by the intrusion. 'Ho! It's you. What do you want?' she asked. She yawned, and pushed her hair out of her face so she could accustom her eyes to the black shape in front of her bed.'

'Queen, forgive me but I have seen the journey of Valas in a vision. He was on his way home, and planned to stop at Stanwix, as before. I fear, there has been some little success with the Carvetii tribe. In the vision, he had not accomplished your orders.'

Cartimandua rose swiftly from her bed, agitated by the pronouncement of Donn's vision. 'I told him not to return until he had success. Do I have to do everything myself?' she spat on the ground and marched round the room, agitated with anger.

'If you please, My Lady, I could undertake to speak to Venutius on your behalf.'

Cartimandua, pursing her lips, began to tut. 'Fetch Valas to me, then I will tell you what will happen next.' She covered herself in a gown of blue wool, flouncing the wrap round her body in a show of determination. 'Get the half-wit here. His days are numbered.'

Donnlugh stalked out of the presence of the Queen. His stride, long and slow, caused his cloak to flip behind him. As it swished, it cast a dark shadow of authority, expelled only on his exit from the room.

Cartimandua paced the length of the room several times. Backwards and forwards she paced. With each length her steps became more rapid than the last. Settling was not an option for her. Agitated and frustrated, she swore at the fire, and at the attendants in the room. Then without much thought, she called.

'Fetch Tormaig. Prepare and saddle him. I will ride shortly. Get Camulo and two others.' Turning to one of the Druids in the hall, she called, 'Is the Druid of Brigcruim here? Fetch Lochru. I want him to oversee the continuation of the build while I am away. Get Donnlugh back. Stop him from leaving and tell him to collect weapons; swords and spears, bows and arrows, and to bring them to me on the route as soon possible.' Then to the ladies in the room, she asked, 'Is there any one of you who knows the warrior ways?

One young girl stepped forward and bowed. She was a pretty girl with dark, curly hair tied back from her face. She wore a *feileadh* over braccae, and a brown tunic of woven flax. The Queen touched the tunic and examined the dagger hanging on her belt. 'What is your name, girl?'

'Elora,' answered the young warrior.

'I like your eagerness, and the fact that you are ready to go, young *scáthach*.' Smiling at her, she nodded. 'You also will travel with me.'

The five rode out of Stanwix that evening, riding to beat the arrival of the night, though it was almost upon them. Camulo, keeping pace with the Queen, asked, 'Lady, have you a plan?'

'Yes, Camulo. I am going to meet Valas. I need to hear the reasons for his failed mission, then I need to address the situation personally. It is no good sending Donn Donnlugh after him. I am angry, Camulo. I am angry, and if what I have been told is true, then I will end the life of the wretched Druid who failed me. And then I will end the life of the pompous king of Carvetii.'

'My lady, I would advise that we rest tonight, and that your plan is given chance to ripen before you storm Carvetii. There are five of us here, and only six when Donnlugh arrives. I doubt that Carvetii will fall at such a small attack, even though you are a great warrior, Queen. Let us rest and talk.'

The wise words from Camulo softened Cartimandua's anger. She laughed. 'Very well,' she agreed. 'We will rest at the next farmstead or sept. Let us pray that it will be a place of sanctuary in Brigantia, and not some *spleuchan boke* belonging to some dolt leader.'

By nightfall they reached a plateau on the route over the Peneinz, which commanded a crossing point at the river flowing by Greta Bridge. Dismounting their ponies, they walked a little distance seeing a small, fortified settlement. They advanced to the gate where a woman holding the hand of a young child advanced to welcome them. 'We are a good people; farmers mostly,' the woman said. 'It is not often that five visitors call at our door at this late hour. Will you wait here? I will fetch our leader, Gallagher. He will greet you in a proper fashion.' The party agreed, nodding at one another, seeking for opinion. Cartimandua waited quietly. Soon a tall man dressed in a brown wool tunic, and carrying a wooden staff, met them at the gate. His hooded cape did not hide his baldness, though the lack of hair on his head was more than compensated by the bush under his lip. His moustache was enormous and flowed down to his belly.

'Greetings, travellers. I am leader of this small farming community. There are about thirty of us, not counting our children. I am Gallagher, known as Gallagher-the-Lip.' Stroking his hairy lips, he laughed. 'What is your purpose on this night?' he smiled again. 'Are you wanting beds?'

Camulo nodded. 'Yes, if that is possible. We are travelling to Carvetii, to meet with our emissary when he returns from business with the King there,' he said honestly.

'Are you Carvetii men?'

'No. We are Brigante, and on a mission from the high Queen, Cartimandua. Have you heard of her?'

'Indeed, I have, and we are pleased to connect with any brothers, and for that matter, sisters, who are like us, loyal to our Queen. Enter, and be refreshed,' he said, smiling at the female warriors. He led them to the home of a weaver woman, whose house held bales of wool in every part. A weaving loom stood proudly at the side of the fire hearth. Cartimandua, looking round the house for somewhere to sit, asked if they might all share a meal together. The woman prepared the food and arranged benches round the fire hearth. Gallagher sat with them for a while, chatting about their journey, and the settlements they came from. When the meal was ready, the woman left the house. Gallagher also rose to leave them. He moved to the side of the doorway, until he was obscured from their sight by the curtain that hung across the gap.

The five sat together, eating the meal of cold vegetables and pig meat. They discussed the way they would deal with the mission undertaken by Valas, and which seemed to have failed.

'Queen. Can we call for warriors to join us on the route? They could follow a safe distance, so we do not appear to arrive at Carvetii with war on our minds,' asked Goron, one of the warriors chosen by Camulo for the task.

'There will be a better understanding of the situation when Valas is found,' the Queen retorted, still feeling anger toward the old Druid. 'But, by all means, send one of the men to seek fighters to back up our plan if needed. This all hangs on Valas. We must find him first.' The Queen was determined to evaluate first, before she continued on the road to Carvetii. 'If I have to go to Venutius, I lose some power. He might think that I am weak, and worried. He must come to me, and I must keep the upper hand.'

So, it was decided, that Cartimandua would send Cuinn, the second warrior chosen by Camulo. 'Find the way that Valas is travelling back to Stanwix, so the results of his meeting with the King of Carvetii can be received as soon as possible.' Cartimandua settled into the roundhouse she had been given. Elora, the young female warrior traveling with them, also stayed with the Queen. Camulo was assigned to guard the room in which she slept. Cuinn and Goron were given shelters close by.

Before he could be found by Camulo, Gallagher-the-Lips moved from the curtained doorway and showed himself to Cartimandua. 'My lady. I apologise, but I overheard some of your conversations. I did not realise that you are our queen.' He bowed low, as Cartimandua sat quietly. Then, standing erect her stroked his moustache. 'Queen, if there is anything we can do to help you, we are willing. I have sixteen warriors among my field workers, who are itching for a sight of battle. It would take but a day to pull them off the land.' He bowed again, so low that it seemed even his moustache brushed the ground.

'Very well,' smiled Cartimandua. 'I will speak to my advisor when he arrives and will give you an answer as soon as I can. But I am inclined to accept your generous offer of support.' She smiled at the man and thanked him. That night Cartimandua slept close to Elora. Both had their swords ready. They talked a little about their early exploits while learning the art of weaponry before eventually falling to sleep. Cartimandua liked Elora and planned to give her a place in her new oppidum when they returned there. 'I have missed female company. I will send for Anna when I return. She also will become part of my new Brigantia,' she mused. 'And Raegan. Yes. I have missed Raegan. Gentle kind Raegan. She was like a sister to me, though sometimes she was more like a mother.'

Cuinn set off as dawn blinked, tracking the likely routes to where the waters meet. Cartimandua waited for Donnlugh to arrive. By noon, the Druid caught up with the five, bringing news of fighting on the southern shores of Albion.

'It is even more imperative that Carvetii unites with Brigantia.' Cartimandua, impatient to proceed, picked up her cloak and went to meet the day. Donnlugh followed. The Queen, seeking insight from her new Druid advisor, asked, 'about Gallagher, the leader of this small community. he has sixteen men ready to join us in fight, should we need them. I need your wisdom here. Should I let him join us in our undertaking?'

'Queen, I see that the more of us, the better. I will ask the gods for a sign, to be sure.'

Donnlugh left the Queen to seek an omen before they ventured further. He visited the waters running outside the village. Lifting his hands above his head, he called to the water goddess Coventina. Then, he threw a ring of bronze into the water as a votive offering to her. He closed his eyes, calling to the one who brings life and fertility to the lands. Stretching her hand into the air to receive the ring, she rose from the flowing water. Her long hair, like green sea tangle, covered her naked frame. Bubbling sounds of the river came from her mouth uttering secrets directly to the Druid, before she disappeared into the depth of her liquid soul. 'All is well, Donnlugh. All is well. Thunder rumbles in the distance and lightning will strike like a hammer but beware the one who bargains for himself. He wears the cloak, but not the heart of Brigantia.'

Two days later, Cuinn returned. 'I have news. Valas and his men are stationed at The Bridge of the Gods, not far from here. They are resting on their return journey.'

Turning to the tall leader of the village, Cartimandua ordered, 'Gallagher-the-Lips. Ready your men and follow us as quickly as you can. We head to *Drochaid Dia*, where we will wait for you.' The six departed in haste, riding with speed toward the Bridge of the Gods.

Riding by her side, Donn Donnlugh took the opportunity to whisper in the Queen's ear. 'Beware the one who wears the cloak, but not the heart of Brigantia.'

Cartimandua found Valas, camping by the side of the bridge. She approached him reaching to the scabbard on her back which held her sword. Drawing it, she readied the weapon. Cartimandua called, 'Valas. Have you succeeded in your mission, Valas?'

'I have had some success, Queen. Venutius is mellowing, but I did not get a definitive answer from him. I think he requires half your lands to unite with you. I think if I return next autumn, when his mind is not so much on the battles with the painted barbarians, then I could be successful in turning him.'

'Next Autumn? Lughnasa? How long do you think we have before our land is covered in the enemies from Rome? How many of my people will be raped and slaughtered before then? We have no time to spare waiting for Carvetii to see the urgency of this situation. And I will cede none of Brigantia to Carvetii. Rather the other way round. You have failed miserably, Valas. You have failed your people, my people, our gods, and our lands. You have failed Bellnorix, and you have failed yourself.' The sounds coming from Cartimandua scaled the heights, growing in volume until her voice could be heard over the gushing water and to the nearest farmstead. Like a carnyx, she bellowed at the fellow, until the breath in her lungs gave way.

Valas sat quietly on the stone spanning the stream. 'I would warn you not to rise against me, Cartimandua. I have warred against stronger than you. I have the ear of Venutius.'

With lungs full of anger, the Queen burst forth, 'This is all I needed to know. My suspicions are real. You wear the cloak of authority. You are a Druid of Brigantia, but you do not have the heart of Brigantia. You are self-serving, and power crazy.'

Cartimandua gnashed her teeth. Her body, hot with the anger boiling inside her. 'You smelly power-driven relic. How dare you threaten me. Do not think that I am naïve to your duplicity. I know of your plans to usurp. I saw for myself in Lopocares, when I sent you to seek godly advice on the life of Vello. When you came back and pronounced that he should live, I knew then that he was an ally of yours and you had been plotting with him. Lochru is loyal to me, and Brochfael of Lopocares. You thought I had placed you to oversee the people of Lopocares after the ending of Vello. But Brochfael oversaw your dealings and your treachery. You have rendered yourself no longer suitable for the position of loyal priest.'

She raised her arm against the Druid. His frame began to distort. A green haze grew from the water, covering him from head to toe, until the young Queen could not distinguish the black cloak of Valas from the black serpent rising above the dank malachite ether. Undaunted, Cartimandua began to make her way to the solid vapour as it began to slither, dancing in front of her, daring her to approach. Her company, including Camulo, surrounded her, they were ready to attack the shape-shifting Druid on the Queen's word. Brigante strength grew in the heart of Cartimandua as she approached the mass which hovered high above her. With raised hand like a hammer, she swung her weighted fist, flattening the monstrous leviathan, and knocking it sideways across the stone. It lay there prostrate; stunned. The mist disappeared revealing Valas, depleted on the slab of stone which reached across the river. A gurgling sound gushed from his mouth.

'Lady, I have seen my ending reflected in the water below. Do what you must do, but for the sake of the loyalty I gave to your grandfather, I pray that my end will be swift.'

'How dare you breathe the name of my grandfather. If it were not for his generosity, you would never have been given the position of High Druid.'

Cartimandua took a step nearer to Valas, carefully watching the men who had gathered. She marked their stance, their hands and their faces. 'I pray these men are loyal to me, or this might be my death, and not the end of this snake,' she thought. Every nerve in her body stood on edge in preparation. Stepping onto the stone bridge, she towered over the slimy mass and with one stab and twist of her sword, she cut his heart from his chest. Her foot rested on the fallen Druid, then with one determined thrust she shoved his carcass into the water and under the Bridge of the Gods. The water ran red.

Wiping her wild hair from her face, Cartimandua stalked away from the dead body, leaving the others in the party to offer it as a sacrifice to the gods of that place. Camulo and Donnlugh followed the Queen; her emotions quietened by now. She wiped the blood from her sword onto the edge of her tunic, and asked of the dark Druid, 'Donnlugh. Do you think you can do any better than Valas?' Cartimandua asked him without thought of the life she had just concluded. Donn smiled; his job now secured as High-Druid of Brigantia.

'Then be on your way. Approach Venutius and seek his desire. I need to know what he would accept in order to unite with Brigantia in this assignment… and Donnlugh, make sure that the bargain you strike is one that I find acceptable.'

Donnlugh said nothing but nodded again. Mounting his horse, he was away, with only the flap of his black raven winged cloak to be seen in the distance.

That night, the party made camp a little distance from the death bridge where the body of Valas was lapped by the water. Her act had raised fear in the men travelling with Valas and the fifteen fighters who arrived by the bridge just as night fell. A restrained mix of awe and dread reverberated among them, whilst they discussed the circumstances of the day. 'This Queen, our Queen is not afraid of the Druids. Even they can be cut down by this diminutive warrior Queen.'

'She holds no fear. I would not want to oppose her.'

The hushed talk continued that night and the following day, as they waited for instruction from Cartimandua. Camulo addressed her, using a low voice. 'My Lady, should we go back and wait for Donnlugh to return to Stanwix?'

'I will wait here but a few more nights. Elora will stay with me.'

Sitting noiselessly, Cartimandua stared into the distance, willing Donnlugh to return at that moment. Listening intently, she perked up. Vibration on the wind brought the sound of galloping to her ears. She stood to get a better view of what the sound might be. Cartimandua saw a pack of seven savage wolvers heading toward the bridge. The decaying wet carcase of Valas swayed at the water's edge as the pack ran down. They tore at the limbs and torso, mercilessly eating the food provided by the gods of the bridge.

'It is done,' said Cartimandua, turning her back on the hounds. 'Brigantia is truly mine!'

They camped at The Bridge of the Gods for two days as the Queen waited for Donnlugh to return. She found her impatience growing with each moon rise.

Gallagher's men, rallied for the venture, were also showing signs of impatience. 'We are itching to spar. Lord Gallagher. Show us where, and we will fight to the death.'

Camulo approached the Queen.

'Take them to the villages and septs beyond these hills, Camulo,' she suggested. 'Take any sept that does not belong to Cartimandua. Those that are against us, miserable ignorant scratters - give them as gifts to Gallagher's men. They may keep the tokens and trophies, but the heads must hang outside the hedges of any sept that does not bear my name. Can you do that? I desire that Brigantia is known for victory and power. No one should stand against us at this time.'

But Queen, it leaves you vulnerable.'

Cartimandua smiled at Camulo, then laughed.' I have an iron fist and a hammer hand, Camulo. I will begin my journey back to Stanwix when I am ready. I will be safe until you return there also. Add another tribe or two to the growth of Brigante power. That would be an acceptable gift for your Queen.'

CHAPTER FOURTEEN

RÈITEACH
Betrothal

D ONN DONNLUGH FLEW AS a black buzzard. His black cloak, inflamed with power, carried the young Druid across the Peneinz to Carvetii within a day. Like a streak across the skies he flew, covering the land in a dark shadow. His raptor eye swept the land offering a pandect of the terrain, tribes and fortified places below. Before he spotted Staena, and came to rest within the gates, he had collected enough information to use in his mission.

Approaching the Great Hall of Venutius, he came across Mugh Ruith, who was bumbling along the path, head bent, mouth uttering unpronounceable words He was also heading to the hall.

The Druid code dictates that should a visitant; a Druid bird in transition, arrive and need help, then fellow Druids are compelled to give that aid. Mugh hailed the black cloak. 'Greetings, my fellow,' he said, raising his hand in friendship. 'Have you travelled far? Can I offer any assistance?'

Donnlugh evaluated the enquirer looking up and down the small Druid. Dismissing his chat, Donn pushed past Mugh and advanced under the great entrance of Venutius' hall. Mugh rushed his step to follow the arrogant cloak, venturing inside the hall quietly to observe.

Venutius was sitting at his throne, eating a staked hare. He tore the meat from the bones and picked at it as the oily juice flowed down his fingers and his chin. His jug of wine washed the food down his throat.

Donnlugh bowed low before the King. Mugh noted the flounce, and thought, 'So this one has a show of respect. I don't think he has much esteem. I would trust him about as much as I would drink poison and expect to live.'

Following on the heels of Donnlugh, Eachann entered the hall. Mugh waved from the shadows, pressing his finger to his mouth. He silently moved over to stand by his side. Mugh whispered, 'this should be interesting, Eachann. Listen carefully.'

'And who might you be?' asked Venutius, without looking up from his morsels. Raigon, who sat at the side of the King, rose to his feet. Several warriors stood to attention, grabbing their sword hilts. Comfortable chatter halted. Faces turned to stare at the intruder.

'I am emissary from the High Queen of Brigantia. I am Donn Donnlugh. High-Druid of Brigantia. I seek an audience with Venutius of Carvetii.'

Still not looking up, Venutius continued, 'What happened to that other fellow? What was his name? Ah! *Grody Saithe*, I think….'

Raigon snickered.

Donnlugh continued. 'Lord. On his return from seeing you, Valas, who was High-Druid of Brigantia, presented your response to Queen Cartimandua,'

'And what was her response?'

'He lives no more. Your response was not found satisfactory to Her Greatness. She had an iron hand and a hammer fist. She is wild but shrewd. Be warned. She will have her way.'

'Is that so?' asked Venutius cocking his eyebrow. 'And what pray does she know of us that she can send a young Druid such as you, against my might?'

Donnlugh spoke calmly and directly to the King. 'She has Druid information which shows weak points across your lands. She has the heart to take Carvetii, and the ability, should she need to. Be warned. You can unite, or her iron wildness will descend and decimate you and your people before you have had time to think about the alternative.'

Venutius glared at Donnlugh. 'What sort of Druid would dare to stand alone yet bring this threat to my halls?' A nervous titter escaped his mouth. 'But also,' he said under his breath cautiously, 'what sort of a queen would end the life of her high priest so callously? What sort of queen would send one man into the halls of a warrior king without a second thought? Maybe it is better not to underestimate this wild horse.'

'You are a wise king, Lord Venutius.' Donnlugh responded.

After several moments, Venutius turned to Raigon and beckoned Eachann. Turning his face so that his lips could not be read, Venutius questioned both for wisdom. 'I think we should retire to discuss this, and seek the gods for wisdom,' uttered Raigon. Mugh moved into the circle as this conversation took place.

'I agree,' he offered.

Venutius, Raigon and Eachann turned to stare at the interrupter, then all three returned to their whispers, ignoring the little Druid. After a few moments, the King raised his head and called for the attention of the folk in the hall. Indicating to one guard by the door, he called, 'You. Send the emissary away for the night. Give him food and a bed. I will see him in the morning.' Venutius waved Donnlugh away. To the rest of the household, he waved his hand again, 'and all of you – go! Only my advisory Druids are to stay.' Donnlugh turned to follow the guard leaving the hall.

When the hall was quiet, Raigon responded swiftly. 'Have his head and send it back to the 'wild queen.' Show her we are not a tribe to be threatened by a woman.'

Eachann shook his head. 'No. Wait. I think there is another way.'

Venutius was keen to listen to Beli Mawr so quietened Raigon. 'Let us listen to all suggestions before we run.' Looking at Eachann, he nodded for him to continue. Raigon snorted but kept his peace.

'Venutius, you are enlarging Carvetii northwards. The Pehtas raid all along the borders of your land, but they also raid along the northern borders of Brigantia. A link with Brigantia could only further your resolve to expand Carvetii. Raigon suggested as much, last time that old man came as emissary from Brigantia.'

'I did, indeed.' interrupted Raigon, waving his head from side to side.

Eachann continued, 'Do not ask for Brigante lands. This queen will be reluctant to give her power. But rather, ask for the hand that holds them.'

Venutius closed his eyes momentarily. Then looking at Eachann, he said, 'I think you may have come up with a plan. I will offer to marry Cartimandua. I will be king at her side. That way, she does not cede any Brigante lands. She will like that. And I do not cede any Carvetii lands. I will manoeuvre her heart into giving me her power. Yes. I like that idea. Eachann. What can I lose?' Nodding in agreement, the Druids moved to retire. 'I am tired now, so we will sleep on it, and should the gods appear in the night with further enlightenment, then add that to the thinking before I see this Donnlugh, fellow in the morning,' yawned the King.

Venutius slept heavily that night. When morning light broke, the Druids were already at his call. 'I am in no mood to think about treaties, or marriage or anything else except my need for a woman,' he said. He called for one of the waiting lasses and did not show his face at all the next morning. Two further mornings delayed the High-Druid of Brigantia from closing the bargain. Those two days made the black Druid impatient with the Carvetii king. He paced outside the room of the King, frustration growing with each step.

Eachann entered the kingly bedchamber as the light was waning on the third day. 'Lord, we cannot delay this Druid any longer. You must make a decision and make it by tonight. The gods have agreed that this is an acceptable offer, and one you should agree to, and move forward with.'

'Which gods, Eachann? Which god spoke?'

'Mugh heard from Taranis, My Lord. He spoke in the thunder. Mugh said he heard him acknowledge the meeting of our two tribes. He said the thunder revealed this —*With strength and courage to overcome, the fire will bring the word.* Then, when Taranis had spoken, the embers of the fire burst into flames. We take that to mean good things, King.'

'Then call the Brigante Druid. Let's get this sorted,' said Venutius, kicking the woman from his bed, and rising to dress. He walked into the hall wrapping his cloak round his frame. Eachann followed. Raigon and Mugh Ruith were already in attendance, sitting with Donn Donnlugh near the fire. Without warning, Venutius called to Donnlugh. 'Tell your queen I would have her hand. Then and then only will she hold my kingdom, and I will hold hers in equal share. If she agrees with this offer, then our two lands will unite against our common enemies.'

Donnlugh bowed. 'Lord King, I think my queen will agree to this plan. But one thing.' Not hesitating for a moment, Donnlugh insisted, 'but Cartimandua will hold the crown and you will be King Consort. This is fair as she will be bringing the most to the table of unity. Her lands extend much farther than Carvetii, and her armies exceed any that you hold. If you will agree to this, I am sure that the Queen will also be moved to agree.'

Venutius remained quiet while he regarded these conditions. He glanced at Eachann and Mugh, who nodded their agreement.

Raigon did not voice his disapproval, but taking a deep breath, his nostrils flared, and his lips pursed.

'I agree to these Brigante terms,' assented the King.

'One final thing, Lord. My Queen required immediate confirmation of these proposals. Can I tell her that you will come to her, and can I tell her when?'

'Rest overnight, good friend, while I discuss with my priests and advisors, the timing of such an awesome event. The answer will be yours in the morning light.' Venutius smiled.

At that moment, a warrior hastened to interrupt the scene, shouting. 'Lord King, Lord I come from the border of our lands. Two nights ago, the Pehtas raided the northern area breaking through the borders from Selgovae. They are slaughtering our people on their move to take Staena.'

Greeting the warrior, Raigon spoke. 'Take a breath, friend.' He offered the warrior a seat. 'Give the details, but first, refresh yourself,' he said. Taking the cup of mead offered, the warrior drank and regained his breath.

'There are forty or more of the naked blue *bodach*. They leave behind them a trail of death and fear. They are five; maybe six days away from Staena.'

'Then gather my army, Raigon. Eachann, bring your fire and

insight too,' responded Venutius.

Raigon turned up his nose, and interrupting, he cautioned the King. 'Lord King, would it not be better if you sent Eachann to meet this Brigante queen, to appease her, while we fend off this outburst? If he can hold her, and even seek her help, then she will not think your lack of appearance is against her.'

'This urgency must be dealt with first,'

'Yes, Lord, But Eachann is quite able to hold the situation in Brigantia, while we uphold our borders.'

'Very well,' agreed Venutius. Turning to Eachann, he said, 'These are my orders. Take Mugh Ruith if you so desire, but go in my name, and appease the wishes of this queen, until such times as I can join her. I ask for her hand, make sure she accepts it.' As an afterthought, he added, 'take gifts. Take things that a queen would like to receive. Make sure that my part of this bargain is received well.'

Raigon sniggered.

Donnlugh, on hearing this decision, responded. 'Lord Venutius, if you will. I will go ahead of your messengers and notify the Queen of your intent. She is keen for you to respond because of the growing threat coming from the south of Albion. I will tell her of your desire, and if she wishes, I am sure she will send men to help you in your battles so that you can be united together as soon as is possible. I will leave after I am rested.' Without waiting for an agreement, Donnlugh left the Great Hall of Venutius without sanction. The following evening, he began his return to Brigantia. Rising into the night sky, his hawk eyes found the road back to The Gods' Bridge, to Stanwix and to Cartimandua.

Brigantia was showing the first signs of summer; the farmed lands outside the oppidum displayed tall grains of wheat, barley and flax softly swaying in the breeze. Although Ostara had come and gone, the apple, hawthorn and blackthorn were still showing a magnificent display of blossom. Bees began to enjoy the nectar from the flowering bean plants, and cabbages were ready for the first pickings. The lushness of the early summer boasted a good harvest to follow. Cartimandua called for the people of Stanwix to gather in celebrating Beltaine. It was to be prepared in time for her return to the new Oppidum.

Fires ready for roast boar and pig were built round the perimeter of the open circle at the centre of the oppidum. Benches and tables were brought into the circle. Food was prepared. Mead, ale and wine in plenty were ready to serve the people of Stanwix. Some travelled from Brigcruim for the celebration, and some gathered from wider afield. Everyone wanted to admire the new royal house and catch a glimpse of the new queen. The largest cauldron that had ever been forged was lifted onto the fire of the Great Hall. Such a display of riches had not been seen before.

Cartimandua was in her hall when Donnlugh returned. The roof had been thatched. The walls had been covered in wattle and daub, and screens had been erected round the hall, giving a sense that there were many rooms within the one great space. The screens had been painted with pictures of warriors, hunters and bhaírds using musical pipes and drums. The 'rooms' used as kitchen, sleeping areas and servant quarters had screens painted with foodstuff, fruits, and trees. The floor was made of chalk which had been rammed in layers and then covered in a top of *chert* collected from the northern regions near the home of Bellnorix. A giant hearth took centre place. Over the fire stood a large spit. Two poles were suspended across the fire, held up by iron legs. One pole had a turning handle at each end ready to roast a full boar or stag, and the other pole held the giant caldron large enough to take two men. On either side of the fire hearth, tables and benches were lined up.

Stars and moons painted on the front of a raised platform placed opposite the door. This dais held the newly fashioned iron throne, positioned centrally to display the full splendour of the power seat. The ironsmiths had created it from long iron slats, weaving them into a basket shape, and fabricating the seat and legs in such a way that the whole structure appeared twice as big as it was. The iron was polished till it shone like gold. Cushions were made of the softest woven purple and red dyed wool. They made the whole throne look regal.

Two warriors guarded each end of the dais. Both stood facing the doorway opposite, where curtains hung either side of this main access. These drapes were pinned back by two enormous iron hooks at either side, and under which two large wooden chairs were exhibited. On either side of these chairs, a box held weaponry, spears, swords, arrows and the like.

Around the back of the throne and across the entire width of the room, plush reds and blue pleated linens had been hung from the roof beams. This created a private area behind the throne where Cartimandua slept. The guard standing on the right of the dais protected the only access from the throne hall to the Queen's bedroom. This room was screened and lined from beam to floor in thick woven linens. The floor was polished flint. At one end of the oval shaped bedroom, furs and skins lay on a mattress of feathers which had been stuffed into a large pillow. Another screen had been built round it for extra protection from any intruders. A single chest sat in the centre of the space, upon which Cartimandua had placed her royal torc and items for her hair. A hand mirror of polished bronze and a comb made of bone had carefully been laid there too.

On the back outer wall, hidden by the chest and curtained screen, was a small hatch giving an escape route if it was ever needed.

When Donn Donnlugh returned, he entered the Great Hall at Stanwix for the first time since the Queen had approved the completion. He looked round, also with approval. 'My Queen. This hall is spectacular, and I am proud to be one of your loyal subjects. Your ability to view a new world is astounding,' he encouraged, spinning round the hall, admiring it all. The Queen was delighted to see him, but more eager to hear the record of his mission. Rising from her throne, she moved to greet the returned High-Druid.

'Well?' she asked impatiently. Donnlugh, flounced his cloak wide, bowing low as the Queen approached.

'Queen. Venutius sends his good wishes and hopes that you will be delighted with his proposal. He does not ask for your lands, or a portion of them even, but rather gives you his lands if you will accept his hand in marriage. You will remain Queen of Brigantia, of course.' The black druid bowed. 'Carvetii will become part of Brigantia, under your joint rule. You will retain the high rule, and Venutius will become King Consort. If you agree to this, then unity between Brigantia and Carvetii is assured. You will become betrothed to Venutius as soon as you agree. The treaty will be confirmed.'

Cartimandua fell silent. 'Marriage? Hummm,' she thought. 'This is a new idea. What is his reputation? 'What does this Venutius look like, Donnlugh?'

'He is dark skinned and rugged but even featured… and muscular. He is about thirty-five-year cycles, maybe thirty-six, with only a few face lines. His ears hold rings, as does his beard. His hair is thick and black, with no balding. I think, my lady, he has a kind heart, though he is known as a brave warrior. He can be ruthless in battle, but he is loved by his people. They see him as a fair-minded king.'

'And your wisdom, Donnlugh?'

'Lady. I think you would do well to join with this man and Carvetii, before the floods break against us.'

Cartimandua thought, 'I wish Camulo was here to advise too, though have I not been able to control many men by just lifting my skirts?' Straightening her posture, she breathed in and then, nodded. 'Yes. I agree. Send word back to Carvetii of my agreement and that we are from this day, betrothed. The marriage will take place on his arrival at Stanwix.'

Turning to look around, she called for Elora. 'Elora, we must plan a wedding!' she said, allowing herself to feel a little excited about the prospect. She began to dance in a circle round the fire. But then with further questions, she returned to Donnlugh. 'When will Venutius come? Is *Litha* the right time for our nuptials?'

Once again, bowing low, Donnlugh replied, 'He has a pressing concern which delays him. There has been a breach of his boundary and Pehtas making their way to his oppidum at Staena. He will send envoys to you with his word on the pact for unity, but until he has secured the situation at Staena, he feels he cannot leave. There is hope that you, Queen, may send warriors to support him, now that you are agreed in the promise of betrothal.'

Cartimandua stopped her excited movements, to consider this edict. 'Yes. Send men. Send some men from Vincobancio and Brigcruim, and some from Taftefield who have little to do here now that most of the oppidum is completed. Send them in my name. The sooner the Carvetii boundary is re-established the sooner we can be united against the real enemy of our lands.'

On the eve of the festival, the Queen stood before her people. Awe struck the crowd as Cartimandua began her oration. 'Hear this, my favoured Brigante people. It is good to come together to enjoy the season of Beltaine; a season with such promise and passion; of fruitfulness and plenty. The gods have been good to us these last few years. But our future could look very different should the despicable Latin army get a foot hold in Albion. They have tried before to take our wealth, our silver and bronze. They have taken our men as slaves and our women as their whores. They have plundered and killed in the name of their gods, while bringing destruction to our own altars and our way of life.'

Cartimandua held her tongue for a moment before proceeding. She surveyed the crowd and smiled. Raising her voice over the heads of the listeners, and her fist in the air, she shouted with passion. 'My people. We will not let this happen again! We will be more than prepared to fight against them. Their threat is real, and so it is with the purpose of strengthening Brigantia, in determination against these invaders, that I am betrothed to Venutius of Carvetii. Our marriage will bring a unity that also brings strength in battle – for battle is before us. Make no mistake.' Taking a deep breath, she uttered, 'But we will be victorious! Brigantia, Brigantia, Brigantia,' she called. The voice of the people followed the chant. 'Brigantia! Brigantia!

The people began to clap in excitement as the celebration of Beltaine commenced in earnest. Music began to play across the oppidum. Bhaírds were singing songs of glorious battles, as young girls tossed their skirts in the air or sat on the knees of the warriors, then cajoled them to join in dancing capers.

Camulo returned.

'Lady, I come with good news.' He shouted, taking strides into the throne hall where the Queen had returned to her seat.

She stood immediately to greet Camulo, rushing to his side, and holding him close. 'Get drinks,' she ordered, waving her arms at the servants and the wine. 'Bring food.' Soon Camulo and the company of returned warriors were celebrating with people in the whole of the oppidum. Ordering a chair to be placed by her side, Cartimandua requested, 'Tell me your story Camulo.'

'We left The God's Bridge and journeyed into Shackles, a small sept where a few farmers and their families dwelt. No difficulty arose as the company moved in, and within the hour, the small village had agreed that they would belong to Cartimandua's Brigantia. But there was tell of another small village not too far away from Shakles, whose people did not acknowledge the banner of the wild pony. We ascertained that this sept was a little larger than Shackles. We then headed to the area known as Lunehead. The terrain was mountainous. Some sheep wandered the rough wild open moorland. As we neared the farmstead, a few warrior-like men exited their roundhouses, and stood facing the visitors. Another called loudly from within. 'What do you want?'

Gallagher, sitting on the step of the dais with his elbow balanced on his knee, interrupted the story. 'Then I shouted back at them. "We have come on behalf of Queen Cartimandua, to add you to the growing numbers of Brigante in the area." Well, there was no immediate response. That made my blood boil. Insolence of the highest order. I couldn't allow that.'

Gallagher stood and swaggered, acting out the scene. 'One shouted back at me with insolence. "Add us to her number?" he called.'

Gallagher glanced at the Queen, and added, 'then he spat on the ground.'

"We do not need to be counted," he said. "There are but a few of us here. We farm and guard the sacred lune stones up ahead of our town, but we will fight if anyone dares to take from us our homes, and livelihood."

'Then fight you must,' I answered. I shouted to them, 'Cartimandua will have your loyalty, which includes your homes and your families.' Gallagher huffed, puffing his chest out, and continued to bluster in front of the Queen. He looked round the hall surveying his audience. Catching the eye of Elora, he smiled, and bowed his bald head.

Camulo picked up the story. 'So, we descended on the small village, fighting with anyone who dared to come against us. Three men lost their heads. Others fled. Going from one end of the village to the other, we dragged the women and children, capturing and imprisoning them along with a few old men and boys and any who stood against us. We tied them together in a line, and we have marched the long trek back to you here at Stanwix,' explained Camulo. 'We have succeeded in bringing more villages and hamlets under the power of the Brigantium Queen because of the capture of these Lunes. Each place we reached on our return to Stanwix, saw the consequences of perfidy. They fell at our feet. The news of our great warrior queen has travelled wide.'

Gallagher spoke up again. 'All have been given chance to think about their futures …and their end.' He turned, beckoning the Queen to follow him. 'Come, see,' he said. Making his way to the gate of the oppidum he called to his guards to bring the prisoners in, so the Queen could see them. Cartimandua went along with Gallagher to the gate, whilst the line of Lune captives marched past. Shaking in fear, all bowed the knee to the Queen on their arrival.

'Their faces speak of hunger and terror,' thought the Queen. Aloud, she said, 'But I need allies, not enemies. These people could be strategic in our war against invaders.' Surprising them all,

Cartimandua ordered, 'take off their fetters. Give them warm clothing. Bring them to my table.' Turning to the freed people, she said, 'Tonight is a celebration. We are celebrating my betrothal to the High King of Carvetii. I want all the people of these lands to come together in a sense of brotherhood. Together, my people, we will prepare to oust the real enemy of Albion from our lands for ever. Long may the spirit of the High Celestis Brigantia move on these shores, and on this land. Our great goddess and holder of great power has breathed into her people an indestructible determination to overcome. Together in a spirit of unity and strength we will overcome! Come my fellow Brigante, whether you are visitors from Brigcruim, Taftefield or indeed Lune Head; eat and enjoy the company here at Stanwix. Tomorrow you may go home. I promise you safe transport for your loyalty to Cartimandua, and Brigantia.'

That night the high spirits continued until the candles had died and the torches had burned low. The freed people of Lune hugged one another, and then hugged the people of Brigantia.

'This queen is a forgiving queen,' they mused. 'This queen is worthy of our loyalty,' they said. 'We are proud to be Brigante!' they cheered.

Cartimandua was pleased with the festival, and all who pronounced loyalty to Brigantia. 'But in all of this, I feel lonely,' she thought. She called to Camulo. 'Camulo, can you find Anna for me? Bring her here. Also, bring Raegan, my nurse. She has known me since I was a child. I want her here now.'

She turned next to Elora. 'Elora, come to me tomorrow. I miss female company. I need a friend and would like to talk to you. I want to plan my marriage, and I want you to help me.' Elora moved closer to the Queen and hugged her as a sister might.

'It would be my honour, Lady.'

But Cartimandua could not shift the shadow which had settled over her head. She began to retire for the night, making her way to the back of the throne, and to her private room. She laid her torc and white cloak down carefully on her bed, then taking a black cloak from a hook on the wall, she unlatched the iron pin which held the little wattle frame between her and the outside world. Crawling through this opening she scrambled into the fresh night air. Cartimandua surveyed the skies as a bolt of light chased the last glimmer of day and the stars shone in a cloudless sky. She gasped at the beauty of the expanse. 'Surely my gods are with me tonight,' she thought. The urge to gallop away to the hills where the wild ponies ran, became an acute need. Cartimandua crept round the outer walls of the hall, until she came to the shelter where Tormaig was stabled. Quietly she stroked him, whispering in his ear, 'All is well. All is well.'

Gently placing a woollen cloth over the back of the animal, the young queen mounted her steed and away. The wind blew her chestnut hair, like a boat sail tossed by the ebb and flow of the wild spirit of the ocean. Her cloak billowed up as the wind took it from beneath her, and then down, almost scraping the ground in the gallop. She felt the wild freedom she had experienced as a child, riding onwards toward the moors and the moon. Harder and harder she drove the pony; his feet galloping, lifting his rider in the air as they soared. Sparks flew in every direction, ignited by the iron pony shoes on the flint-like path. Onwards they rode into the night; her path lit only by the moon and stars.

'I have missed my wild rides, Tormaig,' she called. 'I feel one with the four spirits: the air, water, earth and fire. They call me to the wild depths, from whence my soul was birthed. This is wonderful!' she laughed, feeling the wind in her hair and the shadows lifting from her lonely heart. They rode on, toward the rushing sound of water. 'This must be the river that is called Tés-ti,' she imagined. Listening, above the sound of running water, she thought she could also hear hooves following in her path. She did not want to stop to investigate. She felt reckless and impulsive. Discretion flew to the wind. 'This is enchantment, Tormaig,' she said. 'The water calls, and I will answer.' She squeezed his sides with the calf of her leg, and Tormaig gathered speed.

Suddenly the horse halted, almost recoiling at the approach of a ring of trees by the side of the river. A flicker of light shone brightly from within the wooded ring, rising like dancing faeries, into the midnight sky. Cartimandua, startled, patted her horse to calm him, and with a soothing tone, spoke low. 'Woaw. Softly Tormaig.'

Inside the boskage, two campers sat round the fire. Three horses were tied to one of the surrounding trees. The water from the Tés-ti slicing through the wood, touched the side of the camp as it ran eastward. At the sound of the horse approaching, a sword was drawn. Cartimandua, realising she was unarmed, nevertheless, rode into the thicket. 'The gods are on my side,' she thought. 'I have nothing to be concerned about on this night.' The moon rose high as she pulled her hood over her head and entered the circle.

CHAPTER FIFTEEN

CELESTIS BRIGANTIA
Divine Goddess

THE ABRUPT BALK OF the galloping Tormaig made the flames from the fire flicker, creating a wall of smoke. Immediately everything was hidden by the darkening haze. For moments, nothing could be seen. Cartimandua began to cough, drawing the horse out of the immediate area. As the smoke settled, she could see one of the travellers lying on a bag of straw, as if sleeping. The other had risen from his squatting position to approach the young woman. Tormaig backed off, whinnying, preparing to bolt. Cartimandua held him steady. Her eyes were weepy from the woody smoke. 'Stay where you are,' she ordered the man approaching her. 'Who are you?' she asked.

'I might ask you the same question, Lady.'

Cartimandua felt no animosity in the reply, so began to dismount. She looked at the man standing in front of her. 'A few years older than me, I would say,' she assessed. She examined him from top to bottom. He wore the warrior cloak of a Druid, white with blue linings of wool. Cartimandua relaxed. The cloak could not hide the bulging muscles underneath the cloth. 'Nice body,' she mused. 'I wonder what he would look like if he was naked' He had his sword strapped to his back, but he did not attempt to draw it. 'He is a ready warrior,' she appraised. He had a white tunic under the cloak, held with a belt of leather, and a dagger and axe fastened to it. His hair was wrapped in a white *capote*, tied tightly round his face. The Queen continued to evaluate the good looks of the man before her. 'He has a noble stand,' she observed, warming to his presence. She studied his face and noted the piercing blue eyes. 'They seem to burn straight into my soul.' Flustered by his returned glances, she averted her eyes and asked again, 'Who are you? What is your business here?'

'We are travellers from Carvetii, on the King's business.' Eachann answered truthfully.

Cartimandua began to piece together thoughts of ambassadors from Venutius and guessed that these two might be they. She snatched another look at the warrior, but his piercing eyes met her sly glance. She felt her blood rise, and her face redden.

'What is your business?' she asked flatly.

'Lady. I do not want to appear rude, but this is private business for the ear of the Brigante Queen only.'

Cartimandua thought, 'If I tell him I am she, I have no way of proving it. I might be putting myself in danger. I will keep quiet. In any case, at least until I have more proof that they are who they say.' She moved toward the fire and made to sit. Eachann quickly found a woven cloth and placed it by the fire. She sat. 'Who is this?' she asked, indicating with a pointed finger, toward Mugh, who had not moved at her arrival, but continued to sleep.

'This is Mugh Ruith, a friend and one who travels with me as I seek the Queen of Brigantia. He is 'seeing' in the flames. He may join us soon.'

Cartimandua contemplated the shrivelled Druid snoring, and

wondered how he might 'see' anything through closed eyes, one of which looked scarred and deformed. She lifted her eyebrow.

Removing the hood from her head, Cartimandua allowed her hair to fall. Like molten gold, the deep burnished copper hues shone in the soft firelight. Eachann gasped. 'What is this? I am bewitched,' he breathed silently. His mouth opened and shut again. Eachann stared at the woman before him. 'What beauty is this?' he whispered under his breath. 'I am under a spell. I cannot think straight.' They sat in silence for several moments, neither knowing what to say.

At last, Eachann coughed a little, cleared his throat, and asked, 'I have wine, and food. Would you like some?' He picked up some kindling, throwing it onto the fire. Flames burst a flash of light, then settled into a gentle flicker once more. Light shimmered over the hair and face of Cartimandua. Behind her was blackness, except for the starry sky silhouetting her frame. A halo of stars caressed her head like a castled crown. Eachann made a move as if to bow in front of her, seeking her hand to kiss it. She held her hand out, twisting and cupping it, just as the moon showed itself.

'She holds the moon, like a globe, in her hand,' whispered the warrior to the night. 'I do not want to shake this vision from my sight.' Speaking softly, he asked, 'are you a goddess? Am I dreaming? What magic is this?'

Cartimandua, not knowing how to receive his compliments, asked nonchalantly, 'Give me your name, traveller.'

Bowing in introduction, he lowered his gaze and with stuttered breath, Eachann whispered, 'I am Beli Mawr. Champion warrior and Druid of Carvetii.' He glanced up searching the Queen full in the face, but the face he surveyed remained expressionless. Before he could rise, Cartimandua was on her feet, moving back to within reach of Tormaig. With one movement she mounted the pony and with an easy flick of the reins she turned, riding swiftly back into the night. In an instant she disappeared from Eachann's view.

Silently out of the shadows, Camulo followed.

Cartimandua made her way back to Stanwix, more slowly than her venture out. The warmth of the night shrouded the young woman, and she had no desire to break this feeling. Scrambling back into her bedroom, she thought of the adventures of the night. 'Why is my heart singing?' she thought, allowing her voice to rise in the enchantment of the remembering.

'Lal, lala,
What is this stone I called a heart, now melted in the midnight sky?
La…lalaa.la'

Cartimandua's mellow voice sang out, allowing her feelings to escape into the darkness. 'I feel elated, yet sad at the same time,' she thought. 'I am undone. But is it a dream? Did I really meet anyone tonight? The path was full of shadows and mysteries. I think I might have dreamt this.' The young queen turned over and settled, she said 'I will deal with this at first light.'

Camulo listened at the back of the throne hall to the soft voice of Cartimandua. When he was sure she had fallen to sleep, he also went to his bed.

The following morning brought sunshine to the whole of Brigantia. The passions of summer and the fruitfulness of the season broke out of its spring hope, and into the full light of purpose. Beltaine bowed. Eachann rose early. Shaking Mugh, he called, 'Wake now. I have not slept, but I know it is time to go.'

Mugh sat up, dazed by the urgency of Eachann's shaking. 'What's to do? What is the need of today?' Mugh asked, slowly rising from the ground. He made his way toward the river, wanting to relieve himself, and wash the night away. 'Too much wine, I think,' he chuckled. 'I had the most unusual dream.' He bent down to the water. An arrow whizzed past his head. 'What was that?' Mugh shouted. Darting up, he called to Eachann. 'Danger, Eachann. I have just avoided death! Hide.' Eachann jumped instinctively to hide behind the trunk of one of the trees. Mugh crawled to the tree, keeping a look out with his one eye for further darts. 'The hairs on my neck tell me that the bowman is hiding some distance away, just beyond the circle of the camp.' He pointed in the direction of the bowman. Eachann stooped low. The two sat at the base of the tree for a little while.

Another arrow flew past them, targeting the next tree. Eachann carefully and silently crawled toward the horses, slowly untying his own bow from the backpack of the third horse. Calming the animal, he blew delicately into his ear, then stroked his mane. Soundlessly he pulled an arrow from the pack, then crawled back to Mugh. 'We have one chance here, Mugh.'

Mugh, frozen to the trunk, remained hidden. When Eachann had the bow loaded, Mugh ran from the tree to the next. Briefly the assassin stood proud of his hiding place, the poised arrow pursuing Mugh. Eachann swiftly stepped out and with precision, shot his shaft. The arrow hit. The hunter dropped and his bow dropped with him.

Mugh flew to the fallen man, throwing a restraining spell in his direction. '*Na diathan a cheangal an duine laidir,*' he called. 'May the gods bind you, as death binds.' The man stiffened. His muscles, rigidified by the protruding arrow in his shoulder, took the shock of pain. Eachann grabbed him, swiftly tying him with ropes round his feet and hands.

'Notice his boots, Mugh?' asked Eachann.

'Indeed.'

Mugh searched the area, checking for other bowmen.

Kicking the boots, Eachann shouted at the captured man. 'Who are you?' The man remained tight lipped. Eachann kicked him again. 'Nice boots. They are like mine. Where did you get them? Did you steal them?'

Mugh interrupted. 'Man, you are going to die, so which would you sooner have; a quick death or a slow one?' Mugh took hold of the arrow, still extending from the point it had entered the man's shoulder and twisted it. Blood flowed from the wound and the pain took its grip. Startled birds flew from the branches above the camp as his screams broke the still morning air.

Twisting in agony, the man found some boldness momentarily, 'I have orders from my Lord. He would have your heart, Beli Mawr. A heavy price is offered for it. One way or another, he will have you out.'

Facing the captured man, Eachann asked, 'who is this lord? How many of you pursue me?'

'I will tell you nothing of that. I am dead whether you kill me now or whether I return. My failure to end your life brings the end of my life, whichever way. But my lord knows of your parentage, and he will make sure that your lineage is ended, once and for all, High-Druid of Carvetii.'

'I knew it. I knew it,' uttered Mugh Ruith, who began to pace round the hunter, kicking him each time he circled. 'We should have never come here. Now what are we to do? I was looking forward to the festival of Beltaine and then peace throughout Litha. I was looking forward to a piece of venison on our arrival at Stanwix, and now we have to watch our heads for arrows,' he chirruped.

'Tell me who your master is, or I will end your life here and now,' threatened the Carvetii champion.

'Never.'

'Then may the goddess of the water make the decision for your life.'

Eachann dragged the man toward the river. Mugh stuffed a piece of linen in his mouth, as Eachann rolled him over and into the water. They watched his body dipping in and out of the current, and as it disappeared down the flow.

'We must be extra careful, Mugh. We will travel away from the open paths, and along the riverbank for a while. Keep your eye open, and your wits about you,' Eachann warned, mounting his horse. They took a winding route to Stanwix, and Cartimandua. 'And you, my little friend, must help me to find out what is known of my mother and father.'

Keeping her voice low, Elora called lightly to Cartimandua, 'Queen. Lady, I have brought you food to break your fast.' She moved the curtained wall to one side and entered the bed chamber. She was carrying a basket filled with the most luscious of fruits and berries. She handed to the sleepy queen soft rolls of rye bread, still warm from the fire pan.

She poured fresh milk into a wooden cup and placed it on the chest, just in reach of the young queen. Elora bobbed, a curtsey of respect. Cartimandua sat up and began to enjoy the morning banquet.

'Elora. I have a job for you. I have a task outside Stanwix which requires my attention, but I am expecting visitors who will call for me. I want you to pretend that you are Brigantia's queen. Receive my visitors, and act as if you are me.'

Elora stared at the Queen. 'No Lady. How could I possibly be you? I cannot act as a queen. I cannot,' she protested.

Rising from her bed, Cartimandua began to pull a white tunic from the wooden chest. 'Put this on,' she ordered, 'and pretend you are me.' Elora obeyed. Elora began to act, as she had seen Cartimandua act. She held her head up and spoke with some authority. Laughing together at the pretence of Elora, Cartimandua smiled. 'That's good. It will allow me time to do what I need to do, and before you know it, I will be back. I will warn the guards to follow my instruction and to play along with you. Oh! And one more thing. Here is my ring. It is the signet ring belonging to my grandfather. Guard it with your life but wear it this morning.'

Cartimandua dressed quickly, tucking her skirts up and making braccae in her usual way. She put boots on her feet, and a tunic over her shoulders. 'Get me a brown cloak,' she shouted. Leaving the hall, she fetched Tormaig. She rode in a frenzy through the gate of the oppidum, retracing the route she had taken the night before. The clearing in the trees by the Tés-ti was unoccupied, except for a magpie sitting on a branch of one of the oaks. From this lofty position, his beady eye followed her every move. Cartimandua searched for evidence of the two travellers, but even the fire left no sign. 'How can that be?' she asked herself on her journey back to Stanwix.

As she arrived back at the Great Hall, she heard voices.

'I have come as emissary from Venutius, Lady,'

Peering round the curtained doorway, Cartimandua saw the little Druid from the night before. She sighed. 'Thank the gods I did not dream it. This is the Druid from last night.' Then she noticed Elora, sitting on the throne. Taking a step back out of sight, Cartimandua listened to the conversation, but could not resist a giggle.

'And what have you to say?' asked Elora.

'I believe your High-Druid, Donnlugh reported back to you, so you know that a treaty has been offered. I am here to ratify the agreement and send word back to Venutius of your decision. Then he will come to Stanwix where the marriage will be sanctioned, and the union between Brigantia and Carvetii will be complete.'

Elora nodded. 'Yes. I understand that I am to be married to Venutius, who will become my King Consort, and rule by my side. He will retain Carvetii, and I will retain high power over Brigantia. This I have understood.' Elora reiterated all she had heard from the halls and from Cartimandua over the last few days. Cartimandua craftily glanced round the room, looking for the other warrior Druid she had met the night before. There was no sign of him. She blew her lips out in a sigh. She turned to leave the hall, but in her turning she bumped straight into Eachann. He had been standing behind her, watching her. 'Oh!' she gasped. 'It's you.'

'Ah,' he said. 'It's you.' For one moment their eyes met. As if in answer to unasked questions, a flash of lightning provoked sparks across the sky. They glanced up to see the blaze as it burst across the *heafan*, followed by a thunderclap that shook the hall. Heavy rain started to fall, running within a few moments like a river down the main path of Stanwix. Eachann pulled Cartimandua out of the puddle, which was developing from the sudden deluge, and into a nearby shelter. Sodden, Cartimandua removed her cloak, and shook the water from her unruly hair. The rain caused her untamed tousle to curl and expand even more. She shook her head again and began to flatten the mass with her hands nervously. Eachann removed his cloak. Shaking the droplets of rain from it, he discarded it on the floor of the shelter. She followed his eyes as they moved over her face and body. She admired his muscular arms as he removed his wet headwrap. The glory of his golden mane fell magnificently round his shoulders. He took hold of Cartimandua's hands to stop her movements, then lifting her chin so their eyes met, he smiled kindly. 'The rain will stop in a minute. It's just a cloud burst.'

Cartimandua hesitated but stepped back from the strong arms of this stranger. Bringing herself to task, she said, 'I must get back. I will be missed.' Before Eachann could engage with her again, she was gone.

Cartimandua crept back into her bedchamber while the conversations continued in the hall. She lay on her bed, allowing time to enjoy the feelings which the warrior had sparked in her body and mind. Thinking of his soft voice and then his hands touching her face, she retraced his movements, caressing herself. She slowly lifted her skirt and stroked her groin. 'I am hungry for him,' she thought, moving her hands downward, feeling the intensity of her need. She fingered her pearl until sparks of pleasure shot through her body. 'Why does it feel hard to control my feelings when I am near him? My heart stops when we touch.' She lay there for a while, savouring the sensation of ecstasy before she became aware that time was passing, and Elora was still sitting on the throne. The voices continued from beyond the curtained screen. She deliberated a while, then straightened her clothes. She left the chamber, ready to take over her duties again. Then, she saw him. Eachann stood not far away from the secret entrance. He was talking to Donnlugh. Cartimandua hid in the shadows, listening to his voice.

'Yes, High-Druid. Mugh Ruith is with the Queen now, explaining the treaty we agreed. Venutius will join us as soon as he is able, but until then, I will stay with the Queen and follow her orders.'

Cartimandua smiled from her hiding place.

'Then we will find you suitable shelter, my lord Beli Mawr. Follow me.' The champion duly obliged. Cartimandua crept after them, determined to find out where he would sleep that night. The shelter was not far away from the Great Hall, and soon the champion was settling into his room. Cartimandua continued to hide in the shadows until Donnlugh left, then she crept to the doorway. Holding her breath, she lifted her hand to move the curtain from the side of the opening. She peered inside. A hand reached from within and grabbed her wrist, pulling her into the darkness beyond.

'Who have we here?' asked Beli Mawr, pulling the wrist high so that Cartimandua could not escape his grip. 'Ah! Ha!' he said, laughing a hearty laugh.

'Let go, you brute,' she shouted. 'Let go.'

'I will, my little goddess. But first….' He pulled her toward him, holding her arms behind her till she could not move. Wrapping his strong arms under her waist, he lifted her feet off the ground. His mouth touched hers. She struggled to free herself, but her resistance was half hearted. She felt the strength of his body and felt the weakness of her resolve. She stopped struggling and turned to meet his lips. He allowed her to feel the ground again, but the intensity of the kiss burned in her heart.

'I feel the fulmination of his nearness,' thought the Queen. 'He sends tingles all over. It is like lightning touching my soul.' She met the gaze of the warrior and moved closer to him again, until she could smell his redolence. He ran his hands up and down her arms in a soft caress, tickling her till goosebumps appeared. She could feel the sensation under her tunic. Her nipples became raised and tingly. The urge to remove her tunic became a strong desire. Not wanting to lose the moment, Cartimandua placed her finger across her lips. 'Shhh,' she said, showing with her finger for Eachann to follow her. She made her way to her secret opening at the back of her hall and climbed through. Eachann followed. The voices in the hall continued their conversations, as Cartimandua, gazing steadily at the man in front of her. Easily she removed her tunic allowing it to fall to the ground. Eachann stood, watching every movement she made. She revealed her young breasts, cupping them gently to display their fulness. She untied the braccae belt. The cloth folds fell loosely round her legs. She moved nearer the hulky warrior. Lifting her chin and face, she offered her lips to touch his again. Explosions of desire ran between them as their lips met and their souls tangled together.

'I don't understand what's happening,' the young queen thought, 'but I have never felt this way before. I cannot resist. The passion is too strong.'

Running his hands up and round the shape of her waist and hips, Eachann felt her loosed skirts. He hitched the skirts high, moving his fingers underneath the pleats to touch her thigh. Cartimandua unfastened the pin holding the skirts. They fell silently to the ground. Naked now, she pulled Eachann onto her bed feeling her legs weaken. She leaned backwards, as Eachann untied his leathers to reveal the need growing there. He caressed her body, her neck, her legs, then entered her.

'This is not what I have experienced before,' whispered Cartimandua into the ear of her new lover, as she gave herself to him. Together they rode the passion, driven by urgency but gentleness till they were consumed in each other. The notion that this was special floated in and out of the head and heart of Cartimandua.

Expended, they lay silently, savouring the moment of fulfilment.'

The volume of voices from the hall grew, invading the minds of the two in hiding. Then Eachann lifted himself up to rest on his elbow, as the voice of Mugh filtered through the curtained wall.

'We have come to inform you that Venutius will travel to Stanwix very soon, in order to ratify the union between our two tribes. But Taranis has spoken,' Mugh shouted. 'I heard it in the thunder just now. I know my sight is poor, but my hearing is attuned to my god. He spoke and …'

Mugh's voice tailed off into the mist of love, as Eachann returned to his new love. Cartimandua snuggled into the strong arms of the warrior. She remained silent, but her mind raced. 'What should I say? I don't want to break this moment, but I have to tell him the truth. I am betrothed to Venutius.' Shuffling on the bed, she turned to get up. 'Damn!' she cursed.

Mugh was speaking again. His voice raised in panic, he shouted, 'Fetch Beli Mawr. I need to know what is happening here.'

Eachann, began to dress in haste. As the Queen made to leave the room via the little opening, he grabbed her arm. 'Lady, whoever you are, you are mine. This, this… this thing we have here ……' He stumbled for the words, then almost spat out, '*Anam Cara.*'

'Yes,' she responded, reaching for his hand. '*Anam Cara.*'

Cartimandua left the room circling round to the main doorway of her hall and waited by the curtains. Wrapped in a dark cloak, she shuffled unnoticed into the chair by the door. Elora was still sitting on the throne, and the little Druid was kneeling in front of her.

'I must speak to my fellow traveller. Eachann Beli Mawr,' he said, though with less volume this time. Elora stood, looking round the room she asked, 'Does anyone know where he is? Fetch him to me,' she dictated.

Eachann strode into the hall. On his approach to the throne, he bowed in front of Elora. 'Queen,' he bowed. 'Forgive me for being late to this meeting. I come with my friend and lord Druid, Mugh Ruith, who I see has already introduced himself.'

Mugh's eyebrows were furrowed, his face was troubled. Eachann went to help him up from the ground he had sunk into. 'What is wrong, Mugh?' he asked.

Mugh began to mumble incoherently. 'There was a rumble warning... shock...a shaking. Seeing...now I understand. I have been shown. I have seen.' Then, looking at Eachann, Mugh spoke clearly. 'While you were gone, the thunder roared. The lightning flashed and, in that moment, I saw!' Mugh covered his ears. 'The pain.... oh! the pain... from the thunder.

'What did you see, Mugh?' questioned Eachann, gently.

Mugh stared directly into the eyes of his young ward, and solemnly uttered, 'I saw the seed of Brigantia spilled over the land. The seed was scattered into the land and began to grow. Then I saw the spirit of Brigantia, spread across the land, like a fire that could never be put out. It was the eternal flame of our celestial goddess Brigga; Brigante goddess, and queen. Like an apparition of sacred knowing - directly from Eòlas, I saw the goddess rise up as fire. She held the moon in her left hand and a warrior spear in her right. On her head was a halo of stars around a crenelated crown. The crown burned with an eternal flame.' Mugh took a deep breath as this edict left his mouth and travelled round the room. Gasps of amazement and astonishment rippled from the people in the hall and around the throne. Eyes searched for Cartimandua. Mugh continued, pointing to Elora, 'and I heard the voice of Taranis clearly telling me that this lady...' he waved his finger in the direction of Elora, '.... this lady is an imposter. She is not the queen we seek.'

As if a spell had been broken, the people in the hall began to giggle and laugh out loud. Cartimandua rose and walked forward. She made her way to her throne. Her Druids, warriors, guards, and others kneeled before her, acknowledging her arrival. Elora departed the throne as the Queen stepped onto the dais and took her position on her seat of power.

Looking to Elora, Cartimandua smiled. 'Our ruse is discovered, Elora.' Turing to Mugh and Eachann, she introduced Elora to them. 'This is Elora, my warrior, friend, and helper. Forgive us for the fun we made on this occasion.' Then turning to Eachann, with eyes burning into his, she said, 'I am the one you seek. I am Cartimandua, Queen of Brigantia and the one to whom Venutius is betrothed. Our lands will be united in our battles against common enemies from this day forward, and Venutius will sit by my side as King after our lives are united in marriage.' Unable to hold her gaze longer, without blinking she focussed on the doorway, as she pronounced this message.

Eachann dropped his jaw and gawked at the Queen in disbelief. She held her glance, not allowing her emotions to manifest. One solitary tear traced her cheek. While she spoke, she asked herself, 'What have I done?'

CHAPTER SIXTEEN

CRIDHE IARAINN
Heart of Iron

THE MARRIAGE BETWEEN CARTIMANDUA, Queen of Brigantia and Venutius, King of Carvetii was planned to take place at the festival of Litha, the summer solstice. The ceremony and rituals were ordered with great precision. Elora worked with Gallagher to arrange workers to line the route to the ancient standing stone circle at Lune Head. This sacred place was chosen by Cartimandua to signify the new friendship between her and the people of Lune, as a tribute to that union. In return, and as a gift to their queen, the new allies built a bower in the centre of the circle, one raised high enough so the people could see the rituals being performed and join in celebrating the nuptials on the day.

The women took charge of the main preparations for the wedding meal, and Camulo was eager to help with the kitchen arrangements of foodstuff. He ordered hunting parties to fetch stag and boar, partridge and pheasant, swan, and duckling. Donn Donnlugh was tasked with arranging the formal proceedings. The ladies of the hall took it upon themselves to assemble the wedding gown and cloak for the Queen. Women of good needlework were called to use their skills in the design and embroidery of the regal attire, while others collected wild berries, flowers, and branches to adorn the bower, the tables, and the Queen.

Mugh and Eachann stayed away from the Great Hall, avoiding the Queen whenever they could, until the day that they heard the *carnyx* sound, announcing of the arrival of Venutius at the gates of the great oppidum. Lavish welcome plans burst into reality as the King and his adjutare entered the gates. People carried boughs of oak and willow. They were strewn on the ground in front of the regal cavalcade of horses, chariots, and stag helmets as they passed into the main thoroughfare of the great Brigante town. Others waved flags that had been daubed with pictures of stags, in honour of Carvetii. Ribbons of red, white, and blue tied to branches in the trees, flew in the summer breeze. A short distance from the doorway of the Great Hall, drapes of green and yellow hung from screens. There was clapping, and banging of drums, whistles, and tambourines, along with bagpipes and the like, all sounding off in the open green in the centre of Stanwix. Signs of glee and merriment consumed the oppidum.

Venutius dismounted and walked straight into the hall. 'Where is the Queen, soon to be my wife?' he asked without ceremony.

Cartimandua appraised the man; her eyes shot up and down his frame. She stood in greeting but said nothing.

Venutius in one glance, surveyed the riches displayed round the hall, and smiled. 'My Queen,' he said, approaching the dais where Cartimandua stood. He bowed, a token movement, before he stopped and stared at the Queen. 'Turn, Highness. Let me see what I am getting for our union,' he said, circling with his finger.

Cartimandua sat back upon her throne, and looking beyond the King who hovered over her, called, 'please send the King to me when he arrives, and do not let *plebians* into my hall uninvited.' The two guards at each end of the dais moved toward the King. Taking him off his guard, they each grabbed his arms and lifted him away from Cartimandua. She rose from her throne and stared at the red face glaring at her. 'Oh! King,' she simpered. 'I do apologise. I thought you were some rude *sleekit*. I now see you are the one we have been waiting for.' With a nod from the Queen, the guards dropped their hold.

Venutius pushed the guards away. Straight faced, and serious, Cartimandua addressed him. 'King Venutius of Carvetii. I do not enter this union for my own gratification. There is nothing in me that would require such a joining, though you are a handsome man and known for your fairness and victories in battle. However, I am aware that our enemies are one and the same. The latins threaten with a great threat, and with great capacity, so I am informed. Because of this, and only because of this, I am willing to join with you against our common foe. I am not willing to give my soul to Carvetii without an undertaking from you that we will stand together against any invasion of our lands.

I will be treated as the queen I am. I am not a whore who might give you gratification for a moment. I will be your queen first, and then your wife, and as such I demand your respect, if not your faithfulness. Have we an understanding?'

Venutius grinned. 'I like your guts and spirit,' he spouted. 'I have heard of your fiery spirit. Legend is already weaving a tale of your wild heart. I like a challenge.'

'Have we an understanding?' she repeated.

'Indeed. Queen.' Venutius bowed low, still grinning at the Queen.

The following day, the Druids led the procession from Stanwix on the two-day journey to the standing stones at Lune Head where the marriage rites were to be declared. The prepared spits, roasters, cauldrons, and foodstuffs were loaded onto carts. Other carts were filled with casks of mead, ale, wine, breads, and sweetmeats fit for the regal wedding. Every cart in the sept was used to transport linens, blankets and goods deemed necessary for the making of shelters and teanta by the families joining in the celebrations. The warriors, wearing the full battle armoury; helmets, shields and swords, rode on ponies, also decorated with battle bits and bridles, colourful saddle blankets and ribbons. The wives and children of the warriors rode or walked at their sides. The charioteers riding two abreast, filled the carriages with food for their horses and dogs, and followed the procession out of the great gates of Stanwix. The bhaírd musicians, story tellers and general working groups, walked behind. Then came the vanguard of Venutius, Raigon and the Carvetii stag warriors, riding high on large ponies. Eachann rode as one of the Carvetii. Mugh rode by his side.

Camulo, Elora and the Queen's household brought up the rear parade which surrounded Cartimandua riding her beloved horse, Tormaig. Finally, the Queen's warriors and charioteers guarded the heels of the procession.

Heading to the great river Tés-ti, they followed the route advancing to the crossing at *Cerveltune*. Once they passed over, they headed to the northern bank overlooking the mighty waters. They planned to set camp on the plain where a small, fortified sept stood. The people of that sept had already prepared for the arrival of the regal parade, and gladly opened their gates to their queen and her subjects.

Early sunrise roused the pageant. The steep climb to the ancient stone circle, took them to the crossing of the Tés-ti at Street Ford, through flax fields and small farmsteads, then northwest in the direction of Cotherstone. The amount of baggage and chattels being transported made the gradual ascent laborious, but the expectation of the celebration before them brought energy to the travellers. They arrived at Grassholme meadow where for the second night they camped high up on the rocky ridges, a distance away from the watery peatland. The meadow below was alive with curlew and lapwing, and all manner of wading birds enjoying the water from the river Lune. Blanket bog, heathers and orchids grew as wild as the queen who marched upwards on her wedding day. The sound of bees enjoying the fruits of the wildflowers was drowned out by the commotion of excited babble from the people adventuring on to the circle of *maenhir*. As the sun balanced on the Peneinz summit, and began to shrink behind the ridge, the stone circle though not large, stood proud. Then night followed. The blackness set free a myriad of stars in the summer sky winkling above the people as they slept.

Before the sunrise, Donn Donnlugh, covered his usual black vestment with a white priestly cloak, and set off to the sacred place of ceremony. The stones marked the ancient boundary between Brigantia and Carvetii; an appropriate position for the uniting of the two tribes.

The wild moorland leading to the standing stones was difficult to walk on. The track was made of soft mosses and turf, which grew in clumps. Scattered all around the track were large flat stones, some half hidden under the damp tussock sedge. Ancient rune engravings told of more primordial habitants that once occupied the region. These flat memorial tablets spoke of the gods, makers of an older humanity. They spoke of the Eòlas wisdom gathered from the stars above, the moon and ancient understandings.

The Druids following Donnlugh in procession, fell into silence using every breath to conquer the difficult terrain. Each touched the stones to feel the power of Eòlas, then offered praise and prayer to their personal god. The sound of the prayers created a bombinating drone which spread across the landscape like a swarm of wasps, then settled again into silence.

Raigon walked directly behind Donnlugh. The warrior Druids, seers and judges walked with the educators and philosophers of the groves. They in turn were followed by the bhaírds and healing ovates. They all marched to the single beat from the drummers; their differing-coloured cloaks swinging to the rhythm of the solo strike. As the people began to wake, they heard the thrumming. Scrambling to follow, they assembled into a mishmash of a crowd, eager to fall in line so as not to miss the nuptials.

Venutius mounted his horse, and with Eachann at his side, he rode on.

'Wait for me,' called Mugh Ruith. 'He doesn't think of me. I should be with Raigon in the order. So should Eachann, really. But I suppose he is the King's champion still. Must rush. Must rush.' Mugh hurried to catch up with the two. Chasing at his side was Vellocatus, the second champion of Venutius. Taking a side each, they flanked Venutius and Eachann. Warriors sprang to position, Carvetii and Brigante fell into line behind the King. All rode to Lune Head, and to the standing stone circle.

With Audigus Raigon by his side, the High-Druid of Brigantia, Donn Donnlugh, entered the circle at the south point of the sacred place. He walked erectly to the west stone and stood with his back against the maenhir. He faced east. The Druids took their positions by each of the other stones. The people stood outside, jostling for a good position so as not to miss any of the day's excitement.

The constructed bower in the centre of the sacred ring had been topped with summer flowers; the smell of their scent drifted through the air. Rush, oxeye, corn cockle and the honey smelling bog pimpernel had been laced with ferns and small branches of green. The place was ready for the Queen and her betrothed.

Venutius entered the circle just as dawn broke. Eachann stood by his side. All was ready for the arrival of the Queen. All became silent and motionless as they waited.

The summer sun began her ascent. Cartimandua began her approach. She rode to the hallowed maenhir on the back of Tormaig. Her bronzed hair held back loosely with a gold and red ribbon, fell wildly around her face. A twisted thread of gold metal crowned her head. Her gown of white and red flowed almost to the ground, shivering in the morning breeze. She wore the *torc* of Brigantia, and a gold filigree brooch on her shoulder. Her arms were bare except for the bangles and bracelets adorning her wrists and arms, and on her finger, the signet ring of Bellnorix. Her waist, like her hair, was tied with gold and red plaited ribbons, and her shoes were the softest leather, stitched with beads and patterns of flowers and leaves. Elora rode by her side, holding to display the Queen's red cloak delicately woven with golden thread, so it sparkled in the summer sun.

As the Queen rode toward the stones, the Bhaírds; the keepers of traditions and memory; the minstrels and musicians in their robes of dark blue, began to sing haunting melodies. The euphonous sounds appeared to weave in and out of this world and the other, catching the breath of the summer morning. These sweet melodies invoked dreams of blue skies, golden days, and love. They vibrated in the ear of the bride, but Cartimandua could only think of Eachann.

'I feel like I am riding to my death. If it were not for my own Brigantia, I would not be doing this,' she pondered sadly and silently. Stoically, she jutted her chin out. 'For Brigantia,' she resolved.

The early sun rose slowly. The bright shining fingers of heat hit the top of the east stone, sending rays directly across the circle to Donnlugh. Bathed in glory for one or two moments Donnlugh appeared deific. He opened his arms to receive the acclamation from above. The sight sent a gasp around the people. 'What magic!' the people gasped in awe. 'He is indeed the High-Druid of our people, and judge of us all,' they whispered. Donnlugh held his arms higher to receive the praise and welcome the day.

The musicians continued to sing famed ballads and songs of praise to their glorious Queen, and to the King of Carvetii. Behind the bhaírds and outside the henge, the Queen's warriors stayed their horses. Twenty footmen walked holding spears, while selected charioteers also walked the path toward the marriage place. The folk of Stanwix, still jostling for position, were eager to find the best viewing spot to witness the ritual tying of hands; a sign that Brigantia and Carvetii were now one.

Venutius stood under the flowering *pàillean,* waiting for his bride to appear. He smiled when he saw her arrive at the stones. As she dismounted Tormaig, he turned to Raigon. His broad smile filled his face. 'This could have been so much worse,' he said in a tone of satisfaction. 'And her riches far exceed my own.'

She approached the bower and stood at the side of Venutius. The sun continued to rise, shifting the golden glory to light the bower under which the King and Queen now stood.

Cartimandua acted as if she was made of stone; her heart made of iron. She did not smile. 'I will do this for my people. I will do this to bring us security, but I do not do this for love.'

Instantly, the sun rose higher, pointing phalange of gold and red into the sacred circle. The full impact of the beams rested on the golden locks of Eachann, bathing him in majesty. Cartimandua caught sight of him, and gasped. Her heart fluttered. Her legs felt weak. 'I must not look at Eachann,' she thought. 'I must not acknowledge him.' She glanced round to see if anyone else had noticed the godly phenomena that had taken her breath away. She wanted to look again at the shining one but dare not. Her heart throbbed. Each time she thought of him, she found her eyes drawn to the warrior. Her mind raced. 'Look away. Look away. I am undone,' she thought. 'I long to touch him, his hair, like fire spewing fingers of gold. I long to feel him.' She made herself turn away. 'Stop. Stop it.' She scolded herself. '…Boiling fingers of flames,' she thought. 'His fingers…'

'So now you belong to each other,' Donnlugh was saying.

As if waking from a dream, the Queen glanced at the man who was now her husband. She could not bring a smile to her cheeks, but stilted, she allowed him to hold her hand as ribbons were tied round their wrists, a symbol of the tying of their souls, and the tying of their tribes. Cartimandua felt sick.

All celebrated throughout the day and the night, using the shelters and trappings erected around the great stone circle especially so the revelries could be continuous. When the marriage formalities were over, Cartimandua walked into the teanta specially erected for her and her new husband. She felt faint and nauseous. Once back in the shelter, Venutius moved toward Cartimandua. 'My wife. this is good. I think we will retire,' he said, patting the furs scattered by the fire. He grabbed her hand and began to pull her onto the bed.

'My Lord,' responded Cartimandua, 'There is nothing I would like more than to be with you,' she lied, 'but I am faint through lack of food. It has been a long day, and I did not break my fast this morning, I was so excited to be your wife. May we not eat first?' She asked. 'Drink, Husband. Celebrate.' She poured a cup of wine and handed it to him. There is sport tonight. Cock fighting by the sound of the shouts. Why don't you go and enjoy the exhibition?'

'Indeed. And then we will retire.' Venutius glugged the wine. Cartimandua refilled his cup.

Discreetly Cartimandua called for Elora and whispered in her ear. Elora left without attracting any attention, and shortly a messenger arrived, bursting with information. 'King. Lord Venutius. I have news from the borders near Birdoswald. Swarms of aggressors from the northern regions have amassed there and are moving to take our land. We need your direction, Oh! King. And fast,' he said, without drawing breath.

Cartimandua leapt up. 'Venutius, you must go. Take your men and some of my men with you, but do not delay. This is important. We cannot have an uprising at this stage in our union.' Her voice sounded urgent and concerned.

Venutius also vaulted. 'Get my horse ready. I ride immediately.' Looking at his new wife, he said, 'I will be back, and I will take what is mine.' He reached for her hand, and holding it he kissed it, then clicking his heels, he turned and left.

Cartimandua slept uneasily that night. Relief had spread over her like a warm river as soon as she settled under the furs by the fire. But her dreams were filled with feelings of foreboding. All at once images of golden hair and hands offering comfort, reached out to her. Then dark shadows overwhelmed the corners of her mind, snatching the hands away. Imprisoned in the thick darkness, she knew there was no escape. When she woke the following morning, a dull pain pervaded her head, and sadness penetrated her heart. Tears filled the back of her eyes as she took measures to start the return to Stanwix.

Donn Donnlugh entered the Great Hall of Stanwix calling, 'My Queen, a messenger from Textowerdi has arrived bringing distressing news. There is trouble on our northern borders. It spreads from the boundary of Carvetii, to where it meets the boundary of Brigantia. The Pehtas are raiding north of Taftefield. The painted people are thought to be coming south through Votantii and hitting Brigantia, raiding and killing our farmers and farmlands. What would you have us do?'

Cartimandua rose from her throne. 'Gather the warriors. We will not allow our borders to be breached. Urgency demands.' Eachann and Mugh entered the hall as the Queen gave her orders. Turning to Eachann, she asked, 'Champion of Carvetii, do you return to your king?'

'No, My Lady. My orders are to stay with you until your husband, the King returns. I am at your disposal.' He bowed. 'Give me your orders,' he said, flatly.

'Go with Donnlugh. Prepare with the warriors. We ride at first light.'

As the light dawned on a summer day in Stanwix, Cartimandua proceeded out of the high gates, followed by warriors and riders, charioteers and *saighdear-coise,* a mix of men and women fighters. The count was eighty in all who waved farewell to their families and loved ones knowing that they might not return and knowing that the gods may call them to a higher place. On orders of Cartimandua, they travelled to Taftefield with the intention of using that as a base, from which to mount a counterattack on the nuisance. They stopped only once on the way, to rest the horses and to eat at the side of the running Cong Burn. Cong offered a midpoint between the two Brigante septs; Stanwix and Taftefield.

The place was barren, except for a small herd of *aurochs* roaming the poor moorland, looking for graze and a few wild ponies munching on moor-grass and gorse. The travellers sat to eat. Cartimandua watched the ponies, averting her eyes from Eachann. He approached Cartimandua. 'Lady,' he said gently. Cartimandua turned her eyes to look at him. 'Lady, I offer my apology.'

'For what? Are we not Anam Cara?' she ventured. 'Is what happened between us of no consequence?'

'Lady,' he repeated. 'I am between this world and the other. How can you be mine? You are married to my lord Venutius.'

Cartimandua began to weep. Pain shot to her chest. She grabbed the fabric covering her heart, and screwed the cloth in her grip, in agony. The pain did not subside; anger built inside her. she drew a deep breath. Tears stung her eyes. She wiped the water away with the back of her hand. Through the pain she blasted, 'You will do my bidding, Eachann Beli Mawr. I am queen and you have your orders from Venutius to stay with me till he returns,' she spat.

Eachann moved away from the Queen, standing for a moment as if frozen to the spot. 'Excuse me Lady, but I answer to no one. I choose to whom I give my loyalty, and my loyalty lies with my lord king Venutius. Because of that loyalty, I honour you, my Queen. Make no mistake why I will be loyal to you,' said Eachann.

'Then go. Stay with the warriors. Do not show your face to me again,' she screamed.

Eachann nodded his head in obedience, and left Cartimandua. She witnessed him leave, her lips quivering at the corners. A magpie flew across her line of vision.

Searching the scene, she called for Elora. Elora came to the side of the Queen. Without a word passing between them, Elora hugged her. 'Stay close, Elora,' Cartimandua said, composing herself. She mounted Tormaig and the company quickly followed, continuing their journey.

The messengers had travelled swiftly to arrange safe shelter at Taftefield for the Queen and her army. The people jubilantly opened their gates to Cartimandua as if she had come for a festival and not a war. The old hall of Bellnorix had been prepared for her arrival, and that evening the warriors of Brigante ate and drank together celebrating the victory promised. Cartimandua was in no mood to celebrate, so calling for Camulo she asked, 'My friend. Will you find Anna for me? I do not know where she is, though I hope she will be not far from Taftefield. Can you make discrete enquiries and report back to me? Also. Fetch the woman called Raegan. She is the one who kindly cared for me as I grew.'

Camulo left Cartimandua to obey her orders. All around her, Druids and warriors enjoyed the conviviality. Elora was among them. Cartimandua called for her to sit by her side. 'Elora, tomorrow I wish to go out as a triumphant queen. Prepare my battle armour, the sword and axe. Tomorrow I will show these insolent marauders the consequences of dishonouring the spirit of Brigantia. I will show the world that the soul of Brigantia will bow to no one.' In her heart, Cartimandua thought, 'and I will show Eachann Beli Mawr that he cannot use me then walk away.'

Sitting high on the back of Tormaig, Cartimandua waved the army forward, to Votantii and the pestiferous painted people. They made their way to Water Gates Head where the most fordable point of the river Tinea gave access beyond. On the banks at this ford, they camped and waited for signals from the scouts as to the whereabouts of the offending tribes, and any news mustered secretly from the offenders. The Druids at Textowerdi sent secret messages of support and places of shelter for Cartimandua and her army if needed. 'We are here to support your venture. We will continue to attack these pests, but we are grateful for your help,' they said. 'It is a growing nuisance, but with extra power, we will send them where they belong: to the other side of the border or to the abyss!'

It was three days before Camulo arrived at the camp. His search for Anna, the sister of Bellnorix's wife Riganta had been successful. 'Queen, I have found Anna, and she is willing to meet with you on your return from this expedition.'

'That is good, Camulo. I will return by Taftefield to speak with her.'

The moon had turned its full cycle when Mugh came to Cartimandua. 'My Lady, I have been praying to the gods; to Brigga and to Taranis. I have understood that the people we seek are ready to raid the septs lining this river on the northern side at Trewhitt, and that some have come together to raid the small Brigante farmsteads at Tecket and Teppermoor. And there are others. Troughend and Wardrew too.'

'And when you were enquiring of Taranis and Brigga, did they give size or weaponry?'

'Yes, Lady. In the vision I saw small farmsteads of maybe ten or twelve people, excepting Troughend and Wardrew. They are trading septs and have grown quite considerably. Obviously, they would be lucrative storehouses should they be captured. Together it might amount to around one hundred and fifty, maybe two hundred souls.'

'Call Donn Donnlugh and the Druids. Call my warrior *braint* too. Contact the chief Druid seated at Textowerdi. They will support us in this. We will have strategies found to deal with these pesky raids,' ordered the Queen. The Druid and advisors assembled to discuss the information given by Mugh. They gathered round Cartimandua, sitting on the ground at her feet. Eachann silently crept into the shadow of the doorway, and crouched, so as not to be seen.

'We have five areas to deal with,' assessed the Queen. 'One leader to five depredator units could cover these five areas. We have eighty or so warriors and fighters. That means…' While she worked out the count of men she would send to each place, so they could act simultaneously, Donn broke in.

'…We could send twenty men including three leaders to the smaller septs, and thirty each including leaders to the two larger trading septs.'

'Yes, and the leaders would have charge of at least ten each of the people in the septs, to protect them, while making sure that the enemy raiders do not get away with their lives,' Mugh added.

'This is a good plan. Donnlugh, you head up one group and head north toward Teppermoor. When you have victory over the raiders, make your way to *Corioso* and wait. Camulo, you head up another to Tecket. Call for Gallagher, He is capable. He can take Trewhitt. We will travel together until we reach *Corioso* where we will separate. I will travel with the larger groups and move on one of the two trading stations. Who else have we, strong enough to take a lead at my side?'

Mugh lifted his voice, 'We have the champion of Carvetii, Lady. He awaits your instruction.' Cartimandua fell silent.

'Yes,' agreed her Druid advisors. 'Yes. He is more than capable.' Consensus rumbled round the Druid cabinet.

'No.' said the Queen flatly. The room fell silent. 'Mugh Ruith,' she said, looking at the little Druid. 'Ruith. You can do it.'

'But Lady, this is senseless. I am strong in hearing from the gods, but I am blind and weak in battle. Eachann is a champion. Surely, he should be the one to do this.'

Mutterings and opinions flew everywhere. 'Of course, it should be Eachann Beli Mawr. Of course.'

'It would be stupid to think otherwise.'

'Why would he not be chosen?'

'We have the use of the champion. Why not use him?'

Feeling trapped, Cartimandua tutted. 'Very well. Send for Beli Mawr too.' She did not speak or glance in his direction as the finer points of the plan were relayed to each of the leaders. As the camp was made ready for departure, Eachann came to Cartimandua.

Standing by her side, he bent to whisper in her ear. 'Lady. Mandua'

Cartimandua swung round, flashes of anger escaped her eyes. She glared at him, then turning away, she spoke with venom. 'How dare you call me Mandua! I am your queen. Remember your place. I may have to ride with you, but I do not have to acknowledge you.' Her anger brimmed out of her voice, like a growling hound ready to pounce. Pointing to his horse, she registered his dismissal. As Eachann walked away, Cartimandua could not stop the tears falling from her eyes. 'Pah!' she raged, wiping her nose and the tears. 'Control yourself,' she thought.

The company rode on from the camp heading to the ford from the banks of the Tinea. From there the company split from the men heading north to Trewhitt. The others rode on to *Corioso* before splitting into the different directions. Mugh rode with Eachann, and Elora rode with Cartimandua. The two companies of warriors and fighters followed on horseback or in carts and chariots. The full summer sun had hardened the ground making the journey across the country easier for the chariot wheels and the horses. They made good time and only rested a short while to gather information from local sources. Separating from the group led by Eachann, Cartimandua directed her platoon in the direction of Troughend.

Moving to ready her fighters and herself, Cartimandua tied her skirts into braccae. The warriors, both men and women, removed their tunics and cloak, not wanting to be hindered in the fight by any loosening of the garments. They battled naked, except for their boots and dyed emblems marked on the upper part of their bodies. The Queen also removed her tunic. Starting at her nipples, with wode dye, she painted a spiral round each breast. Fastened across her chest, her sword belt decussate. She donned the regal torc of her position round her neck. Her tousled hair fell loosely over her shoulders. With her sword in one hand and her shield in the other, she was ready for battle, and ready to meet these bedecked alien people who dared to defy the boundaries of her land.

The Brigante soon discovered the camp a few hundred strides outside Troughend where a small farmstead was being used as their base. It seemed as yet, that the Pehtas had not entered the trading centre, but were busy making some of their own strategic plans, whilst drinking outside the farmstead. Silently moving close to the base, Cartimandua listened to the conversations of the raiders bragging about their intentions. The language they used was unusual, but some of the words she understood. The Pehtas waved their arms about laughing and jeering. 'We will have their lands easily,' they seemed to say.

'What audacity,' she whispered to Elora, who stayed by her side. Looking round to make sure that she and her men were well hidden from sight, she signalled for them to be ready to move.

'This is our target' she whispered, spying as they overlooked the site. Holding her sword high, she steadied her army. Without further warning, Cartimandua shouted to attack. 'For Brigantia and for victory,' she called, swinging her sword as she hurtled toward the camp with the thirty warriors following. The Pehtas were surprised by the sudden onslaught, and with little chance of escape they scrambled onto the only route they could take. The cries and screams from the fleeing pests, and the sound of the hooves and chariots following, warned the people of Troughend of the approaching conflict. Unaware of the closeness of the Pehtas, the Brigante of Troughend, gushed from their homes, shouting and collecting spears and axes, and running in bewilderment. But that confusion met the raiders moving toward the sept for safety, head on. They were trapped by the people of Troughend in front of them, and the Queen and her army, behind. Cartimandua descended on the fearful blue arses in their attempt to escape the wrath of Brigantia.

As the fighting continued at Troughend, simultaneously the other trading posts and settlements were being freed from the threat and danger of the enemy. Their attempt to breach the borders of Brigantia was thwarted. Other raiders were slaughtered in the areas where they had edged or sidled into the land belonging to Cartimandua.

Laughing, the Queen took the victory of Troughend, ordering a celebration to take place in every sept and hamlet from the victory field across to the Gate Head. 'Send messengers back along the route,' she ordered. 'Send bhaírds to sing the victory song. Tonight, we will return to Corioso and celebrate our victory,' she cheered.

The bhaírds did indeed sing of the Queen and her prowess on the battlefield; of her fearless attack on the raiders, and of the treasures she gained from the people. They thanked her for saving their homes and families. Twenty-two heads were collected from Troughend and taken as tokens. The bodies were left swinging on trees for the carrion birds to pick at.

That day, as the army rode back to Corioso to meet with the others, Cartimandua was both elated and disturbed. 'I wonder how Eachann is,' she thought, trying to dismiss the flutters she felt in her stomach.

At Corioso, they dismounted. Camulo had arrived early from the smaller battle situation in Tecket. His men had the heads of fifteen enemies tied to their horses. The bodies, they had left as a gift of food to the animal kingdom. Camulo ordered a celebration and the people of Corioso were excited to welcome the Queen of Brigantia to their home. Mead and wine flowed for the victorious warriors. It was handed to them on arrival at the gates of Corioso. Whole boar and stag had been cooking over open fires. The smell of the roasted meats met the company on their approach. When Cartimandua entered under the panoply of iron, which formed the gates of Corioso, the people threw willow branches and flowers at her feet. 'Our Queen,' they called. 'Our champion and victor.' Salutations sounded loudly from all the people as a celebration began in the name of Brigantia.

The chief Druid of Textowerdi was there to greet them. No leader had been found for these people since the death of the great warrior Textowerdi himself. This Druid had taken up responsibility, and it was he who promised Cartimandua the help and support from their tribe. Speaking directly to him, Cartimandua thanked him. 'You are a loyal Brigante *cadre*, and without you to hold the situation, the Pehtas would have overrun. When the *Breehin* of Textowerdi is re-established, you will find your position is always secure. You have my thanks.'

Servants ran round the hall, making sure there was enough food. Platters of fruits and nuts, breads and cakes were displayed at the central table for the delight of the queen. Looking round the hall, Cartimandua searched for Eachann. 'Are all returned from the offensive?' she asked Camulo.

'Lady, Donnlugh has returned, and Gallagher, but as yet, there is no word from Beli Mawr.'

Cartimandua glanced away from the watching eye of Camulo. She fiddled nervously with her tunic hem. 'Bring them to me, Camulo. I wish to hear every account. And let me know when Beli Mawr returns… the moment he returns,' she charged.

Each of the leaders attended the Queen, settling at a bench, ready to give individual accounts of the onrush in the places hiding the raiders. Each had been successful, bringing to Corioso the severed painted heads of the offenders. Each reported that the area had been freed from strikes for the foreseeable future, and that glory and victory had been laid at the feet of Cartimandua. 'You bear the accolade of goddess, my Queen,' smiled Gallagher, stroking his moustache and bowing in front of her.

'And what of Beli Mawr?'

'Queen, we have not heard from him yet. But I am sure he will be with us very soon,' returned Camulo. 'This day has been a great success in keeping our borders from infiltration.' Smiling he added, 'let us celebrate tonight.'

'Yes,' said Donnlugh. 'Tomorrow we must look at ways of protecting our borders more permanently. But tonight, we are safe to celebrate.'

As the wine and mead flowed, so the company of warriors and Druids saluted the victory. Songs of triumph burst from their lips as each cup lubricated throats around the halls. The songs flowed outside into the sept. Voices from all across Corioso joined in, united in the battle praises. They sang the old warrior songs, passed down the generations of Brigante families and folk.

'All through the battle and into the night,
Warrior's fighting with all of their might.
The fighting men battling with iron and gold.
Counting the heads of our foes, all cold.

We are the victors.
Conquerors bold.
Our enemies lie under our feet.'

'Drink in the name of our queen,' they called. 'Drink to our goddess and leader.'

'Brigga rides with us.' They shouted as the tables were drummed with the rhythms of war.

As the voices grew in volume, so Eachann arrived back at Corioso. Mugh and his group of thirty men followed, pushing into the hall to see the Queen. Eachann made his way to face Cartimandua, before kneeling to the ground by her seat.

'Lady,' he said, looking up. His face was covered in blood. The left side of his cloak was torn in shreds. His hands, heavily scratched and gashed, showed skin hung from the bloody sores.

'Where have you been and what is your report of the situation at Wardrew?' Cartimandua did not look at Eachann while she enquired but continued cutting a steak from the chunk of boar on the table, picking at it with her fingers.

'Lady, Wardrew is freed. The Pehtas are dead. They will not be returning to their homes or causing problems again for Brigantia this side of Sanheim.'

Cartimandua's voice grated. 'And what took you so long, Beli Mawr?' She chewed the meat nonchalantly, acutely aware of the nerve ends in her body smarting as if a fire burned them.

Eachann rose from his bent position and sat at the side of the Queen. She moved her hand to stop the action, but hesitated, allowing him the seat. Her eyes did not look away from the plate of meat.

'Lady, after the raiders were slaughtered, we obeyed your command to bring the trophies home. My company began the deed of collecting and tying the heads to our horses. Indeed, they are here with us now. The skulls of twenty-four raiders are our gift to you. But while I was surveying the land, making assurance that no raider had escaped our attack, out of nowhere a hound appeared. He had the appearance of a huge wolf. His fangs drooled, catching the smell of me. His hands were huge like claws with iron nails; long and sharp. He came for me out of the shadows. I was unaware of him until he was so near that there was no escape for me except to fight him. I drew my sword and fended him off for a while, but his continuous ability to attack me wore me down.'

The Queen turned her head to look for the first time at the man she loved. Seeing the blood and the state of him, she started. 'Where were your men? The people who could help in this torturous situation?' she asked.

'I called, and they came. I thank the gods for them, otherwise I would not be here now.'

Mugh and some of the warriors who had been with Eachann, began to speak up.

'He is modest, Lady. To our shame, we did nothing, except help him back onto his feet after the dark occurrence.'

One of the warriors spoke up then, 'Lady, when we heard his calls, we went to help. But what we saw was a brute so huge that we were afraid. Beli Mawr was underneath the *deam*, fighting for his life. He grappled with the evil, while we watched.'

Mugh added, 'Eachann was fighting with the invincible one; *Madaidh Allaidh,* the demon god. We saw the wolver gnash his teeth, preparing to bite into the neck of our leader. We thought it was too late to save him,' he said, looking round the room. The hall fell silent. On seeing all the faces intent now on listening to his account, Mugh continued. 'And don't ask me how this happened, but there was a flash of lightning all around the champion of Carvetii. The lightning struck directly, filling him with starshine and fire. His light grew brighter as the shadows grew darker. The next thing we saw was Beli Mawr grabbing the front legs of the wolver,' Mugh began to demonstrate how the grapple had occurred. 'Then he pulled them apart.' Grabbing the air to show the action, he stretched his fists left and right, making a snapping sound with his tongue. Watching the enthralled faces of the audience he had amassed, he continued. 'In an instant the demon was lying on the floor at the side of Beli Mawr.'

'Then,' continued another one of the warriors, 'we saw with our own eyes, the wolver just disappeared. We searched, but he had gone.'

'Yes, back to the underworld, no doubt.'

'The Shining One of Carvetii fought the blackness of death and came out the other side.'

The people in the hall began to cheer. 'Wonderful Beli Mawr. God of the lightning. Taranis in human form.' The conversations and celebrations continued as the wine was passed round the room again and the singing continued.

Cartimandua scrutinised Eachann. Her eyes revealed what she could not bring herself to profess but seeing the results of this fight scrawled on his face and body, she took his hand. 'Come with me, Eachann Beli Mawr. I will dress your wounds.'

Eachann followed the Queen out of the hall and into a quiet corner of the sept, to a shelter not far away. She called for water and soft cloth to care for his wounds. She called for skins for him to lie on, and a pillow for his head.

'The wolver, Eachann?' She asked. 'What are your thoughts?'

'If I didn't know better, I would say it was a shapeshifter. A Druid of high rank. Do you trust Donnlugh?'

'I do,' she said. '…I think I do,' she hesitated, tossing the thought in her head. 'Who and why would anyone do this, though?'

'I don't know. But after our first meeting out in the oak grove; before Mugh and I left that place, there was a bowman shooting at us. I caught him, and with a bit of persuasion he admitted that he was sent by someone to take my life. He also told me that this person – this assassin, knew of my parentage. This is information I would love to have. I never knew anything of my father, and only that my mother was called Eanna, or something similar, I think. I was abandoned as a baby, until Mugh Ruith found me and brought me to Carvetii.'

'I am sure the gods will reveal your parentage when the time is right. They have a way of opening up the secrets of men.'

'Then, my love, I would like to help them. Will you allow me some time to seek the truth? A moon turn, maybe. You are safe with Camulo for the present. Your journey back to Stanwix is secure. I will find you there.'

Cartimandua began to bathe the bloody mess from Eachann's wounds, allowing him to continue to tell something of his early years. She bathed the lacerations, caressing his face and hands. Eachann's eyes followed her every move. Speaking lovingly to him, she asked, 'What are we to do, Eachann?'

Eachann lay silently, as Cartimandua wrapped his hands and tended to his cuts. But he could hold himself back no longer. Pulling her closer to him, she moved to lay at his side. He enveloped his arms around her frame, until she was encompassed by him. His kisses covered her face, burning into her heart. She felt the strength drain from her body as it had done the first time they met. This weakness, she embraced. Responding to his touch, she untied the shoulder cord to his tunic. Once loosened, she moved her hand to caress his chest. 'I know what is going to happen,' she thought, 'but I cannot stop this. It is too strong for me to hold back.'

In the silence of the little shelter, Cartimandua and Eachann made love. Eachann was kind and restrained so as to give pleasure to his love, but Cartimandua was more urgent in her need. 'I have waited too long, my love,' she said, lifting her tunic and removing her clothes.

The night was long and sleepless; their exigent need for each other, insatiable. When the thought of the morning became a reality, neither of them wanted to move. Cartimandua, although not wanting to think about the consequences of their actions, rose first. 'I must get back,' she muttered into the ear of Beli Mawr reaching for her tunic and skirts.

As she rose to leave, Eachann held her back. 'When we are back in Stanwix, my love, then I will come to you. We will find a way.' Cartimandua nodded.

Lament of Sucellos

'I feel the power,' the hound-God said,
The smell is in the air.
One man I need- to own his soul.
His blood to bring him here.

Bright as the sun, the cloak appeared,
while darkness sucked its stench.
Will you imperil might and love.
For envy thus to quench?'

He vented venom. 'My need is strong.
I need to know the truth.
You know the place from whence he came.
This shining god of youth?
He saps my blood, my strength, my soul.
I live under his shadow.
Slit his gut, so I may live.
His heart with poison arrow.'

Then I will give your heart's desire:
The death which you now seek.'
Answered the bright cloak to the dark.
I will grant that which you need.
I'll give you this, but you must pay.
The cost which now we speak.

This enemy is kingly born.
With godly conservation.
Would you remove the greatest gift
Appointed to our nation?
Do you sell your soul for such a thing?
For power? Not Salvation?'

The hound god snarled. 'I would' he said.
'His blood to flow down crimson red.'
So sent the hound-God, wolf-skinned beast.
From broken fetters all unleashed,
Against the lightning power seat.
The day against the night compete.
Then lightning brightness flashes heat.
Two gods in mortal combat meet,

Taranis breaks Sucellos.

CHAPTER SEVENTEEN

CEACALL
The Eternal Circle

BEFORE THEIR RETURN TO Stanwix, the planned stay at Taftefield allowed the Queen to check on the leadership of the place since the death of Bellnorix. She messaged King Ninniau of Gabrantovices, seeking his help in the continuous security of the Brigante stronghold until a champion could be found to sustain the land she called home. A message returned swiftly stating that his son Branderix would be honoured to hold the position. 'He is young but able to uphold the responsibility. He is also an able warrior, and excellent equester. You will not do better, in the interim,' messaged Ninniau. This pleased the Queen, so she felt able to concentrate on her future plans.

The Queen was eager to meet again with Raegan, and also to meet the sister of her grandmother. Both women were in the hall awaiting the arrival of the Queen. Both bowed low on her entrance.

'My dear Raegan,' Cartimandua rushed to embrace the woman who had been with her since childhood. 'I have so looked forward to this day. How are you? Are you well and in good spirits? You look healthy and just as lovely as when I last saw you.'

'Lady,' answered the maturing Raegan, who had added some weight to her frame in the last few years. 'I grow fat with health.' Laughing, Cartimandua asked if she was married yet. 'No. There is no one special in my life.' Raegan blushed and curtseyed.

'There will be as soon as the moon turns, I shouldn't wonder,' smiled Cartimandua. Turning to the lady next to Raegan, Cartimandua smiled lovingly. 'Anna?'

'Lady, My Queen,' said the older woman. She too bowed before her queen. Her hair was tucked underneath a scarf of blue woven linen, which matched her robe in colour. Her face was given to openness. Lines and creases around her eyes and mouth displaying signs of endured hardships, but a twinkle escaped from her eyes. Cartimandua wondered about this woman's life, but the smile returned to the Queen was kindly, and at once Cartimandua felt her warmth.

Taking Anna's hands in hers, Cartimandua stared intensely at the woman before her, as if trying to remember the face from her distant past. 'Anna, I want you to stay with me. I want to know all about you; about my father and mother and anything you can tell me of my grandfather, the old buzzard!' she laughed. 'Tonight, we rest, and tomorrow we ride on to Stanwix, but I want both you and Raegan to travel with me.'

Lady Anna bobbed asking, 'Forgive me, My Queen, but would you give permission for my Druid to travel with us? He has been my trusted companion for many years.'

'Yes, Anna, and any other friends you need. You are a queen, Anna, and we are kin. You hold a special place in my family. I would like it very much if we became friends as well as kin. Please call me

Mandua, as a sign of our friendship.' Looking round the hall, she continued. 'Now, let's eat and relax.' She glanced round the hall wondering where Eachann was. 'I know he won't be far away,' she thought, 'but I need him very near.' He was nowhere to be seen, but Cartimandua did not fret. 'I know he will meet me at Stanwix. This he has promised,' she mused.

That evening, in the hall of the last great king of Brigantia, Cartimandua encouraged Anna to tell her story. 'What about my mother?' she asked.

'My sister. Yes. She was beautiful and wilful and loving and lovely,' Anna reflected. 'She was older than I and destined to become queen on the death of our father, Textowerdi. He held the land which now bears his name. It was a great tribe, but when Bellnorix sought him with the offer of unity between Brigantia and his northern kingdom, for the sake of peace among our people, it was agreed. Our tribe became a province secured under the banner of Brigantia. My father was happy to do this, because the young king of Brigantia had fallen in love with his daughter, my sister. Riganta.'

Cartimandua soaked up the information. 'It is the first time I had heard this story from one who had the authority to speak. Mostly I heard the stories filtered through the songs from bhairds. I had no way of knowing if truth spoke in the lyrics. But what of my grandfather – Bellnorix?'

Anna sat quietly, crossing her hands in her lap as she moved the story forward. 'Bellnorix was young and strong, and quite handsome in his days. His battle exploits and victories are well told. When he met Riganta, both saw the sense in marriage. He was a fair and just king, and Riganta was happy. Our lands were merged in the union. Brigantia oversaw and supported Textowerdi, and both strengthened as a result. It was the beginning of the growth of

Brigantia, as Bellnorix began to encompass the lands east, west and north of Taftefield. He was a powerful king. It would have been wrong to go against his wishes.'

'And my mother and father, Anna? What of them?

'Ferelith was born very early into the marriage. Although she was beautiful, she was a weak child; something that Bellnorix could not accept. I think he worried about what would happen if Ferelith was one day to be queen. So Bellnorix sought Brennus, the Raven Prince of Roecliffe with the ideas of a betrothal. I am ashamed to say that Bellnorix only seemed to see the Roecliffe lands he would acquire through that arrangement. Ferelith was little more than fourteen at the time of her marriage, and small for her age; a bargaining piece in the hands of the King. Brennus was almost the same age as the Brigante king. He was fat and his jowls hid his neck. His face was marked with scars from pimples, though they had healed some years previously. He was not the warrior that Bellnorix wanted in his growing powerhouse of victors. Indeed, your father was an overindulged body, and though he had an astute brain, there was little bravery in his actions. Bellnorix saw his lack of brute strength only as a weakness. But Brennus was strong in other ways, and eventually I believe that Bellnorix began to appreciate the power of insight, strategy and wisdom that this son brought to the Brigante table.' Anna took a drink from the cup at her side.

She appeared tired, but Cartimandua continued to press her. 'I accept that you may be tired, Anna, and I am grateful for your readiness to give me answers. I will not press you much longer, but please, please continue. I beseech you.'

Anna looked calmly at the Queen, then continued with her story. 'Ferelith was only just a woman when you were born. Her death brought your life. Bellnorix was angry. Not only had he lost Riganta a few years previously, but Brennus, your father, was also lost in an attack. He was captured and beheaded by marauders, who took his head and hung his body on a tree. The body was found a day or two later, and Bellnorix, out of respect for your mother who was due to give birth, ordered a warrior burial for the Raven King. So here you are – both parents gone to the otherworld.'

The young queen sat silently taking in the news about her parentage. 'I think I should weep,' she notioned, 'but I cannot summon the feelings. Am I so cold and hard? Has life given me no warmth and love? I see these people, but they have little meaning to me.'

Anna reached out to touch the expressionless face on the young queen. 'But Cartimandua, has this not made you stronger? You have survived these years learning your own strength and battle skill, and now you have your own kingdom, and…' smiling shyly, Anna whispered, '…and a child; an heir on the way.' The mouth of the Queen dropped open and her jaw fell. She peered around the hall, wondering who might have overheard Anna speaking.

Her hands flew to her belly. 'How did you know? I hardly know myself.'

Smiling the older woman nodded. 'You have a glow about you that speaks of motherhood.'

Cartimandua began to fidget nervously. 'It cannot be known.'

'But would not Venutius be pleased with this event?' The wild frightened look in the eyes of the young queen told its own story. Anna nodded. 'I understand. It will be kept from those who should not know, Mandua. The gods have brought us together, so that this child may be protected. Others who can be trusted will be revealed. You carry a very special bairn, My Queen.'

Cartimandua, flustered and edgy, stood to leave. She pressed her hand onto the shoulder of the older woman but made her way to the doorway. 'I need air,' she thought, gasping, she fled. 'I need Eachann!'

Anna and her Druid travelled with Raegan in a cart lined with soft feathers and cushions. Elora rode at the side of them, while Cartimandua headed up the caravan on its way back to Stanwix. Camulo rode by the side of the Queen. Mugh Ruith and Donn Donnlugh protected the rear of the convoy, along with the charioteers.

'There is much I still need to know about Anna, and my parentage,' Cartimandua mused on the journey home, 'but most of all, I want to be with Eachann.' The thought of him made her belly flutter. She felt a rush of heat surge upward, and tingles flash up and down her body. She rubbed between her legs, enjoying the thought of his body next to hers. She looked back, hoping to catch his eye, then remembered that he had asked leave for a time, but she imagined him riding by her side, and smiled.

Stanwix was ready to receive their queen and warriors, and all was prepared for their arrival. Wild pig roasted on the spits, and drink flowed round the oppidum in celebration of the victory against the Pehtas. All around, people were in high spirits. The sounds from outside the hall spoke of cavorting and exuberance. Music played louder as the evening proceeded. Singers joined in victory songs and others told stories of battles and the glorious champions of Brigantia. Women sat with seers, listening as their futures were revealed through the patterns of sticks and stones falling to the ground. Old warriors spun tales of bravery to the children who listened with mouths open and eyes wide. Laugher rose like the flames of the fire, crackling and sparking in the darkened night.

Inside the Great Hall of Cartimandua, the scene was more

peaceful, but eyes remained alert. The music from outside the hall filtered inside. *Velitas* danced with girls between serving drinks to the people in the company of Her Highness of Brigantia. The Queen reclined on her throne, surveying the scene before her. Anna sat quietly at the side of her Druid and Mugh Ruith.

'The two Druids speak warmly to one another, making connections from their knowledge in a friendly fashion, I shouldn't wonder,' thought the Queen. 'That is good.'

Elora sat with Raegan. 'They also make friendly conversations,' acknowledged the Queen, giving a nod in pleasure. At the table near the fire, Camulo sat watching the Queen, his eagle eye attentive. He joined in conversation with Donnlugh. His hand remained on his dagger hilt. 'Always on guard. My dear Camulo.'

Cartimandua glanced round the room and noticed that Anna was looking directly at her. Anna smiled at Cartimandua as she caught her eye. Cartimandua smiled back. Beckoning to Anna, 'come,' she called. Anna made her way across the hall to the chair at the side of the throne. 'Take my mind somewhere else,' she said. 'Anna, tell me about you, and your life. I have heard that you had an altercation of sorts with my grandfather, and that Bellnorix sent you away. Is that so?'

Anna twitched her lips, 'Ah!' she sighed. 'Ah!' She remained silent for a while before she began to speak. 'A time ago – more than thirty-year cycles now, when Brigantia was young, and there were many other tribes arguing for land and power; back when I was a young girl, it was then that my hand was offered in marriage. I was to be betrothed to the King of Votadini. I could not accept this man even though I would have become the queen of his lands eventually. He was king in a place I did not know. It was too far away from my home. His reputation was of a ruthless warrior, who cared for no one except his own glory. I was frightened and worried. It seemed that my life was but a piece in a kingly game, a political bargaining pledge. But my heart belonged to another. He was a *braint* and warrior and although he was born of a Brigante mother, his father was not. He was king of lands southwards of Brigantia, having his own tribe and territory. My lover-his son was handsome and fearless, with his eye on distant territories of his own. He had a wife and sons and was already establishing himself as de facto ruler and chief among his friends.

The night he planned on leaving to fight for lands of his own, he came to me. I loved him and gave myself to him. The following spring, I gave birth to a son.'

'Oh! Anna. What of your lover? Was he good to you after the birth?

'Before our son was born, I found out where my lover was based. I secretly followed him. When I caught up with him, I told him of my demise. I don't know what I expected, but hoped that he would be pleased, and take me into his life. But his mind was on grander schemes. He saw the threat from Rome, and the threat to the new lands he had gained. He could not afford to be distracted at that time. I understood that. It was a dangerous time for us all. He advised me of his many enemies. He feared for my safety and that of the unborn child. "If anyone found out about the baby, you would be in grave danger," he warned. "You could so easily be used against me. I cannot afford to be placed in that position." He told me that he loved me, but he could not help me, and that I should return home. I should protect the child in the best way I could. I haven't seen him since that night.' Anna turned away, wiping a tear from her eye.

'And your child. What of him? Where is your son?'

'Bellnorix was angry with me. I never told him who my lover was, though I believe he guessed. In any case, it does not seem to matter now that Bellnorix is passed into the other world. I have kept my secret all these years, and intend to continue holding this secret, if you will allow.' Anna gazed at Cartimandua and grasped her hands; her eyes pleading for her support.

Cartimandua smiled and nodded. 'Your secret is safe, Anna.' Cartimandua saw the pain in Anna's eyes. A tear expressed her grief. Pressing a little more, the Queen asked, 'Do you know the whereabouts of your son now?'

I only know that I trusted him into the wisdom of the Druids, with a promise that he would be safe.' Cartimandua nodded. Silence followed for some time, while the two women felt the consequences of the sharing. Then Cartimandua, surprised by her own thinking, jumped. 'Then your son… If he is still alive…he is the rightful heir of Textowerdi. Because of your position, the rule would have been passed to him when Textowerdi, your father, died.'

'I am not sure. Remember that my son was a bastard.'

'But, after you, he is the only direct successor to Textowerdi. Anna, we must find him, for he could rightfully lead the northern tribes of Brigantia.' Cartimandua felt herself getting excited about the prospect of a new king over the northern borders of Brigantia; someone she could trust and who could duly take that place without power battles or bloodshed.

Anna protested.

'Look, Anna. There is no shame in the birthing. If he is alive and able, it is right that he should take up his responsibilities. Would you not want to see your son again before you are too old to appreciate him?'

Anna began to quake. 'I never dreamed there would be a time when that became a possibility. I have never dared to dream.'

Calling for Donnlugh, Cartimandua whispered in his ear. At once the Druid left the hall. He clicked his fingers at Anna's Druid advisor before leaving the presence of the Queen. Together they wandered through the oppidum, heads close, talking together. By nightfall two horses could be seen riding toward the moors.

After a long evening of celebrations, Anna retired, and Cartimandua made her way to her own private bed chamber. She called to the folk left in the hall, 'Goodnight my people. May the gods give you peace and good sleep.'

Only an owl could be heard in the stillness of the moonless night. Eachann made his way stealthily to the secret opening at the back of the hall of Cartimandua. He silently moved the willow door screen and entered. Cartimandua had moved the thick protective curtains to one side of the opening, making it easier for Eachann to enter anytime without struggling through the hanging fabrics.

Creeping on hands and knees, he made his way to the bed. A small candle was flickering on the chest near to where the Queen had placed her torc and sword. She lay on her bed, in a restful sleep; a steady rhythm of breath escaped her open mouth. Eachann approached, removing his tunic and braccae before he pulled the furs and blankets to one side and sidled into the bed at the side of his love.

She lay on her back, one hand gently resting on her belly. Stretched up above her head, the other hand had entangled her fingers in her hair. Eachann gazed steadily at her and smiled. He felt a heightened urge deep within his groin, as his hands caressed her body. A whimper escaped from her mouth as Cartimandua became aware that her lover had arrived. Stirring a little, she moved closer to him.

'At last,' she whispered.

The night was hot and sticky. They could not hold back. The heat only intensified their need and their fused feelings of bliss, in the taking of each other, once, twice and again.

As the dawn moved closer, Cartimandua lay fully awake at the side of Eachann. Slowly she felt his breathing alter, and his hands begin to feel for her again. She cuddled into him, enjoying the protection she savoured from his strong arms. They lay in silence before Cartimandua dared to break the hush of that moment. 'My love. I would that this moment could last for ever.'

'Hmmmhhm.' The warrior responded. He squeezed her bottom closer to him.

'I am worried, Eachann. I am sorry, but what can we do?'

'I have been thinking about this, Mandua, my love. This is why I have not left yet. I need to search for my past, but I could not go without securing my future.' Eachann lifted himself up onto his elbow to face his lover. 'I *will* be with you.'

Cartimandua sat up and shook her head. 'If only it was that simple, Eachann. You know Venutius. How will he receive the news that I have betrayed him? How will he receive the news that his own champion has betrayed him?'

'Well, until he comes to consolidate this promised unity between Carvetii and Brigantia, I am here.'

'I would not wish it like this Eachann, but I cannot live without you by my side. If we can keep our love a secret, then we have a chance, for a while at least, of being together. We must watch for Venutius coming. Scouts must always be looking for him.'

'Then we need a place away from this hall. We are too vulnerable here.'

'Arrange that, my love. Is there anyone you can trust, who might help us?'

'Mugh. Yes. He might not like our need, but he will keep our secret.'

'Can he stop mumbling to himself?'

The champion flexed his arm muscles and nodded. 'He will keep the confidences.' He hugged his woman, placing kisses on her ear and her neck, before pulling her close enough to enter her again.

As the light stretched forward, the lovers could hear the scraping of the fire in the hall. Preparations were being made to welcome the day. Eachann readied to leave the bedchamber before anyone could call for the Queen. On his leaving, Cartimandua held him back. 'Eachann.' In hushed tones, Cartimandua told him of her gestation. 'Eachann. I believe that you will be a father before the next Ostara is celebrated.' The smile on the face of the warrior spread wide. He turned to Cartimandua and hugged her. But Cartimandua could not smile. Solemnly she said, 'this must be kept from Venutius, obviously. So, we must plan our future very carefully.'

'Who knows about this?'

'Anna guessed. I will need Elora and Raegan to help me, and Camulo probably knows. That is all that is needed. Donnlugh does not need to know. Let us keep this as long as we are able. As Eachann made moves to leave, the Queen held his hand tightly. 'Our plan must be that we are never seen together. There must be no talk which will touch the ear of Venutius. We must avoid anything which places Brigantia in danger as a result,' uttered the Queen. 'Send for me when everything is ready.'

Eachann bowed. 'Take care, my love,' whispered Cartimandua.

As the evening entered her domain, Cartimandua called Elora and Raegan to her side. 'I have news, but it must be between us only,' she muttered in a low-pitched voice. 'I need your absolute loyalty at this time. You know that I have Venutius as my husband. Well, it seems that the gods have dictated a different path for me, and while I work that path out, I will need your help.'

Elora nodded. 'Does that mean you want me to continue my stay here with you?'

'Yes. I do. And Raegan, I want you here too.' Both women smiled to each other. 'What are you grinning about?'

The grin on Elora's face expanded with her words. 'I have found a friend, and maybe even a husband, and Raegan is in the same position. There is something about Stanwix that brings lovers together.'

Cartimandua grinned too. 'Who are your men?' she asked.

Elora blushed. 'Gallagher. Gallagher makes me blush every time I see him or think of him. He jokes with me, and I am sure he likes me,'

'Ah! Yes. A good choice, Elora. You have my blessing.'

Looking at Raegan she lifted her eyebrows inquisitively.

'Camulo, My Lady.'

Cartimandua laughed. 'Oh! Yes. My beloved protector. Oh! Yes.'

The three women laughed about their situations, joking about the tall Gallagher-the-Lip and the 'large' Camulo. Each looked at Cartimandua with questions on their lips. 'Will you divulge your secret, Queen?'

'I will. In due course. I will,'

With his hair wrapped in his white scarf and hidden under his deep hooded cloak, Beli Mawr rode out from Stanwix. He did not tell Mugh where he was going or why, but Mugh called after him, 'I am coming with you, Eachann. You are up to something, I can tell. You will need me to cover your back as usual.' Climbing onto his pony, Mugh galloped after the champion. 'Foolishness must be his name.

Headstrong also suits him. Yes – Beli Mawr the headstrong fool, he should be called. Oh! I wish that the Eòlas would deal with him,' mumbled Mugh, speeding to catch up.

Coming upon a suitable resting place, Eachann took his horse to a small rivulet. He sat on the bank while the horse drank. Mugh dismounted.

'I think I know what you are doing, Eachann. I knew when we first arrived at Stanwix, and you disappeared while I sought an audience with the queen, who turned out not to be the queen.' The words flowed from his lips without a breath between them. 'You are besotted with her. I see it in your eyes. But more than that, I see her looking at you. This is wrong, Beli Mawr. She is married,' he said, dipping into his saccus on the side of the pony. He brought out two cakes, forgotten from his last journey but still edible. Soaking them in water from the rivulet, he offered one to Eachann.

Eachann did not respond.

Mugh continued ranting. 'It's bad enough that you looked at her, but what you are doing will be the death of you.' Mumbling under his breath he continued, 'And me probably. I don't want to die yet. I want to enjoy this cake for one thing. Though I hope my teeth are strong enough for the crusty bit.'

Eachann did not look up but continued staring at the bubbling water in front of him. He pulled blades of grass from where he sat, picking till there was nothing but a bald patch left.

Although Mugh's tone had softened, the rant continued. 'You do this, and then you do that. You never consider me, or my advice these days. You fight with the wolver and overcome, and lightning strikes you, but you live. But this - this is something else. Venutius will have your head.'

'This is why I need your help Mugh.'

Mugh began to hold his head and rock it backwards and forwards. 'I know. I saw. The Eòlas told me I would 'see,' and I have. They told me all those years ago that I would gain understanding, and I have. The knowledge is painful to hold, Eachann. I see death. Your life is held together with *withies*. Yet, I know that the gods have planned it this way.' He lifted Eachann's chin so that the warrior could look no other way. He spoke directly into his soul, 'I will help, for I believe that you hold the key to Brigantia, but I wish you could see what I see.' Then smiling, he offered the cake once more.

'I dare not look, Mugh. My life is bound to her. I do not know how or why, but from the first time I saw her, I knew that much.'

'I know this much, Eachann. Eyes are useless to see, when the mind is blind.'

They began the search for a place where Cartimandua could come safely, and from where they might begin the search for Eachann's past. 'I know that my enemies lie on this path,' he told Mugh. 'I must find my enemies. Then I feel I will find my past.' Together, they investigated possible hide-outs. On one of these ventures, they came across a small hamlet just as the Alwent Beck met the rush of the Tés-ti at a place known as Whispering Waters. Here, the wild tree lined mainstem waters running from west to east, offered a place of shelter with a natural food source. Three deserted homes sat on the banks of the Tés-ti at this point, where a shrine to the goddess Coventina had been erected between the houses and the river. This goddess, Eachann worshipped, knowing her magical ability. He had heard her whisper across the waters; her magic drawing the fairies close. He dismounted, eyes alert for any sigh of movement other than the wind in the treetops. He knelt at the side of the old shrine made of three stone slabs built on top of each other. The flat tabletop held a bowl, once bronze, but now covered in verdigris. Into this bowl Eachann offered a token of the cake left over from his meal with Mugh. It was but a few moments before the birds swooped down to receive the offering. Magpies squawked and pecked each other, fighting over a single morsel. Eachann counted. 'One, two, three. This is an omen from the goddess. I feel this augers well, though we need to be alert.'

Once he had decided to make camp at Whispering Waters, he tested the travel times and accesses to the place. He tried several routes, and decided that from Stanwix, a circular route as if moving northeast was the safest way, though not the quickest. He wanted Cartimandua to avoid travelling over the wooded land where wild boar roamed the thickets, and it was effortless for enemies to hide.

The hamlet was in poor repair. Eachann marked, 'One hovel is suitable for stabling, and one, with a little practical thatching, could become weatherproofed from the westerly winds.' He wondered about the reasons that the homestead was empty of life but did not unduly concern himself. People moved on, in their search for a livelihood. 'It is probable that the people who lived here are now ensconced in some new home in Stanwix.'

Once he had settled on the place, he approached Mugh.

Mugh muttered. 'The hovel at Carvetii was better than this. Will you choose this place above the halls of Venutius? I think the madness has taken you.'

'Mugh. If you know so much, you will know that I cannot change things. I must follow the gods.'

'Then if I cannot change your mind, I will take the other shelter for my own. The thatcher will have double the work. I will build a shrine to Taranis, and *you* will help me.'

Eachann set about making the hamlet as welcoming and private as possible. Staking his trophy heads collected from his battling,

Eachann placed several at the entrance of the little hamlet, as a warning and a sign that Whispering Waters was occupied by a warrior. He cleared a dry place for Cahir, Mugh's pony and the other horses he and Mugh now owned. The life of the little hamlet began to awaken.

Vindovium was the nearest settlement to the hamlet. Rather than travelling back to Stanwix for preserves, Eachann disguised himself and made his way to Vindovium for supplies and a roof thatcher, if he could find one. Mugh arranged for an iron wheel to be forged and brought to the hamlet. Soon the shrine to Taranis was finished. Mugh had collected the largest stones he could carry, building them into a mound. It sat at the side of the shine to Coventina and topped with the newly forged iron wheel. The bowl became a shared bowl, but one that Mugh sprinkled with sacred water, cleansing it and offering it to the two gods afresh. Mugh settled as a hermit into his home, watching time portray the skies turning the Earth from autumn reds to winter ice. Warm and comfortable in his home, he rested, studying the stars for signs and omens, until Yule had passed. The first morning that spring kissed the land once more, Eachann sat with the little Druid outside the doorway of Eachann's roundhouse. Mugh sensed there was something on the warrior's mind for he stuttered round conversations for a good time.

'Well? What is it? What do you want from me, Eachann?'

'Is it a truth that our future is defined by our past? I will soon be venturing to find my past, Mugh, and before I do, I would like you to give me what I believe is rightfully mine. You have kept it safe all these turnings, but now I require the ring.'

'I do believe that our future is not defined by our past, but rather we must learn from our past; mistakes, decisions, experiences, and apply that learning to this present day. Then we will see our future revealed in the life we are meant to live.' Mugh silently walked toward his shelter and a hook on the wall where his cloak hung. He lifted the bag from the lining of the cloak and returned to Eachann. Undoing the blue tie around the soft leather pouch, he allowed the fabric to fall open in his hand. A flash of starlight escaped his grasp, as his fingers opened to reveal the ring. 'Here, Eachann. Take great care of this ring. I believe it will prove your birth-right.'

Eachann took the ring, folding it back into the safety of the pouch. He tightened his grasp round it and turned the blue silk around it again. Hooking it onto a leather thong he dangled it round his neck and hid it in his tunic. It rested near his heart.

Cartimandua began to wear looser tunics and longer skirts. Her weight gain was undetected by most, except her most loyal cluster. The Feast of Lughnasa arrived. The harvest had been reaped, the grain stores were full, and Stanwix enjoyed peace as the year headed into Sanheim. Cartimandua carried her royal responsibilities as normal, never taking the fragile peace for granted. She sent raiding parties to check on her tribes. She rode out herself to parley with her tribal chieftains and kings. She led her warriors to war against agitators within Brigantia who thought they could overcome the Queen's battle-power. Her passion, persistence and determination forged together as true grit.

Camulo and Gallagher rode with her, but as often as she could get away, she rode out alone, to Beli Mawr. The summer brought love and laughter to the paramour and his secret.

Donnlugh and Anna's Druid did not return in all those months.

Venutius sent a message to Cartimandua telling her that he could not return to Stanwix yet, though she was to expect him around Imbolc. Cartimandua rode to Eachann the day the message arrived from Carvetii. Jumping from Tormaig the instant she arrived at

Whispering Waters, she called for her lover.

'Eachann, He cannot come yet!' she called, trying hard not to let her voice sound so pleased. 'He is still warring with the boundary breaking painted mobs.'

'We are safe for a while longer then, my love.'

'Yes. But not from the arguments between the farmsteads at Rose Hip Dene near Mythomrode and the tribe of Luddenden. The Ludden are insisting that the pathway between the two tribes belongs to them. It could cause trouble should we need to get to Setantii and Broccos Maglos. Can you go with Mugh? Take men with you, but settle it in my name?'

Cartimandua sent fourteen men from Stanwix to meet Eachann on the way to Luddenden. He was eager for the change and the chance to battle. He had a job to do also.

'Three things must be done while we venture to sort out the affray in Luddenden, Mugh,' he said. They set off.

'And they are what, my friend? To do the bidding of our queen. Yes?'

'Yes. But also, to find a goldsmith. And then to find Donannu.'

CHAPTER EIGHTEEN

PRIMOGENITOR
The Beginnings

A S THE FESTIVAL OF Sanheim arrived, Cartimandua prepared for the great celebration. 'I know that I should present myself to my people. They will expect me to speak to them, and to be there when the omens from the sacrifices show their projections to the Druids for the coming year.' Speaking to Elora she enquired about the return of Donnlugh. 'He should be here to represent the Druids in the sacrifices and reading of the entrails. He must be here. Can you find him; send a message asking for his return? It does not matter that he has not completed my task, but the festival of Sanheim is most important, as we prepare for the Winter Queen to hold power over our land. We must show the people that all is prepared, and we are safe when the winds blow and the frost bites.'

Elora nodded. 'I will, My lady.'

The Queen ordered two new cloaks for the occasion. For one, the finest linen was woven and sewn with the smallest of delicate stitches. Embroidery of horses adorned the cloak, which had a long train at the back. Cartimandua swished the train round from the back to the front, tucking it over her arm, and allowing it to fall in front of her. The excess of fabric allowed the pleats to hide the growing belly of the Queen. The second cloak was made just as full, but black.

Cartimandua ordered that the eating and drinking should be conducted outside on this occasion, without the use of her hall.

'We should all be together for this auspicious occasion,' she said, though in her mind she thought, 'the shadows from the fire will help to hide my growing frame.' She was concerned that Donnlugh had not returned, but sent messengers to Brigcruim, inviting them to join in the celebrations. 'I can ask Lochru, the High-Druid of Brigcruim to lead proceedings if Donnlugh hasn't returned.' Satisfied all would go well, she busied herself with the immediate concerns before her.

'Winter allows us some time of peace and rest,' she thought. 'I should use this time to consolidate my tribal rulers and their kingdoms under Brigantia. Come spring, I hope that the peace will hold, and the Romans do not move before we have gathered the count to stand against them.' Then, trying to calm her own fears, she thought, 'Come spring, my baby will appear. Raegan is ready to take the child under her wing. All will be well.' Though the tremble she felt in her belly made her body tense and fear stronger.

The evening of Sanheim was calm, and still held the last of the summer warmth as the Queen moved to her chair outside the Great Hall. The people had been celebrating since the dawn, but were attentive when Cartimandua appeared, wrapped for a colder night. Lochru had arrived that morning. He presented himself to the Queen, making himself available to her.

'I have brought a small company of Druids to join with your own, My Lady. Should Donnlugh not return in time, I am able to perform the sacrifices and readings in his name.'

The altar table displayed the pig to be slaughtered. Four Druids held the limbs while Lochru drew the breast of the animal. The entrails fell with the harsh gutting. Blood spread all around the table and onto the floor. The guts were placed in a caldron ready for the reading. The carcass was taken to the spit. On the table, the guts were poured. In the falling, the patterns revealed the future of Brigantia. 'My Queen. People of Brigantia,' called Lochru. Holding his bloody hands high in the air, he called. 'Our gods have spoken, and in the blood and the viscera of our sacrifice tonight, I see a time of peace for us all. I see a time when the Queen of Winter holds sway over Albion, keeping us safe for this season. As the Spring comes, our gods will hear us and will guide.'

Cartimandua was satisfied. When she rose to speak to her people, a cheer ascended.

'Dear, dear Brigantia; my people. We have heard the pronouncements from the Druids; some from Stanwix and some from Brigcruim. How fortunate we are to join together in peace across our wonderful land. We hear the words from our gods, Taranis and Brigga. But do not be fooled. Our peace may be short lived. We must be prepared, for the threat from Rome does not disappear. When the spring tides allow, the Romans may be upon us. If not this spring, then the next. Stay alert, my people. We will be ready for them. Make no mistake. Together we will uphold the spirit of Brigantia, and the spirit over the lands of Albion.' Cartimandua poured some wine into her drinking cup. Lifting the cup to the skies, she lifted her voice, 'This night we thank the gods for peace among us. We drink to them. We celebrate Sanheim, and the blessing of a final harvest before the cold moves over us. There is plenty in our stores for the winter. Peace will endure as the cold Queen of Winter holds her power.' Raising her cup, she shouted, 'to Brigga and to The Winter Queen.'

'To the Winter Queen, and to Brigga,' came the response from the people across the oppidum.

Though the winter was harsh, the people across Brigantia prepared for war. The stores were full of new arrows whittled from straight branches of ash or oak, and bows from yew and elm. Matara stood by the doors like warriors on guard, while at their side stood the Lancia, proudly boasting iron spear heads, serrated, flames shaped and attached by rivets to the sturdy oak shafts. Chests full of leather slings filled the rooms, and shields lined the walls of the store armoury. The ironsmiths were tasked with forging new and stronger swords and glaives. New covers for oak shields made into rectangular, oval, square or round jackets of leather were added to the already large amount of accumulated shields. All manner of artisan crafts were used to build up supplies of belts, sheathes and holders for the weapons. Warriors trained; charioteers vied. The oppidum was vibrant in their desire for peace and their preparation for war. The Queen inspected her stores regularly, praising the craft men and women of Stanwix, her warriors and fighters.

Yule arrived, heralding in the darkest of days, and still Eachann did not return.

As the winter began to turn to spring and Imbolc had passed, Cartimandua felt the kicking of her child. She longed to see Eachann before the birth but knew that he might not arrive back in time. 'I should not have sent him away before winter. Now I do not know where he is or when he will be back. Donnlugh is not returned either. I need to know where they are and if they are safe.'

Her agitation spread from her thoughts to her muscles, then travelling down her body to her stomach, she felt the grip of pain. She cried out, bending double, holding her belly. 'Anna,' she called.

'Anna, come quickly.'

Anna entered the hall where Cartimandua writhed. 'My Lady. Come with me. Let me take you into your bedchamber.' Turning to the guards and *velitas* in the hall, she ordered, 'clear this place. The Queen wants privacy today. No one is to come into the hall. Make sure that this order is obeyed.' Helping the Queen to the private place beyond the throne, she began to shout urgently. 'Elora. Elora, I need you to guard this hall. Do not let anyone enter without permission from the Queen…' She then cast around for the young woman who had been there in the Queen's early years. 'Raegan,' she called urgently. Raegan stepped forward. 'Raegan, fetch water and cloths.' Then loudly she called to any ears that might be listening, 'The Queen is ill, but we will have her better in no time.' A buzz of voices could be heard as Elora ushered the people toward the door, encouraging them to make their way outside the hall. Some shouted blessings and good wishes to the Queen. Some called for healing charms.

Cartimandua leaned on Anna, grateful for her help, then feeling for the bed.

'Mandua, I think your child will be born today.'

'But it is too early Anna.' Before the words had fully escaped the mouth of the queen, the water sac broke showing the baby was truly ready to join the world.

'Do not stress, My Lady. Just allow nature to take its course. We are here, Raegan and I. We will make sure that everything is ready to receive the little one.' Anna poured a tincture to ease the pains and offered it to Cartimandua. Speaking softly, almost singing, she whispered an ancient blessing,

> *'May you always have for you and your child –*
> *Walls against the wind,*

And a roof from the rain,
Drinks bedside the fire,
Laughter to cheer you.
And those you love near you.
And all that your heart may desire.'

The pains of the birth gripped Cartimandua for some time, giving little rest between the strong cramps. Raegan lit candles as the light faded, but still Cartimandua toiled, exhausted from the prolonged period of suffering. 'Does this pain never end?' she cried.

As time passed, with great relief, the child was born. Raegan lifted the babe into her arms. She washed the small bundle, wrapping clean swaddling around the small body. 'Oh! My Lady. It is a girl. You have a princess. She is beautiful.'

But still Cartimandua was in pain. She thrashed about in the bed, tossing onto her back, then around onto her hands and knees time again, not knowing how to relieve the travail. 'What is this? I am dying' she screamed. She grabbed for Anna, scratching her arm. She cried out. Then, as the contractions became so frequent, she fell silent, unable to speak, the pain, too intense.

'I think that there may be another, Mandua. I think you have another baby on the way.'

A while later the second child was born. Anna tried to muffle the sound of healthy lungs as the baby took first gasps in the world. 'Shhh,' she whispered, rocking the small bundle close to herself, before offering the child to Raegan. Raegan cleaned and swaddled both, then lovingly handed them to their mother.

'Are they well, Anna? Are they healthy?' Cartimandua asked, concerned about her new responsibilities.

'My Lady they are small, but they look healthy. Their lungs are working well, as you heard.'

Then, exhausted by the delivery, peace fell onto the mother and twin daughters.

A few days later Cartimandua was well enough and had regained some of her strength. She was ready to make plans. Anna asked, 'Have you names prepared for your daughters, Cartimandua?'

'Yes. My firstborn will be named Lilith. The second will be named Layn. I will not disown or neglect my children, but they cannot stay here, where Venutius may hear of them. I have decided that they must go to Whispering Waters, where Eachann has a hamlet. There they will be safe for a while, and certainly till Eachann is back from his ventures.' Thoughtfully, Cartimandua beamed at Raegan. 'Would you take care of my babies, Raegan? Would you go with Camulo and look after them together until it is safe to bring them back? If you go to Whispering Waters, I can come and visit often, but I need them to be safe.'

Raegan bowed. 'I will, my Queen. It will be my honour.'

'Then call for Camulo and be on your way. Can you find a wet-nurse? Take what you need and pretend that the girls are your own. It hurts me to do this, but until it is settled with Venutius, I have no choice.'

'Will the father be visiting too, My Lady?'

'No. No he won't… But Eachann will be there occasionally. He is my champion alongside Camulo, so I will use both champions in the protection of the two.' She smiled and nodded, satisfied with the deception.

Cartimandua sat on her throne as Camulo entered the hall. 'Camulo, this is sensitive,' she said. Explaining to her champion and friend, she kept her voice low.

Camulo smiled and winked. 'I understand my Lady. Everything

will be as you require. I will protect with my life. The babes will be safe.'

She grabbed the arm of her champion and squeezing it till he flinched. Her voice was deep and shaky. 'Venutius must not hear of this,' She warned.

Camulo patted her hand. She was reassured.

Within a few days Cartimandua resumed her regal duties. She sent messengers to find Donnlugh and his fellow traveller. She sent messengers to find Eachann and Mugh. She sent messengers to Belinos, and his cousin, Byrde; to King Ninniau of Gabrantovices, and to King Maglos of Setantii, seeking news of enemy activity in Albion, and updates of any dissension in Brigantia. She called on Gallagher to stand by her as high champion until such times saw the return of Eachann Beli Mawr, and Elora she called to stand at her side whenever she needed her.

'Now I have things in order, I will send yet another messenger to Venutius, to find out when, if ever, he plans to come to Stanwix. I must have warning of his plans.' In her heart, she wished him dead.

Beombran Byrde was the first to return news, travelling to Stanwix to speak with the Queen personally. 'The fighting in Catuvellauni has moved south. There is heavy fighting in *Cantiaci*, but it is necessary in order to defend Albion coasts against the continued threat from the Roman Emperor Caligula. It is only since Adminius took power in Cantiaci, that his father, King Cunobelinos Britannorium has discovered the extent of his son's treason against Albion. Although Cunobelinos has exiled his son for his perfidy, it has left the coast of Cantiaci perilous. Many of that tribe remain loyal to Adminius or are looking to gain the power of leadership for themselves.'

'And what of the emperor of Rome? What is the state now?'

'It is said that as a result of the treacherous Adminius, Caligula most certainly has information and power enough to take all of Albion. Cunobelinos, seeing the urgency, is determined to secure the coastal areas again. Togodomus the Terrible - though you, Queen, know him as Belinos, fights alongside his father. His brother Caracatus also fights beside Cunobelinos. They hold the area, but the wounded are many.'

'Is Belinos well?' Cartimandua asked casually.

'He is, Lady. My cousin is well.'

Looking into the distance, Cartimandua detached herself from expression. 'And what of his wife?'

'She is with me. She has travelled with me to Stanwix. She was eager to see the oppidum now it comes to completion.'

Cartimandua said nothing but twitched her lips. Changing the subject, she moved on. 'I have heard of Cunobelinos and his trading with Rome over many years. Can we be sure that he is on the side of continued freedom for Albion?'

'I think so. He has only ever traded and had dealings with the Romans because of his young years in the court of Caesar Augustus. He returned to Albion on good terms with Augustus, but he never bowed to him. There has been many good influences and riches effected as a result of his relationship with Rome, but not once has Cunobelinos given an inch of Albion territory or even a hint of it. He guzzles power, only for himself and for his sons.'

'It is well that he has this need. He is a great king and one who will fight to the end.'

'Indeed, My Lady.'

Speaking in hushed tones, almost to herself Cartimandua murmured, 'The ways of our people are ancient and deep rooted, Beombran. We will not be uprooted easily, for the bones of our ancestors are entwined in the roots of this land. Our ancestors breathe life to the future of our people. We understand the cycle in the very fibre of our souls. It is not for anyone to give that away, nor to take it.' Cartimandua became silent and thoughtful for some moments, taking in all that Beombran had reported. Then seeming to return from a trance, she returned to Beombran Byrde and smiled. 'Come, you will need a bed for the night, and for the wife of Belinos.'

The following day, the messenger from Venutius arrived back. He fell at the feet of his queen 'Lady, Queen. I arrived in Staena of Carvetii only to find that the King was not there. I was told that he and his army were still pushing the painted barbarians back from the borders, and although weary, were winning the fight against them. The occurrences were not as frequent as they have been over the last *ealdor*. I did not know whether to venture to the borders, or whether my aim should be to return to you with the message given through the High-Druid of Carvetii. I saw him. He said there would be no good come from trying to see Venutius personally, as he would be in the thick of battle, with no time to let up.'

'So, he is not coming yet?' asked the Queen.

'No Queen. He is not. According to Raigon, his High-Druid, the King will be occupied dealing with the enemy for a time yet.'

Cartimandua stood. Without a movement in her body, she stood, allowing the news to filter. Touching her forehead with the fingers on her right hand, she tapped. 'Then Venutius does not know that I have asked for him?'

'The messenger swallowed hard. 'No, Queen' then offering reasons he added, '… though Lord Raigon told me he would make sure that Venutius knew of my arrival. He said the King would know the questions I would be asking on your behalf.' The messenger began to quake, as Cartimandua remained frozen. He began to stutter, stroking his throat. 'I ask for mercy, Queen.' He grovelled on the floor, pleading for forgiveness for his failure. Amazement and relief spread over his face as he saw the Queen begin to smile.

'And still he does not come,' she thought.

Uprising in small villages surrounding Wetfield Slack, where Cartimandua had been encouraging the building of chariots, had lost their leader. Disputes had broken out between the families there and were spreading across the area bringing discord in the surrounding hamlets and farmsteads. Cartimandua had been warned that several tribes had begun to gather. Concern over the issue escalating, the Queen took it upon herself to ride out and settle the argument.

'I will show them how to argue' she vowed, whipping her sword as she rode into Slack, the largest of the farmstead septs. Her warriors had been informed to wait for the signal from the Queen so storming of the villages could be done simultaneously. When it came, Cartimandua was brutal. Anger and dread rode by her side. She ordered the holy men out first. 'Drag them into the centre of Slack, and tie them to the trees,' she ordered. With floggings, they gave the names of the instigators. Cartimandua ordered these agitators into the centre of Slack. Five chiefs died at the hand of the Queen that day. Each, a swoop of her sword, Cartimandua laid low the chief warriors from the area. Then, reinstating the whipped Druids, the Queen gave them rewards for their 'help' and loyalty. She positioned one of each to replace the leaders lost, issuing warnings should they ever act against Brigantia. 'I will hear. I will know. And just as I disposed of your chiefs today, let it be known that anyone – anyone who is not loyal to me, will go the same way. You are my eyes and ears. You are now the High-Druids of these septs.' As Cartimandua spoke these words, a ripple of pleasure escaped their mouths. The grove of cloaked faces nodded with delight. The Queen continued, 'You will guard the unity of my people, so that there is no longer a desire to fight among yourselves. Do your job and teach the Brigante way. Bring our ancient truth and wisdom to my people. Now, hang the heads of the traitors by the doors of your halls, and be grateful that I am a merciful queen.'

Many days passed before Cartimandua, having brought a type of peace to the fraught villages, was sure that the Druids could hold the people. 'I need more tribal chiefs. Ones I can trust,' was her constant thought even though she was assured that the new heads of Wetfield Slack were more than able to hold the situation.

Her thoughts continued. 'Eachann could have sorted that little affray. I will be glad when he returns. He has been away so long now,' she thought.

As Beltaine arrived, the blossom had begun to show itself. The buds were opening to the promise of fullness and a bountiful year. The fields around Stanwix, and indeed across Brigantia had already been ploughed, and seeds sown. Walls were repaired, farm shelters were thatched anew, and animals were turned out into the open grazing fields. The Queen and Elora sat one morning, enjoying the summer warmth. Bees buzzed and butterflies settled on red deadnettle and dandelions which spread callously across the gravel paths of the oppidum.

Plans had been made for Raegan to visit with the two young princesses. Raegan and Camulo had taken on parental roles, so the princesses were protected. Cartimandua fidgeted nervously. Because of her duties at Westfield Slack, she had not seen her babies for a full moon turn.

As Elora and the Queen sat watching the sun strengthen as it rose into the morning sky, they noticed a rider and horse approaching.

Dismounting, the cloaked man 'bowed before Cartimandua. 'Lady. I have come from Carvetii, where Venutius still fights at the borders. But I have other news for you. While I was there, I met two travellers, both Sages, men of the Druidic orders. They told me their story and I promised to take this news to Stanwix, and to you.' The cloaked man bowed low, removing his hood to reveal a soft young face, not yet old enough to grow hair.

'What is your name, young traveller? Are you a Druid?'

'Yes, My Lady. I am bhaírd Brccht Lamfal. I come from Moricambe; a tribal area under the rule of Carvetii, and therefore under your rule now, Oh! Queen.'

A nervous excitement spread a smile across Cartimandua's face. 'Fetch Anna, someone. She should be here to listen to this.' As Anna arrived and sat by the side of Elora, Cartimandua gave her orders. 'Then sing your tale, and we will listen.'

The bhaírd slung back the sides of his cloak to reveal a small willow whistle from under the folds. He began to blow the whistle creating a merry tune, then interjected his high soprano voice in song.

THE TALE OF THE TWO

Two travellers in the hardened night,
walked day and night to find the light.
The path led on, as if through dreams,
to northern lights and fairie realms,
And through the Druid underworld,
where death, yes, death its grip unfurled,
Where desolation overturned the land and its inhabitants,
The two found 'knowing' curled in knowledge.
Then lightning struck just as it vanished

With lightning wheel and magi gleam, the truth is now uncurled.
Oh, the truth is now uncurled. The truth is now uncurled.

The seed was scattered on the land and watered by the lightning
hand.
The sun and moon and stars above watch over as the growth of love
Tends the golden shoot.
With lightning wheel and magi gleam, the truth is now uncurled.
Oh, the truth is now uncurled. The truth is now uncurled.

The god, he thunders from above, speaks deep into the sacred grove.
May lightning from the darkness rise, predicting glory as the prize.
From blind and weak the power grows, until o'er the land it blows.
The seed of being, spirit strong, producing fire and living, long.
The future of Brigantia bloom. Brigante seed - Brigante womb.

The lightning wheel and magi, gleam, the truth is now uncurled.
Oh, the truth is now uncurled. The truth is now uncurled.

Brecht Lamfal fell into silence, finishing the song on an extended low note.

'There is so much I understand, my good bhaírd, but there is a lot that is still not clear. Can you tell me more?' asked the Queen.

'This is the story told to me, by the two Druids, but I guess that they have travelled far, and to the dark places not accessible to us mere mortals. But I believe that they have discovered the very beginnings of our being, and even the future before it unfurls. It is possible that they have discovered the seed of Brigantia, and one that has already been sown into the land. But they are travelling home now and will soon be able to tell you for themselves.'

'This is good, Brecht. I am glad you were able to let me know that they are well and have something special to tell me on their return. Please make yourself comfortable while you stay in Stanwix, and sing more tales for us, if you are able.' The Queen nodding to the young minstrel as he took his leave. She turned to Anna. 'Is there any insight in this song, Anna?' she asked. Her mouth drooped as she spoke.

Anna's eyes fell. Her hands lay in her lap. She turned them over and began to examine her fingers and palms. 'I dare not hope. Does this mean my son may be alive? It is too big a chasm to leap, to even dream that he is alive and that his destiny may be of great importance to Brigantia?'

'Oh! Anna. I think if the gods speak, then there is every chance that your son is alive. Let us hope that Donnlugh knows more, and that he knows of his whereabouts.'

Anna smiled as Cartimandua encouraged her hope.

'And now the children have arrived,' interrupted Elora, running to the doorway to meet Raegan and Camulo, followed by a wisp of a girl, who did not look old enough to wet nurse. Raegan brought the girl forward, in front of Cartimandua.

'My Queen, this is Dera. She is helping me feed the babies.'

Cartimandua nodded, saying only, 'I trust your judgements, Raegan.'

Camulo left the women to their talk of babies, their health and happiness, whilst he visited old warrior friends and drank ale.

As the sun began to set, horses could be seen in the distance approaching Stanwix at speed. Their riders carried torches which burned brightly, creating shadows in the muffled light of dusk. All other 'cepting one, wore black. This one rider stood out against the set of the sky as if his cloak were blazing fire itself. No banner could be seen, no clear identifying standard. Stanwix warriors gathered quickly at the gates and on the high fortified earth ramparts of the oppidum walls. Camulo joined the warriors; shields and weapons ready to deal with the company galloping toward them.

'Halt' shouted Camulo. 'Who goes there, and what is your business at Stanwix?'

The company slowed at the gate. One rider ventured further, holding his torch high.

'Open up. We have urgent business with the Queen,' he shouted.

'Give me a name,' called Camulo.

'I am Beli Mawr! Champion of Carvetii.' called the voice from behind the flaming torch.

CHAPTER NINETEEN

AIRSON BRIGGA
For Brigantia

ACHANN AND MUGH RUITH rode into Stanwix, and to the roundhouse where Camulo had been drinking with his confreres. Wine was poured at once for Eachann and his fellow companions. Camulo slapped his friends on the back, then lifting his cup high, he saluted them. Mugh sat at the side of Eachann and grumbled in his ear. 'I am getting a little too old for that sort of riding. And that slap from Camulo made my back hurt,' he moaned.

Placing a drinking cup on the table in front of the little Druid, Eachann grinned. 'Maybe this will ease the pain.'

'Maybe it will, but a little sweetmeat would help too. Or a cake.' A grin appeared on his face as he noticed a young lass near him carrying two platters, one full of honey cakes and the other full of warm sweetbreads. The company began to relax as the food appeared at the table, and the wine flowed.

'Has your venture been successful, Eachann?' Camulo asked.

'Indeed. The Queen will be pleased with the results, though she needs to keep an eye on that chief at Luddenden. He is a slimy character. He flows whichever way the purse swings. If another leader can be found to move into that area, then I think it would be a good thing. Meantime, all is calm for the present. I have suggested a tariff for the passing on the road, which is to be paid as a tax to Cartimandua. For each week of peace, both sides get a percentage of the toll. That way it is in their interest to be friendly. I have set three of Cartimandua's men to reside there, and it may be that they will be strong enough to handle the sides. They are happy to do that, if their wives and children can join them.'

'On the subject of wives and children, Eachann. I am now the proud father, caring for two baby girls.' Camulo winked. Eachann glanced up in amazement. He stared at Camulo allowing his mouth to drop open. 'Congratulations, Camulo! This calls for a real celebration.'

'No. NO. Eachann!' Leaning forward, he whispered. 'You have been away too long. The Queen will be waiting for you. Raegan and I have the babies at Whispering Waters. But today we have brought them on a visit to see the Queen. They are all in the hall.'

'Babies? Twins?' Eachan stopped, tilting his head to one side. His eyebrows nit for an instant, then he jumped and made as if to leave, but Camulo grabbed his arm.

'Wait, Eachann. Let me go and warn the Queen of your arrival. Let me make sure that there are no prying eyes, or ears in the hall.' Eachann nodded and sat down again. Mugh had the ears of a few men drinking wine and had already begun to spin a fantasy. The attention kept him occupied.

When Camulo arrived back, he smiled, and without a word passing between them, Eachann made his way to the hall.

The hall was empty, except for Elora. She bowed as Eachann entered, then pointed to the curtained screen behind the throne. 'I will be here, should you need me.'

Eachann drew the curtain aside and entered the bedchamber. Raegan sat holding the babies. Cartimandua was fidgeting nervously with her tunic. Eachann beamed at her when he saw her smiling face. Then eagerly he went to the tiny babes. Raegan offered one. 'This is the Queen's first-born daughter, Lilith.' Eachann took the bundle, hugging her close to his heart and kissing her head. Then he passed her back to Raegan. Raegan offered the other child, 'and this is her second daughter, Layn. Both are well and lusty,' she smiled. Eachann kissed Layn and hugged her also. Holding Layn, he moved to Mandua.

'They are beautiful girls. My Lady,' then quietly, he whispered 'I love you so much. Thank you for these precious gifts.'

Cartimandua nodded to Raegan who took Layn, then gathering her shawl and the babies, Raegan left to find Camulo.

Taking the hands of the Queen in his, Eachann pondered long and hard into her eyes. 'I have missed you, my love.'

'And I you,' she responded. Her heart fluttered and her stomach overturned with the nearness of his body. 'Do you want to talk?' she asked.

'Are you well?'

'I am fully recovered from the births, yes. I am well.'

Without a further moment, Eachann picked Cartimandua up into the air, and slowly slid her down his body, allowing the feel of her to invade his senses. 'Too long I have waited for you. Too long,' he whispered in her ear. As their lips met, the passion grew, until each could not contain their need for a moment longer. Eachann ripped off the garment which hid his lover's body. He caressed her shoulders, feeling her smooth skin, allowed his hands to roam to her breasts. 'Hmm.' He said, still whispering, 'these have grown in the birthing. Nice,' he said, nuzzling into them. Cartimandua laughed and began to undo the belt hung round the waist of her warrior, excited with the thought of his exigence. Her hands felt for the fullness, as both tumbled onto the bed. Stripping his clothes from his burning body, he took his satisfaction swiftly, but then returned to heat the fires of her passion. The made love through the night.

Before the morning cockerel called, Eachann woke. Stroking the hair away from the face of his queen, he bent to kiss her.

Cartimandua held onto him. 'Don't go, Eachann. Tell me first of your travels, and of the pouch hanging from your neck. Is this a new lace?'

Holding the leather bag in his hand, he spoke of the completed orders between the arguing tribes at Luddenden. 'The problem with the tribes holding the road at Luddenden has been temporarily solved, though I left three of your warriors there to hold the situation. It took a pair of my trophy boots and a horse to satisfy their manners. I will talk to you about that later. It will wait.'

'And what else? Did you find anything of your past, my love?'

'I found someone who knew of my trainer, my Druid warrior educator. I have a way of finding her. She will have some insights, I am sure. But I got no further than mention of Gabrantovices. One day, if you allow, I will go there and see if there is a path to find her.'

'Her?'

'Yes, when I was a young boy, she told me the story of her training. Since then, she has chosen to remain hidden from me. She is a priestess and a warrior and has *Rí* blood flowing through her veins. I know she has 'seer' understanding. She will be able to help me.'

'Then she must be found.' Cartimandua agreed. 'My news is that Venutius is still fighting the Pehtas on Carvetii borders. I am beginning to think he does not want to come back to Stanwix. And that is good, for I do not want him here. Though I need to know where that leaves our united tribes. But for now, the romans are still holding back. I had news only yesterday, that their leader Caligula has been killed. We have a reprieve. But for how long?'

Eachann took from around his neck the leather bag holding the precious treasure. Untying it, he revealed the ring inside. Cartimandua sat up to take a better look at the ring as Eachann offered it to her. It was made from one long gold thread, wrapped round itself like a coil, then hammered flat at the end. A sun wheel cross, the symbol of Brigantia was etched onto the flat buckle. 'This is the ring given to me, passed down from the Eòlas and to Mugh Ruith for safe keeping. The Eòlas said it was mine. It is a signet ring fit for a king, or queen, so one I cannot wear, but I took it to a Druid who is good at working gold. He inscribed it on the inside with the symbol of the wild pony. See, can you see it?' he asked. 'I want you to have it. Take this and wear it as a symbol of our eternal love. Whatever life has in store, this ring promises we will always be together. *Anam Cara.*'

'But Eachann. I cannot.'

'You can. You are the mother of my children, and the Queen. If you cannot wear it, then no one can.'

She took the ring, seeing the glow of it, and tried it on. Her thumb held it. 'Thank you,' then kissed him. '*Anam Cara.*'

'I must go, but I will wait for you at Whispering Waters. Who knows, but the battles in Carvetii might not finish for a while longer,' he grinned. Opening the hidden screened doorway, Eachann called his love to his side. 'Look, Mandua.' He pointed to the perigee moon in the sky. 'She smiles down on us, beaming an omen of approval, this *Sár Ghealach.* I wonder what she foretells this night?'

Cartimandua touched her belly. Meeting his mouth, she kissed him. And he was gone.

As the seasons unfolded, Cartimandua and Eachann snatched secret moments; moments filled with love and joy. They celebrated as the twin princesses began to grow, and again at the arrival of their third daughter Maawan, just as the spring days showed early signs of blossom. Whispering Waters kept the secret of the nascence, hiding the birth sounds of the child in the bubbling polyphony of unexpected mid-summer fionnas. The heavy rain flooded the river, then just as suddenly as it appeared, the deluge magically disappeared.

Cartimandua had never been so happy. The fire blazed brightly as the Earth grew dark. She looked round the small hamlet which gave her a feeling of home. She felt safe and comfortable. Coming from the direction of one of the roundhouses, Cartimandua could hear the voice of Mugh Ruith chatting to the young girl who had become part of the family there. She had settled into the secret life, knowing that this was a good position for someone with no family, and no protection. Mugh found the waif outside Vindovium when the nights were still blanketed in snow from the winter covering. He brought her to the safety of Whispering Waters. There she had stayed. On the eve of her arrival, as they sat together drinking a cup of hot soup by a warming fire, she told Mugh her story. 'I am Rica. My parents were murdered; killed by Roman traders. Then they raped me.' She said flatly, showing no signs of emotion. 'When you found me Mugh, outside Vindovium, you remember I was distraught and naked. You wrapped your cloak round me and brought me here to the safety of Whispering Waters. I will always be grateful to you.'

'And here you must stay,' assured Mugh. 'Stay with us, and Dera too. All will be well.'

Later it was discovered that Rica was with child. The boy was born as the new princess Maawan arrived, so Rica blessed both her son and the princess with her full flow of milk.

The voices, low and kindly, ran alongside the whispers of the river. The lilt created a sweet-sounding cadence as its music flowed into the night air. The giggles from the two young princesses, mixed into the melody. The sounds lifted the spirits and relaxed the people gathered at Whispering Waters.

'If only this could be my reality,' thought the Queen, as she sat with Eachann and the protectors of her children. She regarded the young Dera who had suckled them, now playing with the twins. They giggled, enjoying the fun of being tickled. Camulo joined in the hilarity as Raegan rocked the new-born. 'I thank the gods for Camulo and Raegan,' she smiled. 'They look like the perfect family.'

'What are you thinking, My Lady?' asked Eachann.

'I am thinking what a perfect day this has been. I have the ones I care about by my side, and my beautiful babies. I wish this life could last for ever.'

Eachann wrapped his arms round his love and hugged her. 'I wish that too.'

'But reality is not here. I must return to Stanwix tomorrow. The messengers come more furiously now, bringing reports from south of our borders. Cunobelinos of Catuvellauni is dead. The great warrior has died in battle. His sons Caracatus and Togodomus Belinos of Catuvellauni head up the resistance since their father's death. But they are battling close to the western borders, and it has given the Romans a chance to take many of the southern areas of Albion. Since the murder of Caligula, the new emperor Claudius is eager to prove his worth. Each fresh report tells of the growing number of Romans landing on our shores. There are boats full of men; legions ready to embark. I have to gather my armies and we need to move down to the lower borders of Brigantia.'

'Then I will be by your side, my love, *Anam Cara*.'

Overhearing this decision, Camulo came over to the Queen. 'Lady, I would like to ask for your permission to marry Raegan. I long to show my commitment to her, and if you agree, I would like to take her back to my home sept at Ellstob.'

'But what about the children? How far is Ellstob?' asked the Queen, as a shaking took over her voice.

'My Lady. If we take the children with us, Dera and Rica too, we will be able to care for them safely; maybe until you know how the situation is in the south. There has been warning after warning coming from the new Latin Caesar, aye, and false alarms too. It may be that the threat is not something to worry about, but Ellstob is not far. The children would be well hidden in the fairie sanctuary [for that is what Ellstob is], and we can visit Stanwix as often as you like.'

Eachann agreed. 'If the children are safe, then we are free to go with the armies, and do what we can to support the kingdoms in the south who are building strength to resist the enemies.'

'While Venutius plays in Carvetii? Ptah!' the Queen spat.

The others moved nearer the fire to listen to the conversation. Mugh sat by Eachann, gazing into the fire. Rica appeared with her sleeping son in her arms and sat close to Mugh.

The Queen did not speak but gazed also into the flames. The thunderous rhythm of her heart spoke loudly into her mind. 'You have to do this. You have to do this. You are the queen, and you have to do this.'

Mugh, in the ancient language, began to mumble into the fire.

'Brigga buadhach. Brigga buadhach.
Dean Seo feumaidh tu.'

A thick and dreadful darkness fell like a shroud over the shoulders of the party. Mugh scoured round, peering into the thick black atmosphere where a hazy mist began to circle. As he stared, a vision exposed a hand-held glaive, slicing deep into the heart of the darkness. From the open cut, an orb appeared. The red burning sphere was elevated above the fire, rising into the night sky, until the red goddess Aurora moved to her proper position in the heofones, to display her fullness.

Then Mugh began to speak again, repeating his mumblings. 'From the darkness, arises the light. *Brigga buadhach. Brigga buadhach. Dean Seo feumaidh tu.* For the victory of Brigantia, do this, you must!'

The fire crackled; the darkness dissipated, and the full moon revealed herself. No longer red, but silver, the wheel in the night sky shone her light on all below.

'For Brigantia,' the Queen assented.

Anna and Elora were waiting to greet Cartimandua on her arrival back at Stanwix. 'Welcome, Queen. Is all well?' they asked.

'Indeed. Indeed. All is well, but I need to convene a meeting. I need to parley with my tribal chiefs and warlords.' Turing to Elora, she ordered, 'Get Lochru. He can help with this. Mugh and Eachann will help too.' To the warrior beside her, she held her open palm so as to introduce him to Anna. Eachann bowed in front of the lady. Anna stared into his face for lost moments, as if searching for the answer to some question asked long ago. She eventually bobbed her knee and smiled.

Elora called messengers, who were dispatched with haste across Brigantia. They each held an invitation to join the Queen in discovering the extent of their armies and weaponry, their practical capabilities and analytic intelligence should they come face to face with the enemy. Cartimandua wanted to corelate all defences at her disposal.

The oppidum was prepared for the influx of tribal leaders and their escorts, at just the beginning of the festival of Litha. Braint arrived from across the land, bringing their own small companies of warriors and Druids. Soon the oppidum was heaving with the guests and visitors. The traders were quick to arrive too, displaying their wares on tables set up on the approach to the great fortified sept. Musicians played, Bhaírds sang, old women read palms, women danced, swinging their skirts to show off bare legs and shaking their shoulders till the tunics dropped to reveal their bosoms. The children played in the dry ground; amusing themselves with checked boards and glass pieces, skipping ropes and stick throwing. The atmosphere took on a jubilance befitting the best festival the Brigante had ever seen. As each lord arrived the people cheered. Druids were welcomed to the largest sacred grove in the country, outside the main Druid Isle at Ynys Mon. The grove occupied a large swathe of land in the sept, hedged by the sacred hawthorn and positioned with a great oak tree central to the plot. Round houses circled the plot, with doorways facing the oak. The extra shelters for the visiting Druids, were teanta slung between each round house. As with the houses, they also faced the great oak. More shelters had been erected to supply the many more beds needed across the oppidum, and extra poles had been erected around the outside walls, to display the heads of enemies and animals, a sign of the prowess of the Queen.

Cartimandua displayed not only her oppidum, but her resources and wealth too.

A great excitement took over the people when the Druids walked out of their grove into the wide space of the central arena. White hooded cloaks mixing with brown and blue, creating a formidable sight in the gathering. A platform had been built to elevate the heavy iron throne of Cartimandua. which had been carried out from her hall for the occasion. Banners on standards hung all around the outside walls of the hall, displaying diverse tribal symbol, each allied to Brigantia. Cartimandua sat on her throne as the Druids, acknowledging her highness, bowed their heads and filed past her. They then formed a ring around the edges of the arena. At the end of the line, she saw Anna's Druid and Donn Donnlugh. 'Donn,' she called from her lofty position. 'You are home.' Donnlugh bowed.

'Come here to me,' she called, beckoning the Druid to climb onto the platform. 'You are my High-Druid. You belong here,' she called. Donnlugh moved swiftly to position himself at the side of the Queen. Bending close to him, but still watching the line of Druids passing in front of her, she asked, 'Have you news, Donnlugh?'

'We will speak later, Queen. I am glad to be home.'

'Then take up your duties this day, and we will speak later about your journey.'

Closing his eyes, Donnlugh inclined his head in a nod.

The procession continued, as the champions walked or rode in front of the Queen. The Queen was treated to a show of the full extent of her greatest fighting men, flexing magnificent thews. Eachann rode among them. Cartimandua could not look anywhere except toward her lover. His body, oiled and naked except for his short braccae, shone in the sunlight. His golden hair fell down his back, like a blaze of fire. Lifting his glaive high in the sky, he revealed his rippling muscles and biceps. The sun glinted, bouncing the light from the dagger like lightning. He smiled at the Queen. Her eyes met his, as if two magnets had locked them.

Dragging her face to look away from him, the Queen undertook to concentrate on the parade passing her by. The chief lords and warriors from across Brigantia led the parade on horseback. Each king bowed, then shouted their name and territory. They were followed by the champions from each tribe affiliated to Brigantia. One by one the kings and chieftains came.

'I am Ninniau, Coria Toutas from Gabrantovices and Vidicum.'

'I am King Broccos Maglos, Breehin of Setantii, and surrounding areas.' Maglos acknowledged the Queen, without a smile, he nodded his head. He rode on.

Next, a young warrior, followed by the Druid Brochfael arrived in front of the Queen. 'I am the chosen chief of Lopocares, along with Brochfael. We guard the northern lands of Vello. My name is Brei Toutoris.' The warrior held his shield high enough for the Queen to see the ensign painted on it. Lopocares had taken as a symbol for their tribe, the wild auroch. Cartimandua nodded her approval.

The next chief to present to the Queen said, 'I represent Belinos, *Coria Toutas* of Brigcruim. I am Onomarix, the wife of Belinos. I stand in his place while he is away.' As Onomarix spoke, Cartimandua stared her full in the face. Steadily, the woman glared back into the eyes of the Queen. Neither smiled, but Cartimandua felt the blush of red creep up her neck and face, as Onomarix continued to stare. 'May I speak with you, my Lady, in private? I have news.'

Cartimandua nodded. 'Come to me after we have eaten. You may speak then.' Onomarix rode on. Cartimandua returned her attention to the parade.

Branderix *map* Ninniau of Gabrantovices rode in the procession, standing for the tribe of Textowerdi. He was followed by Lord Epicus of Epiacum, then Braint Beombran Byrde of Corinota stationed at Vincobancio. Many more followed representing Eboracum, Isuer, Adel, Calatum and Rigodonun. Cartimandua sat for the day, only resting for a short time, before welcoming further lords and kings. The line was finally drawing to an end as the dusk began to settle. Cartimandua yawned.

'I am Venutius, King of Carvetii and King Consort of Brigantia,' a voice shouted. Cartimandua at once sat fully alert staring at her husband riding into her sight. She stood and gazed at Venutius. He grinned and bowed. 'Ah! Wife,' he called, laughing with a hearty laugh.

Cartimandua froze, though her mind did not. 'Oh! No!' she panicked. 'I must let Eachann know before he comes to me.' Even while she thought about the danger Eachann may now be in, she hoped that Venutius knew nothing of their love, or of the children. 'Husband,' she called. 'Let us retire to the Great Hall, where we can talk and eat together.' Having regained her composure, she called to Donnlugh. 'Donn, please fetch Anna. I want to introduce her to my husband. Please make ready our meal for this evening.' Then looking kindly at Venutius she smiled, 'Come.'

Behind Venutius, lurking in the shadow of the King, was Audigus Raigon.

As they settled into the hall, four men carried the throne and placed it back into position on the dais. They placed two chairs at either side of the throne and covered them in thick woven linen of purple. Venutius sat at the right-hand side of his wife and surveyed the hall. He scanned the faces of the high-born guests. 'I see you have many great allies and supporters, Queen. I see from their stance, their demeanour and their age. We have good fighting men here.'

Although the night was not cold, the fire was lit, and candles began to twinkle in the fading light. The kings and lords of the largest domains in Brigantia were among the first to find benches and tables. The wine was already flowing as food arrived. The musicians and Bhaírds were already playing soft refrains, though everyone knew that the music, singing and voices would soon be raised as the wine and ale flowed. Venutius smiled at his wife. He took her hand and kissed it. 'My dear. I cannot wait to be with you tonight. I have waited a long time to savour your tenderness,' he smiled.

Cartimandua shuddered. 'For Brigantia,' she thought. A movement, a flicker, almost unnoticeable, caught her vision. She scanned the doorway, and half hidden behind the door curtain, she saw Eachann. A short gasp escaped her mouth. Then Anna, followed by Donnlugh, brushed past him on their way to the dais. She bobbed at the foot of the throne, and Cartimandua held her hand for Anna to step up to the chair on the left of the Queen.

'Venutius, this is Anna, sister of Riganta, my grandmother, and now rightful Queen of Textowerdi.'

Venutius politely nodded to Anna, then turned again to Cartimandua asking, 'who heads the tribe at the moment?'

'Branderix of Gabrantovices took the leadership until a veritable chieftain can take his place. He is doing a good job of keeping the area, after I took armies to the borders and victoriously held them. But you would know nothing of that, Husband,' she snapped.

'As you know, Queen, I have my own borders to safeguard.'

'As you know, husband, I have five times as much land to safeguard while you play with your piddling bit.'

Venutius sucked his cheeks in. Slamming his hand on the arm of the chair, he stood. Then he sat again, silently staring away from the Queen.

Cartimandua ignored him, calling for attention from the lords and kings in the hall. 'Is there a Druid who is able to use the *tomus*?' she called.

The sages and seers considered among their ranks, but not one was willing to step forward. Eachann entered the hall, revealing himself. 'Mugh Ruith can use tomus. He may be out of practice, but he learned the way of it in his training years. He told me he was quite proficient in his youth.'

Venutius recognised Eachann. 'Beli Mawr,' he called. Standing to greet his champion, he held his hands out, meeting Eachann with a slap on his back. 'Well, Beli Mawr, I had almost given up hope of seeing you again. Raigon told me you were dead. I am glad to see that he was wrong.' He shook the hand of his lost champion. 'Where have you been? I was told that you had been eaten by the wolver… Or hit by a deadly arrow. Or some such thing. Come. Drink with me,' he said, moving his chair, and seeking another chair for his champion. Eachann could do no other but sit by the King.

Cartimandua seethed.

The kings and chieftains gave details to Mugh, so he could account for the warriors, *gaesatae*, chariots, bowmen and fighters that could be gathered. They spoke of the positioning of those armies and how soon they could assemble and be on their way to points of weakness in the southern boundaries of Brigantia and Setantii should they be breached by the threat. Cartimandua asked, 'what about the protection of Ynys Mon, the most sacred place of learning, where the knowledge of Albion had been passed down for so many generations?' The Druids began to add to the *tomus* from their own knowledge of other priest-sages in sacred places and the numbers living across the land. The beginnings of a census across Brigantia began to take shape.

Other chiefs brought news of connections between them and other tribes wider afield. One such connection was King Prasutagus of the Iceni, and his wife, Queen Boudicca. Beombran Byrde spoke up, 'Prasutagus already trades with the romans in his area. He has done for quite some time. Romans brought their wares to Albion and have traded for tin and metals since they first landed on our shores with that farcical Caesar of theirs. That is not unusual. There are lots of areas where this happens, and no one bothers about it, because there is a good living to be had by trading with these foreigners. He, -Prasutagus is quite happy to do that. And I know of others who also trade, in fact, at Vincobancio we have Roman traders visit sometimes too.'

Epicus of Epiacum spoke up then, 'I have been trading my horses with the Romans for some years now. They generally hold to their bargains. Which is more than can be said of some of the tribes in the north of Brigantia. They squabble and argue over a worm in the fields.'

'That aside, Epicus, these Romans have a way of infiltrating our lives.'

'It is not the trade we are against, Byrde, it is what we can expect if the Romans win authority over our island. The thought of losing our way of life is what I find so detestable,' shouted Ninniau. 'We did not allow it when Julius Caesar tried to take our lands, and we will not allow it now!' Ninniau banged his fist on the table. 'Remember what happened to the *Veneti* tribe, and their trade with us over the southern water? Their nobility was massacred, their women and daughters raped and then sold into slavery. Thank the gods that the Veneti were our allies and warned us of the attempt Caesar would make on Albion.'

'We need to be prepared like never before, because you mark my words, and mark them well, if they come again, they will be better prepared than last time,' offered Branderix. 'I am young, I know. But our history shows if we come together against our enemy, then we may be able to hold onto what we value; our faith, our families, and our way of life.'

So, conversations flowed, bringing together the ideas needed to build a strategy pertaining to victory. The hearts and souls of all meeting with Cartimandua that night were encouraged toward bravery, even death, in the name of Brigantia. As the night developed, the lasses from the sept were called. Dancing and singing ensued. Battle songs and songs of victory belted out from the throats of the warlords, like a pack of wolves on the hunt for prey.

Onomarix approached the seat of the Queen and bowed. She spoke quietly. 'Queen Cartimandua, I acknowledge your greatness, and want you to know that I am loyal to you.' Cartimandua acknowledged her approach, nodding. Onomarix continued. 'For the sake of my husband Togodomus Belinos, I come to you with news. He sends greetings. He is well, but you may have already heard that his father was killed in battle near the mighty Thames River a good while ago. Cunobelinos Britannorium Rex is no more, and Caracatus has taken the title. Belinos and Caracatus fight against the Romans who have landed on our shores. They are already in the midst of setting up camps in readiness for the influx of Roman contingents. Belinos sent word that I was to advise you of the current situation. Emperor Claudius rides forward with legions; the most we have ever seen. He kills and rapes, fights and takes slaves of our people. His brutality is of the highest order. Some tribal chiefs and kingdoms, through fear for their lives and the lives of their people, have succumbed to his offer of peace. They have already handed their lands to him. Caracatus is heading up the offensive, but Claudius, determined to have it all, is intent on taking the capital of Catuvellauni, and bring Caracatus under his power. Belinos asks that you be ready on the borders of Brigantia, to fight against their invasion.'

'Thank you Onomarix. I am glad that your husband is well. I appreciate your news. Please let Belinos know that we will be ready.'

Cartimandua indicated to Anna that she was leaving, and without signalling to anyone else, she silently left the hall. 'I hope Venutius does not come to me tonight,' she thought.

CHAPTER TWENTY

AN RUAIG
The Chase

ANNA SAT FOR A while longer, intent on the scene before her. She stared forward, fascinated by the warrior called Eachann. Elora came to her side. 'There is something that I find intriguing about him,' said Anna, indicating the champion standing next to The King of Carvetii.

Elora elaborated on Beli Mawr, explaining to Anna his position as champion of Carvetii, and how he had been ordered to deliver the message of agreements to the Queen, bringing about the betrothal between Venutius and Cartimandua, and their subsequent marriage.

'What do you know of him, Elora?'

'Nothing much, except what I have just said. Mugh Ruith walks with him. Ask Mugh.'

Just then Mugh approached the dais where Anna still sat.

'May I join you, Lady Anna?' he asked, plonking his arse at her side. He started to chat away about cakes and flights, the Queen and Albion. His chatter spread across a range of subjects. He mentioned cakes several times. His jabber was without direction, but eventually he asked a clear question. 'Anna, I believe that you are the rightful

Queen of Textowerdi. Are you happy with Cartimandua's choice of Branderix as leader there in the interim? Do you know of him?'

'Indeed, he seems to do a good job. Yes, he is young, but he has held the boundary for these last moon cycles and held them well. It remains to be seen whether he will do as well against the Roman armies. He may have chance to show his ability before too long, it seems.' She smiled kindly to the Druid, before continuing. 'I will take my place in Textowerdi when it seems right, Mugh Ruith, but for now I am content.'

Mugh sighed with relief. 'I am pleased about this. The Queen needs people she can trust. I am glad you see Branderix as a good ally.'

Anna continued, 'But what about Beli Mawr? Where did you meet him? What is your story about that, Mugh?'

Mugh began to babble, always pleased to be able to tell his tales of magic and lightning in the sky; of the young boy he found on his travels, and how he has been with him ever since. Coming to a natural close to one of his stories, he checked to see if Anna had fallen asleep. 'My Lady, forgive me. You must be ready for your bed.'

'No! Mugh Ruith. I am fascinated by your tales. And where exactly did you find this child?' she asked.

'As I came home from my travels, I found him on the route from the northern lands of the Pehtas,' he admitted. 'Why do you ask?'

'Oh! Nothing. He reminds me so much of one I once knew; a young Brigante warrior, but now I believe. he is a glorious king.' Gathering her cloak, she apologised. 'Forgive me, but my bed does indeed call. I will leave now and wish you the blessing of our goddess.'

'Blessings of Brigga on you too,' nodded Mugh.

Glancing round the room, Mugh's eyes fell on Eachann, who

continued to stand by Venutius, as the King carried on drinking and singing. The throng of battle kings and lords had begun to dwindle. A few remained, singing with less gusto and more dribble as the drink conquered their senses. They stumbled to the doorway, using whatever chair or person they could find as balance to keep them from falling over. In twos and threes, they returned to their shelters and makeshift beds as sleep overtook them.

'Eachann, I will go to my lady now.' Venutius tried to stand also, but the wine had affected his stability. He slumped down onto the bench again. Laughing, he took support from the arm of Eachann. 'Help me,' he ordered. 'Lead me to my wife,' he maffled.

Eachann and Mugh helped the King toward the bedchamber of the Queen. Leaving the intoxicated king propped up on the arm of one of the throne guards, Mugh swiftly ran to the doorway, and Eachann entered the bedchamber of Cartimandua.

'Come quickly,' he stipulated. 'Venutius is drunk. Mugh has gone to fetch a potion. He will sleep until mid-day. I will lay him on your bed, and you, my lady, will come with me.' A smile spread across the champion's face, and a twinkle in his eye met her gaze.

Mugh arrived shortly, carrying a cup of mead with a mix of dried henbane and valerian whisked into it. Eachann offered it to Venutius, who drank it down and flopped onto the bed.

'Now, w ..w.. where ish my wife,' the King asked though his bibulosity. 'Ah. There. Come here. Come here, little lady.'

Cartimandua approached him, then lifting her skirts high enough for the King to see the pink flesh beneath, she raised one leg and pushed him. He fell backwards insentient, onto the bed.

Creeping out through the hidden exit, Cartimandua waited for Eachann. Both Mugh and the champion left the chamber by the Queen's door on the dais, leaving the guard to suppose that the

Queen was in the room with her husband. Eachann ran round the outside of the Great Hall, to the hidden portal where Cartimandua was waiting. 'I have a hidden place away from the hall, my love. We can be together without fear. Elora will be ready to fetch you when the King begins to rouse, and Mugh will stay on guard too. Until then, let us savour our good fortune. Tomorrow I must take my leave before Venutius gives me fresh orders. I must travel to find my past.'

Mugh lit a fire outside the shelter where the lovers slept. He watched the flames lapping the wood fuel. From necessity, he spun a conjuration, an ancient Druid spell of covering, then to help him stay alert through the night, he began to chant the words:

'Ceo Draoidheachte. Cover this place.
Cover the heads. Cover the feet.
Over Mawr and Mandua.
Ceo Draoidheachte.'

The mist began to rise from the darkness, and except for the fire, the place was enveloped in a thick blanket of leafy green. Mugh sat in the midst of it. All around became silent, almost sacred, as the phantom veil anointed the place where the two lovers slept. Mugh allowed himself to drink the remains of the sleeping cup made for Venutius; just enough to enchant his mind. As he entered a trance state, the thunder rumbled across the sky. Mugh listened as Taranis spoke.

Above him was the wheel, the beginning of his journey with Eachann. His legs and arms began to rise as the hand of the god lifted him above the fire. Overhead smoke from the fire thickened; swirled. He pressed through the dense blackness, to find himself back into the broch from so long ago. Floating above the towering wheel in the roof of the broch, he looked down through the open windows to see the Eòlas, sitting together. They talked as if they did not know that Mugh flew above them. Listening intently, he heard Gliocas say, 'The seed has been sewn in the earth. Our job is almost done. Mother Earth will be appeased. Her spirit has been planted in the land where tender shoots will soon begin to appear. The land now has a future. The cycle can continue. Therefore, all is not lost. The knowledge will lie dormant until the awakening, when our ancient spirit will live on. It is time, My good kings. It is time.'

'What of the Cailleach? Should the Winter Queen be told?' asked Misnech.

'No. She will know when it is time to leave. She will see the buds appear.'

'And what of the Druids? The keepers of our world?' asked Neart.

'They also, will lie in the darkness until the new awakening.'

'And what of the Earth, while the darkness hides the growth?'

'Do we not know the size of the Earth and the cosmos and the movements of the heavens and stars? This knowledge will always bring a balance. But while the darkness has the power over the land, the light must be ready to burst forth.'

'But the blood over the land cries out, Misnech.'

'And yes, the cry causes us to remember the cycle of pain and agony as the Earth journeys from the darkness into her new tomorrow. The birth brings many pains, but the spirit of our Mother Earth will live on.'

Like a soft pillow supporting the little Druid, Mugh was shielded by the caress of feathers underneath his body as he floated back to earth. 'I am beginning to see things more clearly,' he said. 'The Eòlas grant me understanding.' Before any time had passed, Mugh was back in his position by the fire. Soft whispers fluttered past his ears. The sounds were indistinct, but odd words landed in his brain as if they were spoken directly.

'Donannu knows something…find her…lord of Gabrantovices.'

'Must go… Discover…find a way…watch the shadows.'

'…meet at Taftefield…'

Mugh checked round to see if anyone else heard the sounds from the make-shift queen's sanctum. 'Only a magpie,' he muttered as the bird flew from the pinnacle of the enclosed sanctuary. 'Only a magpie.'

The day brought a promising start. The sun smiled through the clouds as the kings and chiefs made their farewells leaving Stanwix in good spirits and headed home.

The light broke through the shelter onto the warm bed of the Queen and her lover. Eachann, already risen, went to the stream by the south wall, and took a dip in its waters. The fresh morning met his spirit. He breathed deeply of the summer air. Carefully tracing his steps, he returned to Cartimandua. Shaking her softly, he woke her with a kiss. 'We depart now, my Queen.' With Mugh by his side, he took his leave. Cartimandua went back to her Great Hall, hoping she might sneak into her royal bed before Venutius woke. But Venutius had already risen.

All that morning Venutius did not appear. Cartimandua moved to her throne room and began the duties of her day. Anna appeared, then sat at the side of the Queen. She began to talk hurriedly, 'Have you spoken to Donn Donnlugh yet?' she asked.

'You sound excited, Anna. What is it? I haven't seen Donnlugh yet. What is it? Have you news?'

'Indeed.' Anna smiled and shuffled on her seat. 'I have called

Donnlugh. He will join us shortly.'

Donnlugh entered the hall, his cloak swinging wide from side to side as his stride dictated. At his side, striding with equal width, was Anna's Druid.

'My Queen, I and my fellow traveller have things to tell you.' Cartimandua waited patiently until the two Druids began their report. 'As you know, you gave us instructions to find the whereabouts of Anna's son.'

Cartimandua nodded. 'Have you found him?'

'Not yet, My Lady, but we have information about him.'

Cartimandua looked at Anna's Druid and enquired. 'I know you are Anna's Druid and friend, but I do not think I know you. You have not been presented to me. What is your name?'

'I have been by the side of my Lady Anna for many years. I know she has told you of her son. I am the Druid who held the boy in safety, taking him to a far place for his protection, as the gods dictated. My name is Taragh.' Taragh bowed and swung his cloak wide in a flurry of show. He began to explain. 'In order to find the young prince, Donnlugh and I made our way back to the far lands, where it all started. We approached the broch where the wet-maid placed the baby. The Eòlas took him. We knew he would be safe, because I had seen a godly vision unravelling the cycles of the boy. I knew that he would be taught well by the Eòlas. The prophecy of his birth and standing had been predicted, and all will be fulfilled as told. But our journey took us back to the very place where his life was presented to the Knowledge.'

Cartimandua waved her hand, beckoning Taragh to continue. 'Yes, yes.' She said impatiently.

'We asked questions around the isle. We found a man and his wife who, one night long ago, had taken a Druid and small boy in, until a boat could be found to return them to the mainland. So, this much we knew. It is likely that this boy and Anna's baby are one and the same, though we do not know for sure. We know that the boy was taken by a Druid.'

Cartimandua sat on the edge of her chair, showing her excitement at the news. Anna sat almost as a statue holding her breath. Taragh continued, 'We travelled many miles south, taking the route I walked many years before. We decided to stay at the main settlements or fortified farmsteads on the way. We journeyed through the Pehtas country, risking our lives many times. The enemy were stealth like, and cunning. They knew the territory. But our enchantings were more powerful than any enemy we encountered. The gods watched over us until it seemed that we suddenly came upon Carvetii army.

At that time, Venutius was on the borders mobilizing his warriors against the pests there. We asked around about any stories which might link a boy and Druid together, and one story was repeated several times. It is the story told by Mugh Ruith. The story of Beli Mawr.'

The Queen remained silent. Her eyebrows knit together, puzzling over this story. 'What are you saying? That you think that Eachann Beli Mawr is Anna's son?' Her eyes widened.

'We think so,' the two answered in unison.

'Can this be proved?'

'I do not know, Queen, but Mugh Ruith may be able to give us further information. Where is Ruith?'

Cartimandua hesitated to answer. 'I want to give Eachann enough time to settle his own knowing, before he is told of this news,' she thought. 'I have sent him and the champion of Carvetii to support Branderix in Taftefield. Lord Epicus told of some uprising between tribes east of there, so they are on their way to settle the argument, and check on the situation before returning here,' she lied. Turning, Cartimandua gazed into the eyes of Anna. 'Do you believe this Anna?' she asked. 'Do you think that Beli Mawr could be your son?'

Anna remained stationary a moment longer before she took a deep breath. 'I believe he is. He reminds me so much of the father of my boy, and as I have observed him, I have wondered. But how can we be sure?'

'Sure about what?' questioned Venutius, into the hall. 'Sure about what?'

Audigus Raigon walked behind Venutius, his black and white cloak flapped wildly, stopping the sunlight from entering the doorway. He carried the King's sword and shield from the arena where Venutius had been sparring. The sweat from the practice ran down the King's forehead.

Cartimandua spoke pragmatically, 'Donnlugh and Taragh have discovered the possibility that the heir to Textowerdi; Anna's son, is still alive.'

Raigon stood forward. Alarm showed in his eyes. 'And who do you suppose this son is?' he asked.

'It is possible that the heir to the seat of Textowerdi is Beli Mawr, Champion of Carvetii.' Cartimandua intently marked the King for reaction, as she disclosed this news.

Venutius lifted an eyebrow. 'So?' he responded. 'That's very good for Anna. I am pleased that you may have your son returned to you.' Then causally looking round the hall, he called, 'where is the food? I have not broken fast yet. Bring food, and ale. I have worked up an appetite.'

Raigon fussed round the King, then when a bowl of peas, beans and flax appeared, the two men sat to eat. Raigon began to whisper in the ear of the King. Donnlugh, interested in the conversation, moved closer to sit with the men eating and drinking. As Raigon purred into the regal ear, all in the hall could see that the veins in the neck of Venutius began to tense. His jaw clenched as his face turned the colour of plums. He began to bang his fist into his open hand. Jerking up, he pointed his finger close to the eye of Raigon. 'If this is false, My Lord, then I will have your head, but if this is so, then I will have his head and his membrum virile, and feast on the juices,' he shouted, storming off into the light of day, and outside the hall. Raigon dashed after him.

Donnlugh whispered into the Queen's ear. Cartimandua's face became ashen. 'My Lady, I fear Raigon may know the whereabouts of Beli Mawr, and has accused him of treason.

'Why?'

Talking to both Cartimandua and Anna, Donnlugh unfolded his thinking. 'I can only surmise, my lady. If the champion of Carvetii is indeed your son, then his position as heir of Textowerdi gives Brigantia even more strength. If you, my Queen, should decide to use this new alliance against Carvetii, then you would no longer need to uphold the union into which you have just entered.

Thinking aloud, the Queen murmured, 'Are you showing me a way out of the dreadful situation I find myself in, Donnlugh? But at what cost? We cannot afford the disintegration of our unions. Brigantia is stronger with Carvetii. Textowerdi need not be a threat to Carvetii.'

'It does not need to be, but if Raigon has facts and particulars of Beli Mawr having plotted against Venutius in any way, then there will be a battle, I fear. Also, Beli Mawr is a Druid of the highest order, and one who has been offered an elevated position over Carvetii- a position that Raigon will not want to let go. Raigon stokes a fire.'

Anna gasped. 'Why would he think that Beli Mawr is a traitor to

Carvetii?' probed Anna.

'I did not grasp all of the words, Lady, but I heard him telling the King that he had been watching Beli Mawr. He did not trust him, nor has he ever trusted him. But he said he had evidence that the champion is a traitor to the King and could prove it.'

'Call for Elora and Gallagher. Prepare the horses,' shouted the Queen. 'We must stop Venutius.' With fear and urgency showing in her moves, the Queen mounted Tormaig. 'We must find Eachann, and before Venutius does.' She shouted to Anna, 'Do not worry. Beli Mawr is a gifted Druid and champion. He will meet any action with strength and ability.'

'Please let me ride with you, Mandua,' begged Anna. 'If he could be my son, then I beg of you to let me ride with you. Give me an opportunity to see for myself.'

Cartimandua ordered Elora, 'Bring her, Elora. Keep up with us. All will be well.' Shouting further orders, she called to Gallagher. 'Find Venutius and delay him. Take three warriors along. Make sure he is stopped from his anger.'

Cartimandua rode south, thinking only of protecting her children first. On her heels, Donnlugh, Taragh, Anna and Elora. The horses flew swiftly; all hooves rising in the air simultaneously. Cartimandua was excited to approach the sept. She began to shout, 'Camulo. Camulo,' before ever her voice could be heard.

An old hag sat by the gate to Ellstob, chewing on the seeds from a stalk of flax. Her legs protruded onto the path the Queen travelled. Tormaig pulled up sharply, to avoid the obstruction. He whinnied as if seeing a ghost. The old woman smiled a toothless smile. 'Welcome to Ellstob. Home to travellers, jugglers and *scates,*' she said, spraying saliva from her very large mouth in the direction of Cartimandua.

'Make way for her highness, The Queen of Brigantia,' called Donnlugh. The old hag continued to smile, and continued chewing.

'Spare a token for an old seer,' she begged. Donnlugh threw a tin token onto the crone and made to move. Looking directly at the Queen, the crone spoke clearly. 'Three are yours. One for joy. Two for sorrow. Three for *Brētrā Ōrd Mōr.*' She began to mumble in the old language, shifting her legs out of the way of the visitors.

Cartimandua turned her eyes away from the hideous carlin, though her mind remembered a similar *vistant* face. 'Pah!' she growled, then rode by. Up the central pathway, and around the fairie elder tree in the centre of the sept, the group rode. They passed the thirteen or fourteen round houses which had been built to face the mage tree, before arriving at the chief house and then the Great Hall of Ellstob. Outside the doorway, trophies from past victories hung. Heads severed and oiled to preserve them, swung from the beam across the sides of the open entrance. Skulls of goats and bear displayed on stakes around the pathway, revealed the extent of Camulo's championship.

Raegan ran from the hall to greet the riders. 'My lady, my Queen.' she called bobbing in front of the Queen. 'Welcome.' Then seeing the others, Raegan became guarded. 'Lady, can I get one of our men to show your party where to rest?'

'Yes. Take the men and give them a meal, if you can. Elora and Anna will stay with me,' she replied, winking at Raegan in understanding. When the Queen's party had moved to the drinking inn, Cartimandua asked quietly, 'Where are the children? Are they well? Where is Camulo?' The questions tumbled from Cartimandua, even before she stepped down from her horse. 'Where are they, Raegan?'

'Come,' Raegan beckoned, wearing a smile that spread from one ear to the other. Elora and the Queen followed the woman into her home, where the huge champion of Brigantia sat on the ground, playing with the three girls and the son of Rica. Raegan laughed. 'He cannot tear himself away from the babies.'

Camulo stood to welcome his queen, knocking the dust from his hands. 'All is well, Lady,' he confirmed. 'All is well.'

The queen sank to the ground snatching the children into her arms. She hugged them one by one. 'It won't be long, my babies, before you are with me again,' she whispered to them.

The morning turned and passed noon, but the joy in the heart of Cartimandua, overspilled. 'What a wonderful day,' she beamed. 'Look Anna. These are your grandchildren.'

Elora and Anna gasped. 'Beli Mawr is your lover?' Anna asked.

'Do you now see the urgency to find and make safe the future of your son? These girls are seeds and heir to the Textowerdi kingdom, and also to Brigantia. They need to be hidden, for their lives might well be in danger. Many would like to end the lineage of our glorious tribe, but such a spirit cannot be destroyed easily. It is the spirit of the very earth we stand on, and we will protect this spirit in this world and in the next.'

Anna nodded, and rushing to the children, she gushed with love over the princesses. 'But where will we find Beli Mawr?' Which way would he travel, Mandua?' Anna asked.

'He is searching for that which is already found – his past, his parentage. I believe he will search for his trainer, Donannu. He has learned that she may have a home in the northeast, near the great Northern Sea. He may be on his way to seek the help of King Ninniau of Gabrantovices. If not there, then he will make his way to Taftefield, to ask the son of Ninniau for his knowledge of her whereabouts. I will ask Donnlugh and your own Taragh to seek understanding from the gods, before we quit here.' They ate a meal together enjoying the moments with the three princesses before the need to leave took precedence.

'There is not enough time. I am sorry,' said the queen, as the length of the afternoon shadows began to warn her of the urgency to depart.

The route had been decided upon. The venerable priests sought the guidance of the gods using a sacred chicken running free around the grounds of Ellstob. With a stick in the dusty ground, they drew a circle encompassing the symbols of the four elements. Then, placing the chick on the centre point, they waited. She ran first of all to the sign for air; the east, and then to the sign for earth; north. Donn Donnlugh announced the interpretation. 'We travel east first to visit Gabrantovices. The wind will blow us there in good time, and then, unless the gods say otherwise, we travel to Taftefield.'

Camulo had readied himself to ride with the entourage. Sitting atop his horse, he had regaled himself in his full war clothing. His horned helmet and weapons disclosed a terror not to be overlooked. 'I ride with you, My Lady,' he determined.

Smiling at him and then at her children, Cartimandua shouted, 'Look after them, Raegan.' She waved, as the party pulled out of Ellstob. She blinked, holding back the tears, then, adjusting her posture, she sat upright on Tormaig, and galloped straight ahead.

Two days journey brought them to the outskirts of Gabrantovices, where just a few years previously, the princess of Brigantia had stood with her grandfather on the edge of a cliff overlooking the great Northern Sea. This day, breathing the cold sea air and looking out beyond the bay and toward the distant horizon, she remembered how she had felt that day. 'This is the edge of Brigantia. The fingers of gods protect this place. My gods, please protect my beloved,' she prayed, staring beyond the sea.

Donnlugh drew close to her. 'Lady, I am not needed here. Let me travel on and meet you at Taftefield. I will be discrete but find out what I can before you arrive.'

'Yes. Go,'

Donnlugh bowed his head and turned his horse northward. Hailing the party, Cartimandua led them on toward the gate of Gabrantovices. Camulo shouted, 'Make way for the High Queen of Brigantia. Open up.'

King Ninniau rode out to greet them. 'My Queen. We are honoured. Enter and welcome.'

'We will stay no longer than a rest period for the horses, King. I have but a short time, and need to seek your knowledge,' explained the Queen, who was already fidgeting on her horse, not wanting to dismount, but knowing she must. 'We have little time, Ninniau.'

They walked into the hall, where Cynifrida welcomed the company, offering them a place round a table in front of the chair of the King. Cartimandua was swift. 'We are looking for one called Donannu. When last we heard, she was heading east on the coast. Is she here?'

'May I know the reason you seek her, Lady?'

'I believe that she trained a certain warrior in the art of Druid warfare. It would have been some time ago, but I wish to find her and thank her,' said Cartimandua, sincerely. 'But also, I believe she might have information about this particular warrior, and I seek her knowledge.'

Ninniau took a moment before he responded. 'I told your grandfather at our last meeting, that when my wife Arnemetia died I had found some comfort in the arms of another woman. The truth is, I lay with this woman before my wife left this Earth. She was one of my household servants, and when we found that she was with child, I sent her away, not wanting to cause distress to my wife. Latis, the one of whom I speak- she had a daughter. I was told that the child did not live, though I now know that this is not true. After the departing of my beloved Arnemetia, I was distraught, and Latis comforted me in my sorrow. Now Latis has become my wife, but for many years I did not know about her daughter. I believe that the one you seek is one and the same; Donannu.'

'Then she is the half-sister of Branderix?'

'Yes. Indeed. Donannu returned to Gabrantovices some while ago, and again encountered Branderix. He brought Donannu to my side. Because of him, my wife was able to see her daughter again, and I gained a daughter. I learned that Branderix, over the years had secretly arranged for her training in all things drueidan. He kept in touch with her, when we thought she was lost. I have a lot to thank Erix for.'

'Where is she now? Is she with him now, in Taftefield?'

'Yes. I believe so.'

'Then thank you Lord Ninniau. We will leave as soon as possible on our way to find your daughter. Believe me, My Lord, I have a lot to thank her for. She will receive accolade as soon as I am able to present her with rewards.' The Queen and her company ate and drank, rested for one night before loading up the horses and travelling into the new day, envigored with hope and determination to continue swiftly into the northern territories of Brigantia.

Within two days of leaving the northeast coastline, and only one night's rest between, the speed of the animals brought them to Clach Aicliffe. This was a small hamlet of two houses built from rock and stone. Donnlugh had arrived earlier and prepared for the company to take lodgings for the night. He asked questions of the dwellers there but learned that no other travellers had ventured through the village for a few days. When the retinue arrived, the farmer and his wife came out to greet them, taking the horses to water and rest while the group were given food and mead. As they also rested, Gallagher and his men appeared. One other rode with them. Jumping down from their horses, Gallagher spoke up with an urgency directed solely to the Queen. 'Hail, My Lady. I have news. Venutius is settling in at Taftefield. He stormed up to the old capital and had Branderix in chains before your regent realised the intrusion. The people there know that the King of Carvetii is your husband, so they obey him without question. No lives have been lost. We moved stealthily into Taftefield. I don't think anyone was aware of our entrance. There was no sign of Audigus Raigon, the High-Druid, so, when we had located it, we felt better able to venture to the shelter where Branderix was imprisoned. We managed to release him, and as you see, he is with us. But the hall of Bellnorix has been taken over by your husband.'

Turning to the ousted chief of Textowerdi, the Queen asked, 'Branderix, I am glad to see you. Where is your sister? Do you know?' Agitation would not allow her to remain calm. She shuffled on her seat, then stood, then paced round the room, while Branderix followed her, issuing explanations for his capture. He bowed low. 'Yes, yes,' said Cartimandua impatiently. 'Yes, never mind all that.' She beckoned Branderix to stand, and not grovel in front of her. 'You are safe. What of your sister?'

'She rode away as Venutius entered the gates of Taftefield. I do not know where she went, but I know she is not affected by the King of Carvetii.'

'Good.' Cartimandua sighed, allowing her tense body to relax a little. 'Tomorrow, we head for Taftefield, and for the sake of

Brigantia, I will settle this dilemma.' Stamping her foot on the ground she shuddered with determination. She shook her hair free of the ties Her wildness had returned, 'No one who will stand in the way of the Wild Queen of Brigantia,' she vowed.

Before the dawning of the day, the party remounted the horses, thanked the farmer and rode on to Taftefield, but on the approach to Knocbodhar a heaviness adumbrated the night. They made speed through the copse of oak and ash trees. The horses slowed to a canter as the copse turned into dense forest. 'I feel a foreboding,' Cartimandua whispered to Elora, negotiating the shadowy trail through the thickening forest. The idle chatter of the group waned. A pair of nightjars silently flew around them, only revealing their whereabouts by the doomsayer churring of their voices. The hoot of an owl could be heard in the distance. A magpie flew above them, but then rose high in the sky and disappeared. Stealthily they rode on.

'I think we should suspend our course, Lady,' suggested Gallagher. 'The way is too dangerous to travel without light to guide our path.' He took the lead in front of the Queen in a protective stance.

'Very well, we will travel only until we find a suitable clearing to set camp for the night.'

Progressing a short distance into the gloom of the woodland, Gallagher held his hand up behind his head. 'Halt,' he whispered. 'There is light up ahead. Caution.' Glimmering through the wildwood, a flicker from a fire directed their eyes to a small clearing. Guarded, they dismounted the horses and tied them to a branch of a tree, near a trickling shallow stream. Silently they made their way, one step at a time toward the sight. With still some distance between the fire and the Queen's company, they stopped to listen. Perfectly still, they held their place. Silence.

Cartimandua turned to Donnlugh and Taragh. Mouthing her orders, she asked, 'create a spell of invisibility, can you?' The Druids sank to the ground on their knees, and wordlessly shaped an incantation in the old language, though not a sound was released from their lungs. They raised their arms beyond their heads, waving them backward and forward as if caught like a sail tacking in the wind. As each hand moved, so did the breeze, until they created a squall. Noiselessly, the turbulence blew across the leaf litter lying on the ground causing the debris to circle together as a whirlwind. It created a rotating column wall out of the disorder. The duff completely encompassed the regal group, hiding them in the midst of the conjured verdure. And so, they ventured secretly and invisibly, closer to the light.

CHAPTER TWENTY-ONE

ARD RIGH
High King

T HE FIRE BLAZED BRIGHTLY as the illusive screen of leaves drifted toward the clearing in the middle of the forest. The coterie remained silent, observing the occupants of this camp. The fire light defined the backs of two cloaked men, sitting easily, eating from a small cauldron, while sharing bread. They chattered amicably, as night fell all around them.

Cartimandua gasped, recognising at once the back of her lover and Mugh Ruith. As if in a dream, unable to move while the enchanted curtain hid the group, she could only watch the scene being revealed to her. A young woman sat opposite the two, facing them. Her features, alluring and captivating, were highlighted by the firelight and the full moon. Her black straight hair fell wantonly, framing her face. Instantly, Cartimandua was aware and afraid of this woman whose wide eyes stared into the face of Eachann. She questioned herself. 'What is this? Am I jealous of his past, when I have his future in my hand?' She wanted to move nearer to Eachann but could not. 'We are all bound; held by a great enchantment,' she thought.

Fear stirred deeper in her heart as a magpie flew from a low branch of an oak tree, chattering harshly. It settled in the shadows a short distance away and began strutting nearer and nearer to the cloaked pair as they talked to the woman sitting by the fire. All the while, it picked at the ground as if in search of grubs. 'An omen,' Cartimandua thought, and shuddered as a cloud rode in front of the moon, and momentarily seized the light.

Listening intently, Cartimandua could hear the conversation passing between the three.

'How did you find me?' the woman asked.

'I have been looking for some time, Donannu. I went to Gabrantovices, and there I spoke to the lady Cynifrida, your sister. She told me of your mother and your brother; how Lord Ninniau has confessed to being your father. I know of your past, and now I am hoping that you can tell me something of mine.'

'My brother Erix is the one who told me the story of the daughter of Textowerdi and the great King of Catuvellauni, though at the time he was not a king at all, but a Brigante warlord out to find his own fortune. We now know him as Britannorium Rex. He was already married with three sons, but for many years the secret whispered in the halls of Brigantia spoke of another son: a fourth son for Cunobelinos. Cunobelinos sent his lover and bastard son away. No one knows where this son is, or who he is, or in fact if the story is true. But I knew. I knew. As soon as I heard the tales of your travels with Mugh Ruith, I knew. In my heart I knew you must be he. Taranis called me to you Eachann. And in my heart, I have never left - except to allow you to follow the path ordained by the gods.'

'I am the son of Cunobelinos? He is the King of Catuvellauni? Can this be true?'

Mugh smiled. 'Understanding is flooding my mind, and the

memory flooding it too. I see it all,' he said. 'I have my sight!' Mugh bounced, chuckling with glee at the unfolding of the story. He grabbed the hands of the dark-haired warrior and pulled her to dance with him. 'Oh! Donannu! Gifted scáthach. Gifted goddess. I see it all.' Donannu began to skip round the fire with Mugh, as if the earth under their feet was a bed of hot coals. 'Did I not tell you that I would be given my sight! Did I not know it? Did I ever doubt it?' The little Druid rambled on as the burble left his mouth.

Eachann contemplated the two. A joyous smile spread across his face, followed at once by a puzzled expression. 'You might understand, Mugh Ruith. But I do not. What about Cartimandua? What does this all mean?'

'Eachann. There is one way of proving your birth right. It is the ring of Eòlas, given to you by the Kings of Knowledge when we left the Broch so many years ago.'

From behind the wall of green, Cartimandua followed the scene. Her eyes fell to the ring on her finger. 'The ring of Eòlas,' she whispered to herself.

The curtain of leaves began to fall, as if autumn had returned to snatch the summer. The leaves fell, covering the ground as if they had always been there. Realising that the magical wall had melted away, Cartimandua walked silently toward Eachann. Standing in the shadows behind Donannu, she could see the full expression on the face of Beli Mawr. The light from the fire lit his features, and his golden locks glittered as if the moonlight had sprinkled gold dust over him. He was watching Donannu intently, but then glanced up as Cartimandua positioned herself in his way. His smile widened. 'My Lady,' he called, rising to greet her. 'Mandua.'

The others in the company entered the firelight also, greeting the champion and the Druid. Branderix ran to Donannu and hugged his sister, kissing her head. Elora took Gallagher's' hand in hers and squeezed it. Donnlugh and Taragh busied themselves bringing wood from the surrounds and built the fire till it blazed with warmth for them all. Camulo and Gallagher immediately immersed themselves in the stories from Donannu and Mugh. Then each unfolded the travel tales and adventures they experienced in their search for the truth.

Beckoning the Queen, Eachann held his hand out for her. Sitting down by his side, furtively she took his hand. She felt the prickle of passion between them as their fingers embraced secretly. Relaxing in his presence she dropped her guard. He whispered into her ear. 'This is indeed a night of surprises! I have so many things to tell you, my love. So many things.'

'I know Eachann Beli Mawr. But first I have another surprise for you. I want you to meet your mother, Anna.' Anna had stayed back in the shadows of the forest, but now walked boldly toward the golden warrior. Tears escaped her eyes, but the smile on the face of the Queen of Textowerdi confirmed to all, that the warrior sitting with Cartimandua was indeed her son. Anna began to unfold the story of his past.

'Forgive me, son. I was young and we were in love. Our love was so strong that we could not hold back. But it was a forbidden love, and one that put us in danger.

Eachann stared at his mother, not daring to blink.

'When I told Cunobelinos of my pregnancy, he wanted to protect you, but knew that he could not give you the safety you needed. We could not be married. I did return to Brigantia and to Taftefield, my home. I hid while you grew in my womb. The night you were born, stars shot from the sky and fell to earth as lightning. Taragh saw these signs, omens of a greater purpose at work for

Albion, and heard the prophecy foretelling your greatness.'
Taragh began to speak.

> *'Beli, great rider in the sky, in chariot pulled by horses.*
> *Son of thunder and of light, releases and discharges*
> *Healing and power in his right hand.*
> *Then linked like iron to one another;*
> *warrior spirit and warrior spirit, holding sacred Brigga.*
> *One day Eòlas will require the iron, bronze and stone.*
> *With strength and courage to overcome, the fire will bring the word*
> *When Bel melts into the earth and Brigga rides again,*
> *The soul of Albion once more will burn as fire*
> *Throughout the domain.'*

Trancelike, Taragh uttered the prophecy he remembered from so long ago. Eachann joined in with the telling, his expression showed his amazement. 'Is not Cartimandua known for her iron fist?'

'Are you not known as the embodiment of Taranis, the god of thunder and light?' asked Mugh. 'Indeed, though we still do not understand the fullness of this edict, we can surmise that you and Mandua hold the key to the future of Brigantia.' Mugh smiled to himself.

Anna continued, 'so, because Taragh had heard from the gods, he travelled to seek The Knowledge. He left you at the door of Eòlas. Then you were gone. I never again heard of your whereabouts.' Anna's face quivered. She wiped the tears from her eye. 'When I met Cartimandua, she filled my heart with hope. It was she who sent Donnlugh and Taragh to find you.'

The group of friends listened spellbound as Anna continued.

'But sadness follows. The last time I saw Cunobelinos was the night he left me. He was intent on journeying south to fight against the enemy threat. He gave me instructions to return to my family in Brigantia. I had no understanding as to why I could not be with him, but just as we parted, an owl flew overhead. For me, the owl was a sign that wisdom was involved in his decision. I felt peace in my heart.' Patting her chest, she sighed.

Cartimandua leaned over to whisper in Eachann's ear. 'Now we have heard that Cunobelinos has departed this world. He lost his fight against traitors of Albion, but he will live on in our hearts, always.'

Anna took a breath, pronouncing, 'he will be remembered as the hero he was. You are so very like him. I think I knew who you were, the first time I saw you.'

'There is so much to understand, Mother. But I am so glad to find you, and…' looking round the faces by the firelight, Eachann added, '…and all of you. My friends and family. I am so glad to find you all.'

Cartimandua took the ring of Eòlas and handed it to Eachann. 'Show your mother. She will know its authenticity.'

'It is, indeed, the ring I tied round the wrist of my baby. It is the ring given to me by your father, Cunobelinos. This proves that you are certainly the divine progenitor of the Kings of Albion.' Handing the ring back to her son, she smiled. As he took it, he held her hand for some moments, before restoring it onto the finger of Cartimandua.

That night the talk and songs continued till the early morning. There was so much to talk about, that the voices did not silence until sleep came for all. Scattered around the camp, the company made beds where they could, gathering close together for warmth and comfort. Donannu slept a little away from the fire, hidden in a leafy bed, while Mugh curled up near her, his cloak giving warmth and hiding. Eachann, Gallagher and Camulo took turns to watch for danger. But in the early hours of the night, when sleep is at its deepest, then Cartimandua crept toward Eachann, and whispered 'I need to talk with you. I must return to Venutius in the morning. He rests at Taftefield, waiting for you to appear. Raigon, that old *darach,* has poisoned his mind against you, Eachann, and he will have your head. Raigon has called you a traitor, though I have no knowledge of his reasons.'

Eachann interrupted, 'although three daughters could be the reason…'

'Indeed. If this is so, then it is good that Raegan has them hidden. They are safe for a while, but you must be aware of the danger you are in. I will return to Venutius, and you will leave Brigantia. In time, maybe we will be together again, but for now, we must leave each other.' She began to weep silently. 'Go with Donannu, somewhere far away. Somewhere where I know you will be safe. Go to Ynys Mon. There is a need for the Druid colony to be protected. You will have a great purpose there. Go there.'

'Come with me, Mandua. Bring the children and come with me.' Eachann wrapped his strong arms around his love. 'You could disappear. Venutius need never know. We can be together, you, me and the children.'

The heart of the Queen was torn.

'You give me a choice, but there is no choice. I am not foolish enough to think that Venutius would allow me to disappear. Where would I go where his bawbag of a Druid would not find me? Raigon knows too much already. Maybe more.'

'So, you choose Venutius?'

'It is my duty as queen.'

You choose a life of duty over love?' Eachann searched her face. He searched deep into her eyes. 'Mandua, I cannot live without you.

Anam Cara.'

Sorrow overwhelmed her. 'Eachann. I cannot live without you. It is not life I am choosing. I am choosing the path that the gods have ordained for me. I cannot let Brigantia fracture. The Romans have begun their incursion; already moving to overtake. They have fought against the southern tribes and have advanced to our borders. I must be ready to lead my people against this indignation. The death of your father gives them a reason to invade. His might held back the weak Caligula, till he was only fit to collect seashells as spoils of war from the south coast of our great land. But your two half-brothers, Caracatus and Togodomus Belinos have shown hostility toward Rome which has given the emperor Claudius a fresh reason to subjugate Albion. He is on his way through the south and heading for Brigantia. He has many legions of fighting men, and, I am told, he has war mammoths, giant Luca Bos elephants. It is a mighty army, let there be no doubt.'

Turning to gaze steadfastly at her lover, Cartimandua offered hope. 'One day in the future, there may be a way for us to be together, but I must fulfil my vow to Venutius and to my people. I don't want to lose you now, but look at who I am. I have no choice. I am a queen first, and my duty lies first with my people. For the sake of Brigantia, I must fulfil my commitment.' Her shoulders sank as the onus of her responsibility weighed her down. Sorrow took away her voice; she could speak no longer. She stood to leave, making for Tormaig who waited, still tied to the tree. She wiped her eyes, now blinded by the tears falling heavily. Her body sobbed with grief.

Eachann begged. 'Have not the gods dictated our union? Now I know the truth of my past, I can rightfully take my throne. Brigantia and Textowerdi can truly be as one. Together, we can be the terrible force which saves Brigantia and indeed Albion, from the Latin dog.'

'Indeed, we would be a mighty force, but we would still need Setanti and Carvetii power allied to Brigantia. The Romans have legions coming against us. We are so few against those hordes. Carvetii needs to be ours, and ours absolutely. I must safeguard the Brigante union with Carvetii. If my agreement with Venutius is seen to faulter, then there could be a revolt from the stag people. I cannot afford an uprising from Venutius or his people. It would distract from the real danger ahead of us all; one where we must all draw together against the threat. I cannot take that risk.' Eachann hung his head. Despair sat on the shoulders of the Queen and her lover.

Pulling her closer to his warm body, Eachann whispered, 'Then before you go, Anam Cara, let us be together this one night.' Whispering in the old language, he called to the four pillars upholding the Earth. With drueidan authority he spoke into the thunder and lightning, seeking a covering from the great god Taranis.

'*Cruthaich Sgiath*. Create a shield around us o great god of power,' he pleaded. In response, lightning flashed across the skies as thunder roared an *awen*. The fire burned low. Sounds faded. The hushed tones of the forest fell silence. Darkness covered like a cloak, hiding them from all around. Only the starry sky above gave light. In the centre of this hidden world, this veiled black mantle, Eachann reached for Mandua, whispering into her ear, 'Mandua, Mandua,' Gently he caressed her. Wiping the tears from her eyes he embraced her, then moved his hands lower, he removed the tunic from her shoulders. She felt the pain of losing him, but the exquisite pulse of power from his touch caused every nerve end in her body to throb with delight. Breathless, she began to gasp deeply, moaning with expectation and delight. She arched her back, drawing herself into him. Tension between them, like a magnet, sent shock waves wherever their bodies touched. 'Surely Taranis has heard our prayer,' she thought, 'for only the powerful lightning touch of the gods could make me feel this way.'

He bent to kiss her, then running his lips down her body, he kissed her neck and her breasts. Cupping one breast, then the other he leaned into them, fondling them. His mouth traced the route to her pleasure. His hands and fingers delighted her. Sadness and joy mingled together in her emotions when he placed his hands between her legs to stroke her pudenda. 'I need you,' he whispered, drawing his shaft to enter her. 'I need you. Please don't leave me.' Mandua felt the thrill of his huge erection, pushing inside her, pulling her into ecstasy. His strong arms wrapped round her waist, twisting her frame to lift her closer, as his insatiable need rode her as a wild pony. Exhausted and satisfied, they both slept in the god given space between two worlds.

Without waiting for dawn, the Queen kissed Beli Mawr and mounting her horse, she rode into the morning; his smell still lingering in her nostrils. She did not look back.

'Camulo,' called Eachann, shaking the warrior from his bed. 'Follow the Queen. She needs you right now. She heads to Taftefield.' Camulo and the others shook themselves from the retreating night, and mounted their ponies to follow, leaving Eachann with Mugh and Donannu who still slept on.

The fire burned low, as the morning hinted of its advent. The dark still held authority, so Eachann rammed another log on the fire. He sat motionless. A magpie pecked away near the foot of an oak tree, as the night grappled to hold its power a little longer.

Suddenly the silver face of the moon goddess emerged once again from her hiding place above the treetops and clouds. Her argent luminosity highlighted the black and white body of the magpie growing, altering, unravelling huge black and white wings. Pointing her beams downward, the moon illuminated the enormous silhouette of Raigon against the empyrean backdrop. He flapped his cloak wings one over the other, to hide himself beneath the blackness he was creating and away from the shimmering light of the moon. The wings flapped again and again, causing a sound like thunder to rage through the trees and across the forestland as his whole being shook and shaped into a savage otherworldly beast. Hidden in the dense blackness of his cloak, he moved slowly, showing nothing except two terrorising yellow eyes which peered out from the sinister darkness. Black hair grew over his body and face, thickening into coarse wolf fur; his appearance contorting into a wild *lycan*. His hands grew large and wolflike; his fingernails lengthening, displayed sharp claws. His tongue menacingly gyrated in and out of his mouth stifling his vocal chords, and his sanity. As saliva dripped from the orifice, a deep growl escaped through his fangs. The forest, wakened from drowsiness, shuddered as the sound echoed round the trunks and woody vegetation.

Shaken from her dreams, Donannu saw the giant blackness and wanted to shout out, 'Eachann. Beware!' but her voice was stifled in the shadows of the morning. She moved to stand but a darkling spirit had fallen on both her and Mugh, drawing them into a dream. Mugh shot to attention and tried to shake off the heaviness. He began to hop around the shadows, rubbing his good eye to clear the blurry sleep from it. His voice jabbered, 'What? What? Sleep has taken me.' Stumbling around, he flung his arms out, hoping to feel his way about. 'Eachann. Call for the gods,' he shouted, but his voice too was lost in the shadows. Donannu grabbed Mugh to stop him from falling, but neither was able to help Beli Mawr. They watched from the edge of the camp, powerless, calling silently to Taranis.

Eachann rose; his body still trembled with the anguish of losing

Cartimandua. With sleepiness still covering his sight, he stood blindly in front of the towering evil of Raigon. Then, though the darkness still held the forest, he exclaimed, 'I will bring the light. I will find a way!' Opening his eyes wide to the day he reached for his sword, raising it to the sky in an action of worship. Lightning struck swiftly, as headlong, the glaive of Eòlas captured a ball of fire from above. With instinctive precision Eachann flicked his glaive, tossing the energised sphere into the fire. The blaze ripped, forging an inferno, enough to scorch the surrounding summer verdure. The shock of the flames caused the wolver to back off. Recovering quickly, he roared again, showing his fangs and moving his claws to attack the ball of light as it ricocheted, spinning toward him. Lurching forward, he moved nearer to his prey.

Beli Mawr was highlighted under the brilliance of the full moon. The moonshine stretched a beam from her face to the face of Beli Mawr, ripping the darkest shadows away from Raigon. He reared up on his haunches, while his crazy front claws poised to attack. Eachann moved away from the fire, to meet the wolver.

'Once before, I met with you, Raigon Sucellos. You were not successful then, and you will not be successful now,' called Eachann as the powerful Eòlas liquid in his veins began once again to stir his limbs. Raising the invincible glaive high, like a lightning bolt, he sliced down into the space where the wolver stood. The gash was immediate. Blood flowed down the head of the wolf; thick and black. The roar from the ghoul shrieked across the sky, as Eachann moved in for another swipe. The shapeshifter swung round, raising his crucial strength against Beli Mawr, downing his sharp claws into the champion's head, gouging down to his thigh. Beli Mawr fell. The lycan fangs gripped the arm of the champion, ripping and gorging. Eachann struggled but did not let go of the glaive. Unable to find the strength to move away, he swerved to one side. The weight of the beast held him. Blood streamed down his face. It covered his eyes. The stifled position only allowed short movements, but Eachann stabbed and stabbed, blindly. The black shadow raised his haunches to attack again. Eachann seized the moment, impulsively slashing the throat of the savage. He darted up as Raigon fell to one side. Raising his arm high, Eachann shouted, 'For Cartimandua!' With one hefty penetration, his sword stabbed. The animal screeched in agony.

Shrivelling on the ground, Raigon coughed blood and tried to speak. 'It is too late Beli Mawr. Venutius knows of your betrayal and will have your head.'

Mugh and Donannu stared as the great Audigus Raigon withered until he became a magpie once again. Suddenly aware that he was shapeshifting and might escape, Donannu shook to free herself from the holding spell. She careened forward as if bound hand and foot, and clumsily drew her axe at the floundering bird. She swung it hard into the air as the bird took flight, not knowing whether the weight would meet its target. Blood splashed from the air like rain from the wings of the black and white creature. They all looked toward the sky until the wings could be seen no more.

Eachann fell to the ground, wounded and bleeding. Gently wiping the gore from around his eyes, Donannu held him close. The furrow of missing skin from his head and face left an open wound. The deep gash on his torso exposed the innards of his stomach. Donannu assessed quickly. 'Mugh, we need a healing spell to cover the wounds. Find me a flat piece of wood…Anything,' she called in distress. 'We must bind something over his stomach to keep his entrails from dislodging.' Mugh ran in all directions, looking for something suitable to use.

In his searching, he called to Brigga: Brighid, the Brigante goddess of healing. In the old language he begged Brighid to come and reveal the plants and herbs he needed.

'Brigga soilleir agus mathair an Talamh an.
Brigga bright, and Mother Earth.
Bend your hand to heal.
Bleach these wounds with healing power
And with your herbs make seal.'

Mugh searched rapidly. A carpet of wide leaf Butterbur spread along the bank of a small trickling stream. Mugh picked the freshest and largest leaves and ran back to Donannu. 'Can you find others, Mugh? We need special plants to help with his pain and counter act the darkness of the wound, but these are just right for tying round his body to hold him. He is losing blood and is falling to sleep. Quickly,' she urged.

Where the shallow stream meandered away from the main flow, Mugh found bog Pimpernel. 'Ideal for wound healing,' he mumbled. A patch of Selago and Vervain, natural pain reducers, grew there too. He gathered as much as he could, holding the corner of his cloak as a bag. 'How is he?' asked the little Druid, when he arrived back to where Eachann lay.

Donannu was bending over the torn body. 'Fetch water, Mugh.' She had ripped her tunic into strips and was busy binding the torso of the champion. Each time she moved him, he flinched. Mugh returned with water in his drinking cup and handed it to Donannu. She wrapped the vervain under the butterbur, and then added the selago to the water. Lifting Eachann so he could drink, she offered him a sip. Mugh scrunched up the bog pimpernel until the oil ran in his hand. He bathed the oil carefully into the facial cuts. All day they dressed his wounds, cleaning and retying the bindings. Many times, Mugh took his drinking cup to the little stream then wet a cloth to wipe the sweat from Eachann's forehead. The little Druid continued to seek out food for the evening, though hunger had left his thoughts. He continued to collect fresh healing herbs, quickly blending balms and poultices to stop infection, but the cuts were deep, and the fever was high.

As the day began to approach the impending night, Donannu glanced up from her charge with quiescence. 'We have done what we can. He cannot be moved yet, so we must make a camp, a shelter to protect him, if we can. Then we must wait and pray.'

Collecting willow, and branches from the trees round about, they began to make a teanta using withies to tie the screen together. It was enough to protect the wounded warrior from the night. Mugh shaped a huge fire and began to prepare the wood sorrel, fat hen cabbage and wild raspberries from his progging during the day. Adding it to the two thin slices of pig in his travel sack, they ate a meagre meal. Then they made a shrine by the trickling steam. Collecting a pile of stones, they arranged a totem. 'Brigga, our spirit and our soul. We kneel before you pleading for the life of your king,' prayed Donannu.

'Great god Taranis, who sent to us Beli Mawr, the Shining One. With your thunder and lightning, you have guided us thus far. Continue to guide us, o great god of the wheel. You know the cycles of our life, for it is you who turns the wheel of time. Direct us with your thunderbolts; speak to us through the thunder. We beseech you.' Mugh wept and prayed.

Throughout the night, Donannu and Mugh took turns to guard

against wild boar, bears and foxes, while bathing the wounds of the shining one. The moon took her turn also, to watch.

'The fever is getting stronger, Mugh. We must keep him cool.'

When Eachann slept, it was a deep fever sleep. Delirium caused him to thrash about and shout out with undecipherable ramblings. Then, into the early morning he fell into silence.

As the dawn broke, Donannu knew what she should do. 'Mugh, he has entered the otherworld. There is nothing we can do for him now. Will you help me take his body from here? We must take him back to the Eòlas. Can you shapeshift? Between us, as two eagles, we can deliver him.'

Mugh went to his bag and fetched the phial of bronze liquid so long hidden in the leather pouch. He took a sip and handed the phial to Donannu. Nodding, he encouraged her to drink. 'We might need this, Donannu. The way we must go is far from here. We will need all our strength, and more.'

No further words passed between the two as they prepared the body of Eachann Beli Mawr, the King of Textowerdi. They bathed him in the oil that Mugh had squeezed from the pimpernel. Lovingly, Donannu caressed his torn torso and limbs, anointing him with the oil. She took Eachann's white linen capote that he so often wore to hide his golden locks. She wrapped it over his head and eyes. She began to wrap his glaive and sword also, binding them to his body with the withies they had stripped from the willow the night before. Strapping his arms round her shoulders, Mugh and Donannu lifted the body of the true king of Brigantia between them.

'I am worried, Donannu. I am not good at shifting my shape.' he wittered.

'The gods are with us, Mugh. Our Druidical strength will uphold us in our task.' Donannu grabbed the shaking hands of the little

Druid and held them tightly. Eòlas strength flowed from one to the other. 'Look up,' she called, as their two minds connected.

Looking into the skies, and beyond, the fused minds began to shift their human form into white tailed eagles. Mugh led the way, examining the ground and checking for signs of the path he had journeyed so long ago. Donannu rose behind him, catching the rising currents, then gliding effortlessly holding Eachann on her back. Up into the heafan they soared, carrying their precious cargo northwards over the sea and toward the Eòlas.

CHAPTER TWENTY-TWO

GAOL AGUS DLEASDANAS
Love and Duty

R AIGON TRAVELLED WITH FULL speed, ahead of Cartimandua and
her company. From the skies where his magpie body flew,
he watched the movements of Cartimandua. Coming to
rest outside Taftefield, the bird reformed into the hooded Druid of
Carvetii. Blood covered his face, but the wound, though beginning
to fester, was not deep. He hid in the shadows of the sept, away from
the high hall where Venutius sat in wait for news of Beli Mawr, the
traitor. When Venutius, bored of waiting, decided to ride out to look
for him, Raigon took his place in the Great Hall of Bellnorix.

Donnlugh led the way into the sept by the north gateway,
avoiding the grand entrance by the main south gate. He was followed
by Elora and Gallagher who immediately separated from the group,
to discreetly assess the situation that Venutius had provoked.

Druid Taragh protected Anna, Queen of Textowerdi. Branderix
and Camulo stayed at the side of Queen Cartimandua until she
dismounted and, holding her hand up to stay their action, she

marched toward the Great Hall of Taftefield alone. Her hair swung wildly, blowing up into the sky as if it had been caught in a whirlwind. Shouting hysterically, she called, 'Venutius. Husband. Where are you?' Scowling, she drew her sword, but feeling no fear, she bellowed violently, 'Get here. I demand to see you.'

Venutius was nowhere to be seen, but Raigon stood by the throne in the hall as Cartimandua entered. The blood still ran from the wound on his head and other wounds on his arms and body. The white stripe running down the front of his cloak was covered in red, but he stood erect with little to show in his manner of the terrible fighting between the two High-Mage of Carvetii. He bowed to the Queen who marched toward him. 'Where is he?' she bawled. Anger swelled in her heart.

'He is riding out, My Queen,' answered Raigon calmly. The smirk on his face, enraged the Queen even more.

Jumping at Raigon, she pushed her face into his, and her hands into his shoulders. 'What has he done? What have you done? How dare you usurp my chiefs and run as if you rule in my lands?' Raigon's sneer grew wider. Though his face was covered by the blood, the snigger was not hidden. Cartimandua drew her sword. The point touched the throat of the scoffing Druid. She pushed it precisely until the tip scratched his jugular. He held his head back.

'How dare you raise insolence before me?' she said, twisting the blade carefully. He backed off her threat, lifting his hands up high in the air. The Queen stepped back, releasing her charge. She placed her sword on the great chair of Bellnorix, allowing herself to calm a little. 'Raigon, what do you think you are doing?'

'The ancients speak of the end of our world, when the pillars holding up our faith will crumble. They talk of the 'Shining One' holding the seed of Brigantia, and of Albion too. I saw it in a vision, and thought the gods were showing me the Carvetii champion. But I know about Beli Mawr. I followed him until he led me to you. I know about your treachery with Beli Mawr and how you have both betrayed my king, Venutius. Do you think that I would stand to one side and watch as you destroy all that I hold dear? Do you think that I would give my position over to a deceptive, treacherous flicker of a fire worm like him? Whatever you think, it will do you no good now. It is too late, because Beli Mawr is dead. I finished him. He will not be returning.'

Cartimandua stopped.

Raigon repeated his words. 'He is dead.' Wagging his head he added, 'and along with him go the old prophecies about the shining son of thunder, power in his hand and warrior spirits. Pah! Gone. No more the progenitor of Albion…I made sure of that. And he won't be coming back!' From his gut, a gurgling laughter erupted.

Trying to hold her panic at his words, the Queen shouted, 'Liar!' She ran at him, her fist gripped like a hammer. She swung her fists to beat him on his chest. Raigon flinched but grabbed her wrists to stop her. 'What are you saying? What do you think you are doing?' she sobbed in anger.

Raigon began to speak in the old language. He wove a spell before Cartimandua had time to realise what was happening. '*Ceangail i. Bind her,*' he called. 'This is what I am about, My Queen,' he laughed, forcefully squeezing her arm and holding onto her. Before she had time to think, Raigon had swung her round, pushing her arm up her back to restrain her. He wrapped both his arms round her, tightening his grip. His body was next to hers.

His mouth was near her ear when he snarled, 'I know what you are, Queen of Brigantia. I know you are a whore. I have watched you give yourself to so many others, and make promises sealing them with your pissy hole, including the King's own man. Yes, I saw when he drugged the King and then left to shag you. I followed to where you were in hiding and heard you copulating like dogs.' Raigon squeezed Cartimandua till her breath stopped. 'Now it is my turn,' he menaced. Putting his hand round her throat, he pushed her to the ground. His weight stifled her struggles and her voice. With his other hand he removed his cloak. He was naked but for the short tunic over his torso.

Cartimandua wrestled under his weight but could not rise from the ground nor escape him. Her eyes opened wider when she realised what Raigon was about. 'No. No,' she called, swedging furiously, but her voice and her body had little power under the magic weight of the *darach*. The spell was strong. Raigon pushed her legs apart, grabbing at her thigh till he fetched blood. She lurched away from him. Her back hit the iron leg of the throne. Raigon seized her ankles and pulled her toward him. She called out in pain feeling her ankles wrenched from her legs.

'You will get what you deserve, mighty queen of nothing,' he hissed. With one hand holding her down he straddled her. The other hand fumbled for his *choad*. He attacked her. With all her strength she twisted her body, so her legs closed like pincers. She lurched toward her sword hilt, grabbing it from the chair, and with one weak slash, she ripped the back of the debaucher. Again, she slashed. Raigon reeled back, rolling off her, as the pain from her actions hit him. Crying out in pain he snarled, 'Bitch *Diabhal*. I will kill you for this!' He moved to escape her iron hand, but Cartimandua bounced forward, and with one effortless stab, she pierced the belly of the High-Druid of Carvetii. He fell to the ground, scrawling in agony before her. She lifted the sword high, using both hands, dropping the fatal blow through his back and directly into his heart.

Sinking to the ground, the Queen sobbed.

When Venutius appeared at the door of the hall, Cartimandua was still sitting on the floor, her shoulders convulsing with grief, though her heart was numb. Her dishevelled torn clothing told him of the fight she had been through. At her side, and covered in blood, lay the body of Audigus Raigon.

Taking in the sight for a moment, Venutius stood silently. Camulo rushed into the hall following Venutius. His sword was drawn in readiness. At the same time, Donnlugh and Taragh arrived with Anna. Anna ran to the distressed Queen. 'What has happened here?' she asked, looking at Venutius, then at Raigon.

Still sobbing, Cartimandua whaled, 'Venutius, my husband. This is your traitor. This is the man who whispered lies into your ear, so while you were occupied, he tried to rape me.' Cartimandua sobbed heavily, pointed to the corpse lying at the side of her. She searched the face of the King, hoping that he would not pressure her with further questions. Venutius offered his hand to the Queen, so she might rise. Cartimandua accepted the help. Still weak and shaken from the ordeal, she stood tall, not allowing her fragility to be seen.

'Was it all lies, my lady? What Raigon told me- about you and Beli Mawr. Was it true?'

Her whole body shook from the news of Beli Mawr's death, but she dare not expose her grief. She jutted her chin out and faced Venutius. 'My husband, there are things I have done during my life that I regret more than you will ever know, but my marriage treaty with you has always been my priority. I am yours. You are mine. Whatever Raigon told you, you can dismiss it, as I have dismissed him.'

'The death of a Druid is a serious occurrence, but the untimely death of a High-Druid is serious indeed. Cartimandua. This is not the first time you have removed a High-Druid.'

'And indeed, Venutius. I would remove anyone who stands in the way of the glory of my lands: Mage, Roman or Kings!' she threatened, lifting her face to meet the eye of Venutius, in defiance.

The commotion had ignited the curiosity of some people outside the hall, where a small crowd was gathering. Venutius walked to look at the body of his High-Druid as it lay exposed on the ground. Taking his dagger, he rammed the point down hard into the heart of the body and twisted. Then without concern, he cut off his membrum. Stabbing the penis so it hung on the tip of his knife, Venutius waved it around the room for the gathering crowd to see. 'Let it be known that I have pierced the very heart and manhood of this villein; and I will repeat this action against anyone who dares to take what is mine- Be it lands, wealth or my wife.' Then he shouted, 'Remove the remains of this traitor, and get water and dressings for my wife.'

'May I help?' asked Anna, but as she moved nearer the Queen, Venutius interrupted.

'Lady, Forgive me. I removed your regent without thought of you. Blind jealousy overtook me, when this dog Raigon spoke of Beli Mawr as a traitor. I called for his head, when I should have looked nearer to home for the source of the lies and deceit. I ask your forgiveness and will step away from your throne.' Venutius bowed low in front of Anna. Anna nodded accepting the apology.

'I am glad you see it that way, King. We have discovered that Beli Mawr is my son, and I would hate for us to be enemies in this matter. Peace is what we desire. I will take my throne, and no more will be said.'

Cartimandua surveyed the hall. 'Where is Branderix?'

'I am here,' he answered, stepping forward.

'Branderix, I want to thank you for all you have done to protect the borders of Textowerdi. I am pleased with your loyalty and support. You and Anna of Textowerdi have much to talk about. Anna will decide what is to be done about her tribe. But now, I need to rest.' Looking at Donn Donnlugh, she called, 'Take your lead from my husband while I rest, Donnlugh.'

Cartimandua, unable to put pressure on her ankles, staggered slowly to the shelter inside the Great Hall; a place she had occupied as a child when her grandfather Bellnorix ruled Brigantia. Glancing round the familiar room, she felt warm and safe. Exhausted, she lay on the bed allowing her thoughts to wander where they would. She remembered her grandfather, his warrior strength and his wisdom. She thought of Eachann, and now in the privacy of her own room, she did not hold back her grief. Her tears flowed freely. The great sadness of her loss overwhelmed her. 'How can I ever face another day?' she asked herself. 'How can I ever lead Brigantia without my love, my shining one?' Her body shook with despair. The weight of desolation filled her spirit. She was drowning. Darkness descended. She shut the world from her heart and wrapped a wall of iron round it.

Not wanting to disturb his damaged wife, Venutius did not approach her that night. Elora and Gallagher took up positions nearby, ready to protect her if needed. Camulo stood outside the main doorway of the hall, with his sword ready. Anna spent a little time with the Queen, wrapping her wounds, and making sure she was comfortable for the night before leaving her to sleep.

Drained and weary, Cartimandua slept. In the darkness of her afflicted mind, voices whispered in her ear. 'Cartimandua. You are all but finished,' the voices breathed. 'He is gone and will not return.'

'It was never meant to be.'

'You are queen of nothing.' The voices whispered over again. 'This is judgement for the death of Valas. The gods will have their vengeance.'

'The pillars of our world are crumbling, and it is your fault.'

'You will never see Beli Mawr, in this world or the otherworld.'

'No. No,' she called.

'No. No. This cannot be. *Anam Cara*. We will be together.' She argued with the spirits of darkness and fear, tossing and thrashing about in the black night. '…Promise…for Brigantia… the iron hand…' As in a fever she sweated, troubled and perturbed by the phantasms in her mind. Dreams floated in and out of her night.

From the shadows, the Winter Queen breathing odious rotting smells, moved by her bed. Still wrapped in her dingy brown shawl; her face almost hidden under her veil, she croaked 'Get up.'

Cartimandua sat up, trying to understand how this hag had passed her guard and entered her bedroom. But her fuddled mind could not untie the reality from the dream. She rubbed her eyes and looked again. The rancid breath from the Cailleach rushed into the nostrils of the Queen. She coughed, then spluttered. 'Have you come for the hammer?' she quaked.

'Do you think your job is finished, My Queen? Think again.' An icy finger prodded at Cartimandua, as the Cailleach cackled. 'Do you know that the prophecy is yet to be completed?

> *…. When Bel melts into the earth and Brigga rides again,*
> *The soul of Albion once more will burn as fire through the domain.*

Your love – your Beli Mawr; he is safe in the womb of the earth. He has completed his part of the story, But You! You – you must ride again! You must rise above your own feelings, for these are but selfishness. You must turn your anguish into anger, then turn your anger against the aggressors of our beloved Albion.'

As the Cailleach spoke into the heart and mind of the forlorn majesty, Cartimandua felt phenomenal fortitude grow in her body, invading her senses. Strength flowed through her veins like water turning to ice, then brittle ice to unyielding iron. Into the cold air, the Eòlas spoke. 'The seed has been sewn in the earth. Through death and rebirth, the land now has a future. The cycle will continue. Therefore, all is not lost. The knowledge will lie dormant only for a short while longer. The time is upon us, My good kings. It is time.'

'It is time,' Cartimandua repeated, still in a dream state. 'It is time! For the sake of Brigantia.' Cartimandua awoke to the sound of her own voice, as the light filtered through the cracks in the doorway of her room. Her hair, tousled and wild, stood on end as she rose to meet the morning. Shaking the night from her mind she stormed forward into the sunlight. Across the skies, a single cloud took a new shape. Cartimandua watched as the wheel of Taranis materialised in the heafan. From the dense single formation, a white flash of a thunderbolt escaped. Her heart leapt.

'Do they think we are finished, my love?' she muttered to the cloud. 'I will not lose you *and* my kingdom!' Feeling anger rise in her heart, she gritted her teeth and spat, 'I chose duty, but duty and *Anam Cara* cannot be separated.' Looking full faced up to the skies and into the sunlight, her voice ascended. 'Do those abhorrent Romans think they can take away what is mine? Never!'

Venutius came to stand at her side. 'They are already at our borders, Queen,' he said.

Looking beyond the sept to where the southern boundary of Brigantia lay, Cartimandua raised her right arm skyward. Shaking her iron fist in a vow, she shouted, 'Then, we will have those bastards!'

EPILOGUE

This story - Wild Brigantia -finishes here in the year 43AD.

Under the leadership of the Emperor Claudius, and the command of Aulus Plautus, the Roman army invaded the land known as Albion [Britain]. Not only did they want to expand their empire, but Britain had lots of natural materials including iron, lead, copper, silver, and gold that the Romans needed to support their growing empire and army.

The Romans quickly took control of the tribal areas of present-day south-eastern England, including the tribe of Catuvellauni, which was the most powerful tribe battling against the invasion at that time. The invaders quickly moved northwards.

Legions of soldiers outnumbered the Celtic tribes of Albion, and although some put up a fight against the invaders, many gave over their lands to the Romans without a fight. The Romans began constructing forts and roads, and changed many of the Brythonic place names, latinising the areas as they went.

It is not known whether Brigantia actually fought against the Romans initially, but we know that Brigantia did become a client kingdom, enjoying the benefits of peace alongside wealth and power granted to Brigantia when Queen Cartimandua agreed to cooperate with the Romans in exchange for her continued rule of Brigante lands and people. Her husband, Venutius became King Consort of Brigantia. Together they ruled Brigantia until they divorced in 57AD.

Queen Cartimandua achieved respect from her roman superiors, and alongside Boudicca, Queen of Iceni, she is the only queen to exact that sort of acknowledgement from the writers of history, albeit from the Roman point of view of Tacitus, the roman author.

Tina Zee

GLOSSARY

Adarc	A horn from a ram or some other horned animal.
Ailm	Celtic symbol for 'A' in the ogham alphabet: The Druid letters meaning strength, endurance and purity.
Anam Cara	Anam - soul. Cara - mates
Aurochs	Large wild cattle
Awen	Spirit of inspiration.
Beithir	Large snakelike animal.
Boobrie	Shapeshifting bird.
Boann	Celtic goddess, princess.
Beinn	Hill
Beornraed	High Prince, Chief.
Bescumber	Ancient swear word meaning to spray with faeces.
Bhaírds	Singing poets and musicians in the Druiden orders.
Bliadhna	A Year.
Bodach	Terrorist devils.
Boskag	A wood, grove or thicket of trees.
Braccae	A type of drawstring trouser.
Braint	Aristocratic lord and warrior.
Breehin	Prince, king, lord.
Breith Banrigh	Birth of a queen.
Brētrā Ōrd Mōr	Battle

gcruim	A hill settlement near what is now Hudswell, Yorkshire
Broch	A round stone structured fort.
Cadre	A core group of specialists.
Cailleach	Goddess of Winter, known as 'The Veiled One.' Oftenn appeared as an old wise hag associated with the earth, storms and winter.
Caim	A prayer for safety and blessing.
Cantiaci	Kent, UK.
Capote	Shawl or scarf
Carti Mandua	Sometimes translated as 'Sleek Pony' or 'White Filly.'
Carnyx	An ancient 'S' shaped bronze trumpet with animal head mouth
Carreg	Rock
Catuvellauni	Most powerful tribe, occupying territory north of the Thames
Cerveltune	Small farmstead known as Whorlton, east of Barnard Castle
Chathair	Throne
Chert	A type of stone, of which flint is a variety
Choad	Short and thick penis. A contemptable man
Comachag	Owl. Celts believed owls carried omens of death and darkness
Còmhdhail	Transport
Comraich a-stai	Inner sanctum
Coria Toutas	Peoples' army- Tribal army
Couchen	Sacred drink made with mead and honey and possibly henbane, nightshade or mandrake.
Crannog	An ancient, fortified dwelling build in a lake or marsh.
Daelic	One of two Druid languages

Darach	Dark and evil Druids
Deam	Phantom
Drochaid Dia	The bridge of the gods
Drueidan	Ancient Druid language
Ealdor	Life. Age
Easg	Waterway, river now known as Esk.
Eilidh	River now known as Ellen
Eòlas	The Druid Knowledge
Entresol	Mezzanine floors, balcony
Feileadh	Short kilt type skirt
Fey	Druid wand. A magic staff.
Fibula	Brooch or pin
Fionnas	Freshet: flood of a river from heavy rain or snow.
Gabrantovices	A settlement in the Whitby area, possibly Robin Hoods Bay
Gaesatae	Spearmen
Glaive	Short sword, dagger.
Goidi I	Tribes linked to the Painted people, the Picts.
Grody Saithe	An insult, meaning - Smelly fish.
Heafan	Sky, heavens.
Ignis Fatuus	Ghost lighting, will-o'-wisp, foolish fire.
Ituna	Rushing water. River Eden.
Kirtle	Woman's skirts.
Knocbodhar	Deaf Hill – south-west of Castle Eden in County Durham.
Kringlekarr	Circular marsh area.
Lancia	A troop of warriors who use spears as weapons.

Lolaire	Celtic name for Eagle
Lycan	Someone who can transform into a wolf, or gain wolflike characteristics.
Lithos	Lapis. Grit. Stone. Boulder.
Madaidh Allaidh	Shapeshifting wolf, werewolf, demon wolf god.
Maenhir	Standing stones. Megalithic monuments i.e., Stone Henge.
Mallachd	Hammer, Mallet.
Map	Means 'son of'… Eachann *Map* Belenus – Eachann, son of Belenus.
Matara	Long spears
Menhir	Standing stones. Monoliths.
Murc	Thick mist
Ogham	The ancient drueidan language.
Oppidum	A large settlement with fortified walls.
Pàillean	Form of tent. Pavilion.
Pehtas	Picts
Peitriana	Petteril River, Cumbria.
Plebians	Unsophisticated and uncultured person. Pleb.
Poclin	Now known as Pocklington.
Pollens Nobilatate	Latin, meaning powerful in noble lineage.
Praedetari	Group of predators ruthlessly preying on others.
Rí	Celtic word meaning Royal.
Rig	Celtic word meaning 'King.'
Saighdear-coise	Foot soldiers.
Sár Ghealach	Super Moon.
Scates	Base liar. Ne'er-do-well. Fantasist.

Scáthach	Female 'shadowy' warrior.
Seal Isles	Orkney Isles.
Sept	Iron age settlement of round houses.
Sleekit	Slimy. Deceitful. Fox-like. Weasel.
Spleuchan boke	Swear words, meaning 'bag of vomit.'
Staena	Settlement on the northeast side of what is now Carlisle.
Stanwix	Stanwick North Yorkshire.
Stryx	Bird-like demon
Sulewad	Solway - Tràchd Romhra [Gaelic].
Taftefield	A Hill fort in the area now known as Toft Hill, Co. Durham
Táirneanach	Thunder
Tarraing	In tow; following.
Teanta	Tent
Tés-ti	River Tees.
Tippet	A long narrow strip of cloth. A scarf.
Tomus	Function of weighing, measuring amounts and quantities. Accounting.
Torc	A neck ornament, a solid piece of metal bent around the neck.
Tormaig	Thunder spirit.
Torr Cathair	High throne.
Trinowanti	Tribe located in Essex area.
Ultima Thule	Extreme limit of travel – i.e., Shetland Isles.
Velita	Druid servants. The lowest orders of the tiered Druiden hierarchy

Veniti	A Celtic people who lived in an area of Amorica, northern part of Brittany. By the time of Julius Caesar, they controlled all Atlantic trade to Britain.
Verlamio	Capital of Cantiaci /Cantii.
Voe	A small bay or creek in Orkney or Shetland.
Welkin	Upper atmosphere, where celts believed the gods lived.
Withies	Willow twigs or strips used as bindings.
Ynys Mon	Anglesey. The home of Druid training during the iron age.

Bheir Dhithan siorruidh a' gheamhraidh. Thoir dhomh ord a' chatha.

Translated: Eternal gods of winter give me the hammer of battle.

'Do we not know the size of the earth and the cosmos, and the movements of the heavens and stars."

Pomponius Mela (*De Situ Orbis* § 3.2.18)

TIMELINE

| 13 AD | Eachann Beli Mawr is born in Shetland and brought by Mugh Ruith to Carvetii where he is trained in the Druid methods of magic and arms. |

13 AD   Eachann Beli Mawr is born in Shetland and brought by Mugh Ruith to Carvetii where he is trained in the Druid methods of magic and arms.

21 AD   Cartimandua is born heir to the throne of Brigantia.

31 AD   Eachann Beli Mawr becomes High-Druid and champion of Carvetii under the rule of Venutius, King of Carvetii.

36 AD   Bellnorix, King of Brigantia, and grandfather of Cartimandua, dies. Cartimandua is crowned High Queen of Brigantia.

40 AD   Cartimandua, Queen of Brigantia meets Eachann Beli Mawr. Cartimandua marries Venutius, King of Carvetii, and their respective tribes are united, headed by Queen Cartimandua with Venutius as her consort King. Through her relationship with Beli Mawr, Cartimandua gives birth to twin daughters, Lilith and Layn.

42 AD   A third child, Maawan, is born to Queen Cartimandua and Beli Mawr. All three princesses are taken by the warrior Camulo, and brought up by his wife, Raegan.

43 AD   The Romans begin the invasion of Britain. Cartimandua, united with Venutius, leads the fight to protect Brigantia against the invasion.

CELTIC SEASONS

Samhain   : Beginning of winter and the New Year — *1st November.*
            Representing the final harvest before winter sets in.
            A time to honour ancestors and embrace the dark half of
            the year.

Yule   : Midwinter — *20th / 24th December.*
            The shortest day of the year.

Imbolc   : Beginning of Spring — *1st February.*
            The festival of light, purification, fertility, and new
            beginnings.

Ostara   : Spring Equinox — *20th - 23rd March*
            Time to prepare for the new yearly cycle, and new life.

Beltane   : Beginning of summer — *1st May.* Festival celebrating fertility.
            A season of passion, fire, and abundance.

Litha   : Summer Solstice — *20th - 23rd June.*
            The longest day. Celebration of light over darkness

Lughnas   : Beginning of autumn / Harvest *1st August.*
            A Festival of fire, celebrating harvest.

ACKNOWLEDGEMENTS

Information about Celts in the iron age, the history of Brigantia and Cartimandua, the iron age gods, Druids and other historical facts are few. Over the years I have gathered information from public domain and personal reading. I have woven a story of fiction around a few known facts, choosing actual places in the British Isles to anchor my interpretation of the movements and actions of my characters. I have invented some 'ancient' names for those places, trying to link those names as closely to the local history of the places as is possible. The ancestral line is fictional, though history records the possibility that Bellnorix was the grandfather of Cartimandua. Although I have attempted to fit the dates of events into the known timeline for the Roman invasion of Britain, my timeline is not necessarily correct and should not be taken as absolute.

Thanks to Sandy Wolverson for allowing me to use her extensive library of books on the Celts. I have gleaned numerous insights from that resource, along with the added benefit of Sandy's in-depth knowledge of all things Celtic. Thanks to my friends and story enhancers: Maria Holland, Rosemary Bowyer, Laura Hudson Mackay and Ann Mapplebeck. Thank you for your input and clarity on the flow of the story and pointing out plot holes, bad grammar and my mistakes, [of which there were many]. I love you all.

And of course, huge thanks to my publishers and editors who are the 'DreamEngine'. Thank you, David Baboulene, Edward Marsh, Emma Julian and Caroline Mccudden-Hughes. Your expertise and support have allowed the story in my head to become a tangible reality.

READ PART TWO CARTIMANDUA SERIES

FIRES OF BRIGANTIA

WHEN A QUEEN'S DAUGHTER FALLS IN LOVE WITH A REBEL WARLORD, TWO WORLDS ARE ABOUT TO COLLIDE.

WHEN THE FIRES OF BRIGANTIA BLAZE, CAN TRUE LOVE AND DRUID MAGIC TURN THE CURSED WAR INTO A BLESSING.

Five Stars: Gripping, informative & educational read.

> Really enjoyed the book. Loved it's storytelling of ancient British history and culture whist weaving a story of love, trust, loyalty and bravery through its pages.
>
> -Andrew S.

Five Stars: Plenty of action in early Britain.

> A semi fictional tale of factual characters, make sure you don't skip the prologue which sets the scene very well. Plenty of brutality, tension and (for those who want it) romance, most enjoyable.
>
> -Robin Birkett

ABOUT THE AUTHOR

Tina is a Yorkshire woman who personifies the spirit of Queen Cartimadua. She has firm principles based on the philosophy that a person has to put energy into life if they are going to get anything out of life.

Her positivity is infectious and she is both inspiring and active in helping people to lead a happy life. She is particularly interested in helping older people to continue to feel happy and fulfilled.

Tina uses the power of storytelling, the richness of history, and the place of women central to authentic stories to inspire others to be true to themselves in the world today. In a world where history is sacrificed on the altar of political correctness, Tina questions the need to change those stories, but rather learn from them.

Twitter (X): Tina_Zee_111
Facebook: TinaZeeAuthor
Website: TinaZee.com

Have you got a book in you? Want to get published?

DreamEngine provides extraordinary support for aspiring authors who want education, expert marketing, and an author mythology that actually sells books. Talk to us today!

publishing@dreamengine.co.uk

dreamengine.co.uk

ALSO BY DREAMENGINE

Belleau Wood
by Paul Meachair
When US Marine Liam Kierney reaches war-torn France in 1918, he is thrown into a world of conflict, pain, courage, humour, human weakness and the horror of kill or be killed.

Fires of Brigantia
by Tina Zee
The Roman army. One Yorkshire woman. They never stood a chance.

Monday Monday
by Frances J MacGregor
Vonnie's story starts one Monday in February, when, aged 10, her world changes in ways that will burden her for decades to come.

Lara's Secret
Book 1 in The Pete West Mystery Series by Ray C Doyle
It's not a good story until somebody dies.

The Blind Pigeon
Book 2 in The Pete West Mystery Series by Ray C Doyle
It's a good story. Somebody died.

Life's a Peach
by Steve Askham
Extraordinary fruity business you didn't know that you NEED to know ... The secret life of an international fruit trader.

The Magical World of Lilly Lemoncello
by Carolyn Goodyear
Fate decides Lilly's start in life. So she chooses to let Fate decide the rest of it too. A heart-warming and remarkable work of human goodness.

397

The Shock Tube
by Paul Curtis
Anybody reading this book will learn something uncomfortable. About themselves...

Ocean Boulevard
by David Baboulene
Book 1: An epic and exhilarating journey all the way... from a boy to a man.
"I laughed so hard, stuff came out of my nose." Pete McCarthy.

Jumping Ships
by David Baboulene
Book 2: The global misadventures of a cargo ship apprentice.
"Interesting, raucous and very, very funny to the point that will make your eyes water."
TalkSport

NONFICTION:

The Story Series
by David Baboulene Learn how stories work.

HELPLOVESUPPORT IMPRINT

Where do Tantrums come from?
By Manika Kaur
Little ones will love searching for tantrums in this poetic storybook.
Simple and helpful tools for children with "big feelings bursting through".

Conscious Autism Parenting
By Rachna Malkani
Eight Habits for Looking After Yourself and Making Sure your Autistic Child is the Most Wonderful Gift in Your Life.

The Mental Game Series
by Paul M Maher Ph.D

Soccer Mind
by Paul M Maher PhD
Raise Your Game with Mental Training

Tennis Mind
by Paul M Maher PhD
Raise Your Tennis with Mental Training

Body Building Mind
Think and Grow Muscle with Mental Training

Cricket Mind
Raise Your Cricket with Mental Training

Printed in Great Britain
by Amazon

48088548R00239